OREGON

*The Romantic History
of the Willamette Valley
in Four Complete Novels*

Birdie L. Etchison

BARBOUR
PUBLISHING, INC.
Uhrichsville, Ohio

The Heart Has Its Reasons © 1995 by Birdie L. Etchison.
Love Shall Come Again © 1996 by Birdie L. Etchison.
Love's Tender Path © 1996 by Birdie L. Etchison.
Anna's Hope © 1997 by Barbour Publishing, Inc.

ISBN 1-57748-971-3

Cover design by Robyn Martins.

Unless otherwise noted, all Scripture quotations are taken from the Authorized King James Version of the Bible.

Published by Barbour Publishing, Inc., P.O. Box 719, Uhrichsville, Ohio 44683 http://www.barbourbooks.com

 Member of the
Evangelical Christian
Publishers Association

Printed in the United States of America.

BIRDIE L. ETCHISON

Birdie L. Etchison was born in San Diego, California, and was raised in Portland, Oregon, but she now claims the Washington Coast as home. Her children are scattered in Hawaii, Portland, and Seattle. She also has six grandchildren and two great-granddaughters. Birdie became a Christian when she was eight, after a lady asked to pick her up and take her to a nearby Friends' Church. It is the interest in the early Friends' that started research and eventually led to writing about her grandparents in *The Heart Has Its Reasons*. She knows much about the Willamette Valley, the setting for the majority of her books. She loves to research the colorful history of the United States and uses her research along with family stories to create wonderful novels in a writing career that began in 1963.

The Heart Has Its Reasons

In loving memory of my maternal grandmother;
the inspiration for this story.

Chapter 1

Emily Drake looked admiringly at the even rows of hand-dipped chocolates. With Christmas less than a fortnight away, she had put in a hectic week, working ten and twelve hours a day. Oregon's Finest Chocolates was a popular gift item. Not that she'd be receiving any candy from a suitor. At twenty-four, she had become resigned to the title of "Spinster." She supposed she'd still be dipping chocolates when she turned fifty.

Kate caught her attention from the next table. Smiling, she popped a small imperfect chocolate into her mouth and raised a finger to her red lips. "Sh–h–h," she whispered, her dark eyes flashing. "Don't tell now."

Laughing, Emily took a lopsided one from her row and bit into it. Maple creme. Her favorite. It was okay to eat an occasional chocolate, but she usually didn't. Working at the factory full-time took away any desire for the sweet confections.

Kate wiped her hands on her apron. "There goes a pound." Kate had a buxom figure, which she constantly lamented about. "When I think of all the dresses in my closet I can't wear—I shudder. Look at you—slender as a stick—just as I used to be. I'm truly envious."

Emily's face reddened as it always did whenever she received a compliment. She never quite knew how to respond. Perhaps it was because she received so few. But getting acquainted with Kate these past two months had changed all that. Kate was fun. Daring. Talkative. And beautiful. Emily found herself eager to come to work, eager for each day to start, wishing she could be half as daring, half as beautiful.

"Are you sure you've never been married?" Kate had asked the day after they met. She stood at the production line next to Emily. Emily had been assigned to oversee her, making sure she dipped the chocolates just right. The fondant or caramel had to be completely covered, yet too much chocolate was a waste.

"I—" Emily hesitated, "have never had anyone come calling."

Kate's mouth opened in surprise. "I hardly believe that. You're attractive, even if you are shy."

Shy. The stock boy had said that about her when she turned down his offer to go for a buggy ride back when she first came to work here. That was in 1899. It was now December of 1907 and nobody had asked to come calling since. She rarely explained why she didn't date, the real reason being she couldn't see anyone who didn't belong to the Friends Church. Not that she couldn't, but that she wished not to. There was a difference. It was also her beliefs that kept her from going to dances though Kate had asked her twice now.

"Some day I hope to have a family," Emily said, pausing to look at her row of chocolates.

Kate rolled her eyes. "You have to get married first. And before you get married you are courted. There's another dance next Saturday at the Grange Hall. Why not go with me?"

Emily sighed as she dipped another mound of fondant. "I can't. I explained that already."

"This isn't just any old dance," Kate said. "They have food and toe tapping fiddle music. The people are friendly, and this one man—his name is Ben Galloway—is so handsome and probably the best dancer I've ever seen."

"The Religious Society of Friends doesn't believe in any kind of dancing," Emily explained. "It's worldly and we do not partake of worldly ventures."

"Well, my goodness. Isn't that something! Quite frankly I can't imagine not being able to dance," Kate went on. "It's a good way to meet people."

"If you like this—this Ben so much, maybe you'll get married again," Emily said. She knew Kate was lonely. Being widowed at nineteen had been difficult. It was that loneliness that made her leave the farm in Cottage Grove and move to Portland. She didn't talk much about that period of her life, not even when Emily asked questions.

"Ben's not my type," Kate said. "We're too much alike."

Emily stared at her friend. How did one know if a man was her type or not? The concept sounded strange to her. But, then, she didn't think like Kate, nor did she dress like her. Kate wore her dark hair in tight curls that made her hair net spring to life. Emily's hair, neither brown nor black, was dull. Straight. Her mouth was too wide for her face, her nose small. Her eyes, the color of Persian violets, were her best asset. Not that she should be thinking about such things. Hadn't Grandmother said that beauty didn't count? "It's what's inside that matters, Emily."

Well, if it's what's inside, I guess that needs some changing, too, she thought now as she heard Kate exclaiming about the polka, her favorite dance.

"About the dance. . ." Kate was also persistent.

"Maybe I will go. Just once, mind you."

Once said, Emily couldn't believe the words had come from her mouth.

8

Why had she agreed? How could she even consider it? The Friends would never understand. And how could she begin to explain what prompted her affirmative response? Besides, she didn't have the sort of attire suitable to wear to a dance. Her wardrobe consisted of two dresses: the simple gray cotton she wore to church (it was plain; definitely not a dancing frock), and the brown muslin, her everyday dress. Faded and worn at the seams, it looked like what it was: a work dress.

And if that wasn't enough reason, she didn't have the slightest idea of how one danced.

"Oh, Emily, I'm so glad!" Kate bounded over, hugging Emily hard. "You'll have ever such a nice time!" A smudge of chocolate ran across one cheek still pink from rouge.

Rouge and lip coloring was something else Emily didn't use. Another reason for not going to such social functions as dances.

"I just finished my last chocolate," Emily said, removing her soiled apron.

"Me, too," Kate added.

"I must rush home. Grandmother likes to serve supper at six." A sinking sensation hit the pit of her stomach. How could she possibly get permission from her grandparents? If she mentioned the word "dance" they would first pray, then preach at her for hours.

"You always rush home," Kate said.

It was true. But there were chores to do. Wood to chop and bring in for the night's fire. Water to fetch, the chickens and rabbits to feed.

Kate retrieved her wraps from the cloakroom hook. Her blue-flowered dress flounced as she walked. She wore several crinolines, even to work. Emily wondered how she would look at a dance, a dress-up occasion.

"I can hardly wait for you to meet Ben. I have this inner feeling that he's right for you."

That was something else. Inner feelings. Didn't Kate realize that God put those feelings inside a person? It wasn't luck or happenstance. When you believed, you stood ready for His guidance and direction, what Friends called "inner light."

She moved past Kate. "I doubt that this Ben is a man of God. And that's important as the Bible teaches that a believer cannot be unequally yoked—"

"I didn't say you were going to marry him," Kate interjected.

Emily buttoned her threadbare coat, then reached for her hat. "Just the same, the possibility exists whenever you keep company with someone that this might be the one."

Only, if only she had heeded those words. If only she had listened to her convictions.

"We can't all go to the same church, believe the same things," Kate said then. "Maybe he believes in God. Why not give him the benefit of the doubt?"

"Sorry." Emily waved her hand in dismissal.

"Are you like those Quakers who pray in silence all day?" Kate, all five-feet, nine-inches, stood in the doorway.

Emily tied the strings of her brown woolen bonnet and reached for her gloves. "When George Fox, our founder, said: 'We tremble at the word of the Lord,' people started calling us Quakers, but we prefer the name *Friends*." Emily had heard the story countless times, and it always amused her.

"Come to meeting sometime, Kate. See what it's like for yourself. I play piano for the services."

Kate hugged Emily again, knocking the hat askew. They both laughed. It was one thing Emily liked about Kate. She was loving and kind. You could get into discussions and even though she didn't agree, she never became angry, never judged. She was the best friend Emily had ever had—the only friend. Emily knew she shouldn't bargain, but couldn't resist this one time. "Would you consider going to meeting with me? We could sit together and—"

"Write notes."

"Write notes?"

Kate laughed. "I'm teasing. I meant if the sermon got tiresome I might write or doodle."

Emily couldn't promise that it wouldn't be tiresome. When one wasn't familiar with the teachings of the Bible, or not used to praying, she supposed it could be tiresome.

"Of course I'll go, if only to hear you play."

It was settled then. Emily would go to the next dance on Saturday night, and Kate would attend meeting the following morning.

Kate headed west to catch the streetcar, while Emily caught the one heading east. While Kate's stopped at the corner next to her house, Emily had several blocks to walk since the tracks didn't go that far.

Emily could hardly believe Kate had agreed to accompany her to meeting. She had asked before, only to have Kate scoff, saying she didn't need any church telling her how to live, or what to wear. Kate wouldn't want to give up her brightly colored dresses, the lip color and rouge, the rings or perfume. Yet if she understood the reasons, it might make a difference. Though Kate seemed happy, there was a restlessness about her, and Emily knew she needed God in her life. He could heal all hurts—big ones and little ones alike.

As Emily hurried the half-mile walk home, the evening air nipped at her cheeks. Winter would soon be here and with it came rain, winds out of the east, and sometimes snow. She needed a new coat, but doubted that there would be enough money for one this year.

She thought again about dancing, what it must be like to dance with a man, to feel one's arms around you. Would she ever know love? Was there someone in her future? Or would she be like the Ditler Sisters who owned and operated the Dry Goods Store on Foster Road? It was where her grandmother bought material for their dresses. Always brown, gray, and black. Never red, pink, or blue as Kate wore. She didn't want to remain a spinster, but if that was what God had in mind for her, so be it.

"Thee is late," Beulah said when Emily came in through the back door, bringing a gust of wind. "I've been holding supper."

Emily shrugged out of her coat. Both grandparents often slipped into the old way of talking, referring to her as "thee," and saying "thou" and "thine." Emily rarely used the terms now.

It was warm inside, and the lamp on the sideboard was lit, casting shadows across the kitchen. The smell of fried potatoes and freshly baked bread made her stomach tighten. She hadn't realized how hungry she was. "We stayed to finish an order that came in this morning. Mr. Roberts said it would be extremely busy for the next week."

"More money in thy check then." Beulah, a formidable woman with wide shoulders and gray hair pulled back into a severe bun, regarded her granddaughter. "Not that there will be enough for Christmas presents, however."

Yes, more money, which Emily never saw. She turned her earnings over to her grandparents as that was expected of her. Though most of her money was set aside "for a rainy day," as Grandmother put it, she often wondered what might happen to them if she were to marry and move out. Before she had been old enough to work, Grandfather had farmed the land, but as his rheumatism worsened, he planted less and only recently had sold several parcels of land, banking the proceeds. Now all that remained was the lot the house sat on, and a partial acre.

"Fetch the water, then we can eat," her grandmother said.

Emily grabbed the bucket off the counter and hurried back outside. The water was crystal clear. Cold. She looked at the clumps of green grass poking through mounds of dried, brown maple leaves. The zinnias she'd planted earlier that spring were mere straggly stems with drooping heads. She'd plant more next year. And the year after that. Douglas fir dotted the landscape, giving protection against the bitter east wind. It was this rugged Oregon country her great-grandparents had moved to from Missouri back in the mid-1800s. How she wished she could have known them. Were they as stern as Grandmother Drake? As quiet and deep-thinking as Grandfather? Would they have given up one of their daughters, sending her from California to live with grandparents?

She blinked back sudden tears, as she carried the full bucket up the path toward the house. No sense in dwelling on things from the past.

The dinner didn't quite fill the empty space inside, but Grandfather cleared his throat, saying his usual litany, " 'Tis better to leave the table a little hungry then too full."

The teakettle hummed on the stove. After washing the supper dishes, Emily worked on her quilt squares, sitting close to the kerosene lamp so she could see better. Grandfather might request she play some of his favorite hymns on the old pump organ, followed by a chapter or two from the Bible. Then it would be time to slip up the attic stairs to bed.

"Is something troubling thee, child?" Grandfather asked after Emily had played his favorite, "Count Your Blessings." Emily wasn't a child anymore. Would her grandparents ever see her or think of her as a woman? Yet she wouldn't correct her grandfather. He was old and set in his ways. He was also growing deaf. She wanted to run to him, question him about the dance, ask if he had ever once danced, but she didn't dare. She couldn't risk the anger, the accusations from Grandmother. She would never understand. Never.

"I am fine, Grandfather. Just a bit tired, I guess."

"It's nearly bedtime," Grandmother said from her corner where she rocked the evening hours away. "Thee can read one chapter of the Bible, then go up."

Emily's fingers touched the pages of the big book. She was reading Isaiah now and it tied in with the Christmas story.

" 'For unto us a child is born, unto us a son is given: and the government shall be upon his shoulder: and his name shall be called Wonderful, Counsellor, The mighty God, The everlasting Father, The Prince of Peace' " (Isaiah 9:6).

"Bless Thy word, bless Thy holy name," Grandfather said as Emily closed the book.

She sat thinking about the Christmas story. She never tired of hearing it, and it warmed her heart as she thought about the promise of the coming Messiah, and how the Jews didn't believe that this precious infant was Jesus. Since they didn't believe that, they didn't believe in salvation, and Emily thought that was sad.

Emily bade her grandparents good night and headed for the stairway. Holding the lamp in one hand, lifting her skirts with the other, she climbed the steep attic steps. She *was* tired, but there would be time to pray, to write.

As the house settled to a quietness, Emily stared at the soft, steady glow of the lamp. It was wasteful to use the kerosene, but she must write in the diary. It was one of her few pleasures—something only she knew about. Something Grandmother could not be critical about.

Emily closed her eyes and thought of the dance. Even if it was a little more than a week away, she couldn't get it out of her mind.

She uncapped the bottle of India ink and dipped the pen.

Mama. Emily always addressed the small leather-bound book in that way. It was as if she was talking to her mother, and in turn her mother answering her. It wouldn't make sense to anyone else, and that's why it was a closely guarded secret.

I've been invited to a dance. I know I shouldn't have accepted, but something inside me said yes, do it. Just this once. I want to see Kate dance, Mama. I want to hear the music. Is that so terribly wrong? Did you ever attend a dance? I also want to see this Ben Galloway Kate talks about. Now, that's wrong. I know it is, and yet something is propelling me on. . . . Oh, what is to become of me?

Emily wiped the nib clean and capped the ink bottle. Shivering, she blew out the light, burrowing under the heavy quilts on the four-poster bed. No heat came up the stairs, and as the wind howled outside, rattling the window, Emily was glad she'd read Scripture downstairs in front of the fire.

After warming up just a bit, she flung the quilts back and kneeled on the small rag rug beside her bed—the rug she'd braided from old quilt scraps. She'd been twelve that year. She folded her hands and prayed. "Forgive me my transgressions, O God. Let me be ever mindful that as Your child I must do what is right to bring glory to Your name. Amen."

It was a long time before Emily could shake the dance from her mind, and it wasn't until she'd made the decision not to go that she felt better. She would explain to Kate that it was wrong to put desires of the flesh before godly things. It couldn't be helped, but she must decline. They could still be friends at work, couldn't they? Kate would have to understand.

Chapter 2

It was a sleepless night. Though Emily prayed for forgiveness, declaring she wouldn't attend the dance, she knew it didn't matter. She had succumbed to a worldly desire, and though she might choose to stay away, the fact remained that she had wanted to go—*yearned* to go. And therein lay the problem.

When she left for work the next morning, she carefully rehearsed what she would say to Kate, how she would decline going to the dance.

But somehow she couldn't do it when she saw Kate's smiling face. Humming as she worked, Kate talked about different dances and how she had learned all of them since moving to Portland.

"My husband didn't like to dance. In fact, the only thing he was interested in was farming. I discovered real quick that I wasn't a true farmer's wife."

Emily wasn't sure if she would make a good farmer's wife, if she'd make a good any kind of wife. She tried to tell Kate that she'd changed her mind about the dance, but she'd barely get one word out before Kate started talking again.

"Guess I'll wear my red dress to the dance since red is so Christmasy," Kate continued.

Christmas. There would be little celebration in the Drake household. Emily might receive a new pair of mittens or a scarf. She had no idea what her grandmother knit during the day while she was at work. Emily was working on an embroidered dishtowel set for Grandmother, and warm, woolen socks for Grandfather. He always complimented Emily's work, saying her stitches were tighter than Grandmother's.

"Don't thee tell her I said that," he would say once Grandmother was out of earshot.

Emily would nod and smile, knowing the last thing she would ever do was get Grandfather in trouble. And trouble there would be.

The past week Emily had worked on a muffler for Kate. A heavy black wool, it would lend warmth on cold, windy days. Kate preferred bright colors, but black yarn was all Emily had.

"About the dance," Emily began, her eyes not quite meeting Kate's.

"No," Kate said, interrupting her. "You're not going to back out, Emily. I knew this would happen and I won't let you do it."

"I don't have a red dress, or a green one either—"

"Of course you don't. And believe me, it doesn't matter."

"It's not right for me to go."

"I know you think it isn't, but you're going this once as a favor to me."

As a favor? How could Kate twist things around like this?

"Are God's promises worthless?"

Emily's cheeks flamed. "Certainly not!"

"Then how about yours? Shouldn't you be accountable for your promises?"

Emily stared at her friend. "Of course I should."

"Then I'm holding you to that promise."

"Now, Kate. You don't understand about the doctrine."

"And wasn't it the doctrine you escaped from in England back in the 1600s or whenever?"

"That was different," Emily protested.

"If so, how?"

Emily tried to remember how an older member explained it in meeting one First Day. "We want to better the world, and let ourselves shine as good examples."

"Attending a dance isn't going to send you to damnation, now is it?"

Emily hesitated. "No, that's not the point. How can I be a good example if I'm in a dance hall?"

"Grange hall," Kate corrected her.

"It's still a dance."

Kate sighed. "I sure don't want to be responsible for any wrongdoing, or for any guilt you'll feel."

"If I go, it will be to watch, not to dance."

"That's fine," Kate answered. "The music is good. You'll recognize some of the tunes. 'Turkey in the Straw,' 'Irish Jig,' and 'O Susannah!' Refreshments are also served. Probably punch and cookies. I know it'd do you good to get out, but it's up to you."

The subject was closed for the time being.

Wednesday turned rainy. Grandfather said his rheumatism was acting up and he should stay home from prayer meeting.

"Thee stay home then, but Emily and I are going," Beulah announced.

Emily drove the wagon, not minding the fine mist coming down. Her hat with wide brim kept the rain off her face. She needed to talk to Grandmother about staying at Kate's Saturday, but the time wasn't right. Rarely was the time right when it came to discussions of any sort. Grandmother sat stiff and silent, so Emily remained quiet as well. Maybe tomorrow would be better.

The hall buzzed with voices when they entered. The talk stopped abruptly when Beulah and Emily walked in. Myrtle Lee rushed over, linking her arm with Beulah's.

"We've just heard from Ohio. Pastor Luke Morrison is coming to Portland. He accepted our request. He was pastoring a meeting when his wife died, and he realized he couldn't stay there. Too many memories."

"Wife died?" Beulah repeated. "How old is this pastor?"

"Thirty-five, I believe someone said."

Emily felt several pairs of eyes on her. She knew what they were thinking. Could this be God's answer to her prayers? Might this be a prospect for a mate? She felt a twinge inside. How could she be thinking this way when they hadn't even met?

The bulk of prayers that night were for the man who would be in their midst soon. Times were changing. The old way said that one can discover true belief and righteous conduct from the inner light—that one did not need a minister to lead. Of late there was dissent.

"We are in the twentieth century," a younger man had proclaimed at the last yearly meeting. "With our growth, we need a preacher."

"And perhaps we should abandon our dark attire and drop the formal way of talking," someone else said.

"Never," Grandmother proclaimed under her breath. "I won't hear of it."

In the end, the agreement had been to search for the right man to teach the flock. As for the other two suggestions, they were set aside for the time being. It was up to each individual to do as he or she saw fit. And the meetings would continue opening and closing with silent prayers.

"Yes," Beulah said on the way home. "I think thy prayers have been answered, Emily. Thee needs a husband. Pastor Luke needs a wife. He has had sufficient mourning time."

"Grandmother, I haven't even met this man."

"Thee will." Grandmother stared straight ahead. "It isn't good for man to live alone."

Nor woman, Emily said under her breath. Women get lonely, too. And loneliness leads you to do things such as attending dances. Now. She must ask when Grandmother seemed to be in a good mood. A bit of a smile played about her mouth.

"My friend Kate—from work—you remember my mentioning her?"

"Yes, thee has talked about her. Why?"

"She wants to go to church with me on First Day."

"Is she of our persuasion?"

"No, she isn't."

"Humph!"

Emily took a deep breath. "She. . .wants me to come for supper Seventh Day, then we will walk to church the next morning—"

"Thee doesn't do much, I know."

Emily's heart soared. Was this her grandmother speaking?

"I expect it will be all right this once. If thee finishes all the Seventh Day work and the preparations for First Day."

Emily expected that. "I will," she murmured softly.

"But, I don't like the idea and might change my mind."

Emily swallowed. "She's a wonderful person, Grandmother."

"Still, I don't like you associating with people who don't believe as we do."

"Maybe she will come to believe, too."

It had been a thought, a wish Emily'd had, and who knew? Didn't God work in mysterious ways?

There was much discussion between her grandparents that evening, first about the new preacher coming, then about Emily staying with her friend for the night. Surprisingly, Grandfather was more opposed than she thought he would be.

"Thee better go to bed early Saturday night."

"I will, Grandfather," she promised.

Finally Emily crept up the stairs to bed to think and pray about the situation. She hadn't lied to her grandparents. She just hadn't told the whole truth. Would God forgive this transgression? She felt Him to be more forgiving than Grandmother and Grandfather. Not that they would find out. She certainly didn't see how.

For the remainder of the week, Emily's mind darted from the new preacher coming to thoughts of the dance on Saturday. She had never dipped so many chocolates. She even saw the rows of sweet confections in her sleep. Some day she might not be working in this candy factory. Some day soon she might marry, be the mother of a child, a child who would need her love, time, and attention.

Emily retired early on Friday night. No, she had told Grandfather, she felt fine, even if she did look a bit peaked.

When sleep didn't come, she crawled from under the heavy layer of quilts and tiptoed to the window to look out. No stars shining through the cloud layer. A lantern sent a tiny shaft of light bobbing in the still blackness as someone walked past the lane to the house. It was late. Most people were in for the night. Asleep. Just as she should be.

Her attention diverted, she thought of what it would have been like to share this room with a sister. Why hadn't her parents sent another child to stay? Why had they chosen her? Was it because she was imperfect in some way? What would happen if she went to California for a visit? Would they welcome her? What would her grandparents do? They had come to rely not only on her earnings, but on her help as well. Her thoughts turned to prayer.

"God, I need to learn the lesson of patience. Maybe I should read Job's story again—learn from his experiences. I remain Your child, Your servant. Amen."

The sheets were cold to her touch. Neither the long flannel nightgown or the cap that covered her head helped.

A sister would have helped warm her toes. They might have whispered in the darkness, shared secrets, giggled over the day's happenings. Emily shook the thought from her mind. It was quite obvious that a sister would never come from California. They were grown now.

There had been word at odd intervals. Letters penned in Mama's delicate scrawl. Little Olive Ann had died of a fever when she was but a year old. Paul had broken his arm. Maud, the spirited one, had married a few years ago. Mary was betrothed. Tom had moved away. Nobody seemed to know where.

The one time Emily had mentioned going home for a visit, Grandmother had scoffed.

"And pray tell, where would thee get the money for such a trip?" She stood, towering over Emily, hands on hips. "Goodness sake, child, thee should be grateful to have a roof over thy head. Doesn't thee know there are starving people in the world—those who would give anything to own two good dresses, to go to bed with food in their stomachs?"

Emily didn't broach the subject again.

And now that she couldn't sleep, she lit the lamp again. She would write her thoughts down. One thing to be thankful for was the fact she never had to hide her diary. Neither grandparent would climb the steep steps.

She flipped back through her diary, reading passages from the first year after she'd come to Oregon.

The small leather-bound book had been a presentation by her school teacher for winning the fifth grade spelling bee. It had been the most wonderful gift Emily had ever received, and she wrote in it that very night.

This book belongs to Emily Drake
The Year of our Lord 1893

That first entry read:

Mama,

 How I miss you, Pa, and my brothers and sisters. I remember lying next to Maud with Mary on the other side. Across the room were the boys. Daniel with his straight blond hair, his mischievous grin. And Tom who chopped wood for each night's fire. Even now I can hear the ax sing, see the wood chips fly. Paul. He liked to be hugged more than anything. And Joel. How sick he'd get with the croup. Olive Ann. I remember the morning she was born. So tiny and red, and that plaintive cry.

 Mama, I was the quiet, obedient one. Why did you send me away? Did you ever miss me? Did you cry when you saw my empty space between Maud and Mary? Do you think of me now, and wonder about how much I have grown?

 Mama, I miss you so much. I remember your blue eyes, your plump, round shape. If only you could come to visit. Or send money for me to come on the train.

Emily didn't realize she was crying until something wet hit her arm. No, there hadn't been money for train trips then, or now.

She closed the diary as more memories filled her. Why hadn't she written about the day she'd been bundled up and driven to the train station with Mrs. Barnes, a lady from church? Was it because the memories were too painful? Mrs. Barnes trilled on and on about how beautiful Oregon was and how much Emily would enjoy being an only child.

She remembered swallowing her tears and thinking she didn't want to be an only child. She didn't care about having her own room, receiving all the attention, the advantages. Why couldn't she have had a say in the matter?

She thought of Maud again. Kate made her think of Maud. Maud had laughed a lot and liked to tease the younger ones. Suddenly Emily knew Maud was too spirited to have lived here. She would have been whipped every day and twice on First Day. Emily did as she was told, and if tears or questions came to mind, they were always repressed.

She blew out the light for the second time. Lying in the darkness, she listened as the rain whooshed from one side of the house then, changing directions, whooshed back the way it had come. Usually the rain lulled her to sleep, but tonight was different. Tonight her thoughts kept sleep at bay.

Tomorrow would come too soon as it was. She'd work at the candy factory half a day, come home to do chores around the house before leaving for Kate's. Grandmother would put the beans to soak and bake the bread, but Emily had wood to chop and two buckets of water to fetch.

She planned to catch the last streetcar to Kate's. Together they'd have supper, and later attend the dance. She thought about Kate—Kate who wouldn't let her renege on a promise. Kate with the laughing eyes who was like a sister.

Sometimes God takes, but He always gives back. Yes, He always gives back. Smiling as she pulled the quilt up under her chin, Emily closed her eyes.

Chapter 3

Now that she was really going to the dance, Emily wondered about her simple gray dress. Maybe it was just a barn dance, but people would stare when she came in with Kate dressed in red while she wore gray. The last thing Emily wanted was to be noticed. Still, it couldn't be helped.

At last the chickens and rabbits were fed, eggs gathered, wood chopped and brought in, and two buckets of water drawn and waiting on the kitchen counter.

She was putting on her wraps when Grandmother cleared her throat. Emily froze. Had she done something to displease her?

"We will see thee in the morning" was all she said. Emily nodded and hurried out the door before she might think of something else she needed.

Her cheeks were red from the cold when she arrived at Kate's. Kate greeted her, looking happier than usual. "Emily, guess what?" She took her coat and hung it up. "I found the absolutely most beautiful dress for you."

Borrow a dress? Emily had never done such a thing. What if she ripped it, or spilled punch down the front?

"It's velvet. A royal blue. Come see."

The dress lay on Kate's bed. Emily's breath caught in her throat, as she touched the soft material. With puffed sleeves, a pleated bodice, and tiny pearl buttons, it was the most gorgeous dress she had ever seen. "Oh, Kate, I *adore* it."

Kate's eyes twinkled. "I knew you would. And it's going to fit you so nicely." She held it up. "Just as I thought. The color goes perfect with your eyes."

So this was velvet. Emily was sure she had never seen or felt material as wonderful as this.

"It doesn't suit me because it has no flounce." She slipped it over Emily's head, standing back to examine it. "I'll cut about six inches off."

"Cut?" Emily looked shocked. "You can't cut this. You couldn't wear it again."

Kate grabbed the pincushion. "It's okay. Like I said, it's not my style. Just think of how elegant you are going to look." Elegant. Emily had never looked elegant in her life. Kate made Emily turn as she pinned it up.

"You know I might comb your hair in a different style."

Emily wore her hair two ways. Brushed out, then braided in one long braid before going to bed, or wound into a braided knot at the nape of her neck. No ribbons, feathers, flowers, or fancy clasps.

"Let's hem this after supper," Kate said. "Everything's ready, and I'm starved."

"It certainly smells wonderful," Emily said, not wanting to take her eyes off the dress.

A table was set with a white linen tablecloth, matching napkins, and fine china.

"Wedding presents," Kate said, bringing a covered dish to the table.

"It's lovely." Emily pulled out a chair, hesitating as she looked across the table at Kate. Kate never prayed over her food at work, but Emily wouldn't feel right without asking God's blessing on the meal. Kate touched her arm, as if she knew, then bowed her head.

"Lord, bless this food, this house, and my dear, dear friend Emily. Protect us and guide us. Amen."

Emily opened her eyes, smiling. "I like short blessings. Sometimes Grandfather prays so long the food gets cold."

Kate had baked light rolls. She passed a buttery cream sauce filled with chunks of ham to spoon on top. Raw carrot sticks, dried grapes, and celery chunks rounded out the menu. Emily had never tasted anything so delicious and said so.

"You'll have to come again," Kate answered.

Tea was served in tiny cups with a floral design. Dessert was bread pudding with cream.

After lingering over the tea, Emily pushed her chair back. She felt full. Content. "I'll wash dishes."

"You'll do no such thing," Kate said. "We'll stack them in the dish pan for now. We have more important things to do. Remember the Sears & Roebuck Catalogue I was telling you about?"

Emily nodded. How could she forget when Kate constantly mentioned all the merchandise one could buy through the mail order?

The catalogue was enormous. Emily touched the cover. The only book allowed in the Drake household was the Bible. Once Emily brought home a book of poems from the library and Grandmother frowned. "This reading of untrue things can't be worthy or honorable of our God," she remarked. Emily had returned the book the next day, unread.

"This should be called the *Wish Book*," Kate said, "as I keep wishing for this and wishing for that."

Fascinated, Emily selected a bicycle she would like to own. Kate liked the bicycles, but wanted a sewing machine.

"I plan to order this machine," she said, pointing at a sleek model on page 252. "I've been saving my money and almost have enough now."

A sewing machine would be wonderful. Grandmother had an old treadle style and it worked, but it looked nothing like this one with shiny black paint.

"I'll also pick out a new crinoline and some under things. You can't imagine how pretty they are."

Kate suddenly sprang to her feet. "It's getting late. We better get the dress cut, hemmed, and pressed."

The sound of scissors on the beautiful material made Emily cringe. Noting Emily's discomfort, Kate said, "It was sitting in my closet gathering dust, so don't give it another thought." She handed Emily a threaded needle.

Emily began sewing tiny stitches while Kate checked to see if the iron was hot enough to press.

"I can't keep this," Emily said then. "Grandmother would never allow me to wear it."

"More's the pity." Kate looked thoughtful for a moment. "But we'll worry about that later. Here, you press while I change."

At eight, the two were ready. The red taffeta had a wide, full skirt with white lace at the bodice. A cameo brooch was pinned at the throat while two rings, one a garnet, the other diamond, adorned Kate's fingers. Emily watched as she dabbed perfume behind her ears. It smelled of lilacs.

Emily smoothed out the skirt of her dress. She felt like a princess. Against Kate's advice, she had brushed and rebraided her hair, wearing it as she always did. Pink dots appeared on both cheeks. No rouge needed here, not that Emily would have agreed to use any.

"You *are* pretty with those high cheekbones." Kate made her turn around while she investigated all sides. "I truly mean it. What I wouldn't give for such a creamy complexion."

Kate had agreed to let a friend drive them to the dance, and they had grabbed bonnets and coats when the horses pulled up out front.

"Kurt, this is Emily," Kate said. "Kurt's recently moved here from Germany."

Emily saw how the young, blond man gazed at Kate with an intense look. Kate seemed oblivious, however, as he helped her into the buggy and gave Emily an assist as well. The three arrived just as the fiddlers began tuning their instruments. Several others had come, and a big fire roared in the fireplace. Chairs lined up along two walls, and off to one side was the table with punch and plates of cookies. Red streamers decorated the room. She had never seen anything so pretty. Trembling, Emily followed Kate. Before Kate had a chance to introduce her to anyone else, the music started and Kurt took Kate's hand, leading her to the middle of the floor.

Emily sat in one of the chairs and watched while Kate danced every number. Breathless, at the end of one round, Kate came over, pulling on Kurt. "Emily, Kurt loves to dance. Do you want to try? He'd be a good teacher."

Emily shook her head. It didn't seem quite as wrong if she just watched and listened. "I'm doing fine, thank you. The music is wonderful."

The Virginia Reel started up and Kate ran off with Kurt in tow. "I can't imagine where Ben is," she called over her shoulder. "When he arrives, you'll know," she added.

And she did. The Reel had just finished and another round dance was beginning when the door opened. Emily sensed the sudden quietness though the music was still playing. Every head seemed to turn to view the tall, bushy-haired man who had strode in. Ben Galloway. It must be. He surveyed the dancing people as if looking for someone, then walked over to the refreshment table.

Emily watched, absorbed by the bulk of him. By the dress. His coat, a heavy wool, had a wide collar and huge buttons. The boots looked new, his jeans were bluer than most, and the flannel shirt a bright plaid. "He's Scottish, you know," Kate had said. "That's why we're friends, but that's all we are."

The music was over and seconds later Kate was at his side, giving him a hug. "Ben, I thought you weren't coming tonight," she trilled.

Emily winced. Kate was like that, hugging people all night. It was her way of expressing herself. Besides, she knew everyone.

He smiled, taking her hand as the music started. It was fast. Maybe it was the dance Kate said she liked best. A polka. Kate and Ben started off across the floor, followed by a blaze of color as others joined in. Those who didn't dance laughed and stomped their feet and clapped their hands. It was so merry. Before she realized it, Emily was clapping, too.

When the dance was over, Kate was grabbed by another man. Ben shook his head at a woman with bright red hair and walked toward Emily.

Emily looked down at her lap, knowing Ben was coming over, not knowing what she would say to him.

The boots stopped in front of her and she was forced to look up. "Miss Emily Drake?"

"Yes." Her voice sounded unusually clear. Strong.

"Ben Galloway here. Kate would have introduced us, but as you can see, she is the one every man wants to dance with. And no wonder."

Emily laughed, happy to have the attention drawn away from herself. "Yes, she's so light on her feet. And dancing makes her happy."

"And you, Emily? What makes *you* happy?" His eyes met and held hers for a long moment. She felt the blood rush to her cheeks as she finally looked away.

He stood, as if waiting for her answer. What could she say? She didn't know what made her happy. In all honesty she had never thought about it much. Maybe she'd never been happy. If laughing and dancing was part of it, she doubted she would ever know. Going to meeting satisfied her. She knew she was a child of God, that He loved her and watched over her. That gave a sense of satisfaction. But happy? Perhaps writing in her diary qualified. Or laughing with Kate at work over something trivial.

"Not much, I daresay, if it takes you this long to come up with an answer." He pulled a chair over and sat beside her. His presence overwhelmed her. She'd never looked into such vivid brown eyes, gazed upon such thick, bushy eyebrows. And the hair. It looked as if he'd combed it, but somehow it didn't matter. It was going to stand up like that because it was thick and had a mind of its own.

"I enjoy reading," she finally said. "And writing. In my diary."

A smile flashed across his broad face. "Ah, a writer. A reader. Both worthy endeavors. And I understand from Kate you're the best chocolate dipper in town."

She blushed more than before. "I don't quite agree."

"You are an educated young lady, I can see, and a pretty one, too. Not too many can lay claim to both."

Emily had the sudden impulse to run. Her throat felt dry and her hands seemed to be twisting in her lap.

"I want to dance with you, Emily."

"I—I don't dance."

"Of course you do. Everyone dances."

"No, it's against my beliefs."

"Which are?"

"I belong to the Society of Friends and we feel that dancing is wrong—"

"So, what brought you here?"

"Kate insisted. And since I promised, I had to come. Just this once." She didn't go on to tell him how persistent Kate had been, or how much she wanted her to have fun.

"Anyone in such a beautiful dress has to dance at least once."

Emily could see he wasn't going to go away until she agreed.

"I'll request a waltz, because it's one of the easiest to learn." He pushed a stubborn lock of hair off his forehead. "Then I'll show you how to waltz. We won't say you danced. You can say you waltzed."

Emily began stammering, but Ben had walked across the floor and was speaking to the musicians.

The slower music started and Emily felt herself being drawn from the chair and into the stranger's arms.

"It's simple. A one-two-three, then one-two-three as we turn. We do the one-two-three repeatedly and waltz around the room. Just like this."

She felt tiny in his arms, her forehead reaching the middle of this thick chest. While his right arm encircled her waist, his left arm guided her into the moves. The one-two-three was easy. It was the moving about that took careful concentration.

"There. You are doing splendidly." He tilted her back so he could see her face. "Smile, Emily. This is supposed to be enjoyable."

But how could it be enjoyable when she felt her heart tripping away against the bodice of the blue velvet. She could barely breathe, and she felt as if she might float away.

Then he was humming the tune, his breath in her hair as she trembled against him.

"I grew up in Iowa, and the first time I went to a barn dance, my older brother taught me to waltz. That's why this will always be my favorite dance."

"Iowa?" Emily repeated.

"Yes. I'll be returning one day soon, on the train this time."

The train. Emily thought of her plans to take the train to California to see her family. The corners of her mouth turned up ever so slightly at the thought of seeing her parents again.

"See? You can smile, Emily Drake." He held her even closer. "And you dance wonderfully considering you never tried it before. I think you were teasing me."

"Oh, no." Emily stopped and stepped back. "I wouldn't tease about such a thing. And I don't lie."

The music stopped and Emily's heart beat even faster. "I have never danced. I. . .shouldn't be here now. . ." Emily realized they were the only ones on the floor, and in utter frustration, she tore out of Ben's arms and whirled off the floor and out the door. Tears pressed against her eyelids as she realized what she had done. Not only had she come to a dance, but she had actually danced with a man. Or waltzed, as he called it. And she had *liked* it. How could she like something that was wrong?

Ben was at her side, apologizing. "I am sorry, Emily. I would never want to cause you pain. But I won't say I am sorry for the dance. I enjoyed it and will think of you every time I hear 'The Blue Danube' Waltz."

Emily looked away. "I must go home."

"There's more than an hour left to dance."

"I—must go," she repeated.

"Then let me see you home."

She went to the room to fetch her coat and hat. "Thank you, Mr. Galloway, but I'd rather walk."

"I have a buggy outside."

"No. It's not far and it will help clear my head." A verse came to mind, one from Psalms. *I have gone astray like a lost sheep; seek thy servant; for I do not forget thy commandments (Psalm 119:176).*

"Kate won't be leaving until the last dance is over."

"I know. That's fine. I know my way."

"May I see you again—say in some other way—not on the dance floor?"

Emily wanted to say yes; she longed to say yes, but it would be wrong. Surely God had not put this man in her path. He was not to be her prayed-for husband because she had met him at a dance. God was sending someone else her way, someone who believed as she did and would be a good mate.

"I have a friend," she said then. It was true. Pastor Luke Morrison would be a friend. He would also be her minister. And it was to him she could go to pour out her heart, her troubles. Ask for forgiveness for her wrongdoing.

Ben cleared his throat. "Kate told me you didn't have any men friends. I naturally assumed this to be correct."

"She doesn't know about this one."

"Oh. Someone new then."

Ben stood back and watched the tiny woman at his side. He had danced with scores of women since he could remember, since the first time older brother Jesse introduced him to dancing, but he had never felt this way about any of them. He had always been sought after as a dancing partner, but none of the faces came to mind now. Kate, though beautiful and lively, was a good friend. He could talk to her about anything, but there it ended. There was no special feeling between them. Not like he felt about this woman. He had this sudden urge to protect her, to fight her battles, whatever they might be. From the frown on her face he knew she must have lots of them to fight. He also knew he wasn't going to find them out if he didn't change his tactics.

Emily lifted her chin and gazed up at him. She was proud. A fighter. He had known that at first glance.

"Mr. Galloway, I really must go now."

He tipped his hat and watched while she trudged across the worn path, past the horses and wagons. His heart ached. His whole being ached with the sudden desire to run after her, to take her into his arms and to kiss those soft lips.

"Good-bye, Emily," he called out after her, watching as she sidestepped mud puddles, lifting her dress carefully. Then he went back inside.

The night was clear and as Emily walked a prayer began forming. "Please still my heart, O Lord. It was wrong what I did tonight. I realize why now. This man, this Ben Galloway, is a wonderful dancer, but I know nothing about his other attributes. He cannot know You, Father, or he wouldn't have been at that dance. He cannot believe that I know You, for what sort of witness was I tonight? Oh, please, please forgive me."

The tears began falling as she walked to Kate's. The velvety dark sky that usually intrigued her with its canopy of stars only troubled her more. Now she wished it were raining. Rain would help her forget her sorrows. Rain would also help cleanse her spirit. Tomorrow she would pray at meeting, but for tonight she would read and repent. Read. Did Kate even have a Bible in the house? If so, she had not seen one. But how could one not have God's Word? Here she boasted of the Sears & Roebuck Catalogue, but probably didn't own a Bible.

Emily slipped into the back door and closed it gently. Falling to her knees, she began praying in earnest, then recited the twenty-third Psalm: " 'The Lord is my shepherd. . . . he leadeth me in the paths of righteousness for his name's sake. . . .' "

David's plea in Psalm 51 came to mind next: *Create in me a clean heart, O God; and renew a right spirit within me. Cast me not away from thy presence; and take not thy Holy spirit from me. Restore unto me the joy of thy salvation. . . .*

But nothing soothed her or calmed her pounding heart.

She began washing the dishes, swept the floor. Anything to keep busy. Tomorrow she would feel better. Tomorrow would bring the forgiveness she needed so desperately. Her silent prayers would be lifted to God. In the presence of others she would surely feel His comfort. But tonight all she saw was Ben's face over and over again, feeling the touch of his hand as he guided her into the steps, seeing the smile that took over his whole face. And the hair. That impossible, thick thatch of hair that made a giggle slip out of her mouth as she remembered it.

Ben was not only in her mind, but was part of her heart as well. Without realizing it, he had captured her heart in a way she had never thought possible. She, a child of God, had fallen for the beguiling charm of a heathen, a non-believer. This wasn't as bad as blasphemy, but close. She had become part of the world, enjoying worldly things, and it was the one thing the Friends talked about, how they were inspired by God to do good, to better the world, to change things, and Emily certainly hadn't held up her end. She had thrown caution to the wind and now would pay the consequences of having that memory embedded in her forever. The memory of waltzing with the best dancer in Multnomah County. The man with the twinkling eyes and the bushiest eyebrows she had ever seen. It would be a long while before she would forget Mr. Ben Galloway.

Chapter 4

Emily was wakened by the sound of horses and a carriage pulling to a stop in front of Kate's.

She'd been lying on the sofa with a quilt around her lap, the lamp burning dimly. She hadn't planned on falling asleep, but it had been a full day and evening.

Kate's voice was calling good-bye, then footsteps ran up the porch steps. A rush of wind came in with her.

"Emily?"

"In here." She pulled to a sitting position. The velvet dress lay across a chair where she could admire it.

"Why did you run out like that?" Kate leaned over and turned the lamp up. "Are you sick?"

"Oh, no, nothing like that."

"You could have at least told me you were leaving."

Emily felt the sting of tears against her eyelids. "I'm sorry, Kate. That was very rude of me."

Kate sat and unbuckled her shoes. "I didn't mean to make you feel bad. It's just that I was worried. Of course Ben explained that you wanted to leave and insisted on walking home alone."

"It was a nice night."

Kate sat with shoes off and began removing her jewelry. First the garnet brooch, then a thin silver bracelet. "Ben wants to see you again."

"I. . .I. . ." But Emily couldn't get the words out.

"Don't you think he's nice?"

"Yes, but—"

"And totally polite."

"Oh, yes, the perfect gentleman."

"And how about the dance? You waltzed wonderfully out there, Emily. You two never missed a beat."

Emily's cheeks flushed, and she could feel the pounding of her heart against her rib cage. "I looked good because Ben is a marvelous dancer and easy to follow." And once again, in her thoughts, she was in his arms and counting the one, two, threes under her breath. It seemed she had been crushed against his chest, but she had liked the feeling. It was safe. Comforting. And it was that thought that worried her, nagging at her that it wasn't—couldn't possibly—be right.

"The dress made me look good, too," she finally said.

Kate leaned forward. "Emily, I'm giving you a compliment."

Her cheeks flushed brighter. "I know you are, but it's. . ."

"All you need do is say 'thank you.' Isn't that easy?"

Emily nodded. Yes, it was easy. If she could just think of the right thing to say at the precise moment, but it never came to her. Perhaps it was because Grandmother had done most of her thinking, and talked for her, too.

Four years ago, Grandmother Beulah thought she had found the perfect match for Emily. Jacob Halvorsen and his mother were new to the area. He was unmarried. Thirty-five years of age. Not bad looking, but painfully shy. Emily remembered how Jacob stood back while his mother told him what to say. Emily, equally shy, watched from the sidelines while Grandmother spoke for her. Jacob said one sentence to her, then looked as his mother coached him on what to say next. Then Beulah gave Emily the answer.

Emily pulled away first, knowing if she'd married someone like Jacob, it would be his mother running his life and Grandmother would continue to run hers. She didn't want that.

"Ben left right after you did," Kate said, "though I can't possibly imagine why."

"He did?" Emily couldn't hear his name without trembling. "I can't imagine why either since there was another hour of dancing, and he arrived late."

"I think he was smitten with you—"

"Kate, no!"

Kate merely smiled. "And speaking of smitten, guess who wants to come calling?"

"Kurt?"

Kate began rubbing the arch of her foot. "Yes, but I'm not ready to think about marrying again."

"He seems like a nice fellow, but you are still hurting inside."

"And missing Charles so terribly much."

"It takes time," Emily said, reaching over to touch her friend. She didn't know about losing a husband, but she'd lost her whole family and sometimes she wondered if time would ever ease the gnawing hurt.

"I like Kurt, though, so I told him he could stop by and take us to church in the morning."

Kate's words slammed into her. "Go to meeting with us?"

"Well, yes. That *is* all right, isn't it?"

"Oh, yes, of course." Emily sat lacing her fingers, then unlaced them again. How could she tell Kate she had hoped it would be Ben coming by in the morning. Not that he would have wanted to attend meeting. He was far too worldly for meeting.

"I'm going to coax a fire out of the embers because I need a cup of strong, hot tea." Kate flounced into the kitchen and seconds later she poked a stick of wood into the stove.

"Make a cup for me, too, please."

"Of course. I was going to do that automatically."

Emily crossed the room and touched the velvet dress. It was so beautiful and she'd felt like a princess. It was a memory she'd have forever. Just as she would remember the one time she'd danced, or "waltzed" as Ben called it. She would rock in her chair by the fire when she was old and wrinkled and tell anyone who would listen about the night she'd gone to a barn dance.

Emily tried to still the sudden beating of her heart, as she remembered sweeping across the dance floor, Ben leading the way. It was like magic, not that she'd ever had anything magical happen to her, nor did she even believe in magic. It didn't matter that her hair was plain, her shoes not fancy, nor that she was void of jewelry or a splash of perfume. Her dress had been elegant and for one small moment she, Emily Drake, felt beautiful.

Then came the shock. Like Eve eating the apple. How wonderful it must have tasted. But she had to pay for her sin. Banished from the Garden of Eden. Emily wouldn't be banished. God forgave people of their sins. It would be difficult, though, just trying to get the moment out of her mind, the memory of the waltz and how it had felt to be in the arms of a man.

Kate had changed into a nightdress and robe, and her hair was free of the sparkling combs. "I feel better now," she said. "Those corsets kill me."

Emily didn't own a corset, but perhaps one day she might need one. The peppermint tea tasted good and Emily felt her muscles relax. She certainly hadn't retired early as Grandfather had requested. She'd never stayed up past midnight before, and it felt strange, yet marvelous.

Kate set her cup down. "You need to get away from your grandparents, Emily. Start living your own life. Sure, I know that young unattached women must be chaperoned, but you're not exactly young anymore. And time is a definite consideration here."

Emily sat up straight. "I owe a lot to my grandparents. I could never just walk out the door. You don't understand how it is."

"Then explain it to me."

Soon Emily was pouring out her heart about when she'd first come to live with them, how much she missed her parents, her brothers and sisters, and how she had hoped that some day she would be able to see them again. If she could only get to California.

"Oh, Emily, how tragic." Kate put her arms around her, drawing her close. "I had no idea. I don't know how you've managed to survive."

"Do you think it's wrong for me to want to go to California?" Tears crowded the blue eyes.

Kate pressed a clean, white handkerchief into her hand. It smelled of lilacs. "No, I certainly don't. I'm just wondering how I can get you on the train and down there."

Emily started telling about her baby sister dying and the oldest one marrying, and that Mary was betrothed now.

"We receive letters several times a year."

"Well, I should certainly hope so. I can't believe they haven't come to see you. And wouldn't your father have wanted to visit his own parents?"

"Traveling is expensive."

Kate took the cups and set them in the sink. "And to think I complained about losing my husband. I'm sorry. Everyone has a burden to bear, it seems; some burdens are heavier. It makes my wish for a sewing machine or running water small and insignificant by comparison."

If only Emily dared wish for things. Her wishes were more in the form of prayers, and over the years the only wish was to see her family once more.

Kate leaned over and kissed the top of Emily's head. "I hope you'll be comfortable in the spare room. Wake me when it's morning. I tend to sleep in."

Emily didn't sleep for a long time. After saying more prayers, thoughts of Ben crowded her mind. She didn't want to think about him, she had prayed she wouldn't, but the idea of seeing him again some time made the feelings resurface. What would tomorrow bring?

❄

Dazzling rays of sun hopped and skipped across Emily's face, wakening her. It was early, and the day showed promise of continued sunshine and warmth.

She shivered. If there was wood, she could build a fire. She stopped, remembering they hadn't prepared food last night, and she shouldn't cook or work on the Lord's Day, but water could be heated on top of the heating stove.

The fire started easily, and in a matter of minutes, the rousing fire warmed the small house. Coffee perked in the pot, and it was the smell that must have roused Kate.

Putting an arm into her robe, Kate stumbled into the kitchen. "I haven't had anyone make me a cup of coffee since I left home, and Mama was the first up and got the fire going."

There was a small amount of pudding left and a handful of dried grapes. It would do, especially with coffee and cream, Emily decided. She had dressed and brushed and braided her hair. No dillydallying as Kate did. She was ready and waiting when Kurt arrived.

Emily answered his knock while Kate hollered from the bedroom. "I'm not finished with dressing. Entertain him, Emily."

Emily swallowed. She couldn't entertain Kurt. What could she possibly say to him? She never knew what to say. She'd learned a long time ago it was better to let others do the talking. Like last night. The only time she talked to Ben was when he asked a question. She felt awkward, but it was even more awkward to let his questions go unanswered, especially when he stood over her, watching and waiting.

"I hear you play the piano," Kurt said, breaking the silence.

"Yes, I do. I've never had lessons, though."

"You can play by ear then."

She nodded. "Yes, I guess that's what they call it."

"That's remarkable. I have no ear for music. Can't even sing. I look forward to hearing you."

Emily nodded. She was going to tell him that it had only been in the last few years that here in the West the Friends' Society allowed music in the meeting, and people began having organs or pianos in their homes, but Kate flounced out of the bedroom and across the room. "You are a dear, Kurt, to be so patient. Thanks for keeping him company, Emily."

"It's so nice of you to come pick us up," Kate went on. "It will be the first time I've attended a Friends' church. How about you?"

"Same here." Kurt folded the rim of his fedora, then straightened it out again. "I started meeting with a Lutheran congregation after arriving in Portland."

His eyes never left Kate as he watched her every move. "You look. . . beautiful," he finally said.

Resplendent in a full-skirted pink-flowered dimity, Kate's lips were red, her cheeks rosy with rouge. Her hair, brushed high on top and decorated with pink ribbons, was soon covered with a wide-brimmed hat. Emily agreed with Kurt's comment.

At last they were on their way. Emily in her simple gray dress and hat, Kurt in a dark suit and stylish fedora, ordered from the Sears Catalogue, and Kate looking positively regal. It was the nicest dress she owned, not counting the red taffeta, she claimed. She'd stand out, Emily knew, but it would be all right. She was a visitor. After the stares, people would settle down to the reason they came to meeting in the first place: to pray and worship God.

The meetinghouse was full when they arrived. Horses were hitched to the fence around the meetinghouse and Kurt had to leave his at the end of the line. The two women waited patiently for him to help them down from the carriage, then stood beside the front door.

A man smiled when he saw Emily, nodded to Kate, and offered his hand to Kurt.

"Thee can find room on this side, down in the front pew where Emily sits," he said, pointing to the left. Kate raised her eyebrows, then followed Emily to the front row.

Emily could feel eyes on them, though most were in silent prayer. She slipped into the pew and lowered her head.

The meetings always began with silent prayer. Then Emily would slip out of the pew, go to the piano, and open with a rousing hymn. She was shy until her fingers hit the keyboard. Then she was at home as she played a medley of songs. She ended with her favorite, and one she thought Kate would like: "What a Friend We Have in Jesus."

Guests were introduced and Emily heard a couple of words of exclamation when Kate stood. Her bright dress definitely made her stand out. Kurt's suit was appropriate, but his fedora was much more stylish than the hats most of the members wore.

The prayers went on longer than usual, or so it seemed to Emily. She glanced sideways at her friend, wondering if she would start writing notes. But Kate's eyes were closed and Emily saw a tear roll down one cheek. As Kate's mouth moved, she removed her handkerchief and dabbed at her face. Emily closed her eyes and took hold of Kate's hand. Kate squeezed back.

No longer did Emily feel distracted. She had prayed for forgiveness but now prayed for her friend's problem. Her heart. Her soul. Suddenly Emily's prayers seemed inconsequential.

Later, as they headed up the aisle, Kate whispered, "Now I understand, Emily, why you believe. I truly felt God's presence today. Thank you for inviting me and for praying for me."

"You knew I was praying for you?" Emily asked.

The feather on Kate's navy blue hat pointed skyward. "Of course I knew."

Emily smiled. "I hope you come again, Kate."

"And I loved your playing. Your fingers go up and down that keyboard so fast, it took my breath away. I never saw anyone play with such energy, such verve."

Kurt had gone out to get the carriage. Kate waved her handkerchief, then hurried over, holding her hand so he could help her up. Emily called out good-bye, then joined her grandparents at their wagon.

"Isn't thy friend unmarried?" Grandmother asked.

"She's a widow," Emily said.

"Then who is this man with her?"

"He's just a good friend."

"But she's too young to be unchaperoned."

Emily didn't answer. It wouldn't matter what she said, Grandmother would find something to disagree with.

"Did thee have a good visit?" Grandfather was at her side, touching her arm.

"Yes, Grandfather, I had a wonderful time."

"Thee was missed," Grandfather added. "I'm glad thee enjoyed thyself."

Emily felt good and warm on the way home. The sun was shining out of a clear blue winter sky. Christmas was in three days. Grandmother would bake special sugar cookies to have with their morning tea. There would be additional prayers, and more reading from the Bible, but it would be the Christmas story and she never tired of it.

As for songs, she would play Christmas carols. "Silent Night, Holy Night," "Hark! the Herald Angels Sing," and "O Little Town of Bethlehem." The afternoon would be spent quietly, then the Drakes would attend Fourth Day night prayer meeting. Best of all, there would be no work that day or the next.

"We're almost out of wood," Grandmother said, as she lighted from the buggy. "I know it is Sunday, but thee can bring in an armful before dinner."

Emily looked at the farmhouse. A large two-story, it looked plain with its weathered gray boards, but it was home to Emily. She had enjoyed staying with Kate, but for some strange reason, something she couldn't quite explain, it was good to be home. She was used to the simple way of doing things. Austerity. Prayer time. Quiet First Day afternoons. This was part of Emily's life. She felt shame now to think she had dreamed about a man such as Ben. Ben with his expensive clothes, his splendid horse and buggy, while her grandparents owned an old horse and a plain wagon with a worn canopy.

Yes, this was her life, the one God intended for her to live. Kate had her life and though they could still be friends, Emily knew she'd never fit into Kate's world. There was no sense in even thinking about it anymore—in dreaming about Ben Galloway—or remembering the way his eyes seemed to tease her into thinking she was special. He was handsome, but he wasn't right for Emily. It was that simple. And with that thought, she went to gather wood for the stove, a job she could do and do well. One couldn't waste time thinking about things that weren't meant to be. Her home, her position in life was to be an upstanding member of her church, and community. And maybe, just maybe the new preacher would be the person for her. He was coming soon now. Would she feel about him as she felt about Ben? Or would she feel more stable, more controlled? She was sure the latter were true. If God had His hand in it, she would know, yes, Emily would know. She was certain it was Providence that brought Pastor Morrison to Oregon. Emily did not believe in luck. No. It was an answer to prayer—all part of God's timing, the way God took care of His people.

Emily stood, looking into the sky, breathing in the cold, clear air. Was her life beginning to change? Was it possible that one day she might take the train to California to see her family again? The thought made her tremble. She looked forward to seeing Kate at work tomorrow, just as she looked forward to meeting the new pastor when he arrived next week. A tiny part of her thought of Ben again, but she shut the idea out. He couldn't be part of her life. It wasn't right.

Filling her arms with split wood, she headed for the house.

Chapter 5

Monday Emily had already finished a row of chocolates when Kate arrived.

"Kurt gave me a ride," she said.

"It sounds as if he's pursuing you."

She grinned. "That he is."

"Are you beginning to like him now?"

"Somewhat. But not in the way he wants."

The day went swiftly while they spoke of meeting and the way Kate had felt God's presence. "Maybe I do need God in my life, Emily, but I'm not ready to give up my beautiful dresses, jewelry, or rouge."

Emily smiled. She had heard people make that comment before. It was something Kate needed to struggle with on her own. It wouldn't matter what Emily thought or said about the matter. It was an individual choice. That's what the Society of Friends believed.

At closing, Emily heard what she thought was a familiar voice and looked up as Ben Galloway strode into the room. Her cheeks flushed, and she suddenly didn't know what to do with her hands.

"Hello, Kate. Emily."

His eyes fastened on hers and her heart did a flip.

"Hello," she finally stammered.

"What brings you here?" Kate asked, removing her hair net. "As if I didn't know."

"I came to take Emily home, you, too, if you want."

"Oh, I couldn't," Emily interjected. "It isn't proper that I should go with you."

"Not even to see my new team of horses, and the carriage I bartered for?"

"Well, *I* want to see the new horses," Kate said. "And I also want to hear all about this bartering."

Ben glanced at Emily with a hopeful look.

Kate took his arm. "I've got the perfect solution to that problem. You can take Emily home and then me. That way she has a chaperone."

Emily's heart beat hard against her dress. "Yes. That would be appropriate."

"I'll sit in the back and not even listen," Kate said, fluffing her hair out.

"I think I should sit in the back," Emily said.

Ben looked down at her. She was even more beautiful than he remembered. Without a trace of rouge, her skin was smooth and clear, her cheeks a natural pink. The hair, parted in the middle, was braided, the way it had been Saturday night. He had memorized the way she looked, and the eyes—the eyes that had captured his interest—were now staring at him with that same look. All he wanted to do was touch her hand. Take her home. Walk her to her door. Speak with her. But it wasn't going to be easy. He could certainly see that now.

What need he do to win her approval? For him to call on her? Speaking to her grandfather was the first step. Kate was serious when she said Emily needed a chaperone. Most parents believed that, but Emily wasn't a young girl. She was a woman, in need of love, a husband, marriage, and family. He had sensed that from the first moment they met. Yet her mouth was telling him no, as her eyes said yes, yes, yes.

He helped her with her coat.

Emily took a deep breath. She had to. She couldn't let Ben know what she was thinking. She couldn't believe she was thinking any of these thoughts, noticing again how vivid his eyes were, the thick hair that appeared unmanageable, the air of confidence that penetrated his being. How could this be happening to her? Why hadn't she heeded her own advice? Hadn't she worked it all out in her mind, convincing herself that she didn't need Ben in her life, let alone her thoughts?

Unequally yoked, unequally yoked kept whirling through her brain as he took her arm and helped her into the carriage.

The horses were sleek. Two fine black horses with white markings. They appeared identical. They raised their heads as Ben approached and gave each a lump of sugar.

"They expect it," he said. "And I want to keep them happy."

Kate laughed. "I think you'd make anyone happy that was part of your life," she said.

The words weren't lost on Emily. She might be considered naive, but she caught the meaning.

The carriage was more of a surrey with a square roof covering everyone, even the driver. A bit of fringe dressed it up and the seats were of black, glossy leather.

"I've been thinking, though, about trading these in for an automobile. It's the best way for getting around these days."

"An automobile?" Kate trilled. "Really? That's a wonderful idea, Ben. I rode in one once and nearly lost my hat, but it was fun. A real adventure."

"It would be an adventure, all right," Ben said, his eyes twinkling as he glanced over at Emily. She remained motionless in the seat beside him, and he longed to reach out and touch the side of her face, make her look at him instead of straight ahead on the road.

"I get the second ride, after Emily, of course."

Emily felt her face redden, as she put a gloved hand to her mouth. "Don't be silly, Kate. Ben's your friend. You knew him first. You definitely get the first ride." And even as she said it, she wondered how she would explain the fine horses and fancy carriage to the grandparents, let alone a car with an engine, in the event that she should ever actually ride with Ben. This was happening way too fast. And what was she going to say to Grandmother, who would most certainly be watching from behind the curtained window in the kitchen?

"I've found a partner," Ben was saying, breaking into her thoughts. "We've just finished the Talbot mansion. I build cabinets, you know. This is the Talbots' old carriage and team. Seems Mr. Talbot bought an automobile and it arrived yesterday. This was in payment for all my hard work in the study. They have countless books, so I built fine oak shelves on three walls."

Books. What Emily wouldn't give to own one book, let alone numerous ones. It would be so wonderful, so leisurely to be able to read. And it surely couldn't be a sin as Grandmother suggested. "Idle hands are the devil's workshop" was one of Grandmother's favorite sayings. "I don't believe there's time for reading unless it's God's Word."

They came to the road leading into the lane where the Drakes' farmhouse stood. Emily touched Ben's hand. "I'd like to get out here, please."

"What? So you can walk in that mud?" His twinkling eyes met hers. "What sort of man would I be if I didn't walk you to your door?"

Fear rose in Emily's breast. She couldn't chance her grandparents meeting Ben. At least not yet. She had to think of explanations, reasons for his being there.

"Stop!" she commanded in as loud a voice as she could muster. She hopped out of the carriage, before Ben could put the reins down and walk around to assist her. She knew it wasn't ladylike, but if she hurried in, she would fare better.

"Thank you for the ride." She readjusted the skirt of the brown dress, avoiding his eyes, knowing the gaze was still there, the gaze that had a way of captivating her, making her thoughts all tangled up inside.

"I want to see you again tomorrow," Ben called out as Emily hurried up the road. "Lord willing," he mumbled under his breath.

Emily began bracing herself for the barrage of questions she knew would be forthcoming. Grandmother could see the side road from the kitchen window, and this time of day always found her busy with preparations for supper.

But neither grandparent was in the kitchen or dining room. Muffled voices sounded from the direction of the parlor, and Emily wondered who was paying a call at this time of night. Maybe the new preacher had arrived sooner than expected. She held her breath and without removing her wraps, tiptoed down the hall.

There were no guests, but a tree was in a stand, its lofty branches filling one corner of the room. Emily stood, staring in disbelief.

"Surprise!" Grandfather called out. "Come see what we have done."

Stringed popcorn and tiny candles decorated the Douglas fir, and she recognized it as one of the trees from the corner of the acreage. Each year in the past Emily decorated a tree with material scraps and bits of colored yarn. When one grew too tall, she found a smaller one. She had asked to bring a tree into the house that first year she came to Oregon. They always had one in California and it was just one small part she missed, but when she asked her grandmother about it, she scoffed, saying they didn't have time for such foolishness on the farm.

"Any size would do," she remembered begging those first years. But they had been adamant, especially Grandmother. And Grandfather always went along because it was easier. Yet Emily thought she caught a glimpse of empathy from him. If it were up to him, he would have said, "Fine, let's cut a tree." Now she had her tree, and she wondered at his decision. She knew it was Grandfather who had taken special effort to go chop the tree, then haul it to the house. Chores were difficult to do, so this took extra work and time. How had this come about when Grandmother always claimed it was pure nonsense and in no way honored the Christ Child? It was the same reason Grandmother gave when Emily wanted to cut and bring in a bouquet of spring blossoms. "They look much prettier outside. That's where God intended them to be."

Emily's first few years on the farm had been magical with the forest of trees, their branches forming a canopy over her head when she went on evening walks in the summer. Then as the need arose, Grandfather sold off the timber, then the lot, then more trees, until the only ones left were the few bordering their property. Emily's trees had been on the line. She was surprised Grandfather had cut one.

She clasped her hands, still saying nothing.

"Well, what does thee think?" Grandmother stood back, hands on hips. "It was your grandfather's idea, of course. He wanted to surprise thee."

"And it looks as if we've succeeded," Grandfather said. "Yes, thee is certainly surprised."

Emily took a deep breath. The tree, perfectly round, sat in the corner by the window, its fragrance filling the parlor that usually smelled musty. The window faced east, and that was why they hadn't seen Emily trudging up the lane after hopping out of Ben's carriage. Looking at the decorated tree, at her grandparents, she burst into tears before fleeing from the room.

She heard the sound of her grandparents' voices echoing as they came down the hall. Grabbing the bucket, she ran outside to pump water. Pumping water gave her time to think. It was a day of surprises. The tree made her happy. Seeing Ben made her happy, so why was she acting in this strange way? Why was she crying now? Wiping her tears on the sleeve of the threadbare dark coat, she pumped all the harder. Soon the bucket was full and coming down over the side, wetting her feet. She stopped, jumping back, noticing the small puddle.

The back door opened and Grandmother stood, as if waiting for an answer, an explanation for Emily's unexpected outburst. Emily took a deep breath and lifted the bucket up and moved past Grandmother, who had not spoken. The light from the lamp cast shadows on the dishes, as she hoisted the bucket up onto the small wash stand. The table was set, as it always was, while they waited for her return from work. She smelled the savory aroma of beef stew bubbling at the back of the stove. Big chunks of bread filled the plate, while butter and homemade cherry preserves sat in the middle of the table.

"Now, what was the reason for thy tears?" Grandmother wasn't about to let it go. "You asked for a tree, and now you have one. It was too tall for the ceiling, so your grandfather had to chop off the trunk, then make a stand."

Her grandfather hobbled into the kitchen, regarding her curiously. "Thy cheeks do look unusually bright—"

"A dose of cod liver oil is what thee needs."

"The tree. . .it's lovely," Emily finally said. "I. . .I was crying happy tears, not sad ones."

"Happy tears? Never heard of such!" Grandmother scoffed.

"Yes, thee has," Grandfather remarked. "Thee cried on our wedding day. Now tell me, were those tears of happiness or sadness?"

Grandmother "humphed" and turned her back. Seconds later, the stew filled a bowl, the steam rising to the ceiling. "I say it's time to eat."

They sat and silently asked the blessing.

Emily sat rigid, her eyes filling again. She couldn't explain it. Perhaps it was guilt. Guilt for going to the dance. Guilt for riding home with Ben. Guilt for her transgressions. And then to come in to find the tree, a tree so beautiful it took her breath away. The shock was too much.

"Perhaps thee would like to add the paper chains to the tree after supper," Grandmother said, passing the stew to Emily.

"I didn't know thee saved them." Emily had been surprised to see them in a box, and even more surprised to hear herself lapse into the old speech.

"Yes, I did."

Later they sat in the parlor instead of by the fire. Emily had placed the red and green paper chains around the tree, adding the touch it needed. It was the most beautiful sight she had ever seen. The fragrance filled her being with its piney scent and she wanted the moment to last forever.

"Thee had a good idea," Grandfather said then. "I wish we'd had a tree before this."

They settled against the cushions as Emily read Luke's version of the Christmas story. "And there were in the same country shepherds abiding in the field keeping watch over their flock by night. And lo, the angel of the Lord came upon them, and the glory of the Lord shone round about them and they were sore afraid."

"We are having tea before the prayers," Grandmother said then. "A cup of tea, prayers, and then to bed."

But Emily sat in the parlor long after Grandmother removed the lamp. She wanted to smell the pine, think her thoughts, say her prayers. Things were changing, and it frightened her. It all began with that dance. And somehow she couldn't imagine how that could have anything to do with it. Yet it seemed to. At the thought of Ben she trembled, thinking how wonderful it had been to ride in his carriage. Studying the side of his face, that wild thatch of hair, watching the way he held the reins, the gentle way he commanded the horses to "gee" when it was time to trot.

When he had held her arm as she climbed up, before leaving the candy factory, she had looked just once into his eyes. The same look was there and even now she could see it. It made her cheeks come afire at the memory.

Emily wished she could go riding in Ben's fine carriage some evening. She wished he could come in and see the decorated tree and have a cup of tea with her and the grandparents. She also wished he might come to meeting, that he believed as she did. But "if wishes were horses, beggars might ride," Grandmother always said.

She finally rose to her feet, fetched the lamp by the stove, the one Grandmother always left burning for her. Its flame burned low so as to save kerosene. Even in the stairway she could smell the tree's piney fragrance. It was going to be a wonderful Christmas after all. The most wonderful one she could remember since coming to Oregon.

Chapter 6

Emily could hardly wait to tell Kate about the Christmas tree the next day. She was also eager to give her the gift she'd made, knowing Kate would exclaim over the muffler even if she didn't wear black.

It was Tuesday, the day before Christmas. They would work all day, filling the last-minute orders for Oregon's Finest Chocolates, but they had Christmas and the next day off.

"Well, you're certainly looking happy," Kate said moments after removing her coat. "Almost as good as the night of the dance."

Emily's smile faded.

"Oh, oh, sorry I mentioned it. What happened?"

Emily told her about the tree and about drinking tea in the parlor.

"Maybe they suddenly realized how much they depend on you, and how little you ask for," Kate said. "I've been praying for you, Emily. Praying we'll find a way to get you to California. I just wanted you to know that."

Emily felt a warm glow as she thought about Kate praying for her. Imagine that. It was a good thing she had that to think about because they were so busy filling orders, they cut their dinner time in half. One of the orders had come from Ben. He wanted an assortment of bonbons and insisted that Emily be the one to make the candy. Now as she placed the sweet confections in the small box, she wondered who was going to receive the gift. Not that it was any concern of hers.

Mr. Roberts, pleased with all the last-minute orders, apologized for keeping the girls overtime. "Once the holidays are over, we'll be back to normal working hours."

Emily thought about the box of bonbons several times. Imagine Ben asking her to make them. Imagine Kate praying for her, understanding Emily's need to see her family again. Imagine a tree in the house. Imagine Ben taking her home. Imagine a man looking at her in that way—the way that made her toes all tingly.

"Ben has his train tickets for Iowa," Kate said as they left for the dinner break. "He talked about it while taking me home last night."

"So that's who gets the candy."

"He says he will bring his mother and sister back after he sells the farm."

"He won't be back."

"Yes, he will," Kate insisted. "His mother was widowed last year, and he promised his father before he died that he would look out for her and his little sister."

This promise to his father proved he was a man of his word, Emily thought. Yes, duty prevails. Hadn't she done her duty, too?

"He is coming by tonight," Kate said, biting into a celery chunk. "I'm sure it's because he wants to see you again."

Emily shrugged. He had said something about it, but she hadn't believed him, nor had she encouraged him. She wanted to, how she wanted to, but to do so was wrong, especially when she knew they could never plan a life together.

"I can't have him calling, Kate. You've got to understand why."

"Well, I don't understand why, Emily. Truly you should encourage him. He's a fine man and worthy of you. He's not only intelligent, but has a bright future. There's a demand for good builders in Oregon, and he does wonderful work."

Emily wrapped the remains of her sandwich and said nothing. Then she remembered Kate's gift. They'd been so busy, she'd all but forgotten it.

"I brought you a small Christmas present."

Kate smiled. "I have something for you, also. I didn't mention it before, because I didn't know how you felt about receiving gifts from friends. Let's open them now. Why wait until tomorrow?" Kate said, bringing out a small package wrapped in pale green paper. "Besides, I want to see what you think."

Emily's eyes widened at the beautiful paper. "Kate, I cannot open this. It's too pretty."

"Silly," Kate said. "Go on. It's only paper."

Slowly, meticulously, Emily unwrapped her present, careful not to tear the paper. A silver hair clasp with a scroll design shone under the light. "Oh, Kate, it's the most beautiful thing I've ever seen."

Kate grabbed Emily's braids, unwound them, and pinned the braids together so they fell down her back. "It would go nice like this."

Emily couldn't see how it looked, but she knew it must look elegant. Not that she could wear it to church or around her grandparents, but it was a lovely gift, something she would keep forever.

"Thank you so much, Kate." The words barely escaped past the lump in her throat. "I'll cherish it always." She paused for a long moment. "And here's your gift." She handed Kate the clumsily wrapped present in plain brown paper.

Kate unwrapped the oblong package and exclaimed loudly when she saw the muffler. "Emily, it's wonderful! It's just what I need." She wrapped it around her neck and held her head high. "I truly mean it. It's so warm. And to think you knit it."

"It isn't your color—"

"Maybe not, but it's a good, neutral color and will go with everything I own." She leaned over and hugged Emily hard. "I will wear it proudly."

The women went back to work and Emily kept thinking about the silver clasp, thinking how lovely it was. She was so lucky to have a friend like Kate.

She thought about Ben the rest of the afternoon. What would she say to him? *Hurry back to Oregon?* No. She couldn't encourage him when she knew it wouldn't work. He didn't believe as she did and that was her main concern. The new preacher coming was the one God had in mind for her. It had to be; the timing was right. Emily and he would have a mutual love of the Lord. Together they would pray for the meeting and be good citizens in the community. How could she ask or hope for more?

Ben was punctual. It was five-thirty and Emily had finished his order. He walked to the cloakroom where both women were putting on their wraps.

"May I give you a ride home?" His eyes fastened on Emily with an expectant look.

"I'm not going tonight because Kurt is coming in a few minutes," Kate replied.

"I don't mean to be rude," Emily said, her eyes avoiding Ben's, "but I cannot ride with you. It isn't right."

Ben doffed his hat. "I'm trying to understand, Emily. Kate has explained a few things—about your grandparents."

"There's more," Emily said, not wanting to go into it now. Besides, he wouldn't agree.

"I'll be leaving the day after tomorrow."

"Kate mentioned it."

"I wanted to talk. . .to tell you about my plans. . .to see what you thought. . ."

Emily's breath caught in her throat. Why would Ben want to tell her about his plans? Why would he care what she thought?

"I. . ." the words had difficulty getting out. "I can't see you, Ben. We are too different—"

"Different," he repeated. "But that can be good."

"Not when it comes to honoring God—"

"I see." He turned and without another word walked toward the door. She saw the slump of his shoulders, the way he looked down, and she felt a sudden emptiness. Tears sprang to her eyes. Why was she feeling this way?

How could this be happening to her? She knew in that instant that she must talk to Ben again—that she couldn't shut him out of her life. That she didn't want to, though her brain said yes, yes, it's the only way.

"Ben. . ." It was but a whisper, but he heard and turned.

"Yes, Emily?"

"I would like a ride after all."

He walked back and tucked her hand under his arm.

Kate had wrapped the muffler around her neck and smiled. "Merry Christmas, you two. I'll see you on Friday, Emily. Good night, Ben. And do have a good trip." She leaned over, hugging Emily, then headed for the door.

"I'll see you when I return," he called after Kate.

Before assisting her into the buggy, Ben handed Emily two lumps of sugar. "Thought you might like to feed the horses."

Emily laughed as each horse took his sugar and shook his head as if to say thank you.

Ben made sure she was comfortable before taking the reins. "I'm glad you changed your mind since I may not see you again."

"Kate said you were returning to Iowa the day after Christmas."

He nodded, and she liked the way his chin jutted out. He wore a proud look, one of confidence. Her heart pounded harder than before. It hardly seemed possible that she could be riding with a man in one of the most beautiful carriages she had ever seen. And to think it was his idea—his desire to have her ride with him.

The horses settled down to a slower gait.

"I must convince my mother how beautiful Oregon is. Pearl—my little sister—is ready to come. Together we'll work on Ma."

"And then when I get back. . ." He let the reins fall and the horses stopped. "Emily, I want to come calling when I return. Whatever it takes. If I need to speak to your grandparents, that's fine. I will do that. I will attend your church. Study the doctrine. I am willing to do what is necessary."

She looked away from his intense gaze. How she longed to have him touch her, to pull her into his arms, but of course it wouldn't be right. She mustn't think like this.

He turned her face toward his with his gloved hand. He had to look into those eyes, the eyes he could read so well. Ben knew how Emily felt about him; even without the words, it was there, written on her face, shining in her eyes. If only she could understand it was meant to be.

She raised a hand to her face and looked away. "I have been promised to another man. Remember I spoke of him the night of the dance."

His eyes blazed. "Kate says you haven't even met this man."

"I know, but he is of my faith. He's a good man who lost his wife and baby. He needs a wife."

"Emily," he took her small hand and held it tight. "All I ask is a chance for you to get to know me and me to know you."

Emily said nothing, knowing it was hopeless. Ben could meet her grandparents. He could promise to honor God, to be part of the Friends' Meeting, but he would be doing it for the wrong reasons. It would never be acceptable.

"I can't give you that chance," Emily finally said.

He nodded, his eyes looked straight ahead. "I thought you would say that."

How could he tell her he wanted to change, to go along with the precepts of her church? That his faith was strong and powerful. Because he was of no particular denomination did not mean he didn't love God, or that he didn't serve Him. He did, it was just in a different way. He couldn't believe that God had let Emily cross his path, only to have her taken away to marry someone she hadn't even met, someone who was marrying her because he needed a wife, not because he loved her.

His hand felt the gift in his pocket. Should he give it to her now, or would he wait until after the next church service? He could put off the trip for a few days. All he knew was that it was impossible for him to leave her like this, knowing he didn't have any kind of a chance.

"Emily, I want to see you once more before I go east. I *must* see you again. I'll be at church Wednesday evening."

Her cheeks flamed at the thought. "No, Ben. Go to your family. That's what God would have you do."

"God also wants me to have a wife. I've prayed for one for a good long while and believe that it is you."

Emily didn't know how to respond to Ben's declaration.

The horses started to canter and a wintry breeze blew into the open carriage. She didn't want to go home. She wanted to stay here forever, to feel Ben's strong presence, to go with him wherever he went, even if it was to Iowa. But she knew it wasn't possible. It wasn't right. The time to say goodbye had come. She must not see him again.

The house came into view and she laid a hand on Ben's coat. "Please, stop now. I must go in. I am already quite late."

He stopped the carriage and again she hopped down before he could help her.

"Emily, think about what I said."

She nodded and hurried off, not daring to look back. She wanted to see his face once more, to look into those eyes, to feel him beside her in the carriage, but it was over. She had to return to the life she had known. Another man was on the horizon—a man who was more like her and would be acceptable to her grandparents, to the Friends.

He watched until she disappeared into a house at the end of the rutted road. It was partially concealed by naked maple trees. He wanted to go after her, to touch her again, to lift her eyes to meet his. Even more he wanted to touch her lips, but knew he couldn't. Not now. Not yet.

He shivered from the early evening breeze and picked up the reins. He *would* see her again. Just once more before he left for Iowa. It wasn't a case of "want to" but a case of have to.

Chapter 7

Emily didn't look back once, though she knew Ben stayed at the corner, watching her, waiting for her to go inside. She hoped Grandmother wouldn't notice her pink cheeks. Walking in the winter, though it was only ten blocks from the streetcar stop, usually made her cheeks red, and especially so when it was windy.

When she stepped inside, she smelled the fragrant pine and it made her heart even lighter. Grandmother was already dishing up supper, so she washed up and slipped into her chair.

"I will certainly be glad when Christmas is over," Grandmother said, "so thee can get back to a regular time of getting home."

Supper was eaten, the wood gathered, water pumped, and the dishes washed, rinsed, and left to drain on the sideboard.

Prayers and Bible reading were said in the parlor again that night. The tree seemed to glow from the corner and filled Emily with such gladness, she could scarcely believe it. That, along with the memories of Ben, raced through her mind, making her feel warm and good. She wondered if he really would come to the Wednesday night Christmas meeting, or would he be too busy with his upcoming trip?

She read the scripture from Matthew where it spoke of praying together: *Where two or three are gathered together in my name, there I am. . . .* She wondered if Ben was saying the same prayer she was. *Let there be a way, God. Oh, let there be a way. . .*

Her thoughts surprised her, tormented her. Even as she prayed, down deep she knew to hope was wrong. God answered prayers; it just wasn't always the way one wanted.

The extra work had made her tired, but for some reason she could not sleep, not even after writing in her diary. Ben's face, his eyes kept crowding her thoughts. If only she hadn't met him. How much less complicated life would be now.

She held the silver clasp in her hand before placing it in the nightstand drawer. She wanted to wear it again, but knew Grandmother would not approve.

50

Christmas morning Emily woke to the sound of a gentle rain hitting the roof. No sunshine for the special day. It was okay. She didn't need to go to work. They would eat breakfast, she'd hurry through the chores, and then it would be time to open the few gifts they had made for each other. Grandfather's gift had been the Christmas tree, and perhaps that was part of Grandmother's, too. It was more than she ever dreamed for. She had already received one special gift—Kate's.

"Merry Christmas, Emily," Grandfather called, smiling over his cup of coffee. "May the Lord our God bless thee richly this day."

Emily leaned over, hugging her grandfather. Grandmother turned from the stove, placing a bowl of steaming oats in front of her husband.

"Christmas is like any other day. I can't understand the fuss."

"Thee makes presents every year," Grandfather said, a twinkle in his eye.

"That's because thee makes something for me."

Soon they were in the parlor and Emily looked at her beautiful tree. She handed Grandfather his present.

"Wool socks. Just what I needed." He looked at them with admiration. "You do a better job every year."

"Humph!" Grandmother scowled as she opened her gift from Emily. "Tea towels. Thee does know what I need."

Grandfather gave Emily a decoration for the tree. He had painted a face on a walnut shell, adding cat fur for hair. She placed it on the tree, close to the top. Next was the gift from Grandmother. A black knit hat that covered her ears and had ties. Emily put it on, liking the warmth of the wool.

"Thank you so much." She leaned over and hugged Grandfather, then Grandmother. Her grandmother, not used to such displays of affection, pulled away.

"I'd like to hear some Scripture," she said.

"But thee didn't open my gift," Grandfather said, handing over a bulky looking parcel.

"Oh. Thee shouldn't have."

Grandmother said that every year, too.

A straw basket was under the wrappings and Grandmother actually smiled. "Where did thee find a basket like this?"

"At the emporium that last time we went. I thought thee might like it for thy dried flowers."

Emily read the Christmas story from Matthew and they had prayers. The day flew by quickly and at last it was time for the evening meeting. The rain had stopped and Emily smelled deeply of the night air. Would Ben come? She tried not to think about it, but he kept slipping into her thoughts.

She started the evening meeting with a medly of Christmas carols.

Emily sang as she played, wishing the carols could be played more often than once a year. She had begun the third verse of "Angels from the Realms of Glory" when the outer door opened. She felt the whoosh of cold night air blowing in and turned halfway to see Ben Galloway taking off his hat as he stepped inside. Her heart nearly stopped as one of her fingers hit a wrong key.

He had come, as he said he would. She felt her cheeks flush as she continued the song, chiding herself for trembling inside. How could she have doubted his word? Though she knew very little about him, she knew he was a man of promise. He was also a man of determination, and she couldn't help but wonder what people were thinking as this tall, handsome stranger entered their midst. Would they believe he had just come to worship? It didn't matter. The Society of Friends was open to anyone coming who needed prayer and uplifting.

When the hymn was over, Emily stood and walked over to her usual pew. She could feel Ben's eyes on her, watching, but she didn't dare glance in his direction to acknowledge his presence. She wondered what he would think of the meeting. Surely this was different from other church services he had attended. Most churches did not have long, silent prayers during the service.

Emily's prayer was for a quiet heart, a calm spirit, but neither happened. After the end of the meeting, she rushed to the back of the room.

Ben waited just outside the door. He tipped his hat and smiled. "I had to see you tonight since my train leaves at six in the morning."

"I. . .pray for a safe trip for thee."

"Thank you." His eyes fastened on her. "I enjoyed your playing. It was beautiful and reminded me of my sister Anna. She plays piano and violin."

His voice glowed as he spoke of his sister, and Emily felt herself relax for a moment. "My father used to play the violin when I was little. I'd go to sleep listening to 'Arkansas Traveler.' He came from Arkansas." A lump came to her throat at the memory.

"Come. Can we talk over there by my buggy where everyone can see us, but perhaps not hear us?"

"Let me tell my grandparents where I am—"

But she need not have bothered as everyone's eyes were on Ben. Dressed in tweeds and brown felt hat, he stood out from the others in their simple, plain dress.

Emily saw Grandmother watching her, so she pointed toward Ben's carriage.

"Thee must not take too long," Grandmother said, her voice full of disapproval.

Ben was stroking the neck of one of the horses when Emily walked up.

"It was a nice prayer meeting, Emily. I'm very glad I came."

"I'm glad you came, too." And she meant it, though she knew he was too worldly, and the Friends would never approve. If he had been a Methodist or a Nazarene, he might have been accepted, but not to belong to any church was unthinkable.

"I don't know how long I'll be gone, Emily," he said, his eyes holding hers. "It depends on Ma and the farm and how fast I can sell it. There are many factors."

"I understand."

He took her hand for a brief moment. "I want you to remember what I said yesterday. I meant it. Every word. My heart knows what it wants and needs, and I must see you when I return."

She trembled at his words, wanting to say something, yet knowing she couldn't trust her voice to speak. Must. He had said he *must* see her again.

"You spoke of a man last night. Is he here?"

Luke. He was referring to Luke. She shook her head. "He's due to arrive next week."

A frown creased Ben's forehead. The timing couldn't be more wrong. Here he was leaving, and it was taking all he could muster to do that, and another man was entering Emily's life. A godly man. A preacher. One of whom she would approve, one whom her grandparents and the others would deem worthy and right for her. If ever there was a God—which Ben believed with all his heart—he needed Him on his side like never before. How could he possibly win her over? The competition was unfair. Though Ben had never had a problem convincing a woman of his intentions, this was different. This time it was for real. He wanted her more than anything he had ever wanted.

"When I return I hope to meet this man." He moved closer. "Pray for me, Emily. I need your prayers. I so admire your strong faith."

"I don't think—"

"No, wait. Let me finish." His hand reached out, then stopped. "I will go to your church, Emily Drake, if that's what it takes. I will worship God in the way you do, if that's what it takes. I truly meant what I said last night. I will do whatever it takes—"

"You must worship God because you want to," Emily said then, "not because you think someone expects it. Wanting to is what's important, what counts."

"I worship God now. Always have. My mother taught me prayers and songs from the time I was knee high." He shook his head. "Did you think I was a heathen? That I don't serve God because I dance? That's the real problem, isn't it, Emily?"

Her breath seemed to catch under her rib cage. What could she say? How could she explain that it was the dancing that set him apart from others who believed? How could she discourage this man, who thought it was okay to dance? Even though he believed, which was admirable, it wouldn't be right because he was not of her persuasion.

"Emily, we are leaving."

"I must go," she said as her grandparents' wagon approached. Already she wondered what they would say. There would be countless questions and she would probably end up telling them how she met Ben.

"I can give up dancing," he said then. "It isn't a problem for me."

"You don't know our doctrine—"

"I will learn it then."

"Emily!" the voice was sharper this time.

"I have to go—"

"Emily. . ." His hand reached out. "I will see you again. And that's a promise." He stepped in front, blocking the view of her. Looking down, his dark eyes met hers, and before she could tear away from that penetrating gaze, he leaned over and brushed his lips against her cheek.

"This is for you," he said, pressing a small object into her gloved hand. "A Christmas present. I've been working on it all week long."

"But," she started to protest, "I can't possibly take—"

"It's a gift," he said. "Of course you can take it."

"But. . .I. . .it's wrong to accept a gift."

"I want you to have it to remember me by."

Without saying another word, he jumped onto the buggy seat and shook the reins.

Emily's face, hot from his touch, stood as if suspended in space. Her heart soared as she watched through the darkened shadows at Ben Galloway's retreating back, riding off into the dark night. She unclasped the hard object and held it out in front of her. It was a tiny horse carved from wood. It was beautiful, the hard wood soft and smooth. For her. A gift for her. And he had made it. She swallowed hard as she tucked it into the pocket of her winter coat.

Ben would be gone first thing in the morning and she wondered if she would ever see him again. He said he would return, but would he? Iowa was a long way from Oregon. There were extenuating circumstances. Ben's mother. A sister. Perhaps they wouldn't want to move out West. Perhaps they would talk Ben into staying there.

I'll wait, an inner voice said. *Yes, I will wait, though I know I shouldn't. Though I know it means trouble, I will wait.*

Turning, she walked to the wagon, bracing herself for the words she knew were coming, the lectures, the prayers, and the "how could you even dare think?"

The night sky had never looked so illuminated or so full of stars. And though Emily did not believe in signs, she knew one when she saw it. This was a sign from God that someone cared for her deeply. And she cared back. There was no denying it any longer. And even if he didn't come back, just knowing that he thought enough of her to carve a gift, to come to meeting so he could see her one last time, to kiss her cheek was almost more than she could stand.

Chapter 8

Emily ran to the wagon and, hoisting her skirts up, climbed in. She could feel several pairs of eyes on her, watching, wondering. She wanted to look back to see if she could still see Ben and his carriage, but kept her eyes staring straight ahead. Her heart pounded in her ears as her fingers traced the spot on her cheek where he had kissed her. It had been a gentle kiss, a kiss of promise. It was also the first kiss she had ever received. She knew without asking that her grandparents would never allow her to be courted by someone who didn't belong to the meeting.

They wouldn't get two blocks, she knew, before Grandmother began questioning.

It was one block.

"Who was that man?"

She felt the color rush to her cheeks again.

"Thee knows him from where?" Grandfather asked, before Emily could answer.

"He's Kate's friend," she finally said

"Thee saw him that night thee stayed there."

"Yes."

"Why would he come to meeting?" Grandmother asked.

"He wanted to say good-bye."

"Good-bye?" The grandparents' voices echoed in unison.

"He is returning to Iowa where his mother and sister live. His name is Ben Galloway." Her fingers tightened around the tiny horse in her pocket. The wood was stained a beautiful ebony color so that it resembled his new team of horses.

"When did thee meet him?" Grandmother was persistent.

"Kate introduced us."

Grandmother clicked her tongue. "I knew thee shouldn't go over there that night."

"He's a very nice person," Emily said in his defense.

"But not of our faith." Grandmother drew her wraps closer to ward off the chilly night air.

"No, not of our faith," Grandfather repeated.

"He believes in God. He told me so himself."

"Thee seems to know a lot about him already."

"He came to the factory. We talked there."

It was true. He had come and they had talked. Of course he had taken her home, but she didn't mention that. Still, she had not lied. Every word was true. She just hadn't embellished on it.

"I don't know much. I think he works with wood, building things, like cabinets." Her hand squeezed the small horse.

"Why is he in Oregon?"

"He came with a brother, I believe Kate said."

"Is he returning?"

"He might. He does work for the Talbot family."

Grandfather raised his eyebrows. "They must have paid him well. That would explain the fancy carriage and fine team of horses."

"Yes, I guess so—" Emily said under her breath.

"What else does thee know about him?" Grandmother wasn't through interrogating.

"He leaves for Iowa on the morning train. There. You don't need to be concerned anymore."

"Don't thee use that tone of voice with me," Grandmother said, squaring her shoulders in that formidable way that always frightened Emily.

"I'm sorry." Emily looked away.

"Thee hasn't forgotten about Pastor Morrison?"

"No." And she hadn't. She knew he would be far the better choice, yet there was something about Ben that wouldn't let her mind, or her heart, let go. The night air was cold, but Emily felt warm inside. Her heart pounded and everything inside her seemed to be whirling around and around crazily.

"He isn't right for thee," Grandfather said, giving the horses an extra coaxing with the reins.

"I should certainly say not," Grandmother added. "Did thee see the expensive suit he wore? Obviously he's of the world and doesn't believe in charitable offerings."

"I think it is his brother's suit."

"And that hat. New and fancy. Must have cost a tidy sum," Grandfather went on, seemingly not hearing Emily's comment about the suit.

"We lead a simple life, as you always have, Emily. You cannot put your trust in someone like that," Grandmother went on.

"He is just an acquaintance," Emily repeated.

"Thee would not be happy to be courted by someone who did not believe as thee does," Grandfather said.

They were at the end of the lane and Emily remembered the two rides from Ben. How she had hoped he could come in, to meet her grandparents, see the Christmas tree, sit and have a cup of tea, but he wouldn't have been welcome. They would never accept him, no matter if he did believe in God. He wasn't a Friend. He would never fit in. Kate didn't understand, nor did Ben, but that was the way things were.

"Pastor Morrison arrives next Saturday. All the way from Ohio," Beulah announced, just as Grandfather called the horses to halt. "Myrtle Lee received a letter, and the time of his arrival."

"We will invite him for Sunday dinner," Grandfather said. "Seems fitting, don't you think?"

Grandmother nodded as she climbed down from the wagon. "I imagine he won't go wanting for food for the first few weeks."

It would seem strange, Emily thought, to have a preacher presiding over the meetings. She could never remember that happening before. It might be nice for a change, but what might not be so nice were the expectations directed toward her. Maybe she would have no feeling toward him. What then?

The grandparents went into the house and moments later Emily saw the soft glow from the lamps. She lingered outside, gazing at the canopy of stars overhead. The clear, dark sky promised a nice day, one without rain. *A good traveling day for Ben.* She prayed for a safe trip, and that his thoughts might be of her, even if nothing could ever develop between them. Her fingers closed around the tiny horse in her pocket. She would keep it always in memory of the tall man with thick, bushy hair and eyebrows to match.

Emily opened the door, remembering her forgotten chores. It was a wonder that Grandmother hadn't reminded her. "I'm getting the water and wood," she said, slipping out the back door before removing her wraps.

She was thankful now that she'd chopped so much wood the night before. A bit of kindling, a few large chunks, and two buckets of water should do.

The lamp burned low on the kitchen table, giving Emily enough light to see the water stand. She poured cold water into the basin to wash her face and hands in preparation for bed. The icy water felt good on her hot cheeks. She felt the spot gingerly where Ben's lips had touched so briefly.

"Emily!"

She jumped. "Yes, Grandmother?"

"Thee better go to bed now. We will talk more about this situation tomorrow."

"Yes, Grandmother."

She watched as Grandmother went down the hall carrying a lamp. It was time for bed and she should have been tired, but surprisingly she felt light-headed. Awake. Alert.

The house was quiet as Emily sat in semi-darkness at the kitchen table. Had Ben really meant that he wanted her to wait for him? Would it be acceptable if he were to be dedicated in meeting? Would he then be permitted to come calling? No, she told herself. Why did she think one way one minute, then change her mind? What was wrong with her? How could she have even considered waiting? It wasn't meant to be. How could she dare hope?

Emily paused in the doorway of the parlor, breathing in the scent of the Christmas tree. Ben would be home shortly after Christmas, surrounded by loved ones. She wondered what sort of celebration they would have. She also wondered what his mother looked like and if she was a hugging type of person, or if she was more austere like Grandmother. Somehow she didn't think so. Ben was not standoffish. She could imagine him taking her into his arms and kissing her on the lips. If the Friends hadn't been milling about in the meetinghouse's yard, he might have done that very thing tonight. She would have acted shocked, of course, and he might have apologized. As it was, her first kiss on the cheek was one she would remember for the rest of her life.

She looked at the tree one last time, took the lamp, and proceeded up the steps. She'd left her coat on the hook, but in her right hand was the horse. He was so smooth, so finely carved, from the tip of his head to his tail. The mane was free flowing with ears sharp and pointed. He looked like Ben's horses. Proud as they pranced, heads held high. Her horse might be a race horse with legs that galloped. Free. Oh, to be free like her horse. Free to make decisions. She wondered when Ben had learned to whittle. The horse was something she would always cherish and keep hidden in a drawer beside her bed.

Had she thanked Ben properly for his gift? She'd been so surprised, she didn't think she'd said anything. It wasn't right to accept the horse since she hadn't given him a gift. If only she had knit him a pair of socks. But she didn't know the size of his feet. Closing her eyes, she remembered looking at them the night they had waltzed. They weren't large, nor were they small. Just about average, she decided. Maybe she could guess. Maybe she could work on a pair of socks during dinner at work. If she knit at home, Grandmother would ask questions.

She set the horse on the nightstand next to her Bible and diary. It was her fourth treasure. Besides the diary, a picture brother Tommy had drawn after she moved to Oregon, the silver hair clasp, and now the horse.

The horse needed a name. She thought about Black Beauty after the book she had heard in fourth grade class. Or Belle, after Grandfather's old nag. Ben's team of horses didn't have names, or none that she knew of.

"Black Beauty," she said aloud, and picking it up once more, she held it close to her heart for a long moment. It was the last thing she saw before slipping off to sleep for the night. . .

Chapter 9

Ben Galloway had never felt so alone as he did that night after leaving Emily in the churchyard. Standing there with her hands folded, her eyes watching him, he had wanted to go back, take her into his arms, and kiss her full on the lips. Her cheek felt soft, and he knew his brief kiss had surprised her. Since he had moved in front of her, covering her with his bulk, her grandparents would not have seen anything to construe all wrong. Surely there was nothing wrong with a kiss on the cheek, but from all indications, they were over-protective.

He knew Emily cared for him. The expression in her eyes told all. He now dreaded the trip back to Iowa, wondering how he would manage without her. Her smile would be in his mind, the touch of her hand, the imagined feel of her small, fragile frame.

Would he be able to speed up things? Convince his mother she should sell the homestead and come back with him to Oregon?

And when was this preacher fellow arriving? What if Emily succumbed to his charm? What if he promised to love and cherish her? Since he served the Friends and believed as Emily did, he might win her over, and would definitely convince the grandparents.

Even as he thought it, his hands tightening on the reins, he knew she couldn't love this man as she loved him. It was an unselfish love, for he had it figured out that Emily wouldn't know how to be selfish. It was not something she had learned living with her grandparents. Ben had been selfish when he left Ma and Pearl alone on the farm. Jesse had always been selfish, doing what he wanted, not helping with the farm, nor working with Pa in his wood shop. Jesse fished, hunted, and later drove into town and met women. He never told Ma or Pa, never bragged about his conquests, but Ben knew they knew. They chose to ignore it in the stoic way of the Scots.

Ben's selfish days were past. He now had someone to live for. Someone to pour his heart out to. He had never felt that way before. Was this what it was all about? Could this be the way Pa felt about Ma when he saw her at the edge of the creek bank wading in the water that hot July afternoon? He knew his parents had cared deeply for each other. Ma had borne seven babies. All had lived.

All healthy. She was a raw-boned woman, and it was from that Ben acquired his broadness, his height. Pa had been of slighter build, though tall and angular. He had not worked the land. That had been Ma and the kids' job. And Ma loved the land. Loved growing vegetables. How she would delight in the rich, black earth of the Willamette Valley. He could picture her now, bent over her hoe, breaking up the clods, preparing the ground for spring planting.

Ben had not received this love for working the land, but instead thrilled at the aspect of what one could do with a good piece of wood. Cabinets, tables and chairs were all things he had learned by watching his father measure carefully, then cut. He had taught Ben to whittle, how to use wood, how to be proud of a chest of drawers, a rocking chair, a set of shelves. There had always been a demand for Jebediah Galloway's work, and he'd built things right up until he took so sick he couldn't hold his head up. Pneumonia, the doctor said. Aggravated by daily breathing sawdust. Whatever, it was wicked, and Ben watched as his father grew thinner. Weaker. He seemed to die right before his eyes and there wasn't a thing the doctor or anyone could do.

Jesse had gone off somewhere and didn't even know his Pa was ailing, didn't even know when he died, because he hadn't sent an address or been in touch. He showed up six months after Pa was buried.

"Ben, you gotta come back with me."

"Where to?"

"Oregon. It's great land out there." Jesse's dark eyes glistened with unusual brightness. "Businesses are springing up all over and any man who can do an honest day's work can make money."

Ma had sat, her lips pressed tight. Ben knew what she was thinking. When Ma was angry she got quiet. She was far too quiet now.

"Ma, come with us," Ben urged. "We'll build a new home."

She refused to budge. "I'll be fine right here. This is home. This way I can go to the graveyard every day and talk to your Pa. That's the way it's got to be."

Pearl at fourteen, with waist-length thick, dark hair, begged her mother to go. "Ma, there's nothing to stay here for now. Let's go." But even as she pleaded, she knew it wouldn't work. And being the youngest, her job was to stay here with Ma. That was just the way it was.

Jesse waited a week, working on Ben until he finally agreed to go. On a temporary basis.

"I'm leaving you in charge," Ben said, lifting Pearl's dark blue eyes to meet his gaze. "Here's some money to take care of you, and there are plenty of supplies until I return. I'll be back for you, and if it's as Jesse says, I won't take no for an answer. I have to be the 'man of the family' with Pa gone, and Ma is going to have to come."

"How long will you be gone, Benjamin?"

Ma stood behind him, her hands folded across her ample bosom. She didn't like the conversation she'd just heard and told Ben so.

"Ma, if I can make a better living, then that's what I must do. I'm not a farmer. I can't be. I want to build things like Pa did. Please try to understand."

The train trip had been difficult. Jesse was raging with a sudden fever, and just when Ben had decided to take him off at the next stop to see a doctor—they were somewhere in Montana—Jesse pulled through.

He was involved in a poker game the following day and lost all his money to a rich widow from Eureka, California.

Jesse stayed with the widow and went to Seattle, leaving his clothes with Ben, while Ben got off the train in Spokane and headed on to Portland.

The beauty of the land as the train passed through the Columbia River Gorge surpassed his wildest imagination and he was hooked. Immense fir trees seemed to touch the sky. The Columbia was as long as he could see. He heard it didn't stop until it reached the Pacific Ocean.

At his first glimpse of the Willamette River, Ben lifted his face skyward. He didn't pray with his eyes closed, but always looked up, as if he could see his Maker.

"God, I know this is where You want me to be. What a beautiful spot!"

It was time to settle down, and Jesse was right about the jobs.

"If you can help put on a roof, I'll give you one of my horses," a farmer said.

Another job, another roof. Now he had money for the train back to Iowa. Then he heard about the Talbots and was hired immediately.

Ben rented a room in a boardinghouse and was the best dressed man for miles. Nobody knew he wore Jesse's suits, shirts, and hats. Well, why not? Someone might as well use them.

He shook his head now. If he had followed Jesse to Seattle, he would never have met Emily.

Ben thought back to earlier that day. He had gone out to his acreage, the property he had worked for. The Talbots had changed their mind, building their new home on the opposite slopes of the Willamette, claiming they had a better view on that side. The price for ten acres was reasonable and in no time he had enough to pay for the parcel, plus barter for the team. His partner, John Creel, would lay a foundation once weather permitted and care for the horses until he returned.

He stood on the cliff overlooking the Willamette River. It was a clean river. Deep and clear. A dazzling blue-green, the river was fed by the melting winter snows of Mount Hood. Majestic with rivers, lakes and streams, and snow-capped mountains, Oregon boasted an abundance of natural resources.

Rain fell often in the fertile valley, so the farmer didn't worry about water for his crops. Unfortunately, the rain also turned the roads into slick mud, and mud oozed beneath his boots as he walked across his property.

Rocky bluffs rose on either side of the river. It was a sight he would never tire of, as Iowa was as flat as a sheet. Ben understood why settlers referred to this land as God's country. It was God's country. Hadn't God led Lewis and Clark over this new territory a century ago? Hadn't people been coming to settle it since that discovery?

And though Ben's skills lay with carpentry, he knew the land would always be a part of him. He wondered now how Emily felt about land. The trees? The river? Somehow he knew that she loved the trees, and it was because of that he cleared off only enough land for the house. If necessary, more could be cleared later.

Church. Ben had never been part of a corporate body, but it didn't mean that he did not believe. He believed with all his heart and soul. Too many things had happened in his life not to believe. The wagon accident when the horses got spooked. Thrown clear, he had escaped with a bump on his head. There was the time when he was delirious with the fever and didn't know his own family. Vaguely he recalled cool cloths, mustard compresses, muffled voices as prayers floated over his head. When at last he opened his eyes, his mother said, "Thank You, God, for giving me back my son." There'd been a wintry night when he was caught in a sudden, blinding snowstorm and almost didn't find his way home.

No. God had a hand in his life. He believed it with all his heart. God had also sent him here to Oregon country. Emily had gone to the dance that night, and it was as if God had brought them together for a reason. He was never more sure of anything.

Ben looked out over his land again. As soon as possible, he wanted to buy more parcels so he could build. Houses. Buildings. Shops. Whatever was needed. At thirty, it was time to settle down. To marry. Raise a family. Get going on his business. Yes, he had left Iowa behind, and if it hadn't been for Ma and Pearl and his promise to his father, he wouldn't be returning now.

Pearl, strong and solid like their mother, would find a man in Oregon to marry. Lulu had gone to California three years before, marrying a man in gold country. And Clara, married to a teacher, moved with her husband to his home in Connecticut. Anna, dedicated to nursing, would stay in Iowa. Of course she could find people to care for no matter where she lived. Albert was in Washington State, on some peninsula, fishing the waters of the Pacific, claiming this would be his permanent home. And Jesse. Seattle. Eureka. San Francisco. Who knew where he would be next month, next year.

Ben reached down and picked up a clump of earth. Dark. Solid. Good dirt. He wondered if Emily would care if they didn't farm? Would she be proud to be the wife of a builder? He dropped the dirt and looked into the cloudless winter sky. First he must convince her that he was worthy of her. Convince her that he wasn't a heathen. She hadn't said the word, but her eyes told what her lips did not.

The trip lay heavy on his mind. He wanted to stay to court Emily. All he wanted was a fighting chance. His prayers to God had been clear on that point. Maybe it was time to wait to see what God had in mind. Maybe it was time he learned patience, though patience had never been one of his strengths.

He thought of a verse he had memorized years ago. *I waited patiently for the Lord; and he inclined unto me, and heard my cry (Psalm 40:1).*

He ran a hand through his thick hair. Time for a cut and a mustache trim. Or should he grow a beard? Seemed most men wore beards in Oregon. Not that he needed more hair on his head. Still, beards did look dashing.

He thought again of brother Jesse and the tweed suit. It was the tweed that first caught the eyes of Kate Russell. Happy-go-lucky Kate. He had her to thank for Emily. It was at a dance he told her he had heard the candy factory was hiring. If she hadn't gone to work and met Emily, he would never have seen her and fallen in love.

His heart tightened at the thought of her. The gentle smile. Her high cheekbones. The eyes. Not just the color, though they were a beautiful blue, but the expression. Yes, there were stories in those eyes and he aimed to discover what they were. There was also pain there, and he would find out what caused the pain and maybe help erase it. Even if he couldn't hold her as he wanted to, she helped fill the aching emptiness. And he would forever remember how she had felt as they waltzed around the floor at the grange hall. It had felt good. Right. Surely God understood his intentions.

A breeze flew in from the river and sudden clouds scudded across the sky. Rain was brewing. It was time to go pack.

The train would take three days. Steam engines were a marvel, but Ben wished he could arrive in a day, return in half a day. He couldn't sleep on the trains. They were noisy and soot landed on everything. When he arrived at the farm, he would sleep around the clock, then be ready to sell, to pack, to look forward to his return trip to Oregon. Back to Emily. His mother would love her. He had never doubted it for a minute.

Ben took one last look at the river, turned, and walked down the hill toward the waiting carriage and the new team of horses. Two lumps of sugar waited in his pocket.

Chapter 10

The benches had been polished and a coat of paint applied to the basement walls.

"I think it's silly," Beulah scoffed. "It isn't as if it matters one whit."

"Don't thee like to put thy best foot forward?" Grandfather said. "I think it's fine."

"Humph!" That's as far as Beulah ever went when it came to disapproval of something her husband said or did.

Pastor Luke Morrison was arriving on the train the day after tomorrow. Just in time for the new year. A boarding house was located close to the meetinghouse for him to live in temporarily. He would buy a horse and buggy soon after his arrival and make definite plans then for his living quarters.

Emily tried to get caught up in all the excitement, but her mind kept whirling with thoughts of Ben Galloway. It didn't matter how many times she told herself she was being foolish, she couldn't get the image out of her head and heart. It had only been a few days since she had seen him, but there was an emptiness she had never felt before. A feeling different from when she left her parents so many years ago.

At least she needn't worry about wearing her best dress as she dressed that First Day morning. The gray was the only suitable dress for meeting. She wanted to wear the silver clasp in her hair, but it would remain in her nightstand, just as the blue velvet dress stayed in the depths of Kate's closet. She could well imagine how many eyebrows would be raised if she dared ever wear that to meeting.

She brushed her hair a few extra strokes and braided it quickly.

"Are thee ready?" Grandmother called from the foot of the stairs.

"Coming." She picked Black Beauty up, then set him back in his hiding place.

"I daresay I bet everyone will be there this morning," Grandmother Beulah said. "I just hope he's a true man of God."

When the meetinghouse came into view, it appeared indeed that everyone had come, and had arrived early. Grandfather let Grandmother off, then went to hitch the horses.

They had to sit in the back, except for Emily. She slipped up to the front to play a few opening hymns.

Starting the second song, "Blessed Assurance," she was aware of a sudden quietness, followed by hushed whispers. Emily turned to see Pastor Luke Morrison entering by a side door.

Short with a wiry build, his face was covered with a full, dark beard and mustache. He turned just as Emily looked up and their eyes locked on each other. Emily missed a chord. He nodded, indicating with his hand that he wanted her to stop playing. She didn't even finish the stanza, but took her hands from the keys and waited.

"Welcome, welcome, my friends of God." The voice was low and had a resonant sound. "Shall we pray together." It was a statement, not a question. It was a good, solid, commanding voice and Emily wondered what Grandmother was thinking. Ben's voice had more inflection, and Emily's mind couldn't help comparing. Pastor Luke had a stocky frame, while Ben's was angular and lean. Luke made her think of a picture she had seen of President James Madison. "Short of stature, but mighty of mind," the caption had read. Was Pastor Luke Morrison mighty of mind, also?

Emily took her place on the bench and lowered her head as the silence settled in around her. But try as she might, she could not concentrate on her prayers this morning. Instead, she repeated a few Bible verses and waited.

The prayer time was longer than usual and she wondered if that was Luke's usual custom, or did he want every one to know his heart was open to God's leading, God's command, His will?

Trembling, she thought of that First Day with Kate sitting next to her. It had been a wonderful time, following a night of joy, then pain. Now she had to put that night out of her mind once and for all and listen to what this man had to say. Prepare her mind for what might be forthcoming. If Grandmother had any say in the matter, Emily and Pastor Luke would soon be betrothed. Surely he had been picked by God to be the husband of the spinster Emily Drake.

Emily looked up to find Pastor Luke staring at her. How long had he been watching her? She lowered her head, her face turning pink. What was he thinking? Perhaps he was studying the congregation to see how many mouths moved in silent prayer. She folded her hands, wishing suddenly she didn't have to sit so close to the front where he could see her every move.

He cleared his throat.

"Let's sing another hymn. This is a favorite of mine and I hope yours, too. I've been told that our pianist doesn't need music to read from. Will you please join me in singing 'Faith of Our Fathers.'"

Emily made her way to the piano, her fingers touching the keys and rippling up and down the keyboard.

"Faith of our fathers! living still. In spite of dungeon, fire, and sword. O how our hearts beat high with joy, Whene'er we hear that glorious word!"

There was a brief message, prayer, and again silent prayer. Emily sat straight and felt her hand go numb from clutching her handkerchief so tightly.

At last the meeting drew to a close. She rose and was about to hurry down the aisle when Pastor Luke motioned for her to wait.

"The playing was magnificent, Miss Emily." He held out his hand. "Are there any hymns you don't know?"

His gaze was penetrating and Emily tried to relax. "If I've heard it once, I can usually play it, Pastor Morrison."

"That's excellent. Wonderful." His hand touched her shoulder as he began walking. "I must go talk and meet some of the people. I'll see you later, since I'll be having the afternoon meal at your home."

Emily nodded, but no words came out of her mouth.

"Oh, Emily, what did you think of Pastor Morrison?" Myrtle Lee chortled, suddenly standing at Emily's side. Her dark eyes were expressive.

She didn't say it, but Emily knew what she was thinking. She half-curtsied. "It's so nice to see you, Mrs. Harper. Do have a good First Day."

Myrtle Lee started to sputter, but Emily pressed on, not wanting to be detained any longer. Anything she might say or do would be noticed, and soon everyone would know what she had said. It was far easier to keep her mouth closed.

Emily was glad that Pastor Luke was coming, though she was always tongue-tied around people she didn't know, and if she did say something, it sounded dumb. Of course Grandmother would take over the conversation so she need not worry about it. A simple "yes" or"no" was all that was required.

Since Pastor Luke did not have a horse or buggy yet, and the Drakes' had limited space, Mr. James offered to bring him over. Later, Grandfather would drive him home as there would be plenty of room for just the two of them.

They arrived home and Emily slipped an apron over her gray muslin. She pushed back a loose strand of hair at the nape of her neck. There wasn't time for pins or to worry about what she looked like.

Emily had a good feeling about Pastor Luke. She liked his manner. He appeared confident, as his voice resonated through the meeting. Surely God had sent this man to Portland, to the Society of Friends for a reason. Emily believed that everything happened for the best, that God had a plan for her life, and for all who believed in Him. Could Luke (she could think of him in her thoughts as Luke, but never to his face—it would show lack of respect) be the answer to long-spoken prayers? Would he be interested in remarrying one day? Should she even think about him in that way? One day she knew she wanted to have a husband and children. Yet, even as the thoughts went through her mind, she had difficultly forgetting another face, a warm smile, and the piercing gaze.

Slices of ham, canned snap beans from last year's garden, boiled small potatoes from the root cellar, and chunks of yesterday's bread were placed on the table. Grandmother's berry compote and blackberry jam rounded out the menu. Slices of Christmas fruit cake and Emily's sponge cake would be served with tea and coffee in the parlor later.

Horses pulled up out front, just as Grandmother poked another stick of wood in the stove. Sudden clouds had blown across the sky as rain threatened. The knock came. Grandfather went to answer as Emily felt her stomach churn. "Come in, do come in, Pastor Morrison."

Luke's presence seemed to fill the room, his voice booming out, as he shook hands with Grandfather, then nodded at Grandmother in the kitchen. "Afternoon, Mrs. Drake. And Miss Emily." He removed his hat and overcoat. "I do want you to call me by my first name. Luke or Pastor Luke, if it's all the same to you."

"Dinner will be served shortly," Grandmother said in her no-nonsense tone.

"Here. Come sit by the fire while we wait for the women to set the table." Grandfather motioned to a chair by the stove.

The dining room table was set with Grandmother's best linen tablecloth and matching napkins. Four place settings of the good china and sterling silver were placed on the snow-white cloth. It seemed strange having a fourth person sitting at the table, as the Drakes rarely had company. Emily used to wonder why, but inviting the preacher was different. It was an expected gesture. Emily fetched the butter from the pantry and put the compote and jam on.

"Thee can both come to the table," Grandmother called out.

Emily sat across from Luke, who bowed his head for their silent thanksgiving. When she glanced up, their eyes met. She was the first to look away.

"Oregon is beautiful country, and I 'spect I'll get used to the rain," he was saying. He spoke with a slight accent, a "Midwestern twang" is what Grandfather had called it on the way home from meeting.

"Rain is what makes our crops grow," Grandfather said.

Emily listened to the banter. Words were rarely spoken when there was just the three of them, but Grandfather carried the conversation now and it amused Emily.

She watched out of the corner of her eye, not wanting Luke to catch her looking. She might have entered the conversation—now they were talking about horses—but she would rather listen and let her thoughts take over.

"I'm sure you can get a fine horse if you ask at the livery stable," Grandfather explained. "Ol' Bob will tell you who to see for the best price."

The food wasn't going down at all well. Emily left half a slice of bread on her plate, then smiled at Grandmother when she frowned. She felt a stirring inside, a nervousness, but it wasn't the same as she'd felt toward Ben. Quite the opposite. It was important to look at what was inside a person. And she knew what was inside Pastor Luke. A love of God. Pure and simple. Emily also knew she would never feel about Luke or any man as she had that night dancing in Ben's arms. She trembled now at the memory. Yet meeting Luke was ordained.

Pastor Luke scooted his chair back and nodded toward Beulah. "Fine dinner, Mrs. Drake. Thank you for inviting me."

"Let's take our dessert into the parlor," Grandmother said. "I'll bring the teapot."

Emily carried the tray with the dessert plates, forks, and slices of cake.

The heavy drapes, usually drawn, were opened to let a small amount of sunshine in from the window that faced east. The organ sat in one corner and the French Provincial chair, an heirloom from Grandmother's side of the family, sat in a conspicuous spot in the opposite corner. Nobody ever sat there. Emily much preferred the rocking chairs in the dining area next to the wood stove, over the ornate furnishings of the parlor. She sat on one end of the chesterfield, and watched as Luke chose a rocking chair next to the organ.

Soon they were comfortably settled and Emily watched and listened as she sipped her tea. She couldn't have gotten a word in edgewise if she'd wanted to. *Silly for even worrying about knowing what to say.*

"Rachel, my wife," Pastor Luke began. He looked at the floor, his hand setting the saucer down on the table. "She died six months ago, but it seems like just yesterday at times, and at other times it seems she has been gone forever."

"It must have been tragic for you," Grandmother said. "And thy child?"

"It was a little boy—a breech birth. There was nothing the doctor could do. If we'd lived in the city close to the hospital, she and the child might have been saved, but my meetinghouse was in Fern Hollow, twenty miles from the nearest town. And the doctor was late in coming. Rachel kept saying she'd be all right, that often it takes longer for a first child." His eyes looked tortured and Emily found her heart going out to him. "If only I'd followed my first God-given instinct. I could have wrapped her warmly in the wagon and driven her to town."

"Has thee thought about marrying again one day?"

Luke nodded. "A man needs a woman at his side, especially a preacher. There's the calling on the sick, visitation. I need someone who feels led in that direction." His eyes focused on Emily momentarily, then looked away.

"It's too soon, however," he said, setting his cup down. "I am not over my wife. I feel she is with me. I still love her as if she was."

An awkward silence settled around the four, until Beulah spoke. "Take thy time, Pastor Luke. Thee will know when the time is right, when the right person comes along."

Pastor Luke was again talking about his wife and how she had written his letters, visited the sick, played the piano, and raised a garden, plus keeping the house up and sewing their wardrobe. "One couldn't have had a better mate," he went on.

Emily nibbled on the edges of her cake, then set the fork down. She was afraid Grandmother would begin espousing her virtues, and it would be embarrassing. She didn't look up, not wanting to see Luke's expression, not wanting to decipher what he might be thinking. She sipped the last drop of tea, trying to shake the memory of the night—the one night that would forever haunt her—the night she had gone to the forbidden dance. Would it matter if she never told anyone? She had prayed for forgiveness, so why couldn't she let it go? With Ben gone back to Iowa now, it should be easier. She'd somehow get on with her life.

"Emily, would you mind playing a few hymns before we pray?" Pastor Luke asked, motioning toward the organ.

Grandmother nodded. "Certainly."

Emily rose, wishing Grandmother would let her answer for herself just once.

"Our First Days are spent in prayer and reading the Word," Grandfather said. "A quiet time so we can feel God's presence."

"I'm sure God honors music," Pastor Luke said. "There'll be plenty of the afternoon left for silence, Mr. Drake."

Emily played three hymns and Luke's deep bass filled the room. The sound of his voice sent chills up her spine.

"Now, come sit, Emily. We'll pray before I leave." It was obvious Pastor Morrison was used to having the final say in matters.

They prayed for each member of the meeting as Beulah Drake explained the various needs of the people.

Pastor Luke read from 2 Thessalonians chapter 3. "Pray for us, that the word of the Lord may have free course, and be glorified, even as it is with you: And that we may be delivered from unreasonable and wicked men; for all men have not faith. But the Lord is faithful, who shall stablish you, and keep you from evil."

Emily repeated the words, and her heart plummeted. "For not all men have faith." *Ben.* She did not know about his faith. How deep it went.

The prayers were short, yet meaningful. She knew without looking at Grandmother's face that she was pleased that Pastor Luke knew the Lord and was filled with righteousness.

"It's time for me to go, and I thank thee for the wonderful dinner and your fine hospitality." He nodded toward Beulah, then Harrison. He paused for a brief moment, his eyes meeting Emily's. It looked as if he wanted to say something, but he extended his hand, clasped Emily's, covering it with his other hand. "I need someone to write a few letters each week. Do you think you could do that for me?"

"Of course," Grandmother began, but Luke held his hand up.

"It's for Miss Emily to decide. If she has the time."

Emily nodded, removing her hand from his firm grasp. His hands were warm, responsive. She had felt a safe comfort, and though his eyes held pain, they were sincere. From somewhere deep within, she sensed that he was a caring person, and Emily was glad he had come to Portland, glad he would be their pastor.

"I would be honored to write letters for thee when I am not working. Seventh Day afternoons would be best."

"Good. It's settled." He looked around the room, then bowed slightly. "I will see thee at meeting tonight?"

"Of course," was Beulah's reply. "Bless thee, Pastor Luke, and do come calling again." The meaning was not lost on the other people in the room.

Emily listened as Grandfather went out to hitch up the horses, picking up the dishes and cups as Grandmother stood on the porch, following Pastor Luke Morrison down the steps. She breathed a sigh of relief. There was nothing to fear of this man. His kind gentleness had reached out, encompassing her. It was as if he was assuring her that yes, indeed, she was worthy, and that he was going to bring about a change in her life. She didn't dare to wonder in which way. . .

Chapter 11

Sarah Galloway, never a beauty but coming from good, healthy stock, beamed with pride as she thought about her children. She and Pa had been mightily blessed, though he never thought of it that way. Her heart constricted now. Jesse, the oldest, was the only one to break her heart. He was handsome. Worldly. Too self-centered. He hadn't even cried when he'd heard that Pa had died. What was wrong with Jesse? Only the Lord knew.

Sarah rose and put another log on the fire. Pearl sat by the window, stitching tea towels for her hope chest. She was a good girl. Dutiful. Quiet. Loving. A real blessing to Sarah in her old age. Pearl managed the chores Sarah found too difficult, and had even plowed and planted corn last spring. She had her mother's raw-boned build, her strong constitution. She could do the work of any man and seemed to take pleasure in doing so since she was now in charge of the house.

Closing her eyes, she thought of Benjamin. She never knew why, but she had favored him from the time he was pressed into her waiting arms. The second child, second son, there was something about those eyes that seemed to focus at such a young age, the brightness obvious to others. Jesse, never a loving child, wanted to be left alone, but Benjamin liked to be cuddled. And Sarah had cuddled. And mothered. And loved with all her heart. Now she was troubled. Benjamin still hadn't married, and had chosen to go running off with Jesse to Oregon. Supposedly they would find work there. Was her Benjamin to turn out like his shiftless brother? She prayed not. Yet, why had he left her and Pearl alone to tend to the chores, to eke a living off the land? That wasn't her Benjamin, at least not the Benjamin she knew.

She recalled the morning he left. He had hurried back, giving her a kiss and hug. "Sure you don't want to come, Ma?"

"I cain't," was her reply. "I have to stay here. Be close to Pa."

Pa, buried in the small graveyard two miles down the road, had been Sarah's love, her lifeline. The only problem between the couple had been his lack of faith. She had lived her beliefs, hoping Jebediah would come to believe in the Master, to know there was a power stronger than he.

"Don't take to believing in something I can't see," had been his answer. "It's okay for you, and I'll go along with your larning the kids this 'religion' bit, but just don't expect me to believe, too."

A slim yet strong man, Jeb had earned money as a craftsman. He built sturdy tables, chairs, and shelves. People came from miles to buy his beautiful creations. And though Sarah had prayed that Benjamin would take after her and prefer farming the land, from an early age he showed a keen interest in wood. His dreams were loftier than his Pa's. He had shared them with Sarah, telling her he would one day build her a house.

"I'm not a farmer, Ma. I knew that the first time we planted corn." His dark eyes shined as he talked about his dreams. Like father, like son, yet Ben was different. So different.

Sarah felt sudden tears blinding her vision. Jeb had been a good man. A loving husband. A strict, yet caring father. And Sarah had never given up, never stopped saying prayers, asking God for living proof of His existence so she could show Jeb. Sarah had thought of Thomas and how he, too, had not believed, yet had seen Jesus after the Resurrection, put his fingers in Jesus' side, and come to believe.

Jeb didn't have that opportunity, and as far as Sarah knew, had gone to his grave an unbeliever.

"I'm going to make some gingerbread," Sarah said now, breaking the silence.

Pearl set her embroidery aside. "Ma, you feel all right?"

"Course I do." She turned and smiled at her youngest. At fourteen, Pearl's face was too long, her expression sallow. She missed her Pa and her brothers. Like Sarah, she knew Pearl missed Benjamin the most. And Anna. Of all of them, Anna would be the most likely one to come home for a visit. It was this sudden prompting that told her they needed something to go with coffee.

Christmas had come and gone and though they read the Christmas story in Luke and sang a few Christmas carols, the day had passed by like any other. Sarah had knit Pearl a hat and matching mittens, and Pearl's gift to her had been a pair of warm, woolen socks.

"No use sittin' if I can do something, now is there? Besides, you like gingerbread, and the fire's still hot from supper."

"No use in thinkin' that Benjamin's coming," Pearl said in a wistful voice. "We ain't heard a thing in two months. He's done found himself a job and probably a wife."

Sarah shook her gray head, her hands smoothing the apron over her calico skirt. "Benjamin doesn't have a wife yet. He's a-looking, I know, but he's fussy, and most women aren't to his liking."

"He's found one in Oregon, Ma. Mark my words. He probably won't come back, though he promised."

"Ben's coming home, child. I know him. He wouldn't say so, if he didn't intend to keep his promise."

Pearl said nothing as she picked up the embroidery again.

The fire was stoked, the gingerbread baking. Later Sarah would cover it with a cloth and set it on the sideboard for morning.

Sarah left the bowl and spoons in the sink. She would wash them in the morning's light, conserving the kerosene. Pearl had already gone to bed, leaving Sarah alone with her thoughts.

She sat in the darkness of the house, the only home she and Jeb had ever had. She knew every nook and cranny. Loved every plank from top to bottom. She'd helped build this place. Six months before the birth of Jesse, she'd pounded nails and helped her husband proudly. Let the others roam all over the continent, but she was content to stay in Iowa. On her land, close to Jeb and the cemetery.

She thought about latching the front door, but they were safe in these parts. Never had anybody bothered them; no reason to think things had changed. Sarah looked out the window, noticing how brilliant the stars shone from the black sky. It was late. Much later than she usually stayed up, but for some reason she felt a restlessness.

Tucking the quilt around Pearl's lean body, she slowly walked to her bed, the bed she'd shared with Jeb. Kneeling on the braided rug, she offered first her thanks for her many blessings, then prayers for her children, asking protection for each one.

"And, if You don't mind, dear God, please remember Jebediah. He was a good man, even if he never did come to believe."

It was in the middle of the night sometime. Sarah had been dreaming. In her dream, Jeb was holding her hand as Anna stood over her, smiling. Off to the right were her children, all but Benjamin. Then through the hazy midst, Benjamin strolled in, his face shining, his thick, bushy hair sticking straight out as it always had.

"Ma, I found me someone. I just had to come tell you about her. Her name is Emily."

Sarah shook her head, but the voice was there, and a large, callused hand held hers. She opened her eyes and gasped. "Benjamin! It is you, or am I sick with the fever?"

"No, Ma. It's me. I got home an hour ago, but decided to let you rest."

Sarah gathered the quilts around her as she sat up. "I had the most wonderful dream. We were all together, even Pa. But I remember something about an *Emily*."

Benjamin hugged his mother, then stepped back. "That part wasn't a dream, Ma. It was for real. I'll go out so you can get dressed, then we need to talk."

An hour later, the cow was milked, side meat was frying, and biscuits were baking in the old wood stove. Ben decided to wait to tell his mother about Emily, his land, and the move.

"Ma, you know how to make a place smell homey."

"I should." She smiled, then reached over and hugged him again. "Been doin' this a good long time."

Pearl came in, stomping her feet. "Where'd you get the horse, Ben? He's beautiful."

"A man in town. He's on loan. That and the wagon."

"What do you need another wagon for?" Ma asked.

Ben took a deep breath. He knew this wasn't going to be easy. He realized how Ma felt about the farm. How she wouldn't want to leave Pa. He'd have to do some tall talking. It would wait until breakfast was over, unless she pressed him.

After a second cup of coffee and a third slice of gingerbread, Ben found his thoughts on Emily again. Not that she ever strayed far from his mind. He wondered if she could cook like Ma. Somehow he didn't doubt for a moment that she knew about cooking, planting a garden, and keeping house. That, plus dipping chocolates. He remembered the small package he'd brought for Ma and Pearl. He figured neither Ma nor Pearl had ever had a chocolate-covered bonbon.

"Brought you something special," he said then. "A real treat."

"Just coming home, seeing your face is all I need," Sarah said, drinking in the sight of her favorite son.

"If you don't want them, Pearl will," he said, winking at his baby sister.

Ma's eyes widened when she lifted the lid. "Candy. I never seen anything this pretty before. Where on earth—"

"A friend made them, Ma. A very good friend."

Pearl paused, a chocolate halfway to her mouth. "Didn't I tell you, Ma?"

He hadn't planned on sharing Emily with them just yet, but now he had to.

"You already mentioned this Emily," Sarah said.

Ben nodded. "That's right, I did. And Ma, you'll love her. She's everything I've ever dreamed about. Tiny. A lot shorter than Pearl. And has the prettiest eyes you've ever seen. She belongs to the Friends' Church, Ma. She doesn't believe in dancing and rings and makeup."

"You going to give up dancing?"

"Yes, Ma. I can do that."

Pearl touched her brother's arm. "Does Emily love you, Benjamin?"

"I. . .don't know for certain, but if her eyes are any indication, she cares for me." He remembered how she'd felt in his arms waltzing across the floor, the way her cheek had felt against his lips, but he didn't talk about that.

"There are women here who would marry you, give you children," Sarah broke in. "I can list them on my fingers."

"Ma, I know, I know. But it's Emily that I love. I've never been more sure of anything in my life."

"Do you have a place, Benjamin?"

"Yes, Ma, I do. Ten acres. You'll never believe how rich the earth is. You can have your garden, and Pearl can help out, or go to school. There's a school nearby. It wouldn't be a far walk, or maybe she can take one of the horses." He knew that one of Ma's wishes was for her children to be schooled since she hadn't gone but a few years. Her father hadn't believed in education for "wimmin," as he called them. Benjamin had gone through eighth, two grades further than Pa had.

"Please don't ask me to leave Pa," Sarah said, getting up to pour more coffee. "I can't do it, Son."

"Ma, you're not leaving him. He'd want you to go. He'd want you to be with me, you know he would."

Pearl sat beside the window, looking out, her hands in her lap. Ben wondered why she wasn't helping him convince their mother—why she hadn't said a word on either one's behalf.

"Baby sister, what are you thinking?" Ben asked then, hoping for an ally.

"I'm with Ma, Ben. I can always come to Oregon later." She didn't speak of death, but both knew Sarah wouldn't live forever.

"Ma, I have to go back. I promised Emily."

His mother's mouth pressed together tightly. She was a loving woman, but could also be stubborn. "I only hope you know what you're doing. Having your heart set on someone who, for all you know, may be married by the time you get back to Ory-gone."

Ben knew it to be true, but he had to return. He had asked her to wait, and he had to believe that she would.

"Seems you promised you'd come back here."

"And I came, didn't I?"

"But, not to stay—"

Ben shook his head. "Not when I've found a place more beautiful than you can imagine."

"I'm not going to see Pa again," Sarah said. "I need to be here with him so we can talk over things."

"Ma, life is for the living."

Sarah fidgeted with her apron and looked out the window to the meadow stretching as far as one could see. It was cleared and straight and even as God had made it. How could she leave the land she'd harvested? How could she leave Jeb and his grave? The home they'd built together? Yet how could she stay here and keep Pearl from attending school?

"I'll go to Ory-gone with you," she said finally, "but I must pay your father one final visit."

"I'll come, too," Ben said.

Ben realized now that they had never talked about that day. The words had stayed locked up in his heart until now.

As they trudged up the tiny knoll where Sarah had insisted Jeb be buried, Ben's voice filled the crisp morning air. "He's with the Lord, you know, Ma."

She didn't turn, but placed a tiny bouquet of dried flowers on the barren grave. "Oh, I wish it were so, Benjamin, but I know he never came to believe."

"Yes, he did, Ma."

"No, Son, you're wrong."

"Ma, remember when I was with him that last night?"

Sarah recalled Benjamin sitting beside him, recalled the talk about the first little bear Benjamin had whittled from a piece of soft pine. Pa had actually laughed. She'd left to fix supper so didn't hear anymore, but Ben stayed with his father, helping him drink, saying he would eat later.

"That night, Ma, when you slept in the rocker, Pa asked me to pray with him. I told you—"

"You never told me a thing about praying with Pa."

"He asked me about salvation, and I told him he had to ask for forgiveness and to ask Jesus to come into his heart." Ben couldn't believe he hadn't told Ma. Maybe he had forgotten. He'd fallen, exhausted, into bed, asking Pearl to sit with Pa so their mother could sleep. Ma's anguished cry wakened him at daybreak.

At last it was over and there had been plans to make. A plot to find, a grave to dig. The box Ben had made needed lining. People brought food and blessings. Then prayers were said over the fresh mound of dirt.

It was coming back now. The one time he had tried to talk about it, Sarah had hushed him into silence. Hushed him because she had been aching for her dead husband's soul. Aching for a reason that did not exist. If only Ben had realized.

Ben pulled Sarah up from her knees, and they clung to each other as

Sarah sobbed, "Praise You, Father. Oh, thank You so much for answering my prayers."

She turned once more to look back at the grave. "I'm leaving, Pa, there's no reason to stay now. We're off to Ory-gone and a new life. I'll see you in heaven."

If it had been up to Ben, he would have left for Oregon the next week, but Ma said certain things couldn't be rushed. The farmhouse, land, and most of the furnishings were put up for sale, but many of the items like Ma's bed, the table and chairs, a bookcase, and Pearl's hope chest—all things Pa had made—would be shipped on the freight train. Anna was summoned and would be home soon, to say good-bye before they moved so far away.

While waiting for the house and land to sell, Ben's thoughts were constantly on Emily. She was the force that pushed him on, made him impatient for things to happen so they could leave. Evenings he whittled another horse, then another. One night he sat beside the kerosene lamp, searching for words to write, hoping she would heed them and continue to wait. The letter would be mailed to Kate's house.

My Dear Friend Emily,

It seems like many weeks have passed since I last saw you. There are certain things one cannot write in a letter. There are certain things one must say and do face to face.

I want you to know that I plan to come calling just as soon as I return to Oregon.

My words were truthful that night. I can see you now, eyes glistening as you held the horse in your hand. I am glad you liked my gift.

I beg you, I implore you to wait for my return. My intentions are strictly honorable.

As ever,
Benjamin Galloway

He didn't expect her to answer, but at least she would know he was thinking of her.

People came to look, but Ben held out for a better price. He needed money to get started on his business in Oregon.

When no more offers came by March, Ben went to town to purchase the train tickets. He'd settle for less, for he sensed he had to leave now.

As Ben walked past the station, his eye caught a "BOOKS" sign in the window of a shop. A book. The perfect gift for Emily. Though he had whittled more horses, he wanted to give her a book. He entered the small shop.

"I'm interested in that book in the window."

The shopkeeper handed it to him. Ben opened the volume, *Leaves of Grass* by Walt Whitman. When he read that Whitman came from a Quaker background, he knew it was perfect. He could see Emily's shy smile now, hear her protest that she couldn't possibly accept it. He plunked down the coins and left the shop whistling.

Putting the book into his pocket, next to the train tickets, Ben stopped at the post office to check for mail. Not that he expected anything, but he had given Kate Ma's address and had invited her to write. What he really hoped for was a missive from Emily, or at least some word about her.

The postmaster handed him a pink envelope. Kate. It had to be. Who else would write on pink stationery?

One thin sheet fell out.

Ben,

There isn't much time to write, but I wanted you to know that things have changed since you left. If I were you, I'd hurry back to Oregon. I'm not at liberty to say anything more.

Best regards,
Katherine Russell

Ben read the letter twice, then jammed it back into the envelope. His heart sank. Emily. The "changes" had to do with Emily. And the preacher. What else could Kate have meant? Sudden longing and fear spread through him. He had to get back to Oregon. Could he wait until next week? If he could have found a faster mode of travel, he would have done so. There had been a flight in 1903 out of Kitty Hawk, North Carolina. The Wright Brothers had invented a plane. It had been in all the papers, but as far as Ben knew there were no planes for passengers yet.

Clutching the letter, he closed his eyes and saw those beautiful, violet-blue eyes that had haunted him from the very first moment. His heart ached for Emily's smile, the smile she now bestowed on another man. He saw Oregon. His land. His dream. Emily. She was so much a part of it. God had been so good to him and he must keep believing that Emily would realize that she belonged to him. He must hurry back to court her, to claim her, and to eventually wed her. There was precious little time to waste.

Chapter 12

Emily began working for Pastor Luke the following Saturday. He had located a small house close to the church and had hired Alfrieda, a cleaning lady, to come the four hours that Emily would be there. "Just so people won't talk," was his explanation.

She had gone to work not knowing what to expect. Would she do the work he requested satisfactorily? He'd mentioned writing letters. She felt confident in that area. She knew her grammar and spelling were accurate; she'd received A's while in school. She soon learned she had nothing to dread, as Luke was quite complimentary about her work.

"You have beautiful handwriting, Emily. Spencerian, isn't it?"

Emily felt embarrassed as she always did when someone admired a quality about her, but remembered what Kate had told her the night of the dance. "Yes, it is," she finally said. "And thank you. I copied the style from a letter my father wrote me once."

"My penmanship is horrific," Pastor Luke replied. "I remember practicing those circles and loops, but the teacher cracked my knuckles because my loops weren't wide enough."

Emily tried to stifle a grin.

"I like it when you smile," he said. "It's better than the frown you usually wear."

"I frown a lot?" she asked. Nobody had ever told her that before, not even Kate.

"Yes, even when you play the piano. I figure you must have much on your mind."

She felt at ease and was able to relax after the first hour. Halfway through the letters, he'd called Alfrieda to bring in a pot of tea and something to eat.

"I want to pay you a fair wage," Pastor Luke said as they munched on cookies.

"But I couldn't accept. It wouldn't be right."

"I insist. I know you must have something you wish for. All women do." He leaned forward. "I only regret I did not realize this before my wife died in my arms. She always wanted to take a trip to New Orleans, ride on a river boat."

Emily stared, sudden compassion filling her. How difficult to know his wife was dying, to be holding her when she drew her last breath. Then to lose the baby two days later.

"I'm so sorry about your wife and son. I know how keenly you must feel your loss."

His fingers tugged at the end of his beard. "Tell me about yourself, Emily. I want to know what is going on inside that head of yours."

"I. . .can't say for sure," she stammered. How could she tell him that her heart was riddled with memories of a night at a forbidden dance? How could she say she couldn't get a certain face out of her mind? She couldn't tell him that, but she did tell him about her family in California and how her desire was to some day see everyone again.

"That's where your heart is, and that is where the wage will go." He sprang to his feet. "I think it is high time you paid your family a visit. The grandparents may not understand, but it's an important consideration for you."

Emily's heart soared. Could it be possible? Like Kate said, she could and should go one day soon. Perhaps this was an answer to prayer.

January passed, then February. The first week of March had given way to winds and heavy rains. Luke now insisted on taking Emily home after her four hours were completed.

"It gives me a chance to see the countryside and your grandmother always invites me to stay for supper."

Lawns were turning green and the crocuses had peeped their heads up out of the ground still hard from winter's touch. They talked of many things as they rode toward the farmhouse. Luke never had a choice about becoming a minister since he was the oldest son and his father and grandfather before him had all answered the calling.

"Times are changing," he said one Saturday. "Especially here in the West. Having a preacher at the meetings. Lapsing from the old way of talking. Playing music during the service. All good changes, I might add." Luke paused, as if waiting for Emily's comment.

"I like the changes, too," she said. "And I feel you have a calling, Pastor Luke. I see how people respond to you the few times we've visited the sick."

"And you have it, also."

They had arrived at Emily's home and the glow from the lamps warmed her heart as she lighted from the buggy.

The one thing Emily had kept buried in her heart was Ben. Not once had she mentioned the dance. She didn't know what Pastor Luke would say, but she had a good idea. Not once did she mention how her heart ached with emptiness when she thought of him. Nor did she mention the thoughts buried deep inside her, or her words, *I will wait*. She tried to forget, to push them aside, but repression did not work. Did Ben still think of her, or had he found someone else more to his liking, someone who danced and could carry on an intelligent conversation?

"Does thee want to talk about it?" Pastor Luke said before they entered the house.

"Talk about what?"

"What it is that makes you suddenly hide from the world. It's as if you go into yourself. That's one of my functions, Emily, to listen to people's problems, hear their prayers."

But she could not tell him about Ben. At least not yet. Though she felt she could discuss most any subject with Luke, she still didn't know what he'd say about her transgression, about her attending a dance. She somehow couldn't face seeing a look of shock, or worse, one of disdain.

Soon they were inside, wraps removed as Emily tended to her usual Seventh Day evening chores.

"Thee is late," Beulah said, stirring a pot on the stove.

"Yes. I'm sorry."

"Does thee know something I do not?"

Emily shook her head. What could her grandmother be thinking? Had she guessed about the wage Luke paid her each week? Could she possibly know that Emily was saving for a trip to California?

"I wrote many letters today," she finally said.

Grandmother might have pressed it further, if Grandfather hadn't called from the dining room, "We need another log for the fire, Emily."

Pastor Luke offered to fetch it, but both grandparents said Emily was used to that chore and he was a guest and shouldn't think about doing such things.

The meal was more quiet than usual, and Emily could feel Luke's eyes on her. She didn't know what he wanted or expected, but sensed something was different, but wasn't sure what.

Work went on as usual at the candy factory, and Emily talked of Luke. Kate listened, but said little. A concerned look crossed her face one morning, but she wouldn't say what was troubling her. Emily had that to puzzle over now.

Emily also worried about Pastor Luke. He would be in the middle of a sentence, then stop, staring into space. She knew he had a wounded heart, because she had seen a hint of tears in his eyes on more than one occasion. When he caught her looking, he lurched to his feet and left the room momentarily.

"Is something wrong?" Emily asked when he returned.

He turned and stared at her in a way that seemed unlike his usual nature. "Emily, I have been pondering about something for a very long while now, almost since that first day I arrived in Oregon."

"Is this something you need to discuss with me?"

"Yes. It concerns you." He walked over and stood in front of her and her mind recaptured the memory of that night when another pair of feet had stopped in front of her, and she'd been forced to look up into the deep brown eyes of Ben Galloway. She'd also been forced to answer his question.

"I need to speak to your grandfather."

Emily stared. What could he be talking about?

"I would like permission to call on you."

She gasped. So this was what the changes were about. The reason he had taken her home the previous weeks. Why hadn't she guessed?

"I see this surprises you."

She lowered her head, not quite knowing what to say.

"I thought you knew that I need a wife to help with my ministry."

Luke was kind. Generous. He loved and served God with all his heart and soul. He was many of the things a woman would want in a man. Why wasn't there a stirring inside her at the thought of his coming to call? She had known all along that everyone thought this was the person God had sent, that it was ordained that they might one day marry, that Luke was the answer to many prayers said on her behalf.

"Everyone thought I would marry you. I won't pretend I didn't hear the talk."

"You said you were still in love with your wife."

"I know." He strode over to the window, and stood with his hands folded behind him. "I do still love Rachel, 'tis true, but life goes on, and I need a help-mate. Do thee understand what I am saying?"

Emily nodded, but she wondered why she suddenly felt so awkward, as if she didn't know what to say.

"I'll take thee home now," he said, pushing a book aside. "Forget I said anything. Proper etiquette says I should speak to thy grandfather first."

She was numb as she put on her wraps and went out the door and waited until he helped her into the buggy. Always before they would be chatting, and she'd felt comfortable. Secure. With Luke's declaration, Emily felt sudden apprehension. And then she realized why. Over the past weeks, she'd come to think of him as a brother, the brother she'd left behind in California.

"Are you staying for supper?" she asked.

"I reckon Beulah would think it strange if I did not." His eyes were on her face, but she didn't look at him.

"Emily, I don't want this to change things. I want you to talk to me. I like the way your eyes light up when you tell about something Kate said at work, or how you remembered your father playing the violin. I don't want to lose that special part about you—"

She felt her heart constrict. It was this about Luke that she so admired. He seemed to know what people knew and thought. If only she could tell him about Ben, yet how could she when she couldn't explain it to herself?

Luke let the reins drop for a moment. "I assumed thee knew how I felt."

She had not. Because she felt so comfortable with him, she had let her defenses fall. She had become a person who could talk, who chatted about her family, the needs of the meeting, the desires of her heart. How could she now tell him she thought of him as a brother? Or explain about Ben? What would he think? She wasn't ready for condemnation.

Luke stayed for supper, but left early. He hardly spoke two words to Emily, and he had not asked Grandfather about the courting. She would have known. Out of deference to her, he had waited. Another thing to admire about him.

After Luke left, the scriptures were read and Emily stayed for prayers, but she could hardly wait to be excused to go to bed. Usually the last to go up, she was the first tonight. With trembling fingers, she began writing in her diary:

Mama,

Everything is happening so fast it's hard to believe. I might be coming on the train to visit you and Papa. I hope you will write, sending me directions of how to reach you. I am so eager to come. Our new pastor is helping me with the expenses in return for my writing his letters and helping him in other ways.

Later she wondered why she didn't mention Luke's declaration that he wanted to come calling. Somehow it stayed inside her where she hoped it would stay. At least for the time being.

Chapter 13

Ben Galloway had been gone nearly three months. Often it seemed like a dream, but Black Beauty reminded her of his existence, and she found the more she tried to get him out of her mind and heart, the more he was there. She prayed at length for deliverance of that night and all that had happened, but it seemed to linger and Emily wondered if she'd ever be free of the memory.

She had thought he might return by now, had hoped to at least hear something through Kate. If Kate heard, she said nothing. Emily continued to work for Pastor Luke, though there was a stiffness between them now. She could feel his eyes on her, watching, waiting, wondering. She had never spoken of Ben and couldn't possibly do so now. If he asked her grandfather about calling on her, he might learn of Ben, but she doubted that the matter would be discussed.

And then he brought it up one afternoon.

"God is much more concerned that we be equally yoked than that we be in love," Luke said.

Love. Was it merely a state of mind? Only a dream, a fairy tale? Perhaps so. Had she only imagined that excitement toward Ben? Was she not to expect it to happen again?

"Have you heard of arranged marriages?" he asked.

"Yes," she said. Was that was this was about? Luke didn't love her after all, but needed someone to help him and this was the answer.

"Originally, I thought that's what we would have. It would be convenient for both of us." He paused, as if waiting for Emily to reply. "But after getting to know you, I realized I care for you very much. Perhaps not as I felt about Rachel, but a quieter type of feeling. You're all the things I could need or ever want. We would take the vows before God and others, and have the blessings from the Meeting."

"I think I understand," Emily finally said.

She did understand, but was it right to marry someone when your heart was with another?

"It's good that we can talk about this. Yes, Rachel is part of me, a part that doesn't want to let go, but I realize I need to get on with my calling. I find you proficient in so many areas. You know the Bible, play the piano, write wonderful letters, and you are a sincere person." He paused momentarily. "I have prayed for clearness and for God's continued guidance and help."

She tried to smile as she lifted her face. How many times had she asked for God's help? How many times had she thought she was over Ben, only to have him haunting her thoughts at work, at night when she wrote in her diary, on a cloudless winter day while she pumped water, or in the pouring rain while she lifted her face for the refreshing wetness that drenched her within minutes.

"If there is no fierce objection, I will speak to your grandfather." He paused, as if waiting for her reply.

She said nothing as he brought her wraps and helped her into her coat.

"I have waited, Emily, as you know." She could feel his eyes on her, watching. "I want you to talk to me."

But she couldn't. The words stayed locked inside her. It seemed she was caught in a whirlpool and no matter what she did, there was no escaping. Would she grow to have a deeper feeling for Luke? Would he some day love her in return, or would Rachel and Ben always be there, reminding them of a previous love?

Emily tried to smile. Luke was good and thoughtful. He had many kind attributes. Why couldn't she feel excitement? Why didn't her heart pound as it had when Ben looked her way? Or was it as Luke said, love wasn't that important?

Luke turned and touched her gloved hand. "I will continue to be in prayer about this, Emily. I only want what God wants for me. For us. I will wait a few more days before speaking to your grandfather."

Luke didn't stay for supper, explaining he had to visit someone who was ill. Emily didn't know if it was true, but was glad that they would be alone.

Later that night, as she always did when she needed solace, Emily turned to her diary. She uncapped the ink and wrote in her thin, spidery handwriting:

Mama,

    I wish I knew what your courtship was like, if you loved my father, or if you married because you wanted babies. Was love important then? Did you love my father in the beginning, or did you grow to love him? What if I marry Luke and he doesn't grow to love me? What if he never gets over Rachel? What if I keep thinking about Ben? Those are important things to me. I want marriage. My own home. To have my own baby to love, to dress, to nurse, to just have. I don't think this is wrong for me to feel this

*way. And I really think God understands my feelings, my heart's desire in
this matter. I miss you, Mama. I just wish we could talk about these kinds
of things. I need you so bad sometimes. . .*

After closing the diary and sinking back under the heavy quilts, Emily
knew she had reached a decision. She would say "yes" to Luke's proposal. He
needed someone, and so did she. Ben wasn't returning. If so, he would have
been back by now. After making her mind up, she was able to sleep, but not
before she took Black Beauty and pushed him in the deep recesses of the
dresser drawer.

On Monday Kate came to work beaming.

"It came on Friday! My sewing machine! It's so beautiful, Emily, you
must come to see it."

"Can I use it?" Emily asked.

Kate hugged her. "Of course. We'll both use it. That was my intention
all along."

Kate came the next day with a bolt of the palest pink lawn. "Here. For
you, Emily. Enough to make a dress."

Emily's cheeks reddened as she touched the fabric. It was finer than anything she could ever wear. The color was wrong, yet what she wouldn't give
to have a dress like this.

"I can't accept this," Emily finally said. "It's beautiful, but I could never
pay for it."

"It's a gift," Kate broke in. "A gift from me to you."

"But you shouldn't have bought—"

"I didn't buy it. It was given to me, and I cannot stand this shade of pink.
It does nothing for my complexion."

Emily was tempted, but to take such a gift wouldn't be appropriate.
"Give the material to someone else."

"I don't want to give it to someone else. It's yours."

Emily held it up to her cheek and wondered what it would look like
made into a dress. She put it down. To even think such thoughts was wrong.
God knew her thoughts, the desires of her heart, and He expected her to do
the right thing.

Kate put the pink lawn back into a bag and smiled. "I'll take it home and
start cutting it out tonight. The pattern has tucks in the bodice, and we'll put
lace at the neckline."

"I can't accept it—"

"Nonsense," Kate broke in. "You'll accept it because I have no one else to give it to."

Emily turned back to her rows of undipped chocolates. Where would she wear such a dress? Certainly not to meeting, not when everyone would soon know that Luke was courting her.

She glanced at her friend, wanting more than anything to tell her about Luke, but knew it wouldn't be proper, not before he spoke to her grandfather.

As if reading her thoughts, Kate brought up Ben. "He should be home in a few weeks. It'll sure be good to see him again." She paused, looking over at Emily, waiting for her to say something.

"Did you hear from him?"

"No, but I didn't expect to."

Emily's cheeks felt flush.

"What is it?" Kate asked, not one to let anything slip by her.

Emily looked away. "It's nothing."

Kate smiled and touched her friend's arm. "Yes, it is. Now what's going on? If you can't tell your best friend, who can you tell?"

Emily dared not look at Kate.

Kate sighed. "You're not thinking about that preacher fellow, are you?"

"I still work for him."

"I'm not talking about that." Kate's frowned. "When you get all quiet, I know it's something serious. Please tell me that what I'm thinking is not true."

"Meaning?"

Kate stopped working. "Emily, I saw how you looked at Ben, just as I saw how he looked at you. He may not be of your faith, but you love him."

Love. Had it been love? Could it be love? How could she dare to hope that love was important? Even if they did love each other, it could go no further. Yet, ever since Luke's words on Saturday, she had visualized Ben, not Luke, in a small cabin on the land she had heard about. She would cook his evening meal in the wood stove when he arrived home as his heavy boots stomped off the mud before entering their home. He would always be happy to see her, taking her into his arms, cuddling her head to his thick chest. There would be a kiss before supper, a hug, and lots more of that after the evening sun went down. They would share a life, a bed, love for God and their fellowman, and bright hopes for the future. And a baby. There would be a baby that looked just like Ben with that impossible, thick, unruly hair. And maybe his bushy eyebrows, and ears that stuck out. And children, both looking just like him.

"You're smiling, Emily Drake, and you haven't told me what's amusing. It isn't fair! I demand to know what's going in that head of yours." Kate's red earrings bobbed in the light, her eyes twinkling from teasing.

Emily was brought back to the present, back to the chocolates and her friend's voice, her growing exasperation. "Pastor Luke is a nice, gentle man."

"And so are most fathers, but you don't marry them," Kate said. "Kindness and gentleness do not make up for love."

"I never said I loved Ben."

"You didn't have to. Come on. Let's have our dinner."

The two women left their work station, heading for the small room where they ate each day. They were alone, so Emily could talk freely.

"Luke needs a wife. I need a husband."

Kate shook her head. "You're talking about an arranged marriage?"

"Yes, something like that."

"You can't do it, Emily." She handed her a celery chunk. "You would be miserable."

"How do you know that?"

"Because you love Ben. How many times do I need to say it?"

"We've never spoken of such things."

"No, but he would have before he left. He would have seen you every day if you'd have allowed it. He wanted to speak to your grandfather about calling on you."

"You don't know that, Kate."

"Yes, I do."

"You never said anything to me."

"What good would it have done? What good is it doing now?"

Emily felt tears threaten. Kate was partly right, because Ben had asked her to wait for his return. If that was speaking his mind, then, yes, he had spoken it.

"Luke is a good choice because he loves God and has chosen to serve God and His people."

"What makes you think Ben doesn't love God?"

"He doesn't serve Him."

"No, but that shouldn't make a difference. Not all men can serve God as a preacher. There are leaders, and there are followers. Most of us are followers. In fact," Kate went on, "I happen to know that Ben is a leader. He is going to start his own construction company once he gets back. He told me about it. He's already drawn plans for the house he will build on the Oregon City property. If you had shown the slightest interest, he would have taken you there."

"There wasn't time."

Kate folded her napkin, tucking it into her coat pocket. "You're right. There wasn't."

"Anyway, I've all but decided to marry someone of my faith. Besides," she hesitated, "love isn't as important as people make it out to be. One can grow into love. It happens all the time."

"Yes, perhaps it does. But you, my dear girl, have not taken one thing into consideration."

"Which is—?"

"It doesn't work well when one person is already in love with someone else."

She thought about that the rest of the afternoon. Kate was right. What might happen if she married Luke? Could she forget Ben once and for all, or would the memory of that night slip into her thoughts? It took time. She had to give herself time.

Emily filled a red box with the needed rows of chocolates and closed the lid. There'd been a large order from a company in California, and both women were working on it.

"Emily, if you don't love this man, and you take those vows to love, honor, cherish, and obey, it's like a promise, and we talked about promises before."

Kate was silent the rest of the afternoon and Emily's heart was heavy. She missed her friend's banter, the laughter. Kate always put her in a good mood. Would they stop being good friends?

When five-thirty came, Kate hurried out of the work area, grabbed her coat, and shot out the door before Emily had her apron off.

Emily watched Kate walk in the opposite direction toward the streetcar. She had made her angry, but she didn't understand why. It wasn't wrong to marry Luke. As he said, an arranged marriage benefited both, especially when there was a mutual need.

When Emily turned into the lane to the house, she saw Luke's horse and buggy. Sudden apprehension filled her. He hadn't said anything last night at prayer meeting about stopping by. Had he come to speak to her grandfather?

Grandmother was in the kitchen slicing potatoes when Emily walked in. "Thee took longer than usual."

"We had to fill a large order."

"Pastor Luke is in the parlor with your grandfather."

Emily removed her coat and hat. Suddenly she felt shy again. How should she look at him now? It was all different, and her first inclination was to turn and run back outside.

Grandmother dried her hands on her apron. "Luke has asked if he might start calling on thee."

So, it was true. Trembling, she started setting four plates out.

"Thee certainly is quiet about this," Grandmother said, pausing to cast a sideways glance in Emily's direction.

"Yes," Emily finally answered.

"Thee knew about it already?"

Emily nodded as she filled the glasses with water.

"Well, aren't thee happy? Thee has been thinking about Pastor Luke, hasn't thee?"

"I don't love him, grandmother, nor he me."

"I didn't love thy grandfather, either."

Somehow Emily knew that was what her Grandmother would say. She wondered, again, what it had been like for Mama. Had there been love between her parents? Grandmother might know.

"Did my mother and father love each other?"

"I can certainly say for thy father, but not thy mother."

"And?"

"Thy father needed a wife. Thy mother was pretty. She was also strong and well-built."

"Well-built?" What did Grandmother mean? And why did that matter?

"Men often look at how a woman is built. If she looks as if she could bear children, they ask for her hand in marriage."

"You mean he didn't love her?"

"I rather doubt it, Emily."

Emily found it hard to assimilate. A woman was sought after because she had good bones, sort of like a man buying a cow because she looked strong and healthy.

"Apparently Pastor Luke didn't look for that criteria when he married the first time."

Grandmother nodded. "Yes, thee is right, I'm sure. But that's enough dilly-dallying around. Time to chop some wood and bring in water, then we'll eat."

Always the taskmaster, her grandmother could never talk for more than five minutes, never divulge any of the information about her parents that Emily so longed to hear.

After dinner, which Emily could barely swallow, she and Luke went to the parlor to talk. Now that he had made his intentions known, it was permissible to be alone, if someone was nearby. Her grandparents were in the dining room around the wood stove, as they were each evening.

Luke stood beside the open doorway as Emily entered. It was strange, but she had never noticed how oppressive the room was before. The heavy drapes were drawn and the room smelled musty, and had ever since the tree had been removed.

Luke sat on one end of the sofa while Emily sat in the willow rocker usually occupied by Grandmother.

"I spoke of my intentions today."

"I know. Grandmother told me."

"I intended to wait, but started thinking about it. I need you now, Emily."

She looked into his face. His eyes were warm—kind. She nodded before looking away.

"I think of thee as a brother, Luke. I realized it even more this evening when I saw your buggy in the driveway." Emily raised her eyes to his. "I was excited about your being here, but not in the way you might wish. I think of thee as a friend whom I can talk to freely."

"I understand that, Emily, and there is certainly nothing wrong with that."

"You spoke of love the other day, saying it isn't as important as people think it is, yet you loved your wife. You still love her, or so you said that First Day when we talked here in the parlor."

"Yes, that is true."

"Do you really think one should settle for less?"

"It depends on the circumstances." Luke rose and walked over to Emily. "Is there someone else?"

"I. . .met a man. He's a friend of Kate's, and I try to tell myself I do not care, that it isn't right, that he isn't a man of God."

"Yet he is still in your heart."

She nodded, saying nothing.

"Love is a strange thing, Emily. I know it to be so. Here I buried Rachel nearly a year ago, yet cannot wrench her from my mind. She is in my thoughts constantly, and that is why I could not profess my love for you. 'Twould not be honest."

"Nor I to you," Emily said, lifting her face.

"Does thee think we could eventually get over our hurts?"

Emily didn't have the answer. Luke's wife was gone to him forever, but it wasn't the same for Emily as Ben was very much alive. Time heals all wounds, but if God didn't take away the memory, how could she get over him?

"Your silence has told me what I need to know," Luke said. "I will wait to make the announcement, Emily. And now I must go."

"No. Wait." Emily called as he got to the door. "I know it is what God wants me to do, and I want you to come calling."

"Emily." He took her hands and held them to his face. "You have made me exceedingly happy tonight."

Long after Luke had gone, Emily thought about how he had held her hands. "God be with you, with us," were his parting words. That night she had much to write in the diary.

Chapter 14

K ate wore her new blue gingham on Friday. She'd spent the last two evenings sewing it on her new machine.

Her hair looked bouncier, Emily thought, and a smile crossed her face as she walked into the work area. "Kurt is coming by after work—"

"Kate!" Emily interrupted. "What has happened? You look somehow different."

"You'll know later."

"You said yes to his proposal."

Her dark eyes twinkled. "Maybe yes, maybe no."

Emily popped an imperfect chocolate into her mouth. She didn't like guessing games. "Quit talking so I can do my job right. Here's another lop-sided coconut creme."

Kate set it aside. "If I'm to wear my best dress, I must cut out eating so much."

Emily knew it was true. Kurt had won Kate over. They would marry. Maybe they would marry before she and Luke.

"I want to come. Am I invited?"

Kate rolled her eyes. "Silly thing. Of course you're invited. You can stand up with me as a witness."

The rest of the day flew by. Not once did Emily think about Luke, what marriage to him would entail, whether they might grow to love one another, and eventually have a child. For now she was happy for Kate.

"When is the date?"

Kate looked toward the ceiling. "One doesn't decide these things so quickly."

"What will you wear? Probably a new dress. With that sewing machine, you can make one in a week." Emily could picture Kate in a flowing dress made of palest pink or a soft cream. Since Kate had been married before, it wouldn't be appropriate to wear white.

"I want you to wear the blue velvet," Kate said. "I'll wear whatever goes with the velvet."

Emily wished Kate hadn't brought up the blue velvet dress. She had tried to forget about the dress, the way it had fit, the way she had felt like a princess, as she was swept off across the dance floor, waltzing to the "The Blue Danube Waltz." When she was old and her brow was furrowed with hundreds of lines, she would remember that special night. Thank God for memories—for giving her a night to recall.

"You're daydreaming again," Kate broke into her thoughts. "What are you thinking about this time?"

Emily shrugged, trying not to let the color flood her cheeks as it did when she thought about Ben. "Thinking how beautiful a bride you will be."

"Not any prettier than you," Kate said. "I can't wait to be at your wedding."

Emily stopped dipping. "Oh, I don't think it will be that big of an occasion. I mean, Luke's been married before. The Friends don't believe in much fanfare, you know."

"That's a shame," Kate said. "I think all marriages should be fancy and cost lots of money." Her eyes twinkled with mischief so Emily knew she didn't mean it.

"Luke said we might take the streetcar down to Broadway and have dinner at the Benson Hotel. I understand it's the best place in town."

"How wonderful," Kate said, but her voice sounded almost sarcastic.

"Kurt will insist on giving you a ride home," Kate said then. "He is very fond of you, you know."

"Fond of me? But why? I've scarcely spoken more than two words to him."

"He just likes you, that's all."

Emily was pondering about that when Mr. Roberts walked up. "Emily, we're trying a new candy-making technique, and I'd like you to learn it. Would you come with me, please?"

She ended up in another part of the factory while Kate stayed in their usual work space. She liked learning new things, but she didn't like working alone. She missed chatting with Kate. Still, they could eat lunch together, so that was something.

At five, close to quitting time, Mr. Roberts popped in, saying there was someone to see her. "He's in the waiting area."

Emily wondered who it could be as she washed and dried her hands. Had Luke stopped by for some reason? He had once before and had taken her home. She removed the hairnet and patted her hair into place.

She saw the back, the wool overcoat, and boots and her heart stood still. *Ben. Oh, my. . .* It was Ben Galloway. A little gasp escaped from her mouth.

He turned and in a second, she was in his arms, pressed tight against his chest, tears forming in her eyes, spilling down her cheeks. It happened so fast, she couldn't believe she had fallen into his arms like that, and her a betrothed woman.

"Emily, oh, my darling, I've missed you so!"

He held her at arm's length, studying her face, her hair, her whole being, then he pulled her to him again. "I never knew how much I cared until I looked up and saw your face, the surprise in your eyes. That look told me everything I had asked myself a thousand times since I left Oregon, while I was in Iowa, and on my way back home."

Emily pulled away. "Ben, I'm sorry, but there's something you must know." Her heart twisted inside her as she looked away from his solid gaze. "I'm betrothed to Pastor Luke Morrison. I mentioned him before you left. . ."

"Yes, you did. And why do you suppose I left Iowa so quickly?" He pulled her back to him. "Why did I give up getting a better price for the house, the property?"

"But, you shouldn't have. Not on account of me." She found herself sinking into the look on his face, the dear, precious face she had memorized, the face that haunted her thoughts every waking hour.

"I love you, Emily, and so help me I know it's wrong to make a declaration like this without first going to your grandfather, but I've loved you since that night we danced. No, I knew it before I danced with you." He cupped her chin in his hand, forcing her to look into his eyes. "I'm going about this the wrong way. I'm frightening you to be saying all this. I know the protocol, but seeing you again after all these weeks, and I lost myself. I sort of—" he paused for a long moment, his eyes never leaving her face, "imagined, or at least hoped, you felt the same way."

She wanted to be held tightly against him. She couldn't still her pounding heart, nor could she make her legs even move, though she knew the best thing she could do would be to turn and run as fast as she could. People didn't fall in love after one meeting. *No.* God hadn't intended for that to happen. She knew it wasn't right.

"Miss Drake," Mr. Roberts said, suddenly appearing in the waiting room. "Why don't you take off for the rest of the day? I think you've had enough training for one day."

The inner door opened and suddenly Kate was there, squealing with delight at the sight of Ben.

"Ben! I knew you'd come soon. I just knew it!"

Emily whirled. "You mean you knew he was coming today?"

"Not today." Kate's eyes teased. "Sometime this week, I hoped."

Emily realized that it wasn't Kurt but Ben that was coming, and Kate had wanted to surprise her.

"I want you to meet my family, Ma and Pearl," Ben said. "I don't want to wait until Saturday, but will if I must. Kate can come along as chaperone."

Emily longed to, but how could she? It wasn't proper to be seen with Ben when she had more or less said yes to Luke's proposal. True, it wasn't a proposal in the usual sense, but he was proposing marriage, and they would live together as man and wife in name only. No one else was to know, and it had been difficult, but she hadn't told Kate that part. What if someone saw her with Ben? What might her grandparents and others say? It wasn't right.

"I can't," she murmured.

"You're going to marry a man you don't love," Ben said, taking Emily's hand. She didn't pull away.

"You love me, but you can't marry me."

They stepped out into the late March afternoon. The earlier showers had given way to sunshine, and it felt good on Emily's shoulders and back.

"You know why. I explained it before you left for Iowa."

"I know, but it didn't make sense then and makes even less sense now. How can you marry a man you do not love?"

"I will grow to love him."

Kate walked up, handing Emily her coat, hat, and gloves.

"Ben, I've tried, so help me I have, but her mind is made up. It's the church thing."

Ben squared his shoulders, his voice shouting over the din of two passing carriages. "I won't let it happen," he yelled. "I simply will not."

Emily stepped back, saying nothing.

"I know what we should do," Kate said. "There's that new emporium on Woodstock. Let's go have a soda and talk some more. I've been dying to see what all they have. It's a huge place with all sorts of merchandise."

Always the one for adventure, Kate looked at Ben expectantly.

"Sounds wonderful, Kate. I heard about it before I left for Iowa."

Emily finally agreed to accompany Ben and Kate to the emporium where they ordered sodas. They found a table at the back and Emily slid into a booth, across from Kate. Ben sat next to her. Aware of his presence, she wondered if she could swallow. When she glanced at Ben for a brief moment, it was all she could do to keep from reaching out and touching him.

"I'll come to church on Sunday," Ben said, stirring his soda with a straw. "I will announce my intentions to your preacher after the meeting."

Emily touched his arm. "You can't. Oh, Ben, you can't."

"And why not?" He studied her face, his eyebrows knitting together in a frown.

Emily didn't quite know how to answer. "It would be awkward."

Ben shrugged. "For whom? You or this Luke?"

"For everyone," Emily said in a soft whisper.

"I told you I would attend your church, promised to let our children be raised in your faith. I—"

She heard no more. *Children.* Sudden tears filled her eyes at the thought of a child filling her womb.

"Here, now don't start crying." Ben removed a clean white handkerchief from his pocket, brushing Emily's tears away.

"I think it's the best idea," Kate said. "It certainly wouldn't be the first time two men fought for a woman's hand. Why shouldn't Luke know that someone else finds Emily desirable?"

Emily didn't know what to do or say. What would happen if Ben came to church and spoke to Luke about her? What would Luke do? Worse yet, how would her grandparents react?

"How are your mother and sister?" Kate asked, as if trying to change the subject.

"Fine. They're staying on the property, in the little cabin until the big house is finished. It's been too wet for my partner to do much while I was gone." He turned and looked into Emily's eyes again. "I don't want to wait, Emily. I want to court you as soon as possible."

Emily said nothing. She shouldn't have promised Luke she'd marry him. She knew she could never go through with the vows, not the way she was feeling now. She had honestly thought it would work, but it wouldn't be fair to him. Kate had been right all along. It wouldn't be right to marry Ben, either. She would try to go back to how it all was before. She'd be a spinster. Life was less complicated that way.

"You're too quiet," Ben said, taking her hand again, lifting it to his lips.

Trembling, Emily pulled back. She couldn't believe Ben had done that. She had no business marrying Luke or Ben. The sudden thought surprised her. Of course. It was the answer, or at least one answer. If she didn't marry either man, her life would be smooth once again. Ben would find someone more to his liking, one who loved dancing and could help him build his house on the hill in Oregon City. Not marrying Luke freed him up for another lady in the Friends' Church. There were no single young women right now, but the meeting was growing, and with his dedicated heart and kind manner, there would be someone. She knew this was so. It was all a matter of time.

"I cannot see you," Emily said finally.

"I can wait. If I have to."

It was now Emily's turn to be surprised. She hadn't expected that response. She shook her head. "It will alleviate all problems if I don't marry anyone."

"Oh, no." Ben looked at Kate, as if he expected her to help plead his case.

"That's ridiculous, Emily," Kate said. "You'd be punishing yourself and for what reason?"

"Because it isn't meant to be."

"I don't believe that," Kate replied.

"It's easier this way."

"Yes, maybe so, for you." A pained expression crossed Ben's face. "Your suggested solution is not the answer, however."

They left the emporium, and Emily paused. "Thank you for the soda. It was the first I ever had."

"I have something else for you," Ben said, leaning over and pulling a small package out from under a buggy cushion. He handed it to her.

"For me?" Emily frowned. "But, why are you giving me another gift?"

"Just open it," Kate said. "I love surprises."

Emily fumbled with the string and slid off the plain brown wrapping paper. It was a book. She gasped as she touched the blue cover.

"*Leaves of Grass* by Walt Whitman," she read aloud. She opened the page and read the inscription on the inside page.

> *To Emily, who likes to read.*
> *With love from Ben Galloway.*

"Oh," she gasped again. "It's *beautiful*. I've never owned a book before."

"I know," Ben said, his hand touching her shoulder. "And that's why when I saw it in this store, I knew it was the best gift of all."

Sudden tears filled her eyes. "It's not the best gift," she said then. "My Black Beauty is the best gift."

"Black Beauty?" He grinned. "The little horse I carved for you is Black Beauty?"

"Yes, it seemed the right name."

Kate touched the book. "This is so nice, Ben. I didn't know you liked poetry."

Ben shrugged. "I don't know if I do or not, but thought Emily might read me some of it."

He had known it was the perfect gift, but hadn't realized how much it would mean to her. He watched as her fingers touched the cover and felt the pages and how her eyes skimmed over the first few pages. Yes, it had been the right choice. When he heard that Whitman was a Quaker, he knew that made it even more special. Now if he could bring the smile back to her face when she looked at him. If he could make her forget what she thought she was supposed to do and follow her heart, he would be happy. He was as confident as ever that she cared for him deeply. If only he could convince her of that.

Emily jumped suddenly. "I really must get home. It's terribly late."

"It's off to home then," Ben said, giving Emily a lift into the buggy. Kate had already climbed into the back and sat, waiting for the horses to start.

"I haven't seen Black Beauty," Kate said to Emily. "Bring him to work one day."

"Soon she will have one to match," said Ben, "except the colt is a light brown with a white star on its forehead."

"I simply cannot accept another gift," Emily said, glancing at Ben. "You have given me too much already."

"I don't think so." Their eyes met and her face flushed. She turned away.

"It isn't proper," she insisted.

"There doesn't need to be a reason to give a gift," Kate said. "I'd certainly never turn one down."

"I agree," Ben said, looking at Emily.

Emily didn't know what to say, so said nothing, until they arrived at the end of the road and she had to get out.

"Please let me off at the corner," she said, touching Ben's arm. "I'll walk the rest of the way."

"I don't like any of this," Ben said. "We need to discuss our situation. I'd like to meet your grandparents, tell them my intentions, and go from there." His face was stern.

Emily felt panicky. "No! It can't be that way. Please understand. I have been spoken for."

"I came as soon as possible after receiving Kate's letter. I must speak to your grandfather," he fairly thundered, his eyes shooting sparks in her direction.

"Kate's letter?" She looked stunned.

Kate stammered, "Yes, I wrote Ben a letter—"

"And I wrote to you, Emily," Ben broke in. "Sent it to Kate's house."

Now it was Kate's turn to look stunned. "You did? I never received it."

"I know I mailed it. I thought I had the right address."

It was too late for letters, Emily thought, not that it would have changed anything.

"I want to meet your grandfather," Ben said, more insistent.

"No!" Emily jumped down. "I cannot see you anymore, Ben Galloway. You don't. . .you can't mean anything to me." The minute the words were said and she saw the look on his face, she wanted to take them back.

"Very well, then. I'll let you off here, and do as you wish." His voice sounded controlled. Firm. Emily thought she detected anger, or was it hurt?

The buggy turned the corner, and she realized with a sinking sensation what she had done, how her words had stung. If only she could see once more his look of longing. If only she could have run after him, if only she could have said his name, and felt him reach down for her, pulling her close again. She never wanted to forget that feeling. She never wanted to forget the way Ben had looked at her earlier, before the anger. But the look of hurt and disbelief was repressed from her memory. It would be easier that way.

She lifted her skirts, stepped over a mud puddle, and made her way down the lane to the house. If she was lucky, Grandmother wouldn't have much to say. If she was lucky, she could go out, do her chores, then come in to a quiet supper. If she was lucky, she could soon forget this day had ever happened. If she was lucky, she would soon forget Ben Galloway, his eyes, his touch, and most of all that incredibly bushy hair.

Chapter 15

Luke came to the factory to pick up Emily on Thursday the next week. Kate had just caught the streetcar, so did not meet him. She had been distant since Ben's return.

As Luke and Emily drove over the miles to the farmhouse, her mind went from thoughts of Ben and how he had looked before driving off, to thoughts of Luke and how right and good marriage to him would be.

"Have you thought about setting a date?" he asked. "Would a June wedding be pushing it too much?"

"I don't know." Emily stared straight ahead. "It is such a—commitment—and I. . .I don't think I'm ready to marry anyone."

"If there are still doubts, it would be wrong. When does thee think thee will be ready?"

Emily thought about what it would be like to have her own home. Cooking her own meals. Sewing. Ironing. Washing clothes. Doing what she wanted when she wanted sounded wonderful. No Grandmother peering over her shoulder telling her she had put too much salt in the pot of beans or hadn't sliced the bread thin enough. Emily felt like such a child when Grandmother was around—always had.

And work. She would quit work, as no wife worked unless she was a widow. There would be plenty for a preacher's wife to do. Luke would need her in many ways.

It was tempting. Very much so. Still, she could not get Ben's face out of her mind, her thoughts. As long as she thought of him, it would not be fair to Luke, even if he didn't love her. How could she sit across the table each morning, each night and do for him when she wished he was another man?

"I understand your hesitancy," Luke said as he rose and walked across the room. "Once vows are repeated, one cannot change one's mind."

The air was warm, the sun, a bright red circle setting behind them. Emily turned to look at the sunset.

"It's this fellow, isn't it, Emily?"

She could feel his eyes on her, but she didn't dare look in his direction. She could say no, but she could not lie, especially not to Luke.

"Does he believe in God?"

Emily nodded. "He says he does."

"And do you believe him?"

Sudden tears gathered in her eyes. "Yes."

"I see." Luke sat back, fingering his beard. "You still care, that is obvious."

"I try to tell myself I do not care. . .that it isn't right."

"But it is there, burning inside you, making you experience doubts."

Emily didn't know how to answer. The thought that continued to torment her was the look in Ben's eyes when she said he didn't mean anything to her. It had been a lie, and just as she could not lie to Luke, why had she thought it was all right to lie to Ben?

"We must wait a while longer."

"Yes." Emily glanced over now. "I can talk with thee so much easier than most people. As I said before, it's a special feeling I have for thee, like I would to a brother."

Luke nodded. "I understand, Emily. I happen to believe we could make a wonderful home, serve our church, our community well, but God wants it to be right for both of us."

"My grandparents—they will not understand."

"Thee is right. They will not understand. It's going to be hard for them. They want you to be happy, to have a home provided for you. Thee may not think that, but I know it is so."

"I cannot stay with them any longer, Luke. Kate has invited me to live with her, and I think that is the best decision for me now."

"Yes, this may be good." He reached over, touching her shoulder. "You need to try your own wings. There's a wonderful life ahead of you, Emily. Maybe it's time you found out what it is."

Emily lifted her face to the sky. "What you said makes me think of my favorite verse—"

"Don't tell me, let me guess." He looked upward, too, reciting the familiar passage: " 'But they that wait upon the Lord shall renew their strength; they shall mount up with wings as eagles; they shall run, and not be weary, and they shall walk, and not faint' " (Isaiah 40:31).

Later Emily couldn't believe Luke had understood her feelings. Long after he had gone—and she'd had to make excuses for his not coming in—she sat in the dimness of the dining room, warming herself by the fire. She marveled at how freely they could talk. It was not that way with Ben. Did love have something to do with it? Emily could talk to Luke because she did not love him. Luke could talk to Emily because he did not love her. Love seemed to complicate, to confuse things. Did she *really* know what she was doing? What was God's answer in all this? Marriage seemed wrong for now. The confusion encompassed her, making her full of doubts. Waiting was the only way.

Emily sat, considering her options. Her grandparents would be horrified if she moved out, if she decided not to marry Luke. They would not understand. The ramifications were there, and there were things she could not take lightly. To begin making her own decisions? Time to try her wings. It was good advice, and it came from her pastor. How could anyone argue with that?

She would not tell Grandmother, not yet. She wasn't strong enough to match the volley of words that would most definitely come her way. She'd pack her clothes and wraps, the diary, the book of poems, and the first quilt she had ever made. Black Beauty would be in her pocket with the silver hair clasp. That was all. Kate had extra bedding and a four-poster in her spare room. Nothing else was needed.

Emily went up the stairs. It was quite late, but she knew she wouldn't sleep. She glanced at the quilt. Strangely enough it was the wedding ring design and had been the first one she had made. Her hand ran over the tiny stitches as the memory filled her. It had taken so long, and she'd had to rip out some of the stitches since Grandmother was particular. Surely Grandmother would want her to have it.

She undid her braid and slowly unwound it, letting the brown hair fall about her shoulders. Taking a brush, she brushed until the tangles were gone, then kept brushing as her mind thought over the years, all that had happened since she came to stay with her grandparents. She'd been such a lost, frightened little girl. She had cried herself to sleep many nights, wondering what everyone was doing back home, wishing she could hug her mother once more, listen to her father's happy notes on the violin, feel Mary's arm flinging across the bed, hitting her in the nose. And Maud. Maud who tossed and turned a lot, talking in her sleep. She'd even been known to wet the bed.

There'd been nobody here, no one to turn to, nobody to hug, nobody to cuddle up to, and she had nearly died from the loneliness.

A small mirror on the wall showed her now, a young woman with lean body, hair halfway down her back. Eyes a deep blue, a small bosom, but a nice nose and full lips. Her cheeks were pink from being close to the downstairs fire, but also because of the decision Luke had helped her make. She was giving up both men. She'd go back to being a spinster. Life was less complicated that way.

She opened the diary. Writing in tiny script, saving every last page, every bit of margin until there was no more room, she knew she would buy another book, something else to put her thoughts in. Sometimes she felt writing had been her salvation. It had helped her get through day after day when she felt nobody loved or cared about her. She knew God cared, but He wasn't tangible.

Mama,
I'm moving to Kate's. I need to think about what is right in my life. I love you, Mama. . .I always have.

"Oh, God." Emily fell to her knees. "Is it wrong what I am about to do? Is it a selfish desire? I still feel Your hand in my life, feel Your presence even now in this room, know that You are with me because You promised to love me always."

She looked around the room at the pale walls. Once they had been pink, but were faded from time. She could not take her few belongings on the streetcar. Perhaps Kurt could come with Kate after work. Emily opened her book of poetry, her gift from Ben. She had read the poems so many times, she had memorized them. How had Ben known she had always wanted a book of her very own?

O Captain! my Captain! our fearful trip is done;
The ship has weather'd every rack, the prize we sought is won;
The port is near, the bells I hear, the people all
exulting,
While follow eyes the steady keel, the vessel dim and daring:
But, O heart! heart! heart!
O, the bleeding drops of red.
Where on the deck my Captain lies
Fallen cold and dead.

Tears filled her eyes as she recited the poem word for word. Reaching back into the drawer, she grasped Black Beauty, holding him to her cheek. She loved the maker, but the manner in which they had met had been wrong. Someday she could forget him, but never would she forget the night at the dance, the kiss on her cheek, or how it had felt to be engulfed in his arms when he'd returned from Iowa. And the horse. He had worked on it and even said there was a colt he had made to go with Black Beauty. Of course she could not accept it now. Not after the angry words, the misunderstandings. It was just as well, she knew.

Chapter 16

Kate was ecstatic the next morning when Emily told her about her decision.

Her face lit up. "You're moving in with me and *not* marrying Luke?"

Emily nodded. "I cannot, and he understood."

"He did?" Kate stared open-mouthed.

"Yes. He was nice about it, Kate, said he knew how I felt."

"Emily, I take back all the things I said about him. He must be a very special person."

Emily nodded. "He is, Kate, and he plans to speak with Grandmother and Grandfather about my leaving—help ease the loss."

"How are you getting out of there without causing trouble? I doubt that your grandmother is going to just smile and let it go at that."

Emily shook her head. "I know. That's the part that worries me." Grandmother would say things—sharp, hurting words—and Emily knew she might crumble under the attack.

Kate touched her shoulder. "Kurt is coming by after work, and I'll ask him about picking up your things."

"Would Saturday be all right?" It would take until then for her to work up her courage.

"I'm sure it will be fine."

Emily felt like singing all day. Her heart was light, her mind whirling with exciting thoughts. It would be good to be on her own for the first time ever. Kate might not stay single. Kurt might come to mean more at some time in the future, but for the present, she would make a home with her good friend. She could try to rebuild her life and decide what was best. If her grandparents did not understand why she had to do this, so be it. She would cross that bridge when she came to it. For now she knew she was doing the right thing for her. For Luke. And for Ben, too.

Ben. He would probably always be in her heart, she realized now. It would be, indeed, difficult to get over him, but God could show her the way. Learning to do things for herself was a step in the right direction. She felt better about her decision already. Funny how one decision could free her up like this. She would soar on eagle's wings. She would run and not be weary, walk and not be faint. Yes, thank God, she was on her way.

When Kurt arrived on Saturday, Emily steeled herself. She knew she should have told Grandmother ahead of time that she was moving out. If only she could have talked to her once, let her know how she felt about things, that she was no longer a little girl but a woman who should be able to make decisions on her own.

The knock sounded, and a minute later Kurt entered the farmhouse, hat in hand. "I've come to help Miss Emily."

"Help?" Grandmother asked, a puzzled look on her weathered face. "What on earth is thee speaking of?"

Emily entered the room. "I'm moving to Kate's, Grandmother."

She knew she would remember that look for as long as she lived. The questioning, disbelief, then anger.

"Thee surely couldn't have thought this out."

"I have, Grandmother."

"Thee doesn't appreciate all we've done for thee." Her voice rose and Grandfather hobbled into the room.

"What is wrong? Emily?"

"She's moving out into an unchaperoned home where who knows what will happen. Does Pastor Luke know about this?"

"He does." Emily started up the stairs, lifting her skirts as she went. It would take two trips to carry her valise and the rest of her belongings. Grandmother was going on about the "younger generation" and how they didn't know anything or have respect. Emily grabbed her few possessions and went down the stairs.

Kurt stood, hat in hand, and took the valise from her hand.

"Nice meeting you," he said, but of course neither grandparent responded.

She had done it. Tears filled her eyes as she rode over the miles to Kate's house. There were many things she wanted to say, hugs for Grandfather, but she couldn't. It would have been wrong, and to stay would have meant more verbal accusations. This was the way it had to be. A clean break.

At last they reached their destination and Kate ran out to hug Emily. "I can see you've been crying, but it's going to work out. I know God has plans for you, dear friend." Kate had fixed up the spare room for Emily. Blue gingham curtains, made from the scraps from Kate's dress and with her new sewing machine, hung at the windows.

"Your new dress is in the closet," Kate said, opening the door.

Emily stared at the pink lawn material with ruffles at the collar and one deep ruffle at the hem line. Ruffles. She'd never had ruffles before and loved them at first sight.

"Kate, it's just too much. The dress is beautiful, the room is beautiful, and how can I ever thank you?"

"By being my friend," Kate said. "That's all the payment I'll ever ask."

"I can give you some out of my pay check each week."

"You certainly will not," Kate interjected. "I won't accept it. I want you to start saving to make the train trip to California."

California. Emily's mind raced at the thought. Was she really going to go after all these years? What would her mother say? *And Papa?* She wouldn't even recognize them, she knew, just as they wouldn't recognize her. Too many years had gone by.

Kate held her hands behind her back and suddenly thrust something under Emily's nose.

"It's a teddy bear, named after the President of the United States. Isn't he cute? He's yours to remind you that you are loved and cherished."

Tears welled up in Emily's eyes. She'd never owned toys, except for one doll when she was very young.

Emily placed the wedding ring quilt at the foot of the bed. Kate already had blankets on it, but her own quilt would add color to the room and a welcome bit of familiarity.

Emily hung up her gray dress, right next to the pink lawn, and her undergarments went into the chest of drawers. There wasn't much to put away. She set her Bible, then the diary on the nightstand, then next to that, the book of poems Ben had given her. Her treasures.

"Come," Kate said from the doorway. "Have a cup of tea. Rest for a minute. You must be tired."

Emily sipped her tea and wondered if she should pinch herself. How could this be happening? It didn't seem possible. Soon she would waken and discover it all a dream. She would be back at her grandparents', fetching water or setting the table for dinner.

"It's going to be wonderful having you here," Kate said, her eyes watching Emily. "You're the sister I never had."

"And you're the sister I had to give up," Emily answered.

"I am?"

Kate giggled and soon Emily was giggling. She hadn't giggled for many, many years, and she didn't even know what she was giggling about now. Nothing was funny. Still, one sip of her tea, a glance in Kate's direction, and she started giggling again. It was a good, wonderful feeling, one she hadn't experienced since leaving her parents. She vaguely recalled giggling under the bed covers with Mary and Maud, trying to be quiet so Ma wouldn't scold.

The next few weeks were more precious than any Emily could remember. She and Kate went to work six mornings a week, came home, and fixed a simple supper. They read books since Emily took the streetcar to the library one Saturday and checked out the limit. Some evenings they worked on sewing, embroidery, or darning. Emily baked the bread and churned the cream into butter, because she liked to, not because she had to. Sometimes she'd think about Grandfather, wondering how he was doing, hoping Grandmother was being kind. And sometimes she'd think about Ben. She tried not to, but he was there in her innermost thoughts. And the blue velvet dress hanging in her closet was a constant reminder. She also thought about Luke, hoping he would find a wife soon.

Ben had never worked as hard as he did in those weeks after returning from Iowa. He tried not to think about Emily and the words she had flung at him after she'd jumped down from the buggy. Had she really meant what she said? That she did not think of him, that she had never cared?

He wanted to forget her. He tried to forget her, driving himself from sun-up until well after dark. The Oregon City house was coming along well. It was a new bungalow style with dormers and a good-quality wood siding. Even now as Ben looked at it, he knew he would not be able to live there. It had been Emily's house, designed with her in mind, but he had discovered it was too far from most of his jobs. He needed to be closer to town. He started buying up lots on Foster, not far from Kate's. There was one nice lot, right on the streetcar line, that seemed perfect for a house. He had another set of plans drawn up. More bedrooms this time. He didn't know who he would marry, and right now he didn't even care. Maybe he could have one of those "prearranged" marriages, too. He'd been a bachelor long enough, and it was past time to settle down.

Ma was happy in her new surroundings, and already had a garden planted, in between rain, that is.

Pearl's cheeks had filled out and were rosy and pink. She liked school. She helped in the afternoons after getting home, and soon the garden was flourishing. Ben went out on Sundays to visit, but the rest of the week he stayed at the boardinghouse where he'd first lived when coming to Portland. He hired a man to help with the framing while he did the finishing work. He would always have cabinets to build since he was particular about the measurements, and his name was in demand.

"I've never seen such fine work," Mr. Talbot had said before Ben left for Iowa. Ben alone could keep busy with more work than he could handle. He now left most of the building up to John Creel and the new hired young man. John was honest and forthright and worked hard.

Still, Ben's heart ached. He attended the dances at the grange and heard about another dance and a special music concert held at Canemah Park. It was on Sundays, and he took Pearl one Sunday to hear the music. Dressed in a calico with her hair pinned up, she looked older than fourteen.

Ben looked out over the crowd, looking for Emily. Always looking, always thinking about Emily. Once when he'd danced with Kate, she said to be patient, that Emily wasn't sure what she wanted.

Patient. He had never been patient about waiting to see what God had in mind, and how could he be sure that his life would ever be in order? Once again he found himself thinking about the verse in Romans: *And we know that all things work together for good to them that love God, to them who are called according to his purpose (Romans 8:28).*

As the house on Foster neared completion, Ben worked evenings on the cabinets. The electricity was hooked up, so there was no reason he couldn't work after dark. There was indoor plumbing, and he planned to put in a telephone once he moved in.

He looked around the vacant house, thinking again how much he needed someone to help fill the rooms. A wife. Children. He surveyed one room longer. It looked out on the back side at a forested area. They were in town, but because he had left several trees, the lot retained its desirability. The room that was originally to be a bedroom now made him think of a study. Yes. Why not? He would build shelves along one entire wall, enough shelves to hold hundreds of books.

When he saw his mother that Sunday, she told him to sit, to relax while she fixed him a hot noon meal. "You're looking peaked these days, Son. You're working too hard, and all for naught."

"It isn't for naught," he said, running a hand through his bushy hair. "Nothing is ever for naught."

"I know why you're doing it, and I think it's time to forget and to go on. One cannot wait forever."

His mother, so dear to him, sat sipping her tea, rocking in the chair that had finally arrived from Iowa.

"Ma, I know you're worried, but don't be. I'm going to be fine. Hard work never hurt a soul."

"I pray you know what you are doing."

He knew what he was doing, all right. He was trying to get over a broken heart. He was trying to forget a pair of deep blue eyes and a shy smile and eyes that gazed with meaning into his own. *Forget? Give up? Never.*

He left and made it back to the boarding house well after dark, but he was singing a song, humming "The Blue Danube Waltz."

It was the following Saturday he saw Kate, and she told him the news that Emily was not working for the pastor anymore. She wasn't living with her grandparents, and that bit of news shocked him. Could it be true? He knew, as he had always known, that fear was what drove Emily. Fear of her grandparents' wrath. She didn't do anything that did not meet with their approval. He couldn't understand it. Kate had said she left her family in California years ago and had come to live with the grandparents. Why were they cruel? Ben had never known anything but love in his family. He had always assumed that that was the way it was.

A thin shred of expectation grew inside him after that night, and he felt a renewal of optimism. Emily wasn't as far out of reach as she had once been. Yes, God had opened the door just a crack, and Ben was going to make certain it didn't slam again.

Chapter 17

Pastor Luke came visiting the week after Emily moved to Kate's. He had agreed that it would be better if Emily didn't come to work for him.

Kate answered the door and stared at the short, intense man standing on her porch.

He took off his hat. "I'm Pastor Luke Morrison. And you must be—"

"Katherine Russell." She extended her hand. "I'm so glad we finally get to meet. Come in, come in. Goodness, where are my manners?"

Luke smiled. "Yes, I've certainly heard a lot about you through Emily. Is she here?"

Emily appeared around the corner, wiping hands on her apron. She'd been making muffins, and a smudge of flour graced the tip of her nose.

"Pastor Luke, how nice of you to stop by." She had feared she might feel awkward around him, but one look at his smile, and she relaxed.

"I've just finished the baking, and the water is hot for tea. Would you like a cup?"

Kate, never the quiet one, nodded. "Oh, yes, do please come sit down."

"I'd take you to the parlor," Emily said, "but the parlor is now the sewing room. The kitchen is much warmer, anyway."

"Well, my goodness, I guess I could at least offer to take your coat, Reverend." Kate seemed flustered.

"Yes, to all things," Luke finally answered. "I have time for tea, I much prefer the kitchen, and yes, please, thank you for taking my coat and hat." He smiled in Kate's direction.

He handed Emily a small envelope. "From your grandparents. Your money. They said they wouldn't take it. I'm sorry they feel that way."

She sighed and pulled out a chair. "I suppose they have disinherited me."

"Maybe they will get over it," Luke said. "Give it time, Emily."

"You don't know Grandmother. She will never get over it. She'll carry her hurt and anger to the grave."

Kate placed cups in front of them and sat at the far end of the table. "I hope you don't mind if I sit in on this conversation."

"No, by all means, do join us," Luke said.

"I was thinking you might want to pray with us and perhaps read some Scripture," Kate said then. "I know Emily misses church. I just wish I had a piano for her to play here."

Luke's eyes showed surprise at Kate's suggestion. "I'm happy to hear your request for prayer and Scripture reading and am most happy to oblige."

"I have a few questions to ask," Kate said, setting her cup down. "I believe in God, but my God seems to be different from Emily's and your God."

"How so?" asked Luke.

Emily said nothing but stared into her nearly empty cup of tea.

"I believe that God is a God of love."

Luke leaned forward, flexing his fingers. "We Friends believe that, also."

"If that's so. . ." Kate paused for a long moment, "why are there so many restrictions?"

"Restrictions?" Luke looked puzzled. "Could you expound on that a bit?"

"Such as dancing." Kate tossed her head. "I see nothing wrong with dancing."

Luke nodded, looking thoughtful. "I see what you're asking—is it all right if I call you Kate?"

"Oh, yes, please do."

Emily rose and put her cup in the sink. She was as surprised as Luke at her request.

"I'm sorry, Kate, but we do think it is so. Dancing is a worldly pleasure, and we try to keep ourselves pure and whole for God."

"But David danced," Kate said, taking Emily's Bible and pointing to the Scripture: "And David danced before the Lord with all his might. . ." (2 Samuel 6:14).

Luke nodded. "This pleases me that you've been searching the Scriptures. Emily, you're quite the proselytizer."

She sat again. "We read Scripture together every evening."

"Well, Kate, to get back to your question, it was different then. David danced before the Lord. He did not dance with a woman in his arms—."

"And if he had?" Kate interrupted.

"It would have been wrong, and God would have told him so."

"I'm having a problem with that," Kate said, signaling Emily for more water for tea.

"The very backbone of our doctrine teaches humility," Luke continued. "Servanthood. Modesty. We feel we are yoked with Jesus, and thus believe in upholding the Scriptures."

"Which also means 'thou shalt not wear color'?"

Kate stood and her lavender gingham with its layers of crinolines flounced out. Her cheeks were bright with their usual touch of rouge. "I wear bright colors, as you can see, because they make me happy. And," she pointed to her hair, "ribbons and combs to dress up my hair."

"And on you they do look lovely."

Emily could scarcely believe her ears and turned to see Kate flush scarlet.

"But God gave color to the birds, animals, and beasts. How about the wild flowers in the meadow? Why would He expect His people to be colorless?"

"It goes back to the humility, Kate. It isn't that it is one of the great commandments, but we Friends believe our strengths lie in God's Word, not in things and desires of the flesh." Luke nodded as he continued. "We believe we are humble instruments of God and declare more to the world by refusing to enter battle. We live our lives happily, peacefully, and quite satisfactorily by showing that certain pleasures and daily pursuits are not necessary. Simplicity keeps our minds on the real reason God put us on this earth in the first place."

Kate raised an eyebrow. "Which is? Do go on, Pastor Luke."

"When Jesus came, He said there are only two commandments we need worry ourselves about—"

"Two?" Kate broke in. "What happened to the ten?"

"If we but follow these two, the others are taken care of automatically. It's recorded here in the tenth chapter of Luke, verse twenty-seven: 'Thou shalt love the Lord thy God with all thy heart, and with all thy soul, and with all thy strength, and with all thy mind; and thy neighbor as thyself.' "

Kate seemed impressed as she reread the passage. "Yes," she said, her eyes widening. "It makes complete sense. If we treat our neighbor right, we will not bear false witness, kill or covet, or any of the other things."

Emily broke into the conversation. "I'm beginning to prepare some supper. Won't you stay to eat with us, Pastor Luke?"

"Oh, yes, you must because there are more things I want to ask," Kate said.

"Very well. I shall stay for supper." His eyes twinkled. "Since you both insist."

"I need to know if God forgives us for our sins," Kate continued.

"Of course He does," Emily said, looking up from the potato she was slicing. "I've explained that."

"But, if He does, why would one not be happy and rejoice? Because I found in Philippians where it says, 'Rejoice in the Lord always' " (Philippians 4:4).

Luke grinned bigger than before. "And so it does, Kate. Yes, Paul taught that."

Emily felt her heart sink. She knew what Kate was getting to now. She was referring to her and how she wasn't able to forget the words spoken to

114

Ben in anger. Or how she couldn't put out of her mind the night she'd gone to the dance.

"We believe a person is forgiven if he truly repents and promises to sin no more."

"So," Kate went on, "if a person asked God to forgive him, it should be over."

Luke glanced at Emily, but she turned away from his gaze. "People are often misled by a passion of the moment. It's a weakness of the flesh. But we are only human, and the person must also forgive himself. And that is why we believe in meetings, as we are mighty in number and uphold each other in daily prayer."

"I do believe that," Kate said.

"Do you love God, Kate?"

"Yes, Pastor Luke, I believe I do."

"Don't test God. Love Him with all your heart and soul, mind, and strength, as the Scripture tells us, and everything will fall into place."

Emily stirred the potatoes, but she couldn't see for the tears crowding her eyes. *Everything will fall into place*, she repeated to herself. Why had she not remembered it? Yes, she had not been joyful. Her heart had been laden with guilt and remorse. It didn't take much to rid herself of the feeling.

Sighing, she moved the pan off the stove and fell to her knees. "I am the one Kate speaks of, Luke. It is I who has not felt like rejoicing. I need forgiveness for my moment of weakness. I also need to own up to my own feelings and get on with my life."

Emily had never in her entire life delivered such a speech. Her eyes brimming, she felt Luke's hand on her head as he knelt beside her and prayed.

Kate was on the other side, her arm around Emily's shoulder. And just as they had done last Saturday, giggling like two schoolgirls, now they cried together.

"I must ask for Ben's forgiveness," Emily said at the conclusion of the prayer. "I hurt him deeply. I know because I saw it in his eyes."

"Yes, that is what thee must do," Luke said, standing back up. "I think everything is going to work out for thee now."

The supper was simple fare with fried potatoes, leftover butter beans, and thick slices of bread.

Luke finished off the beans and potatoes, then pushed his chair back. "It's been wonderful seeing you again, Emily, and meeting you, Kate. I'm glad we had this time of prayer. And remember, you're always welcome in meeting."

After handing him his coat and hat, Kate walked him to the door while Emily cleared the table.

He paused, regarding Kate closely. "If you'd like, I could come again and we could talk more about God's Word."

"I think I'd like that."

Long after he had gone, Emily sat staring at her embroidery work. Kate was in the sewing room, making white pinafores to wear over their dresses. She had been more quiet than usual after Luke had gone. Emily wanted to ask her what she was thinking but knew Kate would talk about it when she felt like it. Emily wondered if Kate would stop wearing her bright dresses and jewelry.

The prayers for forgiveness made her feel so light and free. Emily hadn't liked herself very much. And she certainly hadn't been truthful. But her new feeling of release nearly overwhelmed her.

"I like your Pastor Luke," Kate said as she emerged from the bedroom with both pinafores completed.

"I'm not surprised," Emily said. "I knew the first day that he was going to be a wonderful, warm person."

Emily took her pinafore and put it on over her brown dress. "This looks nice, Kate. It's like an apron."

"I didn't tell you this earlier," Kate said, "because I didn't want you to get the wrong idea."

"About what?" Emily removed the pinafore.

"Kurt is leaving for Seattle next week. He has taken a job there, and doesn't plan to return."

"Kate! No!"

"It's okay, Emily. He asked me to accompany him—after we were married, of course—but I told him though I cared very much for him, like you, I could not marry a man I did not love."

Emily's eyes filled with tears. "It wasn't because I'm here, was it? Because I can move. I can find somewhere to stay."

"Emily, I realize that. You have enough money now, with what Pastor Luke brought today, for your train ticket to Monterey. It wasn't you holding me back, but my own heart knew it wasn't right."

"Will he stop to say good-bye?"

Kate smiled. "As a matter of fact, he wants us to go for a Sunday drive and will be by early. Almost as soon as the sun is up. We have a long drive ahead of us."

"We do?"

"Yes, and I want you to bring plenty of wraps and some blankets, as mornings are cold, though the afternoons are warming up nicely. I'll pack a lunch tonight."

Emily chose the pink dress, one of the first made on Kate's sewing machine. Kate selected a flowered chambray and her new navy blue cloche, and they both planned on wearing the new pinafores.

Emily thought again about what Luke had said about color. Did she dwell on her clothing too much now? Could it be true that such things took one from thoughts of God and serving Him? She didn't want that to happen. She wanted to attend church again, but perhaps a different one. It would be difficult to sit with her grandparents in the Meeting. They would stare, especially Grandmother, and it would be uncomfortable.

Where were Kurt and Kate going that would take all day? She'd asked, but Kate had said she would soon see. Kate loved surprises and assumed that everyone else did, also.

Before blowing out the light, Emily scrawled a few lines in a letter she would soon mail to her parents.

Mama,

It's getting closer now. I will come to see you and Papa, and I hope all my brothers and sisters are nearby—except for Tom, of course—unless you have had word from him. I truly pray you have.

I know it will be such a lovely time together and I look forward to catching up on everything that has happened. I love you, Mama! Tell Papa I am eager to hear "The Arkansas Traveler." And if you have a piano, I will play music for you. I play much better than I used to. I send you best regards.

Your loving daughter,
Emily Drake

Emily set the letter aside and said her prayers. She thanked God for the forgiveness and for the riddance of the pain she'd felt for so long. She also thanked Him for her friend Kate and for Luke's caring, gentle manner. She then said a special prayer for her grandmother and grandfather. Some day, she hoped, they would want to see her and speak to her again. Some day, she hoped they would forgive and Grandmother would not feel bitterness toward her. Until then, she would carry on in her new life and continue to be thankful and confident she was in the Lord's will.

Chapter 18

Kurt arrived ten minutes early. After removing his hat, he called out, "Good morning. It's certainly a wonderful day for a ride in the country. A bit nippy, perhaps, but it's bound to warm up."

Both women had warm coats, hats, and gloves, and Emily smoothed down the skirt of her pink dress. It was the first time she had worn it, and she didn't feel wrong for wearing a light color. She felt good inside and had lifted praises to God for His provisions and promises.

Emily had not seen this part of town before, nor had she seen the Willamette River, since that day when she was ten and had arrived on the train. She breathed deeply of the cool, crisp air. Never had a day seemed more perfect, nor a Sunday so wonderful.

They traveled south, taking in the flowering cherry and apple trees. From where she sat, Emily studied her two friends, wishing Kurt wouldn't move to Seattle, knowing she would miss seeing him, and wondering if Kate was the reason for the change. If only things had been different, but, then, life was full of disappointments. She'd learned that early on.

They began climbing, and Emily thought they would never get to the top of a huge hill. The area was wooded with very few houses in sight. A buggy passed them and Emily laughed when the driver doffed his hat and waved.

"Look back over your shoulder," Kate called out.

Emily did and the breath caught in her throat. Never had she seen such a hill, such a sky that seemed to take over, and the river, blue and clear way below them. It was a beautiful view.

"Another half mile and we're there," Kurt said.

Emily wondered where they were going, but that was part of the surprise. She felt the little horse in her pocket. She liked to keep Black Beauty there. It made her think of Ben, made her remember that night, made her remember his face and the snapping eyes, made her wonder if she would ever see him again, wonder if he even wanted to see her.

And then they stopped. Emily peered around the corner and saw a large lot cleared. A foundation and siding were up, and off in one corner sat a smaller house with smoke coming out the chimney.

"Yahoo! Anyone home?" Kurt called.

The door of the cabin opened and Emily froze. She'd recognize that stance anywhere. *Ben*. Even from here, she could see his thick shock of hair, remember how bushy the eyebrows were, and her heart wouldn't stop pounding so hard.

"Come on in. Meet my family!"

Emily's fingers tightened on the collar of her coat. Would he know she had come, too? He couldn't see her in the back like this. She reached up and tugged on Kate. "Why didn't you tell me this was where we were coming?"

"Because you wouldn't have come, that's why," Kate retorted.

"You're right. Probably I would have protested. Still, I need to apologize."

"Ben has wanted me to meet his mother and sister, and I thought you should meet them, too."

So she was going to see Ben again. What might he say to her, or she to him? She felt uncomfortable, but there was no place to hide.

The horse rode over the deep rutted land, threatening to bog down. "This wouldn't be so bad if it hadn't poured last night," Kurt said.

And then they were there and Ben walked up to the buggy.

"Kate! Kurt! I am so glad you both came. Ma and Pearl have wanted to meet some people. This is splendid—" his voice cut off in mid-sentence as his eyes suddenly focused on Emily.

"I. . .didn't know you brought someone."

"Ben, I want you to meet Emily. She's staying with me, and I could hardly leave her home, now could I?"

Emily's cheeks flushed at the game the two were playing. Pretending that Ben didn't know her.

She extended her hands. Well, two could play this game.

"I am happy to meet you, Ben."

His eyes didn't leave her face, nor hers move from his. He reached up, helping her out of the carriage. She lifted the pink skirt, and still slipped on some mud. Ben bent down and scooped her into his arms and held her high as he walked over to a long plank leading up to the house. She was too shocked to even protest.

"There you go. Now it's your turn, Kate."

Kate laughed. "Ben, you silly thing, you."

Soon they were inside the small house, and introductions and greetings were made. Emily felt two pairs of eyes on her once her name was mentioned. She nodded slightly, holding her hand out to Mrs. Galloway.

"I'm so pleased to meet you."

"And I, you," the tall, raw-boned woman said. Her hand was warm and callused from many years of hard work. Emily liked her immediately.

The furnishings were meager, but there were enough chairs for everyone.

"This is temporary," Ben explained. "The new house should be finished end of next month." Even as he spoke, his eyes never left Emily's face. He could hardly believe she was here. And her cheeks all rosy and pink, matching the dress that flounced as she walked. What had happened to the gray and brown? Life had changed for her since she'd moved in with Kate. And he was glad for that.

A girl with waist-length, thick hair stood up and smiled shyly. The hair. Emily couldn't help noticing how like her brother's her hair was. She wondered if his children would have hair like that, then stopped her thought midway. What on earth had led her to think about such things?

"Of course you'll have tea and some nice hot gingerbread right out of the oven," Sarah Galloway said. "Baked it just a bit ago."

The room was warm. Cheery in spite of the lack of space.

Kate took over the conversation to Emily's relief. Emily was getting better, but still had a problem knowing what to say, especially when a certain pair of eyes stayed fastened on her. She didn't dare look in Ben's direction. She would really blush then.

"Do you like it in Oregon?" Kate was asking.

"Very much so. And my Ben was right about the rich earth. I have already planted onions, carrots, and corn. Radishes."

"Mom's a real gardener," Ben said. "She gets anything to grow."

Emily relaxed and reached out for the cup of steaming tea. Kurt, who had been outside, came in and accepted his tea and gingerbread.

"I'd like to show you around," Ben said, his eyes still locked on Emily's. "I know where we can go to avoid most of the mud."

Emily nodded. "I would like that."

"Why did you come?" he asked once they were back out under the cloudless blue sky.

"I didn't know this was where I was coming."

"Oh. I knew there was a catch to it."

"But I would have wanted to come," Emily said. "I had to see you again to apologize for what I said that last time. It was entirely rude of me."

"You meant it, though. About not caring."

"No, Ben, the words were not true."

He stopped walking and looked at her closely. Was she telling him something, or was it only his wishful thinking? How did one ever know?

She watched him out of the corner of her eye, wondering what he was thinking as a frown creased his brow.

"If the words spoken were not true, then what is the truth, Miss Emily Drake?"

"That I need not to only listen to my mind, but to my heart, also. The heart has its reasons, you know."

"And what does your heart tell you?"

"That I want to be your friend again."

His hopes and dreams seemed dashed against a cement wall. Friends. So all she wanted to be was friends. How could he convince her otherwise?

"I'm glad, Emily, for I will always be your friend."

Emily looked into his eyes, knowing she hoped to be more than friends. She wanted to tell Ben that he was in her morning thoughts, her afternoon thoughts, her evening thoughts. But to admit such a thing was too forward. It simply wasn't done.

Ben took her hand and held it gently. "I hear that friendship is a good base for lasting relationships. And my heart tells me to seek more. My God tells me I am ready for more."

Trembling, Emily's eyes met his and in the next second she was pulled into his arms as his head bent down and kissed the tip of her nose, first one cheek, then the other, and finally at last his mouth found hers. She felt pulled under and soon freed herself from his grasp.

"I'm sorry," Ben said. "Forgive me."

"Only if you forgive me first." A smile tugged at the corners of her mouth.

"Emily, is it possible that we might start over? Pretend the dance never happened?"

Emily felt her heart soaring. "I would like that, Ben. Yes, I would like that very much."

"I can come calling?"

"If you'd like. But I am going to California soon to see my family."

"You *are*?" He felt happy for her, knowing how important it was, but to lose her, even for a week, maybe longer, when he'd just found her, troubled him.

As if reading his mind, she touched his arm. "I'm coming back, though. I promised Mr. Roberts."

"How about me?"

She smiled. "I can promise you, too."

"I'm building a house I want to show you." His eyes gazed into hers. "I think you'll like it."

"What sort of house?"

"It's large with a balcony on the second floor and big, wide rooms. One even has bookshelves."

The meaning wasn't lost on Emily. "I would very much like to see your new house, Mr. Galloway."

He took her hand and together they walked out into the open, looking up at the blue, blue sky. Her spirit felt free as she lifted her face.

" 'They that wait upon the Lord shall renew their strength,' " Emily started.

" 'They shall mount up with wings as eagles,' " Ben said, finishing the phrase.

She turned to look at him. It was a sign. Her sign from God that yes, indeed, Ben *did* know Him.

Good-byes were said and the trio started on the homeward trek. Emily sat in the back, keeping the words, the thoughts, the sight of Ben tucked inside her heart. Her face glowed, her hands felt warm though it had grown cold and windy. Ben was coming tomorrow after work. She could ride in his carriage. She could talk to him on Kate's porch if she wanted. She might even wear the pink dress again. She felt free, yet she knew she would never be free from God's hand, God's rule on her life. And she didn't want to be.

Emily looked out from under the canopy at the heavens. "Thank You, dear God," she murmured. "I know You have guided me thus far and are certainly going to guide me even further." She finished the verse from Isaiah: " 'They shall run and not be weary, and shall walk, and not faint.' "

She closed her eyes and saw Ben with his thick hair smiling at her, and over him it was as if God held out His arms to both of them, encompassing them as one whole, as a committed pair willing and wanting to serve their Lord and Master.

A light rain began to fall. . .

Love Shall
Come Again

This book is lovingly dedicated to my mother, Naomi;
my Uncle Clifford and Aunt Margie;
and to the memory of Isobelle, Hazel, and Benjamin.

Chapter 1

Kate Russell put the final touches—one last stitch—in the hem of the pink dress she'd sewn for her dearest friend, Emily Galloway. She held it up and inspected it carefully, from the delicate lace collar to the pleated bodice and down to the nine-gored skirt. Plenty of room for the growing baby. Though there were only two months left, it seemed babies grew a lot during the last weeks. At least Emily could put off her dreary gray muslin, with its faded material and seams stretching to the limit, though Kate knew she wouldn't wear pink to church. The Society of Friends didn't believe in wearing bright colors.

This baby, a first for the Galloways, had Kate caught up in their excitement and anticipation. It seemed like only yesterday when the two women had worked side by side at Oregon's Finest Chocolates Company, dipping chocolates. Then Emily met Ben, and though they never had a real courting period, they finally realized that love would have its way and were married in a quiet ceremony with Pastor Luke Morrison officiating. Kate had been the matchmaker.

Wrapping the dress carefully, Kate hoped the frothy pink creation would bolster Emily's spirits, but then Kate already knew Emily would be pleased, simply because Emily loved everything Kate did for her.

The mantel clock chimed five times. Kate jumped. She didn't have much time to get ready for the Saturday night dance. Usually Kate danced at the local grange hall, but tonight she planned to take the streetcar downtown to the new ballroom. Perhaps it wasn't proper for a young lady to attend a dance without a chaperone, but Kate was a widow and the rules were different for widows—or so she told Emily.

She held her new dress—a full-skirted, dusty rose taffeta—up against her face and waltzed around the bedroom. Multiple layers of crinoline would add the needed flounce. New patent leather shoes, from the latest edition of the Sears & Roebuck Catalogue, had arrived on Friday, not a moment too soon.

Perhaps this was the night Kate would meet that special someone. At age twenty, she thought it was time to think about settling down again, though she doubted there would ever be a man as sweet as her late husband, Charles.

Kate twisted the gold wedding band she now wore on the ring finger of her right hand. Had Charles died only two years ago? Some days it seemed much longer. Her brief marriage had been happy, for she had discovered how nice it was to have someone care about her. Even now she remembered his gentle hands sifting through her hair, his eyes filled with love. Kate needed good memories after her life on the farm in southern Oregon—nothing but that hard work each day, only to repeat it again the next day.

Kate shook the thoughts away as she slipped the taffeta over her shoulders and pulled it past her full hips. Perhaps there was a man out there like Ben Galloway: good, solid, and dependable. For reasons she could not explain, Pastor Luke Morrison's face flashed through her mind. She tried to push it aside, but the thought persisted. Luke was kind and thoughtful, but he was short—shorter than Kate—with a stocky build. They were complete opposites not only in looks, but in religious beliefs. Luke was of the "Friendly persuasion," while Kate wasn't even sure she believed in God. They argued—or "discussed"—it as he put it.

"You know, we'll never agree on this subject, Kate," he'd said more than once.

Kate laughed her tinkling laugh, her dark eyes fairly dancing. "You're so right, Pastor Luke. We never see eye to eye when it comes to God and the church."

"It doesn't mean we can't be friends, however," he'd said once, and his gaze had held hers. She wondered at the intensity of it. Could he possibly have feelings for her? It was impossible, considering her pagan ways. Yet they did share a commonality: being widowed. His loss had given Luke deepened compassion and understanding. Not only had Luke lost a wife, but also a child—a son.

Kate's thoughts turned to the evening ahead. Before the dance, she'd catch the streetcar to the Galloways'. While Emily and Kate chatted about the coming baby and the goings on at the candy factory, Ben would sit on the front porch, reading the *Daily Oregonian* or whittling on a piece of wood, carving another horse to add to Emily's collection. Then there'd be the traditional chicken dinner followed by thick wedges of warm apple pie.

Kate touched the rustling folds of the rose-colored taffeta. Her slim waist didn't match the rest of her well-rounded figure, and the new shoes made her even taller, but she liked being tall. . .like her mother. . .

Brushing back her thick, dark hair—also like Mama's—she secured a silver clasp on one side. Kate smiled at her reflection in the oval mirror in the hallway. If only Mama had lived. What wonderful times they might have had.

Kate pressed a spot of rouge on her left cheek, her fingers touching the nearly invisible scar. She winced for a brief moment, but she never allowed herself to dwell on that scar nor the reason for its being. As always, she pushed the thoughts down and set her mind on more pleasant memories. That sultry August afternoon was a secret she'd carry to her grave. . .

Grabbing the box with Emily's dress, Kate headed to the corner, arriving just as the streetcar came clanging down the street. She boarded, dropped a coin in the box, and found a seat. Straightening her full skirt, she knew her dress was far lovelier than any she had seen in the Emporium where most people shopped. And her shoes were the latest, so the catalogue advertised.

Kate looked out the window at the Portland countryside. It was 1909, and everything was changing fast—it was called progress. Families came to the Willamette Valley to raise better crops. They filled the city and made new towns. Homes sprouted across the landscape, as businesses opened on both sides of Foster Road in the new district called Lents.

Kate smiled as she watched houses being left behind. The streetcar was a wonderful invention, and she was glad the company had extended their service for this special Saturday night dance. Soon she might ride in a motor car if Ben had his way. It had been his dream ever since hearing about them, but Emily said she preferred a horse and buggy, just the same. An automobile drove by, and the driver honked. Kate laughed and waved.

The dirt road, hard-packed from the heat of summer days, was far easier to travel than during winter months when rain turned everything to thick mud. Kate enjoyed summers, especially here in Portland where the heat didn't penetrate as it had in southern Oregon. Beauty abounded around Portland, with immense Douglas firs, snow-capped Mt. Hood to the east, and the hillside across the Willamette River, Portland Heights and Council Crest, where the affluent lived.

Feeling eyes watching her, Kate turned to see an unkempt man leering her way. His eyes reminded her again of that afternoon when she'd been alone in the house. If Mama had lived, things would have been different. Mama had kept her safe in the little farmhouse sitting at the edge of a hill. Kate remembered the warm nights before the last baby came. She and Mama would sit on the front porch to catch a breath of fresh air, watching while the sky changed from blue to orange and red. Mama had so loved sunsets. She loved sunsets, the farm, roses. . .and Pa. . .though Kate had not understood how she could love Pa when he was often mean.

"Things will be better after the baby comes," Mama had said, her hand pushing back damp strands from Kate's face. "Pa needs another son to work on the farm." Pa's first wife had given him two sons, but all of Ma's babies, except for Kate, had died at birth. "This time I'll give him that boy." She smiled. "And I want you to name the baby. Any name you want. . ."

"Moses if it's a boy," Kate had said, "and Ruth for a girl." They were biblical characters from Kate's favorite stories, the ones Mama used to read from the family Bible—the Bible Kate had left behind.

But when Mama's labor had started, it was long and difficult, and Kate heard the midwife telling Pa the baby was dead inside. Kate prayed it wasn't so as she heard Mama's cries. Then it was over and the baby—another girl—was born, stillborn. Kate was finally allowed in the room. Mama's pale face and inert body frightened her, as she ran to the bed and took Mama's hand.

"Cherub?"

Kate smiled. "Yes, Mama? I'm right here." Cherub was Mama's pet name for her, though she was nearly a young lady now. She thought of how Mama pulled the quilt up under her chin each night, murmuring softly, "Sleep tight, my cherub, and God bless and keep you."

"I'm so. . ." Mama murmured, and Kate bent closer to hear the words, "so very tired."

"You'll feel better tomorrow," Kate said, "because I've been praying to God," but tentacles of fear clutched at her as she sponged off Mama's face. Surely God wouldn't let Mama die when Kate needed her so.

But Mama died later that night, and there were now two to bury.

Two days later, Kate lay a scraggly bouquet of wild daisies on Mama and baby Ruth's grave, wishing she had the roses Mama loved so well. She turned, gazing at Pa in his threadbare black suit, flanked on each side by his sons, John and Carl. They didn't own suits, but wore starched white shirts. Scowling, Pa motioned for Kate to come. "It's time to go. No use in staying any longer. Tears don't bring back the dead."

Kate took short, deep breaths, knowing Pa's heart couldn't be breaking as hers was. How could she say good-bye to the only person she truly loved? And didn't he care about the baby who had died? Aunt Lucy, Pa's sister who had come from Seattle to visit, touched Kate's shoulder. "Your pa is right. It's time to go."

Kate nodded, saying nothing.

"You're a big girl now. Practically grown. How old are you? Twelve? You'll take over for your ma now."

No, Kate wanted to say. I can't. I won't! She whirled away from Aunt Lucy, darted past her brothers and Pa, and ran across the meadow. How could she possibly do all the chores Mama had? She could bake bread and knew how to soak beans, then cook them with a bit of fat, but there was so much more to do. So very much more.

In her mind's eye, Kate could still see the small pine casket, the knoll of freshly dug earth as she raced back to the farmhouse. Maybe she could return with Aunt Lucy to Seattle. Pa had said Aunt Lucy had married money, which was difficult for Kate to comprehend. Didn't people marry people?

She flew into the house and to the small room she called her own. Breathless, she picked up a pair of socks from the mending basket. Who would she talk to now while darning socks in the evenings beside the oil lamp? Who would give her a good-night hug? Surely not Pa. Nor would Pa kneel beside her bed as she said prayers. The door opened and voices filled the small house as Kate sat, holding her fear and grief inside her.

"What a mercy the child did not live," Aunt Lucy was saying. "Heaven knows why she kept trying to have a baby when all of them died."

Kate felt the tears burn her eyelids again. It was true. Mama had lost many babies, though each time they prayed for a healthy child.

"A motherless child wouldn't have much of a life here in this God-forsaken spot," Aunt Lucy went on. "By the way, where is Kate?"

"In her room," Carl answered. "She always goes there when things don't go her way."

"Kate!" Pa's voice boomed out. "Come and make supper!"

A few people had dropped in with covered dishes, and one of Mama's friends had brought a beautiful white frosted cake. Kate dried her tears and smoothed her skirt down.

"We'll just have the food people brought," Aunt Lucy said, "but you can slice the bread and get butter from the pantry. I'll put coffee on."

Aunt Lucy's starched percale dress, with layers of crinolines, seemed to fill the whole kitchen, and Kate dreamed of owning one just like it. Though she missed Mama terribly, there was no bringing her back. Surely she would go home with Aunt Lucy.

Not so. Pa had other plans.

"You'll cook and take over the chores your ma used to do," Pa said when Kate asked about leaving with Aunt Lucy.

"Oh, please, no," Kate cried. "I don't know how without Mama here—"

The chair scraped back, and Pa's look withered her. "You're staying, and you'll learn, just as your ma did."

Kate was sent to bed, and listened to the hum of voices late into the night. Pa's voice grated most of all. "Isn't that just like a woman? Leaving me in the lurch at haying time?"

There was a sound of chairs moving and coffee being poured. Pa's next words plunged like a knife in her heart. "I knew I shouldn't have married her. Not with a kid like Kate in tow, being a girl and all. And she was so skinny, and never could carry a son to full term. Took pity on her, though."

The rest was lost on Kate. Pa wasn't her real pa? He had married Mama after she was born? But if he wasn't her real father, who was? And why had he married Mama if he didn't love her? Confusion filled her mind as she finally drifted off to sleep.

"Get up, girl! It's time to fix breakfast!"

At first Kate thought she was dreaming, then she realized Pa's voice was ripping through the house. Kate shivered as thoughts of the previous day passed through her mind. Mama was gone, and she must now do all the things as Mama had. She slipped from bed and into her worn petticoat and brown dress. There was leftover food for today, but what about tomorrow and next week?

As Aunt Lucy packed her trunk, and John, the oldest son, brought the wagon and horse around, Kate saw her last chance fleeing away. "Please, couldn't I go with you? Oh, please, please, Aunt Lucy."

"Your job is here," Aunt Lucy said firmly, not quite looking Kate in the eye. "You'll get used to the work, and you'll be much closer to your ma that way."

"But—but I don't want to stay—"

"You're lucky to have a roof over your head, child. I've heard tell of children who work twelve and fourteen hours a day in factories in New York. You should feel thankful your pa came along when he did, that he gave you and your ma a home, what with your own father dying of consumption when you were just a year old. The least you can do is repay him by cooking and keeping his house up. He's a good man. He's hard to understand, but he's just."

Later, Kate realized why it wasn't permitted. If Pa wasn't her real pa, then Aunt Lucy wasn't her real aunt, either. Aunt Lucy's voice seared her mind, and Kate had never forgotten those words. She was worthless, and Pa treated her as such. When he hired a man to help with the harvest four summers later, Kate was mistreated in another way. But she only let it happen once. . .

She had stolen the money hidden under the floorboards in the kitchen, taken the old mare, and run for the train depot. Sometimes it seemed like it had just happened yesterday, though four years had passed since she'd left the farm, and eight years since Mama died.

Kate sat up straighter, adjusted her hat, and looked with pride at her new shoes. Times were different now. She'd never go back to a farm. It was all behind her. What had happened had happened. The dark secret she had never bared to anyone—not even her best friend Emily—would stay inside her. Life had been good and promised even better now with good friends to love and care about.

"Foster Road," the conductor called out.

Kate lurched to her feet, smoothing out her dress as she lighted from the streetcar, then held the skirts up, not wanting the dust to soil the hemline of her new dress.

She walked across the street, holding onto the package containing Emily's dress. The scent of roses made Kate smile as she opened the gate. No wagon in the side yard, so Ben was still at work. She hurried up the steps and called out, "Yoo-hoo! Anyone home?"

Emily came around the corner and the two hugged.

"Kate! I see you've finished your new dress. It's gorgeous! Makes me think of the color of my climbing roses on the west side of the house."

Kate waltzed across the floor, making the skirt swing out. "That's not all I made," Kate said, holding the package out.

"But it isn't my birthday or Christmas—"

"I know. But mothers-to-be need something new to wear."

Emily fumbled with the string, her eyes widening when she saw the dress. "Kate. It's ever so pretty!"

"You go try it on, then we'll sit a spell before you start the chicken," Kate suggested.

Kate brought the potatoes out of the cellar, and then Emily was there, her face pink as she emerged from the bedroom.

"Oh, Kate, it's a perfect fit, and I like it very much." She put her hands over the mound that was Baby Galloway. "But, you shouldn't have."

"Yes, I should have, so there. Now let's go out and sit on the front porch. It's too hot to cook just yet."

The two chatted about the weather, about Ben's new house, and about how Sarah Galloway, Ben's mother, liked the country here much better than in Iowa, until a streetcar lumbered up the street and pulled to a stop at the corner.

"Nobody ever gets off here," Emily said, fanning her face.

"Except me."

"But you come from the other direction."

A large man with a suitcase stood at the corner after the streetcar left. He turned and walked slowly across the street. Kate noticed immediately the cut of his clothes and his expensive fedora. There was something familiar about him, but she didn't know what.

Chapter 2

The stranger stopped at the gate, then tipped his hat. "Afternoon, ladies. I see you're enjoying this absolutely divine Oregon sunshine."

Kate nodded. "That we are. How may we help you?"

He put his suitcase down and wiped his forehead with a white handkerchief. "Just came in on the afternoon train—the Great Northern—and I'm looking for my brother. Haven't seen him for almost two years. Last I knew, he was planning on settling right here in Portland."

"You're in Lents, Sir," Emily said.

"Yes, so I heard from a lady on the streetcar." He flashed a smile. "I think he planned on building houses in this area."

"And what is your brother's name?" Kate asked, her eyes taking in the self-assured man standing before her. For some unexplainable reason, her heart began pounding.

He walked closer, putting a foot on the bottom step. "I'm Jesse Galloway, and my brother's name is Ben."

Emily gasped, her hand going to her mouth. "Why—you're—you're—"

"We know Ben Galloway," Kate said, taking over for the surprised Emily. "In fact, if you must know, you're standing on property he owns, and this is the house he built for his wife here. This is Emily—Mrs. Ben Galloway."

Jesse couldn't believe it. Not only had he found his brother, he'd found Ben's house—quite an impressive house at that, surely large enough to put him up for a few days. But more important, he'd found a beautiful woman, one more stunning than Miss Priscilla Palmer, whom he'd met on the streetcar, and far more lovely than the Widow Jarvis, whom he'd left behind in Seattle.

"I'm Kate Russell," Kate said, standing to shake his extended hand, "a good friend of the family."

Emily cleared her throat, as if she found it difficult to speak. "Ben's talked about you," she said, then turned toward Kate. Kate sensed a reluctance on Emily's part, as if she wasn't sure about this situation, but all Kate knew was that the handsomest man she'd ever laid eyes on was standing in front of her, and he was Ben's brother. This very afternoon, she'd wondered about finding a man to love, someone who would honor, cherish, and love her in return. It was as if God had dropped him right before her eyes—and she wasn't even sure she believed in God!

"Goodness gracious," Kate said. "Come sit down a spell. I suppose you must be thirsty. Can I get you a glass of water? Emily's fixing to fry chicken, and there are two apple pies in the cooler."

"A glass of water would be nice," Jesse said, "but I can fetch it myself."

Emily, finally composed, nodded. "Of course you'll stay for dinner. We have plenty. Ben will be home shortly. He comes home earlier on Saturday. And won't he be surprised!" She turned and went in to start dinner.

Kate felt her cheeks flush as Jesse Galloway held the door open. He had Ben's same intense gaze, that same unruly hair, a short beard and mustache, but he was taller and bigger. Not that Ben was a slouch, but Jesse had immense shoulders. Kate felt something stir deep inside her, but shook herself back to reality. Perhaps he wouldn't be staying, so there was no sense in thinking of him.

"I just bet Ben will be surprised," Jesse answered Emily, as he swaggered into the kitchen and pulled out a chair.

"Maybe you'd like to wait in the library," Emily suggested. "Ben says it's really a study, but I call it a library. It's our parlor for guests."

"I ain't a guest. I'm family," Jesse said then, smiling as if he was amused. "I'd rather sit here and visit, if you don't mind."

Kate liked the deepness of his voice. She washed her hands, aware that Jesse's eyes followed her every move. Emily floured the chicken while Kate peeled potatoes. They were small potatoes from the garden, and twice she nicked her fingers. She'd better start paying attention to what she was doing, she admonished herself.

"Haven't you been living up north?" Kate asked, trying to remember what Ben had said, the one time he'd talked about his brother.

"Yes. In Seattle. Decided it was time to move on."

"But you and Ben came out on the train from Iowa the same time," Emily added, turning around to look at her brother-in-law.

"Yes, we did," Jesse answered, his eyes staying on Kate. In fact, he couldn't keep his eyes off her. She was different from the prim and proper Emily. He could well imagine why Ben had fallen for Emily. But Kate. . . well, hadn't he always been able to size up women? Yes, she was definitely worth getting to know.

"I thought I'd like Seattle, but I missed my family there." Jesse hesitated, knowing he must make a good impression, not only on Kate, whom he hoped to court, but on his new sister-in-law, so she'd talk Ben into letting him stay. Knowing Ben, he might still be angry. Ben thought Jesse was lazy, and partly that was true. Lazy in the ways that were important to Ben, but not lazy in ways that Jesse deemed important.

"You wouldn't know about Mama or Pearl—would you?"

"Oh my, yes." Emily put the cast iron skillet on the wood stove and dumped some lard in it. "They live in Oregon City and are quite content."

"Oregon City!"

"Yes, it's not that far away. Ben looks in on them at least once a week—"

"Mama is—all right?" Jesse asked, interrupting. "And Pearl?"

"Mama's healthy as can be, and Pearl wants to start school next month. They have a big garden, and Mama takes in washing and ironing—" Emily smiled then. "I know it may sound strange, my calling her Mama, but my mother lives in California, and I never get to see her. And Sarah—Miz Galloway—said she'd be honored for me to call her Mama."

"I call Sarah Mama, too," Kate said, turning to look at Jesse again. "My own mother died, and I think of your mother as my own."

Jesse smiled and Kate dropped the potato. Why was she so fluttery? She was never nervous around men. If anything, men became distracted around Kate, but Jesse was so charming and handsome, she wanted to keep looking at him.

"Mama's always had that effect on people," Jesse said then.

Kate pushed a strand of hair that had slipped out of the clasp. "I—don't know, Emily," she said. "I may not stay for supper after all. Suddenly I feel—"

"Not stay!" Emily broke in.

"Maybe it's just that I'm eager to get to the dance—"

"Dance?" Jesse interrupted. "Did I hear you say dance?"

Emily answered for her friend, as if she knew Kate could not. "Kate dances Saturday nights. Ben and I don't," she paused. "Not that I think it's wrong for Kate to—it's just not right for us."

"That's how Ben met Emily," Kate said then. "At a grange dance I insisted Emily go to."

"What's wrong with dancing?" Jesse asked, suddenly getting to his feet. This was even better than he could have hoped for. Kate liked to dance, and there was nothing Jesse enjoyed more.

"It's against their religion," Kate said. "Pastor Luke says it's a worldly desire, and it takes one's mind off the Lord."

"Which reminds me," Emily said. "Luke may stop by for dinner, too. I invited him on Wednesday after prayer meeting."

Kate gave her friend a quizzical look. Was Emily still trying to match her and Luke? She knew it was hopeless. Kate could never give up dancing, nor would she wear the drab gray dresses the women of the Friends' Church wore. And she'd never stop wearing rouge.

"I'll come another time," Kate said with firmness.

"Now, Kate," Emily started to protest.

"If you don't stay, then I won't, either," Jesse said, setting his cup down. "I want to get to know you better, Miss Kate, and how can I do that if you go running off?"

You could go to the dance, Kate wanted to say, but for some reason she was shy at the moment, and the words wouldn't come.

"You're both staying," Emily said, "so that settles it. I want Brother Luke to meet you, Jesse, and Kate needs to eat before going to the dance. It's going to be a perfectly wonderful evening." She paused, her hand going to the small of her back.

"Are you all right?" Kate asked, instantly alarmed. Ever since Emily announced she was expecting a baby, Kate had thought of her mother and all the babies she'd lost. Emily had the same frail, slender build, which didn't ease Kate's concern. Surely Emily was strong enough to have a healthy child. She didn't have to work as hard as Mama had—Ben saw to that—and that made a big difference. Kate knew she couldn't bear it if anything happened to this child that Ben and Emily wanted so badly.

"I'm fine," Emily said, forcing a smile to her lips. "It's just one of those pains—a contraction—that I understand are perfectly normal. I'm fine. Truly."

"Why don't you go lie down, and I'll take care of dinner."

"I don't know," Emily said with hesitation. "You burned the potatoes last week." Emily's eyes were teasing her friend. "Cooking has never been your favorite thing to do."

"I won't burn a thing. I promise."

Emily left the room, and Kate was alone with Jesse. She wanted to be, didn't she? But it was almost frightening. The bold eyes seemed to penetrate her very being. "I—I think it's wonderful that you've come to Portland," she finally managed.

"Not any more wonderful than I think," he answered, his look turning to one of amusement. "I also think it's going to be much more interesting than I ever dreamed possible."

Kate felt her face turn red and looked away, but not before she saw the mischievous twinkle in Jesse's eyes. He unnerved her—and he knew it, that was the problem.

"You are lovely, Miss Kate. Has anyone ever told you that?"

She forced her eyes to look at him. "My husband said that once. On the day of our wedding."

"Husband?"

"He passed away. I'm a widow."

"Oh, I am sorry. You're far too young to be widowed."

"Thank you, but I'm doing fine."

Kate turned back to the stove and flipped the chicken over. It was darker than Emily's, whose chicken always turned out a golden brown, but it would be good. Emily wouldn't fret too much.

"I may get fired as cook," Kate said with a laugh.

Jesse came closer and checked it out. "It looks great to me."

They were laughing when a knock sounded. "Goodness, I didn't even hear Pastor Luke drive up," Kate said, drying her hands on her apron before going to the door.

"Luke! We're having a celebration tonight. Ben's brother Jesse is here. Come in and meet him."

Luke stood in the foyer, hat in hand, his eyes landing on Kate. "I hoped you would be here," he said with a slight bow.

"It is tradition, you know," Kate said, turning from his intense gaze.

Moments later, Kate ushered Luke into the library. Its large, wide windows faced the west, and sunshine filled the room with light. Emily's books lined one shelf, and there was room for more.

"I know Emily prefers company to visit here. I'll be back with Ben's brother just as soon as I check that chicken."

"And where is Emily?" Luke asked.

"She's resting. Overdid it today, I suspect," Kate said.

There was a sound at the door as Jesse ambled in.

"So you must be Mr. Jesse Galloway, the long-lost brother," Luke said, rising to his feet.

Jesse towered over the shorter man, and his shoulders seemed twice as broad. There was a noticeable bit of hesitation on Jesse's part as he extended his hand to the minister. Though short of stature, Luke looked strong in the face, and Jesse disliked him on sight. Jesse always felt uneasy around men of the cloth anyway. He sensed, too, that Luke found Kate attractive, as his eyes followed her out the door. Jesse knew another thing: He wasn't about to let Kate out of his sight. He'd fight for her if that was what it took.

Luke walked across the room, standing in front of the bay window. "Are you planning to stay, Mr. Galloway?"

Jesse hesitated a moment before answering. "That all depends."

"Depends? Depends on what?" Luke turned back, staring at the tall, suave man before him. He knew the type. Hadn't he always been a good judge of character? That's how he led people to God, how he got to know his flock and helped them see the error of their ways. This man was not open to

God. Though he'd heard little about Jesse Galloway, Luke felt that he was no stranger to the man standing before him.

Kate was back, smiling. Luke had never seen her look so alluring, so beautiful. "Emily's up, taking care of that chicken," Kate said. "She wants to know if you want coffee or tea before dinner, Pastor Luke."

"Nothing for me," Luke said. Without waiting for Jesse to answer, he nodded toward Kate. "You're wearing a new dress, Kate. It's lovely."

Again, Kate felt her face burning. "I made it to wear to the new ballroom downtown."

"You won't lack for dance partners," Luke said, walking back to the window and looking out, glad he could turn away for a moment to regain his composure. One glance from Jesse to Kate and back to Jesse again, and Luke knew that Jesse was more than casually interested in Kate. A sudden uneasiness hit him again. He had always admired Kate Russell, enjoyed conversing with her, having Saturday night dinners here with the Galloways. Though she was not a member of the Meeting, she came on occasion with Emily and Ben, and in his heart and mind, Luke prayed that Kate might receive the inner light and come to know God in a real, personal way. Someday she might admit that she needed God in her life. They'd certainly discussed it enough, and Luke had always felt it was just a matter of time—God's time. Sometimes God worked quickly; other times it was slower, and with Kate Russell, it was definitely slower. Yet Luke had never stopped believing the time would come, and when that happened he wanted to be there.

A sound of horses sounded out front, and Kate jumped up. "Ben's home. I can't wait for him to see you." She darted through the kitchen and paused to give Emily a hug.

"I wonder if Ben will notice my new dress," Emily said, checking on the buttermilk biscuits in the oven.

Kate shook her head. "He's going to be more interested in the fact that his brother Jesse has come."

"I'm afraid of what he might say about that."

"You act as though he may not be pleased," Kate said. She thought she'd noticed hesitation from Emily when Jesse first introduced himself. There was just something on her face. Emily wore her heart on her sleeve, and Kate knew Emily better than anyone, even Ben.

The back door opened and Ben stalked in. "Smells good, as it always does." He smiled at Emily, putting his arms around her, then saw Kate.

"Hello, Kate. I should greet guests first, but when I smelled that chicken frying, I thought I'd better hug the cook first."

"I have a new dress," Emily said, standing back.

Ben smiled. "Kate's been busy at the sewing machine, I see. It looks—well, comfortable."

"There's another surprise—" Kate started to say, but she didn't finish, for Jesse suddenly loomed in the doorway. Kate felt her heart race to her throat at the sight of the handsome man.

"Hello, Ben." Jesse extended his hand as he walked forward. "Bet you're surprised to see me."

Ben shook his hand, his jaw tightening. His tension wasn't lost on Kate. "I thought you were in Seattle."

"I was."

"What happened to the Widow Jarvis?"

Jesse's face looked stricken for a brief moment. "She's doing well. We decided to part ways."

Ben nodded. "I see. It didn't have anything to do with money, did it?"

"It isn't like you think—" Jesse stopped, as if realizing ladies were present, especially one he hoped to capture for his own.

Luke entered the kitchen and nodded to Ben. "Ben, I wonder if you might not have too many guests for dinner tonight? I can certainly return another time—"

"Nonsense! Of all the people I know, you are the most welcome, you and Kate, that is." Ben turned and winked at Emily.

The uncomfortable moment seemed to be over as Jesse pulled a chair out and sat down. "I understand how you might feel, Ben, but I wanted to see you and to hear about Mama and Pearl. I just couldn't go back to Iowa without stopping by to say hi first."

Kate wondered at Ben's reaction. He was showing a side she didn't know existed.

"Mama and Pearl are here in Oregon," Ben said. "I brought them back with me over a year ago."

"So Emily told me."

"What else did Emily tell you?"

"That was it, except that you are building houses. I hoped you might give me a job."

Ben dried his hands. "Let's go in the study to talk. Please excuse us, Luke, Kate."

Once the door was closed, Jesse could feel the coldness surrounding him. Ben had changed. This wasn't anger now, nor disappointment, it was something far worse. Rejection smoldered in Ben's dark eyes.

"I don't think it'd work for you to stay here in Portland."

Jesse looked ruffled for a moment, but recouped his courage in his usual quick fashion. "I knew you'd think that, and I ask for your forgiveness, Ben. Being a godly man, you should understand and forgive me my transgressions."

"Don't use those big words with me."

"Ben, Ben, what's happened to you? You're not the happy-go-lucky little brother I remember so well. I guess it's because you had to give up dancing and—"

"Leave the dancing out."

"Of course, of course." Jesse removed the remains of his last cigar from the breast pocket of his coat.

"You can't smoke in here—"

"All right. I'm not surprised."

"You can stay for one night, maybe two, then I want you to leave. Go back to Seattle or wherever."

"It isn't like you to hold grudges."

Ben paced across the room, not wanting to look at his older brother. Jesse. The dreamer. The wanderer. Why didn't he just stay away? Nobody was safe with him in town, especially not Kate.

"I don't hold grudges. It's just that I know a leopard doesn't change his spots, and I don't want you breaking hearts in this part of the country."

Jesse winced. So Ben knew he had found Kate attractive. Ben also knew he would do anything to win her over. Jesse'd have to think of something to do fast, or he might lose out on the most beautiful woman he'd ever had the good fortune to meet.

"Your friend's not sweet on that preacher fellow, is she?"

Ben signed. "I knew it. Figures you'd notice Kate right off."

"Well, is she?"

He shook his head. "No, I expect not. Brother Luke isn't Kate's type—"

"Exactly," Jesse interrupted. "I could tell that immediately, and so I figured all is fair here."

"Kate is too decent a woman to get hurt, Jesse. I think of her as a sister and feel somewhat protective."

"Don't you think I know a true gem when I see one? Don't you think the time has come for ol' Jesse to settle down?"

Ben walked toward the door, then turned around to face his brother. "I wish I could believe you. I wish I could say it was okay for you to stay here. I wish I could welcome you with open arms. But you hurt everyone you get near, Jesse. It's always been that way, and you know it."

"I'm telling you I've changed, little brother." Jesse studied his long fingernails. They were clean. No dirt or grime under them. It was one thing the Widow Jarvis had liked about him. And his smell. Women liked the fact that he didn't smell of sweat or a barnyard.

"I'm warning you, Jesse, if you hurt Kate, I'll—so help me I'll come after you, and that's a promise."

Jesse pounded Ben on the back. "That almost sounds like a threat, Ben, but never fear. I know when I'm licked, and if anyone could lick me or tame me, it's that woman standing in the kitchen helping your wife fry chicken."

Ben opened the door and motioned for Jesse to go first. "Let's go eat. I'm starved."

Food was heaped up in large serving bowls, and Emily had set the table with her best china. Luke nodded, and they all bowed their heads as he asked a blessing on the food.

Jesse sat across from Kate and saw that she hadn't closed her eyes for grace. Of course he hadn't, either. How else would he have noticed? Grinning, he put a finger to his lips, shaking his head slightly. Blushing, she looked away.

Chapter 3

Kate could scarcely eat the dinner Emily had prepared. She was hungry, because she had skipped lunch to save room for the chicken, mashed potatoes and gravy, and at least one slice of apple pie, but the food stuck in her throat. She swirled the potatoes and gravy around with her fork and tried to still her thumping heart. Finally, she pushed her plate aside.

"Kate." Emily was the first to notice her friend wasn't eating. "What's wrong?"

Kate felt the color rise to the roots of her hair. It wasn't unusual for her to find herself the center of attention. Normally, she liked it, but it was different now, as she felt all three men, Ben, Luke, and Jesse, staring at her.

"It's the heat," she finally said, fanning her flushed face with her hand. "It's been so hot."

Luke pushed his chair back and helped Kate to her feet. "Perhaps you should stay home from the dance tonight."

Kate knew Jesse was looking at her and wondered what he was thinking. "Oh, I'll be fine soon. Once the sun goes down, I recover quickly."

She began removing the dishes, telling Emily to stay seated. "I can certainly dish up the pie as well as you can."

"I've got a contract to build in Portland Heights," Ben said then. "We're getting mahogany shipped out from the East Coast for the inside woodwork."

"Word travels fast when a person is a true craftsman," Luke said, his eyes following Kate's movements.

Ben could make anything out of wood. Like his father, he made chairs, tables, cabinets, chests, and carved small items such as the horses he had made Emily before they were married. They sat on the chest in their bedroom, right where Emily would see them first thing each morning.

Jesse, acting bored, pushed his chair back, walked over, and stood behind Kate. "If you cut the pie, I'll help serve."

Kate felt his breath on her neck and suddenly was lightheaded. She'd never had a man help in the kitchen before. And why was Jesse having such an effect on her? What was wrong with her, anyway?

There were two slices of pie left and plenty of chicken for the next day.

Sunday was Meeting day, and the Galloways adhered to the practice of no working or cooking on the Lord's Day.

"I'll wash dishes," Kate said, setting a second kettle on to boil. "Then I'll be off to the dance."

Luke stopped talking and glanced her way. "Do you need a ride across the river?"

"Oh, no, Pastor," Jesse answered quickly. "I'll accompany Miss Kate and make sure she's all right. I understand the streetcar is running a late schedule tonight."

Kate felt her cheeks flush again as she removed the apron and left the room before Jesse could see how flustered she had become. She stared at her reflection in the hallway mirror. Her cheeks were pink. No need for more rouge. She patted her hair into place, secured the silver clasp, then checked her dress and shoes. Everything seemed fine.

She wondered if Jesse would stay on. She assumed he would, but Ben seemed reluctant and was watching him closely. Kate wondered what had transpired between the two when they spoke in the privacy of the library. She suspected it was far more than even Emily knew.

Ben and Luke sat on the front porch discussing President Taft. "He's nothing like Roosevelt, but maybe he'll govern fairly," Ben said.

"I know," Luke added. "Remember when Roosevelt traveled to California and visited Yosemite Park with the Scottish-born American naturalist John Muir? Imagine setting aside park lands for future generations to enjoy."

"He certainly was the most colorful president we've had," Ben said with a nod. "He's off in Africa now."

Jesse was in the side yard, smoking, keeping to himself. Emily sat inside by the light so she could see to embroider on a flannel wrapper for her baby. "You be careful, Kate," she said, setting her sewing aside.

"Careful?" Kate couldn't believe she'd heard her friend right. "Why do you say that?"

"Ben's worried. Didn't you notice the way his eyes narrowed when he looked at Jesse?"

Actually Kate had not noticed, but perhaps it was because she'd been busy trying to settle her insides, making an effort to stay calm. Who had time to notice anything but a handsome, captivating man such as Jesse Galloway?

"Are you going to be okay?" Kate asked, wanting to shift the attention away from herself. "How's the pain?"

"I'm fine now. Guess it was just hunger." Emily smiled as she looked at her dress. "And thanks so much for my lovely dress. Ben didn't say much—not with Jesse being here, but he'll mention it later."

"Will you wear it to church?"

Emily shook her head. "It's back to my gray for church. You know how the people feel about wearing color to the Meeting."

Kate glanced at the clock on the mantel and leaned over, kissing Emily's cheek. "The streetcar is due in five minutes, so guess I'd better mosey on out there."

Kate was only too aware minutes later of Ben and Luke watching as she and Jesse hurried down the sidewalk.

The two chatted like old, comfortable friends as the streetcar went toward town. Jesse was full of questions and Kate found herself answering them.

"How long have you been dancing, Miss Kate?"

"Since I left the farm and attended my first dance."

The memory of that first dance and the feeling of freedom, the knowledge that men watched her and wanted to dance with her, was as memorable as if it had happened yesterday.

"Mrs. Harris—the lady where I boarded—loaned me a dress to wear. It was red, and one of the prettiest I'd ever owned." Kate smiled. "Later, she taught me to make my own dresses and to sew for others, too. She helped me in so many ways."

"You are a beautiful woman," Jesse said, his face coming closer. "I want to dance every dance with you." Yet even as he said it, he wondered about Priscilla and knew he should dance at least once with her, should she come.

Kate and Jesse talked all the way down town and across the river.

"You'll like it here in Portland," Kate offered.

"I'm already liking it here," he said, his arm suddenly going around the back of her seat.

"Ben and Emily are my two closest friends."

"So I gathered." He leaned forward. "What I'm wondering about is Pastor Luke."

"Pastor Luke?"

"Yes. He was watching you with a look that showed possession."

"Possession?" Kate sputtered. "Never, Mr. Galloway. Luke is just a friend —someone I can talk to."

"Are you sure he knows that?"

Kate felt her cheeks flush again as she turned and looked out the window. "I suppose he's concerned for my soul, being a preacher and all."

"And are you concerned for your soul, Miz Kate Russell?"

"I'm not sure I believe in God, if that's what you mean," Kate said finally. "I was taught to believe, but after my mother died, it was as if my heart died, too. A lot of things happened, and I began doubting that there was even a

God, at least not a God Who cared."

Jesse's eyes lit up, and Kate felt she was losing herself in them. "At last, someone who thinks like I do," he said. "My mother taught me and the others —there were seven of us, you know—about God and why we should believe, but I was a skeptic then, and I'm definitely a skeptic now."

Kate leaned against the seat, feeling comfortable and wishing this moment would never end. Soon they'd be at the dance hall, and there would be lots of women wanting Jesse's attention. She had an idea that Mr. Jesse Galloway was like his brother Ben in the area of dancing. She just knew by looking at his long, muscular legs that he could waltz her clear around the floor and back again before the number was over. She trembled as she realized she could hardly wait to be dancing in his arms—to dance with someone who loved dancing almost more than anything.

"I'm sorry to hear about your mother," Jesse said then. "It sounds as if you were close."

"Mama was everything to me," Kate said, lowering her head.

"You're not smiling." Jesse leaned forward, and for a moment Kate thought he might even kiss her. She hoped not. It was fine to ride the street-car unchaperoned, to go to a dance without a partner, but to kiss on the day she first met someone was more than she could allow. She moved back.

"There," Kate said. "I'm smiling now."

Jesse's eyes looked at her for a long moment. "Don't ever stop smiling, Miss Kate. You are too beautiful to think about the past. Look to the future."

"I am," she said. "I'm looking forward to the first dance."

"Which will be my dance."

And all the others, Kate wanted to say.

"I do need to dance with the young lady I met on the streetcar earlier this afternoon. In fact," Jesse fingered his beard for a long moment, "I'm going to have dinner at her house tomorrow to meet her family. A formal introduction, I'm sure."

Kate's heart fell. Of course a handsome man such as Jesse would have a girlfriend already. She wondered if she was pretty. She was probably much smaller and definitely younger, Kate surmised.

"I'm sure she's your type," she finally said.

"Oh, I don't know about that. If I'd known I was going to meet you, I'd have never said yes to her invitation."

Kate smiled again, feeling better.

"She may not even come, anyway," he said, thinking Priscilla might have meant another dance, though she'd said across town, over the river. He wondered why he had mentioned Priscilla Palmer. He didn't like it when Kate looked serious. He wanted to keep her happy, so she'd fall for him and be his completely. This was what women did with him, and he really didn't think, under all her trappings, that Kate Russell was any different. Women were the same the world over and once a man got to the point of being able to read them, he could get anything he wanted. And he wanted Kate. Desperately so.

Emily, now, was different. She cherished Ben. One look at the two of them together, and he knew. Not that he would have wanted Emily anyway. Emily didn't dance, and that made him even more positive that Kate was the woman for him. Kate with the tinkling laugh, the velvety dark eyes that melted when he looked at her. And she wore her clothes so well. The fact that she had made her dress made Jesse even more favorably impressed.

"The night is going to be special because you're with me," Jesse said, leaning toward Kate. "It's going to be the first of many, I can tell you that."

Kate trembled as she smiled. "I truly think you might be right, Mr. Galloway."

"Cut the Mister business," Jesse said. "It's Jesse to you, and I hope I may call you Kate."

"By all means, please do."

The new ballroom was more lovely than Kate had imagined.

A huge chandelier, hanging from a high ceiling, dominated the entire hall. It sparkled down on people, and Kate was sure she'd never seen anything so beautiful. There were dozens of smaller lights along all four walls, and the floors were made of oak and highly polished. There was three times the room the grange hall had. Kate looked around at the women in lovely ball gowns and the men in suits and ties.

"This is certainly different from the grange dance. Look at the lovely dresses."

"You are easily the loveliest woman here," Jesse said, drawing her into his arms as the orchestra began playing a waltz. Kate's breath caught under her rib cage as Jesse whirled her out across the floor. He was even faster, with quicker, more even strides, than Ben, and she could scarcely keep up. Of course her heart wasn't acting as it should.

Soon the ballroom was crowded with couples. Heads turned in their direction, but whereas Kate was used to people looking to see what she was wearing, this time all eyes seemed to be on Jesse Galloway, noticing the tall, regal-looking man.

Priscilla arrived and Jesse introduced her to Kate. "This is Miz Kate Russell, a dear friend of my brother's wife," Jesse said.

Kate held out her hand, trying not to notice Priscilla's intense stare. She wondered why Jesse hadn't explained that he was escorting her, but she guessed that would come later while they were dancing.

"I'm pleased to meet you, Miss Palmer."

"Likewise," the young girl said, but Kate knew she wasn't sincere. Priscilla liked Jesse, but that didn't surprise Kate. Who wouldn't like Jesse? Unless you counted Ben. But that went back a long way, and sometimes bitter disputes happened between brothers. It didn't have to enter into her relationship with Jesse.

"I've come with my brother, but it's okay if we dance," Priscilla said. She looked at Jesse with clear longing in her blue eyes. Her gown, a deep purple silk, had rows of lace and scallops.

Kate watched as Jesse whirled Priscilla out onto the floor. She tried not to feel envy, but couldn't help the pangs of jealousy as she watched the two dancing a fast jig. Was there any dance Jesse did not know? He must have learned to dance as an infant, she decided.

The rest of Jesse's dances were with Kate, except for once when an old friend cut in. Kate had never felt so exhilarated.

The dance was over too soon, and the streetcar ride home ended too quickly. When the Galloways' home loomed in the distance, Kate wished her house was right here on the very next corner, but she had to ride another mile up Foster Road.

The lights were shining from the kitchen and living room. "Waiting up for you," Kate said, glancing up at Jesse's face, with its strong lines. The darkness made him look all the more romantic, she decided.

"I should go home with you."

Kate's heart nearly stopped. "No, it's fine. You're staying here, and I've ridden this streetcar a good many times. I'll be home and in bed before you know it."

He jumped off and turned and waved, then stood in the middle of the street until she could see nothing but his thin shadow.

She pressed cool fingertips to her face and discovered it was hot, just as it had been earlier at the supper table. She wasn't used to feeling this way. It was so different from any emotion she'd ever felt before. But she liked it. Yes, she definitely liked it. And after their conversation tonight, she knew Jesse was staying in Portland. There was nothing or nobody to drag him off to any other part of the world. They would go dancing every chance they got, and there might be more dinners at Ben and Emily's, not just the traditional Saturday night one.

Emily. She wondered how Emily was faring, remembering how wan her face had looked earlier. Surely everything was going to be all right with her and the baby. Kate couldn't bear it if anything happened.

Her stop was up ahead, and Kate pulled the chain.

She didn't notice the horse and buggy until she'd lighted from the streetcar and turned toward her little house, all dark except for wide shafts of moonlight dancing across the front. And then a familiar voice spoke.

"Thank God, you're finally home."

"Luke?" She could see it was him, leaning against the wagon, his hat in hand. He stepped forward after she spoke his name.

"It's Emily," he said. "You've got to come."

Chapter 4

Kate's heart nearly stopped. Not the baby. It was too early.

"I'd better pack a few clothes, as I might be staying," Kate said, hurrying inside.

Within five minutes she came out, handed Luke the valise, and held her dress up as he helped her into the wagon. "I can't believe this is happening," she said, straightening her skirts.

"I know." Luke shook the reins, and the horses started off at a fast trot. "Shortly after you and Jesse left, Emily suffered severe abdominal pain. I didn't think she looked well earlier. She's far too pale to my way of thinking."

Kate nodded. "She had pains before dinner, but she said they went away. Has the doctor been called?"

"Yes, I fetched him before coming after you, knowing you'd be gone until the dance closed."

Kate blinked back the sudden tears that threatened. "I wouldn't have gone if I'd thought there was any danger—"

"Of course you wouldn't have." Luke reached over, touching her hand. "Emily knows that, too."

Kate swallowed hard, thankful it was a short distance. Soon she would be at her friend's bedside, encouraging her, and praying. . . She stopped short. "Have you prayed for her, Luke?"

A slight smile turned up the corners of his mouth as he stared straight ahead. "It's the first thing I always do. It's second nature to me, you know."

Kate turned and studied his profile. He was a good person, a caring, loving man. His jaw jutted out in determination as if he could command God to make everything all right. Kate knew differently. Nobody could tell God what to do. It didn't matter how many prayers one offered, they weren't always answered—though Luke had told her once that prayers were answered, it just wasn't the way one might have hoped.

"It was kind of you to come after me," she said then. The night air was chilly, and she drew her shawl closer. "I don't know what I'd do if anything happened to Emily."

"I'm thankful I stayed to visit. I don't usually, with tomorrow being the

Lord's Day and the last-minute preparations."

"I'm glad you're such a good friend to the Galloways," Kate said, touching his arm gently. She wanted to say, *And my friend, too,* but she held it back. Then it hit her, as she looked at his tightly lined face. Of course. He was reliving the time when his wife had been in labor, when the midwife could do nothing to help, and both child and mother died. Luke would relive that scene for the rest of his life. No amount of praying would ever completely take away the pain.

"Luke, I know how difficult—this must be for you now—" Kate's hands trembled in her lap.

Luke sat ramrod straight, his hands gripping the reins tightly. "Yes, the memories have a way of coming back—" He turned away, anguish crossing his face.

She found herself wanting to comfort him, as a mother would a small child. The thought surprised her, and she quickly shook it from her mind. It was silly to think such things, yet she knew she had a compassionate heart. She might be a heathen, but she cared deeply for her friends and fellow man, as Luke well knew.

Sitting next to a woman he admired greatly, Luke's thoughts shifted to what it might be like if Kate held him close and comforted him, her thick, dark hair cascading down her shoulders, her soft cheek against his. But the memory of her and Jesse sauntering down the sidewalk, heads held high, as they headed to the streetcar and the evening dance, played in his mind.

Luke had never danced, though he'd often wondered what it would be like. The Friends felt it was wrong. At times he had questioned that stand, but no more—not now, when his thoughts of dancing included dancing every dance with the woman sitting next to him. His intentions were wrong, and that's what the Meeting objected to. His thoughts were not of righteous things, but of holding a woman he loved.

Loved. Luke couldn't believe the thought had entered his head. It was ridiculous to even consider such a thing as loving Kate. She was nothing like Rachel. She would never be a preacher's wife. She claimed she didn't believe in God and was quite open about it. At least one always knew what Kate thought and felt. She hid nothing. Or did she? He took a quick sideways glance and saw her mouth tremble.

"Did you and Mr. Jesse Galloway have a good time at the dance?" Luke asked, staring straight ahead.

"Yes, it was a lovely ballroom. I hope to go back," Kate replied.

"What do you think of Jesse Galloway?" He had to ask, though he knew what her answer would be without asking.

"He's an accomplished dancer."

"I was referring to the person inside."

"Well—I don't know him that well yet."

"Ben is worried—"

"Worried? About what?"

"It seems Jesse has never settled down, has had one woman friend after another. He—"

Kate held her hand up, not wanting to hear more. "Just because he isn't like you or Ben doesn't mean he isn't a nice man."

"I realize that, Kate—"

"He's had a tough life being the oldest—"

"Yes, I imagine he has." Luke paused for a long moment. "Just be careful, and consider that Ben might know what he's talking about."

"I know how to take care of myself," Kate said, looking straight ahead.

"That's what I told Ben, but he says all women are susceptible to Jesse's charm. Yes, Kate, even you." *Especially you,* Luke said to himself, fearful that Kate had already fallen for the handsome, rugged Jesse Galloway.

Luke turned the corner and was thankful to see the dim light ahead at the Galloways'. The talk had not gone well. He pulled the horses to a stop, and Kate was down from the buggy before he could offer a hand. "Thank you, again, for coming after me." She looked him defiantly in the eye, then averted her gaze.

"I was only too happy to do so, as you must know."

Ben opened the door and grasped Kate's hands. "Emily is resting now, but go on in."

Emily's dark hair fanned across the pillow, her eyes shut. The doctor was preparing to leave. "She's in a weakened condition," he said slowly, motioning for Kate to sit. "I don't know if rest will help, but she's definitely got to stay in bed if she's to keep this baby. The contractions have stopped, but there's been some hemorrhaging."

"I can stay," Kate said.

"That would be good."

Ben stood in the doorway. "Your job, Kate?"

"The job doesn't matter. Taking care of Emily does."

Emily's eyelids fluttered as her mouth moved. "Kate—you came—"

"Of course I came," she said, taking hold of the cold hand.

"We need extra blankets," she said to Ben. "It isn't cold in here, but she feels cold to me."

"There are quilts in the spare bedroom. I'll fetch one."

"Emily," Kate whispered, smoothing the hair back from the side of her face. "You're going to be okay. You must believe that." Kate knew that a confident, positive attitude was what Emily needed. She had to get stronger for her own and the baby's sake. But if worst came to worst, Kate hoped that Emily would be spared. There would always be more babies, but there was only one Emily.

Ben came back with a thick quilt and covered Emily. "I love her so," he said in a bare whisper. "I don't know what I'd do—if—"

"Don't even think about it," Kate said. "Here, you sit while I go out."

Luke was on the front porch, gazing straight ahead. "Is she—well, do you think she'll be all right?"

"I hope so. I truly hope so."

"I've been praying, Kate. The Bible tells us it helps when two or more are gathered. Do you believe that?"

Kate shook her head. "I don't know what I believe. It's like when Mama died. And I don't know if I can bear to go through that experience again."

"That's why God comforts us—"

"God never comforted me," Jesse said, coming around from the side of the house, where he'd been smoking a cigar. "It didn't matter what happened. It was as if God always forgot me."

"Perhaps you prayed for the wrong things," Luke suggested.

Jesse puffed on his cigar, staying at the end of the porch. "Yes, brother, perhaps I did."

Kate looked at Jesse, her heart doing its wild beating again. "Hello, Jesse," she said.

"Evening, Kate. Had no idea I'd get to see you so soon."

"I'm staying over to care for Emily, so you'll be seeing me every morning at breakfast."

"I'll like that," Jesse said, grinning. He snuffed his cigar and tipped his hat. "I'm going on to bed now. It's been one long day."

Luke nodded to him.

"Good night," Kate said, as Jesse went in.

"I've got to leave, also," Luke said. "I was wondering something, though."

"Yes?"

"Would you attend church tomorrow?"

"Tomorrow? But why would you ask that?" Kate thought it a strange request with the way Emily was and all.

"It's important that you do so. Emily cannot, and she hates to miss, so I thought you could come back and tell her about it. Lots of prayers will be said for her. I also," he stopped and took a deep breath, "I thought you might speak with her grandparents. . . ."

So that was it. The grandparents who had abandoned Emily when she married Ben. It didn't matter that Ben had embraced the Friends' persuasion, or that he had accompanied Emily on the train to see her parents for the first time in nearly fifteen years. No, they stuck with their rigid ways and would not bend enough to attend the wedding or come to see the new home that Ben built, not even for Christmas or Easter dinner.

"I doubt that anything I might say would matter. And I'm quite sure they dislike me for luring Emily away."

Luke nodded. "You're probably right, Kate, but it's worth a try." He did not tell her the rest of the reason behind his request. If Jesse was sincere about changing, as he so boldly stated to Ben, he would forget his self-centered ways and attend the Meeting with Kate. If he refused—well, that would speak volumes about Jesse Galloway.

After Luke left, Kate took her valise to the small room next to Emily and Ben's bedroom, as she needed to be close. It was to be the nursery, and the walls were painted a sunny yellow. Kate stretched out on the small sofa Ben had brought in from the living room. At least she would feel happy in this bright room. She would sleep for a few hours, then relieve Ben so he could rest. If he would leave his wife, that is.

Kate had promised Luke she would attend church, and Ben would prefer staying with Emily. She wondered now, as she settled down on the small bed, if Jesse would go. Should she ask him? And if he said no, would she be disappointed? She knew she would be, but she'd understand. She herself was only going as a favor to Emily and Luke.

The next morning shone bright, promising a day of heat. Kate put a pot of coffee on and got out cold biscuits, knowing Ben would prefer she not cook. That was fine. As long as she was staying in their home, she'd abide by the Galloways' wishes.

Jesse wasn't there until just before Kate brushed her hair and prepared for church. He came in, holding his hands behind him.

"For you, the most beautiful lady I ever saw."

She laughed, her eyes sparkling, "And what have you behind your back, Jesse?"

It was a bouquet of pink roses.

"But where did you get these?"

"That's a secret."

Here she'd thought Jesse was sleeping in, but he'd been out getting flowers for her. "They are beautiful and smell divine." She buried her nose in the soft pink petals. Mama's favorite color. It was uncanny, as if Jesse had known.

"Thank you so much," she said, looking for a vase. "I'll share them with Emily—put them in her room."

"They're for you. I can get more for Emily."

She wondered where he'd gotten the money since he'd said he was down to just a few coins last night.

"I'm going to church this morning. Would you like to come?"

Jesse's face darkened suddenly. "I thought you didn't believe in God."

"I didn't say I didn't believe, Jesse. It's open to discussion as far as I'm concerned. I'm going so I can report to Emily, and to ask for prayers for her, and to—well, to speak to her grandparents."

"I'm staying home," he said, pulling out a chair and pouring coffee into a cup. "I might go to work for Ben today—"

"Not on Sunday you won't," Kate broke in.

"Oh? He's that dedicated?"

"Oh my, yes."

"And it's all that Brother Luke's fault, I dare say."

"Fault?" Kate thought that seemed strange. "I wouldn't blame Luke for anything, Jesse."

"Yes, well, we'll see about not working on Sunday." He turned and held his cup up. "Does this no working on Sunday mean you can't fry up some ham and eggs?"

Kate nodded. "That's right."

"What if I cooked my own breakfast?"

"I suppose you could, but it might upset Emily." Kate looked at Jesse, noticing the way a lock of hair hung down over his forehead. She wanted to push it back, but shook the thought from her mind. "Emily believes strongly in not cooking on the Lord's Day, and she wouldn't want anyone else in her kitchen cooking—it would make her feel uncomfortable. You can have some chicken and apple pie left over from last night."

Jesse turned and left the room. He knew it would be hard staying here. Too many rules for him. Worse than when he lived at home, where his mother had rules and his father had rules. Why did everyone have to live by rules? Now that he was older, he didn't obey any rules unless he had to. Of course he wouldn't go out and kill a man, but he wasn't afraid to steal money, and lying didn't bother him even a whit.

He was on the porch when the buggy pulled up and Pastor Luke hopped down. In his dark suit and hat, he looked more distinguished than he had last night, and sudden fear lurched inside Jesse. This man was competition. He hadn't realized before how deeply the pastor cared for Kate. It showed now as he assisted her into the buggy.

Kate looked into his eyes before turning to wave good-bye. "You take care of Emily, you hear?"

"Enjoy church," was all Jesse could think of to say as the buggy rode out of sight. *Yes, my dear, you'd better enjoy it by yourself because that's one thing you'll never get me to do—step inside a church.* There'd been women who tried, but Jesse got around it somehow. He'd do it with Kate, too. He knew how she felt about him already. It was quite apparent when their eyes met that he had an effect on her. He also knew she was unaccustomed to feeling that way around a man. It was going to be fun to woo and love Widow Kate Russell. The fact that she'd been married once meant he had found someone who already knew how to please a man. He thought how warm and responsive Kate might be. Priscilla could not compare, though he would go to dinner at her house as earlier planned. No sense in burning all his bridges behind him just yet.

For now there was strategy to figure out. Kate had loved the roses, and it had been easy to sweet-talk the little lady down the road out of them since she had hundreds of blooms in her yard. And he'd buy Kate jewelry. All women liked jewelry, especially gold, and surely Kate was no exception. Yes, he'd find a special piece for her. He'd have to wait until he was working and Ben paid him. Or would he? There was a jewelry store downtown. He could talk someone into selling him a piece, a bracelet or a locket, with the promise to pay when he received his first paycheck.

Jesse put the remains of his cigar back in his pocket and walked back inside with a knowing smile.

Chapter 5

K ate wore a navy blue muslin, one of her older dresses. The blue had faded from wear and many washings, and she thought it the most suitable thing she had since she did not own a gray dress.

"It's a wonderful morning," Luke said, smiling.

"Yes. I just hope it doesn't get so hot."

"Did you ask Jesse to accompany you to church?" Luke asked as Kate adjusted her dark blue velvet hat. He figured it had to be one of the most conservative she owned and found himself wishing she'd worn the bright red, wide-brimmed hat he had seen her wear one Saturday afternoon.

"He prefers to stay out of church," Kate said simply.

"I thought as much."

"And why do you say that?" Kate asked.

"Something led me to believe—oh, forget I said anything."

"Just because he dances doesn't mean he is a heathen," Kate retorted, raising her chin and staring Luke straight in the eye. "I suppose this is something else you and Ben talked about. You don't even give a person a chance to defend himself."

"Kate, I'm sorry."

"As you should be. I don't know what Jesse has been, but what's more important to me is what he wants to be now."

"I hope you're right, Kate."

"Pastor Morrison, I seem to recollect a lesson from the Bible you spoke on one Sunday when I attended with Emily and Ben. It was something about people casting off the old and putting on the new."

"Yes," Luke replied. "That's when they become a new creature in Christ. They give up the old ways and take on the new."

"Then who's to say Jesse hasn't done that very thing?"

Luke nodded. "Yes, indeed. Who's to say?"

Luke stared at the petulant face of the woman he had grown so fond of, and wanted to reason with her, but he knew Kate was stubborn. Once her mind was made up, that was it. You are searching for love, he longed to say, but until you turn to God, you will keep searching. God is the only true source of true, unconditional love.

"Kate, I have a duty to protect my flock. Do you remember the story about the shepherd boy who went back after one lost lamb?"

"I'm not a lost lamb."

"I didn't mean to imply that you were. My illustration may be wrong, but you must know that God cares for every one of His people, and I, as His messenger, must carry out His commandment."

Kate didn't want to sit and talk to Luke about her soul, about God's love. She knew all that, and what had it gotten her? A mother who died in childbirth, a father who had died before she had a chance to know him. No real brothers or sisters because God had seen fit to take them home. If there was a heaven—well, she wasn't sure she believed in heaven at all.

Kate found it difficult to concentrate in church. Her mind kept wandering from what Luke said to worrying about Emily. She listened when Luke called for prayers. There was such a long, silent prayer time, she almost felt herself slipping off to sleep.

Coming to speak to Emily's grandparents was fruitless because they had not come to meeting. Grandfather Drake had a bad cold, someone reported. Kate wondered if it had been a conspiracy—getting her to church, giving Luke a chance to preach at her, to warn her about Jesse. Well, it wasn't going to work. Kate knew what she wanted, and that was Jesse. Now that she'd found someone who liked to dance, who could provide for her, maybe father her children, why was Luke saying it wouldn't work? How dare he? How dare Ben ask Luke to warn her? She was a grown woman and could take care of herself. Hadn't she taken charge that summer afternoon when she'd been widowed? She could take charge again and didn't need anyone telling her what to do.

At last Luke had greeted everyone and was ready to take her back to the Galloways'. They were silent as Luke headed the buggy west.

"It was a nice meeting," Kate finally said.

"I'm sorry the Drakes weren't here. I'll stop by tomorrow and tell them about Emily's condition. They can at least pray for her."

Jesse was gone when Luke dropped her off at the Galloways'.

"Said he had been invited to have dinner at someone's house," Ben said with a shake of his head.

"Oh, yes, that would be Priscilla Palmer. He met her on the streetcar," Kate said, feeling a stabbing pain in her heart.

Kate stayed with Emily all that week. Mr. Roberts had said his daughter could fill in and do Kate's work until she returned. Emily kept saying she could get up, that she had things to do, but Kate insisted that she stay in bed:

"Remember, the doctor said complete bed rest." Kate brought Emily's food on a tray and tended to the meals and general clean-up. Often Kate sat with Emily, and they talked, read Scripture, or recited poems from Emily's favorite book—her second gift from Ben. They also cut out diapers and sewed hems. Soon Emily had a dozen, but she needed more. When Kate went to work in the kitchen, Emily wrote in her small leather-bound diary about the happenings in her life, and as always, wrote the weekly letter to her mother.

Kate thought constantly about Jesse. Though she had expected to see a lot of him, it seemed she did not. He worked with Ben from early in the morning until dusk. After dinner and a bit of talk, Jesse went to bed in the shed out back. He'd insisted that was the best place for him. "Sometimes I can't sleep, and get up and walk around. I wouldn't want to disturb anyone, now, would I?"

When Jesse was with Kate, he was attentive, bringing yellow roses one day, dahlias the next. "And there's more where those came from," he said, beaming at Kate, obviously pleased with her pleasure.

One evening after Ben had gone in to sit with Emily, Jesse sat on the porch with Kate, enjoying the cool evening breeze. "Ben doesn't want me to court you, Kate. He's convinced that I'll be moving on shortly."

"Will you?"

"What do you think?" Jesse took both her hands, kissing the fingertips. "Why would I bring you flowers if I didn't love you? I know I've done wrong in the past, but if anyone can turn me around, it's you, Kate. You've got to believe that."

"Are you going to visit your mother next Sunday?" They had talked about it the evening before, and Jesse had agreed that it would be a good idea.

"I will if you'll accompany me."

"Of course I'll go with you." Kate laughed. There was nothing she'd enjoy more than a trip out to see Sarah Galloway.

Ben stood in the doorway. "Emily's asleep now. I'll go to bed now, if you can stay with her.

"I'll be right in," Kate answered.

Jesse rose from the step. "I'm tired. Think I'll turn in."

Kate liked watching Jesse walk. He had purpose in his stride. She knew part of that purpose was because of her, and that thought excited her. "Good night," she called to his retreating back.

After Jesse'd gone, Kate sat as the night sounds surrounded her—crickets calling to each other, and an occasional horse trotting by. Should she be worried? What if Jesse hadn't changed? But she'd know, wouldn't she? Wouldn't she be able to tell? Were Ben's objections based on jealousy of his older brother? Often brothers and sisters had envious feelings. Kate had not experienced such a thing, but, then, she had no sisters. She'd never felt as important as her step-brothers, so was that a bit of envy?

Finally, she got up and went inside to check on Emily.

The next morning when Kate came to the kitchen to start breakfast, Jesse had already gone. "Said he had to see someone. I have no idea what that was about." Ben pulled out a chair and took the plate of ham and eggs Kate offered him. "I'll fetch Pearl tomorrow," Ben said. "She would love to come stay and help out with Emily. That way you can get back to work."

"We can get her on Sunday—Jesse and I. He said we were going out to see Sarah and Pearl."

"Just the same, think I need to get Pearl sooner than Sunday."

Kate wasn't sure she wanted to leave. It'd been fun being there in the morning as she cooked breakfast for Jesse and Ben. Sometimes, when Ben wasn't looking, Jesse would reach over and squeeze her hand.

Thursday, when Pearl came home with Ben, Kate wondered why Jesse hadn't come. She had hoped he might take her home, giving them time alone. She went into her room and packed her valise. Maybe he'd come after dinner.

He did not.

Ben pushed his plate away. "C'mon, Kate. I'll hitch the horses back up, give you a ride home."

Pearl had jumped up to clear the table and wash dishes. "It's nice seeing you, even if it's just a short while," she said, holding her hand out to Kate.

Kate ignored the hand and pulled Pearl close, hugging the tall girl. "I'm just so glad you could come. I know Emily's in good hands now."

Ben was more silent than usual as they left for Kate's. It was dusk, and Kate shivered as she drew her shawl closer. "You're so quiet, I know you're worried about Emily, but I think she's going to be all right, Ben," Kate said finally.

He turned and met her gaze. "I'm thankful you could stay, Kate. And I'm really not worried about Emily. It's you I'm worried about."

"Me? But—"

"I fear Jesse is going to break your heart."

So that was it. What was this—a conspiracy between Ben and Luke to make her stop seeing Jesse? She just didn't understand.

"I'm sorry, Kate. We've always been friends, always been able to talk, but I know you're not hearing me on this."

"You're right, Ben. I'm not," Kate bristled. Didn't either man believe that a person could change? She believed it, why couldn't they?

"I won't say another word."

Kate sat with head held high, wishing she were home now, wishing with all her heart it was Jesse sitting beside her—wishing they were already man and wife, and he could prove he had changed, prove he loved her.

Later, after Ben left, Kate thought of his brief hug and felt like crying. She didn't want to lose her friends, but she loved Jesse. It was that simple.

Chapter 6

J esse came calling the Friday evening after Kate returned home. Dressed in dark blue pants, a white shirt with tie, loose-fitting coat, and his favorite fedora, he looked debonair, and Kate's heart skipped a beat at the sight of him.

"Been thinking of you all night and missed seeing you in the morning," he said, stepping inside.

"How did you get here?" Kate asked, realizing there was no horse outside.

"I walked."

"All the way from Ben's?"

He grinned. "Wasn't that far. Nothing's too far when I want to see you, Kate."

She blushed. "You were gone the morning I left—"

"I had business to take care of."

"I trust Emily is all right?"

Jesse's eyes narrowed for a moment. "Yes, the little family is doing fine, but I didn't come here to talk about them. I want to talk about you. About us."

His eyes twinkled now as he took in the beautiful woman in front of him. Though she wasn't wearing the rose taffeta which had made him first fall for her, the green gingham with a lace bodice and short, puffed sleeves still made Kate stand out. Jesse knew that it wouldn't matter what Kate wore; she would always look wonderful.

"I was hoping you'd come by. Shall I make coffee?" She had to do something to keep from trembling as Jesse kept watching her. Occasionally she'd look up, and he'd be staring, that smile tugging at the corner of his mouth. His hair was thick, and she found herself wanting to touch it.

"Coffee's fine." He pulled out a chair in the kitchen and looked around. "So this is your place. It's cozy looking."

"Yes, it is." Kate turned around from the stove, glad she'd started a fire when she first got home.

"How was your first day back at work?"

"Twice as busy." Kate laughed. "Mr. Robert's daughter doesn't work very fast, I fear. And how was your day?"

Jesse followed her to the stove and stood inches from her. "I can find better things to talk about, Kate. Here we are, with no chaperone. People are going to talk—" And then she was in his arms. She gasped as his mouth touched hers, first with a gentle kiss, then one filled with ardor. This was wrong. This was not what she wanted to happen. She pulled away.

"I—I think I'd better get that coffee made." Her hand automatically went to her hair, patting the curls into place.

Jesse stood back, watching her again, an amused look on his face. "Yes, perhaps we do need a chaperone, Miz Russell."

"I'll slice some cake—this is Emily's special sponge cake—to go with the coffee," Kate said, trying to ignore the comment. Why did he have to look at her so intently? It only made her more nervous and apprehensive.

They didn't kiss again, though Kate knew how easy it would have been. Jesse talked about real estate in Portland, and about his going to town to buy her something after getting off work the next day.

"Goodness, I don't need a gift. You've given me all those lovely flowers."

"Which you left with Emily."

"Well, yes, I thought she needed them to cheer her up."

"And what do you need to cheer you up, Kate?"

Her face burned as she tore her eyes from his penetrating gaze. "Seeing you, Jesse, is all I need," she finally said.

"Well, I like giving my women gifts. How else can I show my love?"

Kate flushed again. "I really don't need anything now. I—"

"Nonsense! All women like pretty things. And when we get married, you'll quit working at that candy factory. Sounds like drudgery to me."

Married! Had he said married? But she hardly knew Jesse. She'd heard of whirlwind courtships, but she'd never believed they actually happened. Of course, Charles had wanted to marry her the first week they met at the boardinghouse, but it was several months before she'd finally said yes.

"Don't you agree about the job?" Jesse said, getting up and stalking across the room.

"I like working at the factory, Jesse. Mr. Roberts is a good employer. I don't think I should quit, at least not for a while."

"No wife of mine will work," Jesse said adamantly.

"Of course if I were expecting a baby right away, that would be different."

Jesse stopped pacing, and his face turned pale. It wasn't lost on Kate. Did this mean that he didn't want a family?

"I think the children should wait," he said.

"But you do want children?"

"Yes, eventually."

Kate couldn't believe they were discussing such important matters. If Ben could hear Jesse now, he'd have to accept the fact that Jesse had changed. Of course, she and Jesse did not agree about her work. She supposed she enjoyed work because it gave her a sense of independence. She had money saved from her labors, as well as some of the estate Charles left her, and Mrs. Harris, the lady she'd first met and worked for after leaving Pa and the farm, had provided her with a little something. Kate had decided long ago that she never wanted to be poor again. She wanted always to have nice dresses in her closet and new shoes to wear to her next dance. As long as Kate worked at the chocolate factory, she would have enough. Now here was Jesse wanting to provide for her instead, and saying they would soon be man and wife.

Jesse stood up when darkness fell and Kate had to light the lamps.

"Well, I do believe that's a sign for me to be heading back. Tomorrow is a work day, you know."

She watched as he sauntered down the walkway and out onto the road. Did he mind walking the two miles back to Ben's? She hoped not. He'd promised to take her to the grange dance the next night. He would stop by after work.

Her heart sang as she made preparations for bed. It was only after lying in bed and dreaming of Jesse, remembering his kiss, that she realized she hadn't eaten dinner. Strange, but she didn't even feel hungry.

The next day dragged by slowly as she waited for the moment she would see Jesse. They would be off to the dance, and she'd be in his arms again. But Jesse wasn't waiting when she came out of the door of the candy factory. She decided to take the streetcar home and wait at her house. Still he didn't come, and soon it was too late for dinner at the Galloways. Surely he'd come in time to take her to the dance.

Kate changed into a red bombazine dress, knowing Jesse would like it. Her best shoes were scuffed from the last time they'd danced, and she hadn't gotten around to polishing them. Oh, well, they wouldn't show anyway because this dress had a long, sweeping skirt.

It was after seven when she heard the sound of a horse pulling up out front and someone shouting, "Whoa!"

Jesse. He'd arrived and with a small wagon and horse. She ran to the door and opened it.

"Where did you get this rig?"

"A friend loaned them to me."

"Someone at work?"

Jesse leaned over, putting two fingers across her lips. "You ask too many questions, lovely lady. You look like a woman wanting to go to a dance. That's a beautiful dress, Kate."

She smiled and turned around so the dress flounced out. "Glad you like it. Did you eat dinner?"

"Yes. Picked up something at the store earlier. How about you? I know you were counting on going to Emily's."

She ignored his comment. "I made a sandwich."

The dance floor was crowded when they arrived. Kate danced with Jesse, until an old friend cut in. Afterwards, when she looked around for him, she noticed him waltzing with someone she didn't know. It wasn't Priscilla. Jesse had never talked about that Sunday dinner at the Palmers', and Kate assumed he had forgotten all about Priscilla by now.

At last they were dancing together again, and Jesse murmured against her hair, "You're the prettiest woman at the dance."

"And you're the handsomest man!"

"Some pair we make, right?"

They danced together the rest of the evening, for Jesse refused to relinquish her to any other man. Kate felt happy, secure, and loved.

Then it was over. As they went outside, Kate gazed up at the sky. It was filled with stars, and a full moon shone down on them. She'd never felt more content.

Jesse drove the horse slowly, and Kate leaned against his shoulder for a brief moment. She thought of the grand wedding they'd have, with Luke officiating and Emily as matron of honor.

"Wouldn't it be nice for Luke to marry us in the church?" she said, breaking the silence. "Ben could stand up for you, and Emily for me."

"Married in a church?" Jesse stiffened. "Is that what you really want?"

"It would make Emily and Ben happy, and Luke would be honored to marry us—"

"No," Jesse broke in. "Brother Luke wouldn't be honored, that's for sure. He's sweet on you."

"Jesse! That's simply not true."

"Don't you think I can tell when a man is sweet on a woman?"

"He's just concerned about my soul. It doesn't go any further than that."

"It does, but you don't see it because you don't want to see it. In fact, you like men fawning all over you. Look how you were at the dance tonight."

"I wasn't being fawned all over. How can you say that?" His words shocked her. She couldn't believe Jesse accusing her of flirting. She'd danced with one man who happened to cut in. Sure, she had laughed and talked to him, and she'd talked to other men friends at the refreshment table. But that was because she'd known them since first arriving in Portland. They were friends, that was all, just as Luke was a friend.

"I don't like that implication," Kate said finally.

Jesse's jaw tightened. "Can't help what I saw."

"Don't you have friends, Jesse? What about Priscilla? And that woman you danced with? She sure hung onto your arm when the dance was over."

"Are you spying on me?"

"No more than you're spying on me."

"It's different for a man."

"It is?" Kate moved away, sitting straight up. "I don't think so."

"You have a lot to learn about men then."

"Perhaps so." Kate's face felt hot, and she knew tears were pushing close against her eyelids. "Yes, perhaps so."

When her house came into view, she didn't wait for Jesse to come help her down. She managed to get down by herself quite well. Pulling her shawl close, she felt his eyes boring into her back as she started up the walk.

"Don't go away angry," he called after her.

"Don't you go away angry, either," she said, flouncing up the steps and into the house. She banged the door hard on purpose.

It was their first argument, and Kate leaned against the door, letting the sobs finally come. Why had she gotten angry so quickly? And why had he said those mean things about her? Kate had never been accused of being a flirt before. Ben had never said such things! But, then, Ben had not loved her. Perhaps when you loved someone, you did, in a sense, own them. Was she wrong in thinking it shouldn't be different for women? Why shouldn't women have a say about the flirting? If she was guilty of flirting, Jesse certainly was, as well. Still, did it matter? Was it anything to get angry over?

And then Kate realized what it was really about. Getting married in a church. Jesse didn't want that. He'd actually bristled when she'd suggested it. Was it because he was so against churches—all churches—or because she'd suggested Luke marry them? It was something to discuss later, when Jesse came over. Tomorrow was Sunday. Surely he'd come then if he still had the borrowed horse and wagon. They were supposed to go visit Sarah.

Kate readied herself for bed and slipped under the covers, shivering. Why did she feel so cold? So anxious? She'd apologize tomorrow and everything would be fine again.

Jesse didn't come around the next day. Or the next. Of course, it was all her fault. Yes, she had flirted, but that was easy to solve. She simply wouldn't dance with anyone but Jesse. The part about Luke would be harder to resolve. It wasn't true that Luke was sweet on her. Luke was merely a friend, and because of his love for Emily and Ben he treated Kate with special care.

Yes, Kate decided. She would definitely apologize when Jesse stopped by. She hadn't realized how much she'd miss him. After asking herself how she'd feel if she never saw him again, she knew she couldn't bear it. She didn't want to go back to how life had been before Jesse came. She'd been in the wrong; she could see that now. She was too outspoken. Too unconventional. But, then, Jesse was unconventional, too. It was for that reason they got along. She didn't have to marry in a church, nor did Luke have to marry them. She didn't really believe in God, anyway, so why did it matter?

Kate found herself remembering things about Jesse, his confident air, the way he walked and held his head, the way people stopped and took notice of him. She knew everyone had watched while they danced. He was so swift and sure on his feet. It was so easy to follow him. What could she do to make things right again? Would Emily offer any suggestions? She knew she could never ask Ben, and she would definitely not mention it to Luke, either. They wouldn't understand why she loved Jesse as she did. No, she'd go over to visit Emily tomorrow after work. Besides, she needed to make sure that Emily was feeling fine and that Pearl was managing all right. Yes, tomorrow would be a better day.

Chapter 7

It was Friday evening, six days since the argument, and Kate had just gotten off work. She had rehearsed a thousand times what she would say and do when she saw Jesse again. Apologize was the first thing.

She removed her work apron and slipped a shawl over her shoulders. It was mid-September and still warm and balmy. An Indian summer, some called it. She walked out into the dazzling sun and heard horses' hooves coming down the street. Shielding her eyes, she looked in the direction of the sound.

A pair of matching horses was pulling a new carriage. As it came closer, Kate's heart leapt into her throat. It was Jesse Galloway riding high on the seat, a broad smile covering his face.

"Timed that about right, didn't I?"

"Jesse—" Her hand flew to her throat. "I'm—sorry about last Saturday night. I was wrong—"

"Hush, now. We're not going to talk about it, okay?" He hopped down, holding out a small package. "I've brought a peace offering."

When she lifted the lid of the small box, the breath caught in her throat. A gold bracelet sat on blue velvet. "Oh, Jesse! It's so beautiful." She held it up and examined the delicate engraved scrolls. "I like it!"

He beamed. "I knew you would. You were meant to wear nice jewelry and fancy clothes."

"I'll wear it at the next dance."

"And all the men will be looking at my gorgeous Kate."

My gorgeous Kate. Had he really said my? "You say such nice things," Kate finally answered, looking away for a brief moment.

"I know you've never had anyone treat you as you should be treated," Jesse said, leaning over and pulling her into his arms with a sudden fierceness.

For a moment Kate stayed there, liking the feel of his strong chest, the way his hands felt on her back. Then she paled. "I don't—this isn't right—"

"You are a woman who needs lots of attention and special gifts," Jesse said, moving away finally.

"I—"

But the words wouldn't escape past the knot in her throat. She'd thought she loved Charles with her whole heart, but she had never felt this way about him. Perhaps it hadn't been real love. What she felt for Jesse was real and wonderful. Everything was bright and beautiful when he was there. How dare Ben think his brother wouldn't do right by her? Jesse was proving his love by his attention, his gifts, and his sweet words. What more could any woman ask? She smiled inwardly. So that's the way it would be with Jesse. If they argued, they'd pretend it never happened and go on as before. She could certainly accept that.

"What are you doing with these adorable horses?" she finally asked.

Jesse grinned. "How can I court the most beautiful woman in Portland if I don't have a matching team and a nice carriage to boot?"

"But, how—"

"If I told you, you wouldn't believe me, so let's just say I paid some money down and the owner says I can pay so much with my weekly paycheck." He leaned over, kissing Kate soundly on the cheek. Kate was so surprised she forgot about propriety, but stepped back. "It's too nice a day to stand in the middle of the street, Miz Kate Russell. Let's go for a ride."

"The carriage is lovely, too," she said, touching the soft, velvety upholstery.

"The horses are Molly and Lolly, and they're three-year-old bays," Jesse added as they walked around the carriage.

Kate went to the horses' heads, patting one and then the other. They were smaller than the work horses she was used to seeing, and she liked their thick manes and pretty markings. They seemed downright sassy.

"C'mon, let's go some place where we can watch the sun set. Then maybe we can stop and get an ice cream cone at the emporium."

"I only have my work clothes," Kate said, looking down at the old blue calico. Her cotton was faded, and her hat was the oldest one she owned. How could she possibly ride in such an elegant carriage with work clothes on? Jesse was wearing dress pants and a coat, and his fashionable fedora.

"Nobody will notice you, anyway," Jesse said with a sly smile. "Not when they'll be admiring my new team and carriage."

Kate knew he was right on that count. The horses were perfect for Jesse. He obviously liked owning nice things.

She got into the carriage with Jesse's assistance and soon they were heading west of town. Jesse shook the reins, and Molly and Lolly flew over the rutted road. Kate laughed, holding onto her hat, afraid it'd fly off.

"I knew you'd like to go fast," Jesse said, as he shook the reins again.

"No," protested Kate. "That's fast enough. Slow down, Jesse!" she cried, clutching the brim of her old straw hat. Her cheeks were flushed, her heart pounding. She hadn't had this much fun in a long, long time.

"We'll take lots of drives with this team," Jesse said. "I have another surprise for you."

"You do?"

Jesse nodded. "Found a house I thought you might like," he said after they got past the candy factory and other businesses.

"A house?" Did this mean. . .Jesse had said that he wanted to marry her, that he would marry her. Surely it was just a matter of waiting until he had enough money to get married properly.

"But where? And how large is the house?" Kate finally asked.

"Bigger than Ben's."

She glanced at Jesse's profile, her head spinning. Bigger than Ben's? But he had built a large house for Emily. Three bedrooms upstairs, one down, plus the library and living room, dining room, and kitchen. They didn't need a house that large.

"You look surprised." He smiled in that intimate way that made her heart pound. "I can afford nice things, Kate. Don't you know that I'll always take care of you? Provide the best for you?"

Kate smiled as she slipped her hand through the crook of his arm. "Of course I know you'll take care of me."

And of course she wanted to marry Jesse. It was the only thing she'd thought about since the night—had it really only been two weeks ago?—when they first met. Emily's complications had worried her, but that seemed to be fine now.

"What would you say if I suggested we move down the valley a ways?"

"Move? Down the valley?" Kate felt sudden fear. "But why would we want to move, Jesse?"

He leaned over and cupped her chin with his large hand. "The valley is where people are going. The land is wonderful. People are going to need houses. I know enough to start my own business, and Ben doesn't need me. I thought you'd like to be part of an exciting adventure." His eyes were watching her, and she burned under their close scrutiny.

"But I—" Kate's head was spinning even more than before. How could she get excited about leaving her friends? She liked Portland. It was home to her, the first place she'd ever felt was home, and she had work she liked. A nagging little doubt spread through her as she studied the face of the man she loved. Was he always to be this way? Having wanderlust in his veins? Wanting to move on to newer pastures? Kate knew that many of the pioneer men left farms and families as they ventured west across the Oregon Trail. They were ready for adventure, and their women went along, because they had no choice. Was that how Jesse was? Always seeking something new? Bigger and better?

Kate trembled, and Jesse's arm went around her shoulder, pulling her to him. "I see this is a bit of a shock."

"I'm surprised, that's all."

"I won some land in a poker game last night."

Kate's head jerked away. "Poker game? Last night?" So that's why he hadn't come to pick her up from work!

"It's also where I got the money to buy this fancy team. Aren't you proud of me?"

"But you said—"

"I know, I know, but I was afraid to tell you about the gambling. Some women don't approve." Jesse pulled off to the side of the road, his eyes catching and holding hers. He grabbed her to him, touching her lips gently at first, then with force and persuasion. Kate felt herself succumbing to his kiss, then pulled away abruptly.

"We mustn't do this. Not here."

"Aw, Kate, this is the beginning of the twentieth century. The Victorian days are over."

"It's not proper—"

He moved over to his side of the carriage and picked up the reins.

"I thought you had given up gambling," Kate said inanely.

Jesse laughed. "So now you know. It's part of me. And I'm good at it, too. Where do you think the money comes from to buy fancy clothes? Ben doesn't pay that much. The only reason I decided to stay awhile and work for my dear brother was to see you. I thought you knew that." He touched the side of Kate's face. "I knew I had to have you the first moment I laid eyes on you."

Kate tried to still the fierce beating of her heart. These were words she never tired of hearing, and it wasn't the first time Jesse had told her this. She knew he loved her—in the way he knew how. Words floated back to her mind. . .words about Jesse having an eye for women, and something about playing poker. It was why he had gone on to Seattle with that widow woman. Would he tire of her? Kate wondered. Sudden doubt washed over her, as she feared she knew the answer.

"Kate, what is it? You're frowning, and I rarely see you frown. That's what I like about you. You're always smiling and happy, even laughing. That's the kind of woman I need at my side," he went on. "Heaven knows I didn't have it when I was growing up. It was always, 'Jesse, don't do that, Jesse do this. What's wrong with you, Jesse? You lazy?' I heard enough of them words to last me a lifetime. I never did anything right to hear Pa tell it. As for Ma, she always liked Ben best."

"I can't imagine Sarah not loving you," Kate said, adjusting her skirt, searching her mind for the right words to say. She loved Jesse, but could she convince him not to think that everyone was against him? She wanted to marry him, and she believed with all her heart that he loved her. Men could change. Men had been known to give up drinking, gambling, and chasing women. She knew it could be true. She'd change him. Once they moved down the valley, he'd change. And she'd come to see Emily once in awhile. That had to be part of the bargain, for Kate knew how difficult it would be to leave her best friend.

"I'm going to be gone awhile, Kate," Jesse said, interrupting her thoughts. "Goin' to go over to look at my land. Ben'll get along without me for a few days."

"How far away is the land?"

"It's over by Salem, a good day's travel. It's been said that it's some of the richest land around."

"You aren't going to farm—"

"No, Katie, I've never been, nor will I ever be, a farmer."

Suddenly Kate wasn't hearing his words. When Jesse called her "Katie," all other thoughts vanished. She hadn't been called that since the afternoon when the hired hand's eyes followed her every move. "Katie," he'd said against her throat. "Oh, Katie. . ."

"I can lease some of the land to a farmer and pay someone else to raise crops for me. You can stay here in this house I was telling you about while I get a house built on the acreage—"

Kate hadn't responded, for the words "Katie, Katie, Katie" pounded through her brain. Her mouth pursed up tight as she turned and stared Jesse in the eye, stopping him in the middle of his sentence.

"Don't ever call me Katie again. I can't abide it."

Jesse let the reins drop for a moment. "I kind of like the name Katie."

"Well, I don't—for reasons I can't explain now."

"All right. You don't need to be so touchy about it. No more Katie."

Jesse pulled up in front of the house. It was big and new, with a white picket fence around the yard. Climbing roses covered one end of a long, wide porch. She hopped down before Jesse could assist her. "It's wonderful, Jesse. But so big for the two of us."

"It's going to be ours," Jesse said then. "Your house to stay in while I tend to various business ventures."

When Jesse dropped Kate off that night, she was forming plans as she dreamed of what it would be like to live in that house. They could entertain, have parties. And there would be children to fill the rooms. It was the children she thought about as she lit the lamp and undressed for bed. Yes, she would love to have children, but would she have problems like Mama? It was something that terrified Kate. How did one know? What could be done to assure a healthy baby? Plenty of bed rest as Emily was getting? For the first time in her life, Kate wished she could turn to God as easily as Luke did. She wished she could pray for guidance and courage.

Chapter 8

Kate took the streetcar to the Galloways' after work on Saturday. There'd be no dancing tonight, since Jesse would be gone for a few days.

She found Emily and Pearl in the kitchen making pies. Emily sat coring the apples, while Pearl stood rolling the pie crust out.

"Kate!" Emily cried, starting to get up.

"No, stay right where you are," Kate said, leaning over and kissing Emily on the cheek. She took an apple slice out of the bowl, then laughed when Pearl playfully hit at her.

"You two look as if you're getting along quite well."

"Pearl's a real gem," Emily said. "She brings me breakfast in bed, but I insist on getting up later in the day, especially at dinner just before Ben gets home."

"Any more pains?"

"Nary a one. You'll have to come see what I've been working on," Emily said, slowly getting up from the table. "It's for the baby."

Pearl continued on with the pies while Emily and Kate headed down the hall to the bedroom.

"Jesse won't be here tonight," Emily said then.

"I know he won't."

"You do?"

"Yes, he's going to look at his property in Salem. Surely he told you about it—"

"So that's what's been going on," Emily said. "Ben and I wondered."

"He won the land in a poker game. Perhaps that's why he didn't mention it." She touched Emily's arm. "Please don't tell Ben. Jesse's the one to tell him, not me."

"We haven't seen him at all, Kate."

"But, he stays here. Surely he comes home sometime to eat and change."

"Not in the past week." Emily rose slowly, her hand automatically going to her protruding stomach. "Jesse moved his things out last week. Ben said he's been at work two days at most and left earlier than everyone else."

Kate felt a sinking sensation. Had Jesse lied to her? She racked her brain, trying to remember what he'd said about work. He hadn't said much, so he hadn't lied; he'd just sidestepped the whole issue about work. But why hadn't he mentioned that he wasn't living at Ben's? And if he wasn't living here, where was he staying?

"Kate—" Emily's hand went out to her friend, as if wanting to comfort her.

"No, it's okay, Emily. I expect there's a logical explanation."

"Yes, I am sure there is. I'm making gowns now. Ben bought this flannel at the new dry goods store. Isn't it soft?" She held it up to her cheek.

Kate looked the gowns over and nodded. "They're nice, Emily. You did such a good job on the seams."

"Ben says I'll need more." She smiled. "I think Ben knows more about babies than I do. I don't remember much from when I was growing up and Mama had her babies."

"You left when you were just ten. How could you possibly remember?"

Emily sighed. "I just wish Mama were here to see this grandchild. I know it's not her first, because both Mary and Maud have babies, but it's my first, and I'd like her to be there."

"At least you got to see your father before he died," Kate said. What she would have given to have had that privilege.

"I know," Emily said, as if knowing Kate's thoughts. "I don't think Mama will live much longer—it's just a feeling. And then there's just Paul at home. I rather think he might come to see us one day. Ben offered him a home, if he ever needed one. Ben's so good that way."

Kate thought about Jesse, wondering what he might say if she asked if one of her brothers could live with them. He'd probably object. Yes, somehow, she knew that to be true.

Kate sat and held the nightgowns up again. "I could have hemmed these on my sewing machine."

"I know, but I feel much closer to my baby if I do the work myself."

"It shouldn't be much longer now," Kate said, laying the nightgown on top of a little chest of drawers Ben had built. She wondered if Jesse could build things, but thought not. If he had that interest, he'd never mentioned it.

Minutes later, they heard horses coming into the side yard. Emily got up, her hand suddenly going to her back. "Just another one of those pesky pains. It'll go away soon enough."

"How can you be so sure?" Kate asked, her hand touching the spot Emily had rubbed only seconds before.

"Mothers-to-be just know, that's all," Emily said as she left the room.

Ben's voice echoed through the house, and soon he took Emily into his arms, holding her as close as possible. "I will be glad when I can hold you even closer," he said, nuzzling his mouth against her ear. His eyes glanced up as Kate walked into the kitchen.

"Kate! What a pleasant surprise!"

Kate poured warm water into a basin. Emily kept it on the back of the stove where it wasn't quite as hot. It was always just about the right temperature for washing up.

"We've been looking at baby clothes."

"You should be in bed," Ben said to Emily, almost gruffly.

"I have been most of the day, Ben." She smiled shyly. "Pearl made the biscuits and the pies. She's out gathering eggs now."

Soon they sat down to a pleasant dinner, as Ben talked about his latest house. "The cabinets are wonderful. I just wish I'd had cherry wood to put in this house."

"I like what I have," Emily said, setting her spoon down.

"Is something wrong?" Kate asked.

"No. Guess I'm just not hungry. Think I'll go lie down. You two finish eating and talk. I'll be all right."

"Why don't you go with her?" Ben instructed Pearl. "I'll be there in a moment," he said to Emily's retreating back.

"Luke may be over later on. We'll leave the food on the stove, just in case he hasn't eaten. I don't think he likes to cook that much, and his housekeeper just left to go back to her daughter in Massachusetts."

"Oh, I didn't know that."

"If we ever saw you, you might know what's going on." It sounded harsh, but Ben winked at her. Kate found herself smiling for the first time that evening.

"It will be good to see Luke again."

Ben lifted his coffee cup, staring at Kate over the top. "What's happening with you and Jesse?"

"We want to get married. Surely he mentioned it to you."

Ben pushed his chair back. "My brother and I do not talk. We never have. But if he says he wants to marry you, I'm not going to argue with that. He's getting a terrific bargain is all I can say."

"Now, Ben, I can hardly believe you'd say that."

"I'm not saying anything else because I gave my word once, and my word is worth something—unlike some people I know."

There was a noise outside the window, and Ben opened the door.

"Luke, come on in. You're late for dinner, but we saved you some."

Luke entered the kitchen through the side door and clapped Ben on the shoulder. Ben stepped aside, and Luke saw Kate.

"Kate! I had no idea you'd be here, but it is Saturday night, isn't it?"

She smiled and held out her hand. "No dancing tonight. I just came to visit."

"We'll go out and talk later. The night is warm and clear."

"That sounds nice. Now, tell me, have you eaten?"

"No. Why do you suppose I stopped by?" he joked.

Kate dished up a plate of chicken, potatoes, and gravy, and set biscuits, butter, and preserves in front of him. "And apple pie for dessert. Your favorite."

She began clearing the dishes, and Pearl appeared to help. "This is my job, Kate. Why don't you sit? I know you've been working hard."

"I can help, you know."

In no time, the table was cleared. Luke had finished eating, and he and Kate went out on the front porch to gaze at stars. Kate felt more at ease than she had in a long time. If only she didn't have this worry about Emily.

"Where's Jesse tonight?" Luke asked.

"Jesse's out of town."

"Oh? Doing what?"

"Looking at property in Salem. We might move there after we get married."

"I see." Luke's voice sounded stiff.

The door opened and Pearl slipped out, sitting in her usual spot on the top step. She halfway faced the road and also faced Luke and Kate. "Did I hear you say you and Jesse are getting married?"

"Yes, that's our plans."

"That means we'll be sisters!" Pearl clapped her hands. "I couldn't ask for a nicer sister."

"Nor I," Kate responded.

"I never had a sister," Luke said then. "And I always wanted one."

"So did I," Kate murmured.

"Well, I had a-plenty," Pearl said. "And I love all of them. My brothers, too, except—" She stopped short, her hand going over her mouth. "It's just that I don't know my oldest brother. He wasn't around much when I was growing up."

"Familiarity is important," Luke concurred. "You can't love someone if you don't know him."

Luke started talking about his childhood days.

"We'd sit outside to cool off. It's much hotter in Ohio than it is here, mind you. We'd watch the fireflies, and sometimes catch them in jars to use as flashlights. 'We' meaning my cousin Roger and me. He was my mother's sister's boy."

"I've never seen a firefly," said Kate.

"Oh, I have," Pearl broke in. "They had lots in Iowa."

Soon they talked about games they had played as children.

"Tag was our favorite game."

Kate remembered no games. Her only memories were of the farm and working, first helping Mama, then doing it all herself.

"I had a happy childhood," Luke went on. "My father was my source for information, my strength for times of weakness. And just when I thought I'd really done something wrong, he'd put his arm around me and say, 'Now, son, you've learned from your mistake, haven't you?' and of course I had."

"Mama loved me," Kate said, "but my father died when I was just a year old. And then I had a step-father and two brothers. And then Mama died. . ." Kate's voice trailed off.

"And you were young?"

"Twelve."

"That's a hard age to lose a parent," Luke said. "My mother died when I was fourteen."

"I was eleven when Pa died," Pearl offered. "I don't remember much about him."

Kate pulled one of Pearl's braids. "But you have a mother who is one of the most wonderful people I've met."

Pearl smiled. "I know. And I miss her a lot when I'm here."

"I'm sure you do." Kate stood. "I think I'd better be going home. Ben said he'd take me."

"I'll take you, Kate," Luke offered. "Let Ben stay with Emily. I've got to be getting home to finish preparations for tomorrow."

"All right. That sounds fine."

As they drove off toward Kate's with the sunset to the side, Kate couldn't keep from watching the bright, orange ball. "I think this is my favorite time of evening."

"Mine, too. Though mornings are just as beautiful." Luke let the reins go slack for a moment as he turned and looked at the sky, too. "How could any-one ever doubt God's existence after looking at such vivid colors?"

Kate shivered unexpectedly, but said nothing.

Moments later they were home and Luke helped her down and walked her to the door. "If you ever decide you want to go to church again, let me know. I'd be happy to pick you up."

"Thanks, Luke. I'll remember that. And thanks for the ride."

Kate stood on her porch, enjoying the last bit of color, watching Luke as he turned and headed east. It had been a fun evening, even if Jesse wasn't here. In fact, she realized, she hadn't thought about him as much as she usually did. At last she went in and closed the door.

Chapter 9

A week went by, and Kate kept wondering if this was the day Jesse would return. Surely he'd had enough time to look his property over, talk to folks around town, and decide if they needed someone to build homes. Wasn't there a lot to know about building a house? Kate wondered how Jesse could know everything. Ben had men working for him: pouring cement, making the frames, and putting on the roof. Would Jesse find enough men who knew how to do the required labor?

"We'll get married one day," Jesse had said, and Kate believed him. Still, where could he be? Why hadn't he come around? Kate had trouble eating. Food stuck in her throat and wouldn't go down. Maybe Jesse wasn't coming back. Maybe it was for the best, she told herself as she worked. Maybe Jesse wasn't the man for her. Maybe Ben was right all along. But then she'd shake her head. No, he cared for her. She knew he did.

And then he was there one night after work, taking her into his arms, telling her that everything was okay, that he loved her.

"Took care of my business, then stopped off to see Mama. She was sick."

"Oh, and Pearl isn't there to help."

"I know, but she's a tough ol' gal. She was much better when I left this morning."

"What about work?" Kate asked.

"Ben will understand when I explain."

Jesse stopped by the next night, and they drove to Johnson Creek. It was a small, shallow creek. The water was warm, though it was fall. Kate slipped out of her stockings and shoes and went wading. Jesse laughed, saying she would be eaten up by the crawdads.

"There aren't any crawdads in here."

"You wanna bet?" Jesse reached down and came out with one in his hand. Kate screamed and jumped out. Soon they were laughing, and Jesse kissed her.

Kate pulled away. "Jesse, you mustn't."

"Why not? We're getting married."

"I know. Oh, how I know. I've been dreaming about a dress, but can't decide if I want to wear satin or organdy."

178

"Knowing you, you'll look lovely no matter what the material is."

"Oh, Jesse." She leaned over and kissed his forehead. "You make me so happy. I feel so much better when I'm with you."

"That's what I like to hear." His arm slipped around her shoulder as he pulled her close. "I wish this moment could go on forever."

"Me, too."

"But," and he rose, brushing off his pants, "I have business to attend to tonight."

"Oh, Jesse, must you? You just got back."

"I know, but if I'm to provide for you—"

Too soon, they were back at Kate's, but they planned to go to the Saturday night grange dance after dinner with the Galloways.

Kate was humming at work again. Three days until she saw Jesse again. They had made plans for the announcement. Jesse would tell Ben and Emily that he wanted to marry Kate, and would ask permission from Ben. It was a formality, she knew, but one she approved of.

She was halfway finished with a sweater for the baby. She'd have it done by Saturday if she worked on it each night. A pale green, it would look good if the baby had Emily's coloring.

Saturday she rushed home from work and got ready for the dance.

But Jesse didn't show up. Kate waited for Molly and Lolly and the regal carriage to pull up in front of the house. It was five, then six. Too late for dinner now. Perhaps he was detained and would make it in time for the dance.

Kate sat on the sofa, waiting and wondering. Finally she went to the bedroom, removed her newest hat, a creation ordered out of the catalogue. She loved the wild array of flowers on the wide straw brim. Her dress, a blue and white striped percale, was one Jesse had not yet seen, but she knew he would like it.

The hat went back in the hatbox. Kate closed the lid and walked to the kitchen. She thought about catching the streetcar, but it was way past dinner time. She knew Emily and Ben would wonder what had happened, but Jesse might still come to her house. Could he be tired of the Saturday night dinners? He still claimed that Luke liked her, though she'd pooh-poohed the idea.

Twilight settled into the corners of the house as Kate sat on a hardback chair in the kitchen. She was hungry—her stomach told her so—but nothing sounded good. In fact, her entire life didn't seem good right about now. What would she do without Jesse? How could she stand to hear Ben say, "I told you so"? No, it was like before. There'd be an explanation. Perhaps Sarah Galloway had taken sick again. If so, Ben might be there, too.

She still didn't move to light a lamp when she heard a buggy pull up out front. Kate knew without looking that it wasn't Jesse. Jesse always rode up fast, and she'd hear his voice in the house, even if the door and windows were closed.

The gate creaked open, then shut, but she didn't move. If she didn't let on, the caller would leave. Footsteps hit the porch, then a knock on the door. Kate took a deep breath and held it. The knock grew louder. And more persistent.

"Kate? Are you in there?"

Pastor Luke. But why was he here? Why wasn't he at Ben's having chicken dinner?

"Kate, you are in there, aren't you." It was a statement, not a question. "I must talk to you. It's important."

She knew she was acting silly, childish, but she just couldn't bear facing anyone just now.

"It's Emily. She's going into labor—"

At the sound of Emily's name, Kate leaped to her feet and ran toward the door. "No! She should be fine with Pearl there—"

"Pearl went home because Sarah needed her." A frown creased his forehead as he stood in the doorway, his hat in hand. "Kate, what's wrong? Why are you crying?"

It wasn't until then that she realized her cheeks were wet with tears. "It's nothing. I'm—fine. Really."

"It's early," Luke said. "About a month. Ben sent Jesse after the doctor."

"Jesse? Jesse's there?"

"Well, yes, where did you think he'd be?"

"I thought—that is, well, I thought he was coming after me."

"Well, I don't know about that. You'll have to straighten that out with him."

"I—the dance—I—" But how could she possibly even think about the dance or Jesse at a time like this? "I'll get my coat and hat and be right there." Kate paused in front of the hat box, wondering if she should wear the new one. Lifting the lid, she decided, yes, she needed it to cheer herself up.

Luke helped her into the carriage and put a blanket around her feet. "It's cold this evening. Winter can't be too far off."

They started off immediately, but Luke's team of horses didn't match, nor were they particularly swift—not like Jesse's. The buggy was well-worn and quite old, but it felt comfortable as Kate leaned back.

"I hope the baby's all right. Lots of babies are early, but it's difficult when—" Kate stopped the second she realized what she'd just said. Of all people, she didn't need to relay this information to Pastor Luke Morrison. He knew only too well about babies and wives not surviving the delivery.

"I told Ben we should take her to Providence Hospital, but it's a two-hour drive, and it would have been hard on Emily. Besides, she insisted on having the baby at home."

"Sounds like our Emily."

"So what's been troubling you, Kate?" Luke asked, his eyes on Kate, but she didn't turn to look at him.

"I, well, I just didn't feel like talking to anyone then."

"Unless it was Jesse?"

"Well, I had been expecting him as I so wanted to go to dinner—"

"There was no dinner. Well, a half-dinner I guess you could call it."

"Oh, I wish I had been there. I should have gone over on the streetcar, but I thought Jesse was coming."

"It's okay. We'll be there soon."

He watched the huddled figure sitting next to him. What had happened to the sparkle that was Kate? The ready smile, the silvery laugh, the eyes that snapped as she talked? This wasn't the Kate he'd always known. It was uncanny, but it was like Ben predicted. Jesse could do that to a woman and had done it more than once. Of course, there'd be some glib excuse, and Kate would forgive him, and things would continue on as before, as if nothing had happened. At least that's what Luke surmised. He wished now that he'd been wrong about Jesse—almost wished he hadn't warned her about him. Now it caused a stiffness between them. She was probably waiting for him to say, "I told you so." Luke would never do that, but Kate had no way of knowing.

"I like your hat," he said finally, wanting to break the dreadful silence that clung to them like fog on a winter evening.

"Thank you, Luke. I hope Jesse likes it, too."

Of course. Jesse. That's all that mattered in Kate's world just now. Jesse. What would Jesse like? How would Jesse act? Did Jesse still love her?

"Ben is beside himself," Luke said then, wanting to talk about something besides Jesse.

"I can imagine he is. He's so devoted and such a good husband. He'll make a wonderful father."

I would, too, Kate, he wanted to say, but quickly admonished himself for thinking along that line again. Yet, the more he tried to push Kate from his mind, the more she came back to haunt him, to enter his brain and dwell in his innermost thoughts. If only things could be different, but God knew what He was doing. He was in charge, as always.

The house finally came in sight, and Kate was down off the wagon before

Luke could come around to assist her. Holding the blue and white skirts high, she dashed in ahead of Luke.

Ben grabbed her by the shoulder as Kate headed for the bedroom. "Wait here. We can't do anything in there. I've got hot water boiling. Jesse just left—"

"He's gone?"

"He'll be back."

"I want to see Emily." It was better if she didn't think about Jesse just now. "I can probably help. Birthing babies is woman's work."

"Okay, if you think it best. Luke and I'll be out here praying."

Emily's face was so pale, Kate almost didn't recognize her. She clutched the sides of the bed, and Kate went and took her hand. "Dig into my palms if the pain's too bad," she murmured. "I'm here, Emily."

"The baby is turned, as best I can make out," the doctor said. "Not uncommon to have a breech birth, especially for a firstborn."

"Can't you do something—turn it around?" Kate asked. She didn't really know much about birthing, just the fear from what she'd seen when Mama had given birth—her pale face, the cries from the pain.

Another grimace, another contraction, and Emily bore down and pushed. "I—hope—my—baby's—okay—"

"Shh. Save your strength. Don't think about the baby. Get ready to push."

Kate didn't know how much time passed. The light was gone from the sky, and the lamp that sat on top of the highboy was lit. One more pain, and the baby came into the doctor's hands. A red, squalling mass of humanity was brought into the world, and Kate marveled at the miracle of birth. Emily's eyes were closed, but her mouth was moving.

"How is—my baby? What—"

"It's a girl," the doctor said, holding the baby up with one hand. "It's early. We need to get her in a warmer. I'll wrap her up and put her behind the stove where she'll get all the warmth she needs." There was a loud squall, then silence.

"Isobelle," Emily said then. "Isobelle for Mama." She squeezed Kate's hand. "And Katherine—for you." Her eyes closed, and she slept.

The doctor wrapped up the baby tightly and carried her to the kitchen. "What do you think, doctor?" Ben asked. "Is she going to be all right?"

"I don't know. She's tiny—so fragile."

"I mean my wife. How's Emily?"

"Emily needs lots of rest, but she should be fine in a week or so. As for this one, I don't know."

When the doctor went back to Emily, Kate and Ben hovered over the tiny baby, who seemed only half alive. Her eyes opened once, then closed as she slept. There was a rattle in the tiny chest, and Ben said that probably her lungs were not fully formed.

Luke stood over the warming basket and prayed aloud. Kate only half heard the words, but it gave her comfort just knowing that prayer was being offered. Ben held her hand tight, then Luke took her other hand as they continued to pray in silence.

Isobelle Katherine lived twelve hours. The next morning, she left the world to go to heaven. Ben's face was haggard and drawn. "How can I tell her this, Kate? How can I?" His eyes pleaded with her to help him, to say the words he found difficult to speak.

Luke had left for his church duties, and Jesse, for whatever reason, had not returned since the night before when he'd gone off on some errand.

"We'll both tell her, Ben. That's the only way it can be."

"I can't believe this has happened after all these months, after all the plans and preparations. She was so looking forward to having our baby."

"I know." Kate began weeping. It was just too much. First being with Emily as she struggled with each pain, then to see her baby so tiny, so frail, and to be so honored by having her named for her. And Jesse, Jesse, whom she loved with all her heart, should have been here to lend his brother support, to give Kate the words she now needed to hear. Where was he?

At last they went into the bedroom. The pillows were stacked behind Emily, and her face had never looked so pale, yet so beautiful. Kate's heart swelled nearly shut. What was this going to do to Emily? How would she take it? Would it keep her from getting well?

"Emily—" Ben's hand touched her forehead as he leaned over and kissed her gently on the cheek. "I love you, sweetheart. You did such a good job."

The eyelids fluttered. "I—want to see our baby."

Ben looked to Kate for help. "I'm sorry, honey."

"No," Kate said, touching his arm. "She must hold her baby. Even though —you know—Emily must be able to hold her."

Kate went into the kitchen and picked up the tiny bundle wrapped in a soft yellow blanket. She looked at the tiny lifeless body, wishing she could perform a miracle and bring life back into the lungs. She carried baby Isobelle back to the bedroom where Ben was talking while holding Emily's hand. Kate leaned over and put the small bundle into the crook of Emily's arm.

"Tell her good-bye, Emily. You must tell her good-bye."

Emily's eyes opened then, and Kate knew that she understood. "But she cried. I heard her."

"I know, darling. She did cry. Once. But her tiny lungs weren't able to breathe on their own."

Tears spilled down Emily's cheeks as she struggled to see the tiny face. "I so wanted our baby to be healthy and happy, to know your love. Ben, I'm so sorry."

"I know. I wanted the same thing, also, but there's nothing for you to be sorry for."

Kate left the two of them and went back to the kitchen. Nobody had eaten last night. She put food away mechanically, needing something to do with her hands. The stove was still warm, and the basket was there where Isobelle had lain. Kate turned from the sight, eased into a chair at the table, and let her head fall into her hands. So little. So wanted by two people. How could God allow this to happen? Why couldn't the baby have lived? Just like Mama who so wanted a healthy child, a son for her husband. Why did these things happen?

She let the tears fall on her arms, then soak the tablecloth, but she didn't remove the handkerchief from the pocket of her dress. Footsteps sounded in the kitchen, but Kate didn't move.

"Kate, what's wrong? The baby?"

She looked up through her tears and saw Jesse standing there, a stern look on his face.

Kate lurched to her feet. "Jesse. You weren't here. You said you were coming back, but you didn't."

"I meant to, but I saw an old friend, and we got to talking—"

"I don't want to hear it," Kate said. He'd been gambling. Only gambling took his mind off of work, Kate, and everything else. It had happened before and would happen again. She turned and walked from the room.

"Now, Kate, don't be like that," came the pleading voice. "You have to understand what happened. Let me explain." But Kate had gone out the back door, out into the morning sunshine, letting it dry her tears. Jesse did not follow. She had somehow thought he might, but wasn't surprised when he didn't.

I love that man, she said to herself. *Heaven help me, but I love him, and I thought he loved me. What went wrong?*

She was still in the yard when she heard horses' hooves trotting down the road toward town. Jesse was not even going to stay to give condolences to his brother or sister-in-law. How could he not care?

When Jesse left Kate and drove to his boardinghouse, he found himself wondering if this was going to work out. He wanted Kate more than he'd ever wanted any woman, but he didn't want to wait until marriage. Jesse ran his hand through his thick hair. He knew he was more handsome than Ben. He thought he had more going for him. Sure he liked to gamble, he got tired of working daily on a puny job like cutting lumber for Ben while Ben got all the credit for the houses he built. He, Jesse, should be able to get some of the credit. Why not build his own houses? He could do that in Salem. It was a growing community, just waiting for Jesse Allen Galloway.

He was tired of Ben's bossing him around. After all, he was the eldest. He should be the one doing the bossing. Besides, Ben was beginning to remind him of Pa, and Jesse could do without thinking about Pa for the rest of his life.

And Ma. She never seemed happy to see him. Kate said it was his imagination, but he knew better. He knew how Ma had her special, secret looks. The looks she gave Ben were always different from the ones for Jesse. He wasn't stupid. He knew he wasn't wanted. Ma was waiting for him to go wrong, to do something bad. How could he stand to stick around in that kind of environment? And even Pearl watched him out of careful eyes. Pearl, his own sister, acting like he was some kind of bum. What had Ma and Ben been saying about him?

Thanks, but no thanks—he didn't have to put up with anyone he didn't want to. As for women, there were bound to be pretty ones in Salem, just like the little gal in the pool hall who flirted with him. She was always happy to see him. Yes, maybe it was time to move on.

That night, Jesse played in another poker game and ended up losing big. He couldn't believe it was happening. After winning so much the last three times he'd played. How else could he have bought the team and fancy carriage? Won the land in Salem?

But he lost, and the more he played, trying to recoup his losses, the more he lost. Soon the acreage was gone. The horses and carriage. He lost what little money he had on him and the last thing to go was his favorite hat. It was humiliating, but Jesse had been humiliated before. Soon he'd be back up and fighting. No, he never stayed down long.

Ben hadn't paid him, and so he thought of taking money from his brother's library, where he knew Ben kept it. It wasn't much and wouldn't last even a week, but he'd get in a game, and his winning streak would start. Jesse was used to losing from time to time. One had to change strategy or find some funds to hold him over for a spell.

Then he remembered Kate's money. She'd told him about the coffee can in her bedroom. Not that he'd ever been in her bedroom, but she'd told him she was saving money, and it was that money they could use to buy land for their house. He would just borrow some of it. Not take the whole bit. Kate would understand when he told her why he had to do it. She wouldn't want him to do without. She loved him too much.

It would be easy to slip in the back door after Kate had gone to work.

Chapter 10

A small funeral was held at a nearby cemetery with Ben and Kate and friends from the church attending. Emily was too weak to go, though she begged Ben to take her.

"You need your rest," the doctor had cautioned.

The sun stayed behind the clouds as Pastor Luke delivered a brief message. "God has decided to take this little one home, for what reason we do not know. But God's ways are not our ways, neither are His thoughts our thoughts. We must accept His will and go on. This child's life has not ended. She has merely gone to be with Him Who said, in Mark 10:14, 'Suffer the little children to come unto me, and forbid them not: for of such is the kingdom of God.' " The tiny casket was lowered into the ground, and Kate turned away. She couldn't watch this final act; it was too painful. She wondered how Luke could say prayers over a baby. It must bring back terrible memories for him of another time, another baby.

People stopped by the house, bringing food, enough food to last the rest of the week. Kate remembered the food after Mama's funeral and how she'd been unable to eat a bite. She felt the same this time. Emily's grandparents—who still refused to speak to her—had sent a loaf of bread.

"At least it's something," Ben said to Kate. "It will mean a lot to Emily."

Emily sat up in bed, several pillows propped behind her head. Her face was drawn and pale, and this worried Kate. She had to get her strength back, but her broken heart kept her down.

Kate's heart was broken, too, for a different reason. *How could she compare the two?* she thought, chastising herself. Now she had two things to worry about. How could Jesse be so insensitive as to disappear when Ben and Emily needed him—and when Kate needed him? Had he no feelings at all?

Emily drifted off to sleep, and Luke stayed with her while Ben said good-bye to the last caller. Kate began stacking plates in the sink.

"You must be exhausted," Kate said, when Ben came into the kitchen. She knew how worried he was, how devoted to Emily. They were so right for each other, just as she'd known they would be before they even met.

Ben stared past Kate, out the window. "It all happened so fast, I still can't believe that our baby is gone."

"There will be more," Kate said, wishing there was some way to console him. "It takes time, Ben. Time to get over a hurt, but God is there to comfort, to help you through this time—" Kate's words hung in the air as Luke entered the kitchen. Standing in the hallway, his eyes on Kate, he had a pleased look, yet one of near disbelief.

"Did I hear you right, Kate? Are you saying that God will comfort our dear brother?"

"Of course, because I believe it to be true for him," she said, her eyes not quite meeting Luke's. "It's right for Ben to think that, don't you agree?"

"Oh, I agree all right. It amazes me that thee is saying this, yet pleases me to hear thy words."

Luke on occasion slipped into the Friends' old way of talking with thees and thous. Kate liked hearing the Quaker way of talking; it was a comforting sound.

"Does thee want some coffee?" she asked then, her dimples showing as she tried not to smile.

"Yes, please, if thee wouldn't mind pouring it."

Later, after Luke had left and Ben had gone on to bed, Kate walked in the garden, her heart crying out to God.

"I do believe in You, God. I know I do. My problem is understanding why there has to be so much grief. Why can't there be more happiness? Fewer things to worry about?"

The tears began falling again, and Kate cried not for the baby Isobelle Katherine but for Jesse Allen Galloway, the man she had given her heart to. Was he coming back? And if so, would he still want to marry Kate, or was there someone else? What was she to think? How could she go on?

Kate was to stay that night and leave the next morning. Ben would go fetch Pearl to come again to help nurse Emily back to health. She was a good cook and would be happy to fix the needed meals, even if it meant she had to drop out of school. Sarah might have come, but there was the garden to harvest. They would need plenty of vegetables and fruits before winter came.

That night, Kate slept in the unfinished attic because she couldn't bear to think of staying in the nursery. There were too many memories.

She loved this house. It was the perfect size for a family, and she knew there would be more babies. Emily had said she wanted at least half a dozen to fill the rooms with laughter. She'd get a dreamy look in her eyes when she talked about lots of children. She'd been the oldest of seven and missed her younger brothers and sisters so much when she'd been sent to Oregon to live with her grandparents. She'd vowed to Kate then, if given a chance, and if

God willed it, she would have children to love.

Kate stared at the studded walls and the unfinished ceiling the next morning. It was time to get up, for she must go to work, but she could hardly move. It was as if she didn't care if she got up or stayed right here in bed all day. Who even cared what she did anymore, anyway? It was Ben's voice calling from the foot of the stairs that finally made her move.

"It's six o'clock," Ben called. "I'm going to fetch Pearl now. You don't need to stay, because our neighbor Miz Blanchard will come over until I get back."

Kate called down her thanks to Ben and finally got dressed. Emily was awake and smiled weakly when Kate peeked around the corner. Her Bible was open.

"I know that God has a message for me here somewhere. I'm trying to find it now."

"He loves you, Emily. That's all I know, and if we can believe what Luke says, that's all we need to know."

"And trust," Emily said, closing her eyes briefly. "We must have trust that things will work out for the best."

"What's that verse about all things that work together or something like that?"

Emily turned to Romans 8:28. "Yes, here it is. Read it to me, Kate. I love hearing your voice. It's so melodious."

Kate took the Bible into her hands and read the verse: "And we know that all things work together for good to them that love God, to them who are called according to his purpose."

One heartache was being borne. Between the two women, they would survive this test, but Kate had one more heartache to bear: Jesse. What was she going to do about Jesse? When was she going to start feeling better? How was her heart going to heal?

Kate was soon on the streetcar heading for the candy factory. Mr. Roberts came into her section after she'd finished dipping a row of chocolates. Two were lopsided and she knew she must concentrate and do better. An order had to be filled by nightfall.

"I heard about Emily's baby," Mr. Roberts said. "Here, please take this box of chocolates to the Galloways with my condolences."

Kate smiled. "I know she'll appreciate your kindness, Mr. Roberts. I'll thank you for her."

"I wish I could let you have some time off, but I must get this order out today."

"I know. Besides, work is what I need," Kate said.

It was true. She knew that she must stay busy to keep from thinking about baby Isobelle and Jesse.

❄

Kate left work later than usual, catching the streetcar home. What was the use of hurrying? There was nothing at home but emptiness. The rooms seemed hollow, and she couldn't take delight in her furnishings or the fancy sewing machine. They were fine possessions, but what were possessions without the person you loved? Yet Kate felt Jesse would come back some day. He'd come bearing gifts, or there would be a surprise like the time he came with the horses and new carriage. How surprised she'd been, and how he'd smiled when she laughed as they raced over the rutted road back toward Portland.

"I love it when you laugh," he'd said, touching her face. She'd stopped laughing for a moment and gazed deeply into his eyes, wondering if it could be true. She had found someone who loved her and someone she loved with all her heart.

Kate sat on the sofa and sighed. How quickly things changed. One moment Emily and Ben were expecting their first baby, and Kate was planning a wedding. Now this.

Dinner seemed unimportant as Kate sat thinking. How devastated Ben must be, not only losing his baby, but with Emily being ill. She hoped Pearl had come and that she would bring laughter into the house again. Though a quiet girl, she was sweet and dedicated to her family. It should work out fine.

Kate went to work the rest of the week, barely able to navigate, yet knowing she must keep busy. She ate little and ignored the gnawing ache in her stomach. She didn't even test the imperfect chocolates but just worked harder to make up the loss. She recalled the times when she and Emily had laughed as they ate chocolates. Never more than one or two on any workday. The imperfect ones could be dipped again, and sometimes Mr. Roberts sold them to friends who didn't mind a lopsided vanilla creme.

On Friday, Kate looked at the calendar in her kitchen. Six days since she'd seen Jesse. Six days since she'd heard his voice. Six days since he'd spoken her name, or touched her hand, or looked into her eyes. How could she bear it any longer? She had to know what had happened, but how? Ben wouldn't know. If he did, he would have told her. So far everyone had sidestepped the issue about Jesse, as if they were trying to spare her any more pain, yet she felt the need to talk about it. She couldn't keep the hurt and pain inside her much longer.

Kate went to her box where she kept her savings. She knew banks were safer, but she liked having the money there in case she should need it. If it would have helped, she would have paid for Emily to go to the hospital.

Could they have done something more to save the baby's life? She'd never know now.

She lifted the tin lid and gasped. The money was gone! Every last bit of it. How much had there been? Forty dollars and a few coins. But when? And how? Who could have. . . ?

She sat holding the box in her hand and looked around the room. Nothing else had disappeared. There hadn't been a robbery. She had other valuable objects. The gold bracelet was in her jewel box and the necklace, too. The sewing machine sat in the corner of the spare bedroom. Jesse. Her heart nearly stopped. It couldn't be. Not Jesse. He wouldn't have taken it. How could he have? Yet he knew about the money. She'd told him that sunny day when they'd had the picnic at the park. She'd made sandwiches, packed cookies and fruit. The sun had been bright, and it seemed as if nothing else mattered but the two of them.

After eating, Jesse'd held her hand as they walked along a winding tree-lined trail, and she had told him about her savings, including where she kept it.

"I'm saving money for land or furniture," Kate had said. "Or a trip. I don't want to be poor like Mama was."

Jesse looked thoughtful, but only for a moment. "You'll never be poor, Kate, not if I can help it. And you'll have your nice furniture and lots of pretty things."

Laughing, Kate had tickled his chin. He'd laughed, too, grabbing both hands so she couldn't tickle anymore.

"If you're not careful I'll tickle you back."

"Oh, no, you don't," she'd cried, running away as if she was scared.

They'd left the park soon after, and Kate had been filled with love for Jesse, feeling she'd always love him.

"This has been the most enjoyable day of my life," Jesse had said later as he stood on Kate's porch and lifted her face for a good night kiss. Kissing was permissible. After all, they were going to be married soon. And then she wouldn't have to stand on her porch and say good night. He would come inside with her. . . .

"Stop!" she cried out now. That day was gone. It was today now, and her savings were gone.

Kate put the box back on the shelf and fell across the bed, sobbing into her hands. "I loved him, God. You know how much I loved him. And believed him. Trusted him. He was my whole life. What am I to do now?"

Later she got up and paced the floor. Should she call the police and report the theft? What if it wasn't Jesse? What if it was someone else? Yet even as she thought it, she knew it was Jesse, and she couldn't bring herself to report it. She didn't want to embarrass him that way. Besides, he was going to pay it back. Of course. That was it. He had simply borrowed it. He'd show up on her doorstep tomorrow, bearing flowers or some gift, sweep her into his arms and tell her how beautiful she was, and then hand her the money. She had to believe that was the way it would happen.

Kate tried to sew a new dress Saturday after work. She had stayed late at work again. She wanted to go over to Emily and Ben's to see how Emily was doing, but she couldn't bear facing her friends. What if they asked her if she'd seen Jesse? What could she say? No, and he's stolen my money, too.

She was dressed in one of her older calicos, having no heart to attend the grange dance. Of course Jesse might be there, but somehow she knew he wouldn't be, just as she knew he wouldn't show up on her porch again. She'd go to the Galloways' after all. It was better than staying at home, moping.

The porch was deserted when Kate lighted from the streetcar. Usually Ben was there, with the paper. The wagon was there, so she knew he was home.

The house smelled of spice and sugar, and she remembered Pearl had come again. "Is that apple pie I smell?" she called out from the side door.

"Yes, and you can't have any," a voice answered.

"Pearl!" A second later the girl was in Kate's arms, and she was holding her tight against her bosom. She hadn't expected to cry, nor did she think Pearl had expected to, but they were both crying, and then they stopped, looked at each other, and laughed.

"Emily's been hoping you'd come, and I fried extra chicken for you and Pastor Luke."

"Is he here?"

"No, but he's coming in a bit."

"Did I hear my name mentioned?"

The door opened, and Luke entered the room. Kate had almost forgotten how quiet he was, compared to Jesse and his loud ways. He looked good and strong, and she found herself happy to see him.

"I just got here and the delightful smell drew me to the kitchen."

"Yes, our little Pearl is a great cook."

"Taught by my Mama," Pearl said, her cheeks flushing bright red from embarrassment.

"Well, how's our patient doing?"

"She sat up on the porch swing this afternoon," Pearl said. "Ben's with her now."

"Is dinner ready?" Ben said, his bulk filling the doorway. "I think my friends are hungry. I know I'm hungry, and Emily says she thinks she could eat a chicken leg and a heap of mashed potatoes."

"And apple pie," Kate said. "I must go see her."

"Me, too," Luke said, following Kate down the hall.

The dinner was a celebration of sorts. Kate felt better than she had in a long time, and there were two pink spots on Emily's cheeks, signs that she was going to be all right.

"I'm just so happy to be here," she said, lifting her face and smiling. "Now if you'll ask for God to bless this food, we can eat." She nodded toward Luke.

"Oh, God, we come to You grateful, humble people. We've had pain, but thank You, God, that joy cometh in the morning. . . ."

Kate closed her eyes and listened to Luke's deep voice offer thanks to a God she wasn't sure even existed. But one thing she did know was that time does heal all wounds. Emily was getting better each day, and Ben's face didn't have that lost, hollow look. Someday she would be able to forget Jesse, too. She had to hold onto that thought and know that for whatever reason, it wasn't meant to be. Now she held her broken heart out for God to heal, if He really was there and if He even cared. . . .

Kate heard the rattle of forks and realized the prayer was over. She opened her eyes and glanced up to find Luke's eyes on her, watching. . . waiting. . . .

Chapter 11

The next few weeks became a blur to Kate. Jesse did not return. Emily was on her feet and had strength to cook and do a few housekeeping chores, but she was listless and pale. There were dark circles under her eyes, and though she smiled as she talked to people, it was a false smile, as if she knew it was expected of her. Ben worried about her, as did Kate, Pearl, and Luke.

"Get your strength back and have another baby," Kate suggested one Saturday afternoon as the three women sat on the porch. While Kate and Emily took the swing, Pearl sat on the steps, her back against the beam, her arms hugging her knees.

"Mama says no baby takes the place of another one," Pearl said.

"And that's right," Kate said in agreement. "It won't be a replacement because nobody can replace baby Isobelle." She set her smocking aside. She'd thought she could work on the bodice of a new dress for fall. It was really for Emily, a navy blue linen with lighter blue smocking, but she hadn't told her about it.

There were chickens to feed, so Pearl left to do that chore. Ben had brought home rabbits two nights ago, and they were also Pearl's responsibility.

"Pearl should be back in school," Emily said then. "I know how much she enjoyed it."

"I think she'd rather stay here with you."

Emily poked a hairpin back in place in her hair. "I'm more of an obligation to her than anything else."

"Perhaps so. Ben will be the one to decide. Whatever he says, Pearl will abide by. With the garden winding down, perhaps Sarah could come stay," Kate suggested. "The house is certainly big enough for four of you."

She almost said five, but one could hardly count Jesse since it was doubtful he would return.

"Sarah's too independent," Emily said with a sudden shiver.

"That breeze is cool," Kate said. "I'll fetch your shawl." It certainly wouldn't do for Emily to catch cold on top of everything else.

Neither Emily or Ben had spoken about Jesse, nor had Pearl. It was as if

Jesse had never existed, but it was hard for Kate to think that way. Jesse did exist and had taken part of her heart with him when he left. There was always the question, the fear that something could have happened to him. What if he lay in a ditch somewhere out of sight? He could have fallen with the horses down a ravine or up by the mountains where it was steep and heavily forested. Still, Kate said nothing.

"Kate," Emily's voice broke through Kate's thoughts. "I don't want to make you unhappy, or more unhappy than you already are, but I'm worried about you."

"Worried about me?" Kate turned and stared at her friend. "Why do you say that?"

"Look at you. Your clothes hang limp and your cheeks are sunken. And you haven't been going to dances or doing much of anything."

Kate's fingers touched her face. She knew her face was drawn, and her clothes did hang on her tall frame like a dress on a hanger. "I go to work, and that's enough to keep me occupied."

"It's Jesse, isn't it? You can't get him out of your mind."

Kate sighed and leaned back in the swing. She knew it was over, but how could she admit defeat? How could she go on as if nothing had happened? She could never return to the carefree days she'd known before. Jesse had stolen not only her heart, but her money, as well. Stolen. There, she'd said it. She'd always said he was going to return it one day, but the days had turned into weeks and now with winter just around the corner, she knew it wasn't about to happen. She'd have to wear the same coat she'd worn the last two winters. And what would she do if an emergency arose or if she needed to take her doctor's advice and get away from it all? He had suggested a train trip to California might be just what she needed.

"I loved him, you know."

Emily touched her arm. "I know, Kate. It was hard not to love Jesse. He had a little-boy quality about him, didn't he?"

At last, the tears came. Tears that Kate had bottled up inside burst forth, rolling down her cheeks. "I believed him. Trusted him so completely." She wiped at the tears and tried to smile. "Go ahead and say, 'I told you so,' Emily."

"I would never say that to my best friend."

"Well, you could, and you'd be right."

"What purpose would it serve?"

Kate shrugged, then laughed. "None, I suppose. It might make you feel better."

"But it wouldn't make you feel any better, and I'd never intentionally hurt you, Kate. You know that."

"Yes, I know."

Pearl came around the side of the house, holding the egg basket high. "Found six more eggs—" She stopped when she saw Kate's tear-streaked face. "Is something wrong? Kate?"

Kate shook her head. "It's just Jesse."

Pearl slumped down on the steps, nodding. "Yes, my brother. Jesse seems to hurt everyone wherever he goes. He borrowed money from Mama, and she didn't have much to give away."

"Borrowed money!" Emily gasped. "Why, he took money from us, too, but it wasn't borrowed—though I'm sure he figured he had earned it. Ben said it was way more than Jesse ever earned, and that he was just thankful that all his workers weren't shiftless like Jesse." Her hand clapped over her mouth as if she'd said more than she should have.

Should Kate add to the story?

"He took money from me without asking," she said finally.

"Kate! No!"

The silence was stifling as the three sat, staring out at the road with horses and carriages trotting by on their way to town, or on their way home.

"When I tell Ben this—"

Kate stood then. "No, Emily. Please say nothing to Ben. I don't want him to know."

"But he should, and maybe he can help repay—"

"I wouldn't dream of letting him repay me," Kate remarked. "It's a lesson I've learned." *And have I ever learned it well,* she wanted to say, but the words stayed tight inside her.

"If I decide to take a trip to California, I'll sell the gold jewelry Jesse gave me—"

"California! Kate, you never mentioned anything about a trip to California." Emily's eyes widened in dismay.

"I know. I've been contemplating the idea. It's just to get away—to try to sort things out."

Emily nodded then. "I'm sure it would help, but what would we ever do with you gone?"

Pearl agreed wholeheartedly, reaching over and hugging Kate. "I just want you to be happy again."

"I'm trying," Kate said. "So, let's talk about something else."

As if in answer to her request, one of the buggies pulled up and stopped.

"Hello, ladies. Isn't it a nice day?"

It was a peddler who had stopped by once before. "I have some new lovelies to show you."

Kate and Pearl went out to look at the wares, while Emily stayed on the porch.

Kate bought a comb for Emily's hair, remembering how much she'd loved the clasp she'd given her the first Christmas they'd known each other. When Pearl admired some ribbon, she bought a yard of that, too.

"That's all I can afford today, though I love your new dishes," Kate remarked. She might have bought them if she were planning to get married, but there was no reason to now.

Pearl rebraided her hair, crossed the braids in back, and added the new red ribbon. It was time to start dinner, so she went inside and left Kate and Emily alone.

"She's been such a blessing to me, Kate, you have no idea. How could two such wonderful people have a scoundrel of a brother like Jesse?"

Emily thought back to the one time she and Ben had talked about Jesse. Ben claimed that once Jesse got gambling in his blood, he couldn't stay away from it. He'd always gamble away any money as fast as he could make it. "He needs the Lord, Kate, but he'd never admit to it."

"He told me that Sarah never loved him as she did Ben and the others. I don't believe that of Sarah, though. She's so kind and gracious, I can't imagine her not loving all her children the same," Kate added.

At the mention of children, Emily's frown appeared. "I'm going back in to rest until dinner."

Kate watched Emily rise from the swing and go into the house. She wondered why Ben hadn't come. Usually he was home by now. Of course there was a house he was trying to finish by the end of October, so maybe he decided to work until dark.

Kate was walking out back to the orchard to see if there were any apples on the ground, when a large wagon made its way down the street. It looked like Ben driving. On closer inspection, she saw that it was indeed Ben.

"Yahoo, Kate! You won't believe what I got my hands on today!"

There was a huge object in the wagon, covered with gunny sacks and blankets. What had Ben brought home now?

Kate walked out to the side gate and opened it. "Something for Emily?" she asked.

"A piano."

"A piano? But how did you ever get a piano?"

"The fellow I'm building the house for ordered this and then changed his mind. It's perfect for Emily. Just maybe it's what she needs to bring the color back to her cheeks."

"And how will you get it out of the wagon?" She looked under one of the blankets, admiring the smooth, shiny black ebony. It was the largest piano she'd ever seen—a baby grand.

"When Luke comes, we'll unload it, with Pearl's help, and maybe you can guide us into the house."

It was so exciting. Kate knew how proud and happy this gift would make Emily. More than anything, Emily missed playing the piano at home. She played at church sometimes, but hadn't gone in a long time now.

"Is she resting?"

Kate nodded. "She'd been up more than two hours."

Pearl came around the side of the house, clapping her hands. "A piano! Oh, Ben, it's so beautiful!"

Luke always seemed to come at precisely the right moment, and he arrived just in time to help. He nodded at Pearl, his eyes meeting Kate's for a long minute.

"Kate. Haven't seen you for two weeks. How have you been?"

"Could be better, but I'm on the mend, thank you."

Luke removed his coat and pushed up his shirt sleeves. "I can certainly tell when I'm needed."

Soon they had pushed the piano up the steps and into the house.

"I know Emily suggested we put a piano in the library some day," Ben said, "but I want it right in front, by the window, so all can see it as they pass by."

Emily, hearing all the commotion, came out of the bedroom and clasped her hands, her mouth falling open. "A piano! Ben, you never told me you were buying a piano."

"Didn't know it until this afternoon. How do you like it?"

Her hands touched the keys, playing several chords as a smile tugged at the corner of her mouth. "It's more beautiful than I could have imagined. And listen to that wonderful tone."

After supper, Emily played five hymns, a concert of sorts. Kate helped Pearl with the dishes and set things out for the Sunday meals. She could hear the men talking on the porch. Not that she could hear a word they said, but it was a comfortable, buzzing sound. She realized that in all the weeks that Jesse had lived here, he'd not once sat on the porch to talk with his brother. He was always off doing something, keeping busy in his own way, which Kate now knew to be gambling—and possibly wooing unsuspecting women.

She dried her hands and said she was going out back to sit under the apple tree. "I just want to think, Pearl. Don't feel you must keep me company."

Pearl smiled her warm, happy smile. "I hope someday you will find a man that is every bit as good as Ben," she said.

Kate leaned over and gave her a quick hug. "The same goes for you, Pearl. You're becoming a fine young woman, and one day you'll want to have a home and a family. I hope there is someone out there who will love you, too."

The evening was much cooler than she'd expected, and Kate wished she'd brought her shawl. She sat on the ground, drawing her skirts up under her legs. Proper ladies didn't sit like this, but she liked sitting on the ground. It was soothing to her for some reason.

As darkness descended, she thought about the dance tonight. There would be music and, oh, how she loved music and dancing. Probably some might be looking for her, or at least asking about her, but she didn't know if she could ever go back to the dances. Not with Jesse gone. It wouldn't seem right, and it would be far too painful. It was better to stay away, though her heart longed to go and be part of the fun once again. How much longer would she grieve? Would it take another man to bring her out of her doldrums, or would a trip be the answer?

She leaned back and drew a breath of fresh air. The chickens and rabbits had bedded down for the night, and it was quiet and peaceful. What she wouldn't give to have a man to cook for, to have a child with, to grow old with, but she didn't think her heart would ever let her love again.

"Kate? Are you out here?"

It was Luke.

"In the garden, under the apple tree," she called out, standing and brushing the dampness off the back of her skirt.

"I thought you might need this. There's a sharpness in the air." He held her shawl out to her.

"Thank you, Luke. I should have realized the night air would be cold."

He nodded. "Going to be a beautiful day tomorrow, the kind I like. Look at how clear the sky is."

"Winter's not far off," Kate said.

"Are you all right?" There was concern in his voice, and Kate trembled unexpectedly.

"I'm going to be fine, Luke. And you?"

"It's not me that I'm worried about."

"You're always listening to other people. When do you get a chance to tell someone your innermost thoughts?" Kate had always wondered this about preachers. Whom did they talk to?

"I have God to share my concerns with," he said, nodding as he looked into the heavens.

"God isn't tangible."

"To me He is, Kate. How could one ever deny His existence when looking into a starry sky?" He cleared his throat. "I need to talk to you. Just for a moment. . ."

"Like the other time?" The minute Kate said it, she wanted to take the words back. Why bring it up, when all she wanted to do was forget?

"Not like the other time, but perhaps as important."

"Yes?"

"I am worried about your health. You've lost weight. Pardon me for noticing, but a person would have to be blind not to see. Remember, my profession is to notice people."

Yes, thought Kate. *He is paid to get the message out, and here it comes now.* She braced herself.

"You don't go to the dances anymore."

"You don't believe in dancing."

"For me, no. But for you, it's all right because you deem it to be right."

"I—don't know what to say to that."

"I think you've been in hiding too long, Miz Katherine Russell. It's time you started living again. There's hurt in your heart, but it will heal. Just give it time, and it will go away."

"I'm trying to forget. I really am." She snuggled deeper into the shawl, wishing it were longer. Should she tell him now about California?

"Don't try to forget. Remember it as something that happened to you. Now it's over, and it didn't work out for whatever reason, but life goes on and so must you."

He moved until he stood directly in front of her. "Kate, I only wish things could be different for you—and for me. I'm not saying this very well, but I know Jesse is not the first hurt you've experienced. There's been another hurt, an even deeper hurt. I wish you could talk about it. I wish you would let me help you."

Another hurt. It was not something she wanted to tell Luke. He wouldn't understand. Even if Luke was a minister, he would look at her in a different way if he knew about that hot afternoon, if he knew what had happened to her.

"I would rather keep my problems to myself," she said.

Luke touched the side of her face, his fingers on the scar, tracing it gently. "Let it all be over, Kate, so you can love again."

Kate swallowed hard, not moving. Luke was so close, she could feel his breath on her face. Why was her heart suddenly racing like this?

She stepped aside.

"Kate—"

"I have to go in," she said, shivering as she pulled her shawl closer.

"Here, you can have my coat." He removed it and put it around her shoulders. She noticed it had a nice, woodsy smell.

Finally, she looked up. "Thank you, Luke." She paused. "I'm going away," she managed to say, "to California on the train."

In the brilliant moonlight, Luke's face revealed shock, then he nodded. "I see."

"It was my doctor's suggestion."

"You can't run from your problems."

"I know that."

"How long will you stay?"

"I'm not sure." She took a gulp of night air, unable to look up. She knew how his face looked, that his eyes were on her, and she couldn't stand the intense gaze. "Probably not long, I'd miss Emily and Ben too much—"

And me, he wanted to say, but did not. It would never work out, anyway, and Kate knew it as well as he did. "I hope this is a wise decision, Kate."

"I've given it a lot of thought."

"When will you leave?"

"Friday. Ben said he could take me to the train station. Good night, Luke," Kate said, as she slipped out of the coat and handed it back to him. She started toward the back steps.

"Kate!" He walked toward her. "If ever you should choose to love again, I'd like to be the one you turn to." Without waiting for an answer, he opened the gate and disappeared around the corner.

Kate stood motionless. Had she heard right? But, no, that couldn't be what Luke meant. They were good friends, nothing more.

She trembled and went into the kitchen, still warm from dinner, and sank against the door, Luke's parting words buzzing around in her head. *I'd like to be the one you turn to.* What did his words mean? Was she making the right decision? How did one ever really know?

Sounds of music came from the front room as Kate slipped out of her shawl and thought of how Luke had brought it out to her. He always thought of other people. She'd seen it time and again. When she knew how his heart must be breaking at the memory of his dead son and wife, he had held the service for the Galloway child. He had comforted Emily and been there for Ben, too. He was such a good, decent man. How he could ever think of Kate in that special way was incomprehensible. Luke was such an enigma to her, coming up with things that made her stop and think. He had just said that he wanted to be the one to help her forget. Surely he wasn't implying that he—no, it could never be, not when she had no faith. What little faith she'd once had was extinguished when baby Isobelle died and Jesse left her. Luke must know that, so how could he even intimate that he cared?

She walked into the front room and watched Emily's hands flying over the keys. Such talent. She was another one who thought of others when she herself was in pain. You never heard her complain. It seemed strange to Kate, now that she thought about it, that Luke hadn't been right for Emily. Together they would have made a terrific team, preaching and teaching about God's love. God's love surely shone through them, and Kate smiled for the first time that evening. Perhaps she thought of God more than she'd admit even to herself. Perhaps God was becoming real to her for whatever reason.

She applauded when Emily finished the song "Count Your Blessings."

"I see you couldn't leave the piano alone."

Emily smiled brightly. "No, I couldn't. And I feel so much better already." She turned and stared at Kate. "Your face is all pink. It must be very cold outside."

Kate's fingertips touched her cheeks. They did feel warm. "Yes, it is cold outside," but down deep she knew that wasn't the reason for her flushed face.

Chapter 12

Luke knew he shouldn't have said anything to Kate. It had just sort of slipped out and there the words were in front of them—between them now. Of course she was shocked. Could he have expected anything different? He'd been Kate's friend since that first afternoon in her kitchen when she'd barraged him with questions. How could she possibly think of him in any other way? But when she'd mentioned going to California, he was crestfallen. To lose her forever was something he couldn't quite comprehend, even though she wasn't his to lose.

Besides, what did he, Luke, have to offer someone like Kate? She's beautiful. . .gregarious. . .loving. . .beautiful—oh, did I already say that? He had to laugh at himself, even in his perplexity. In truth, she was not the kind of woman a preacher needed. She was too controversial, plus she made no bones about not believing in and questioning God.

But she believes, he declared to heaven. *I know she does. I've heard her say things. The way she acts. She believes in You, God. She's just fighting it—for who knows what reason.*

The night air was nippy, but Luke scarcely noticed as he coaxed his team toward home. Perhaps there he could put Kate from his mind, yet he doubted it. Kate constantly puzzled him. There was an inner person that nobody got to know. And it was this she was running from, not realizing that she could not run from her problem. What secret lay in Kate's heart and mind? What had happened so long ago that she kept buried inside? It was something she had not told anyone, not even Emily.

Luke had guessed a long time ago that she had a secret heartache. And he now knew that the scar on her left cheek, usually hidden by her thick hair, was part of the secret. He wanted to know what had happened, but he could not press her. In fact, his declaring his mind had so surprised her that he feared things would have been awkward between them from now on if she weren't going away.

Kate still loved Jesse, though he had hurt her deeply. Luke had seen her tremble, watched her face and her eyes, when Jesse's name came up—not that it had come up a lot lately in conversation. Ben refused to talk about his brother.

"Let sleeping dogs lie," he'd said the one time Luke had asked if he knew about Jesse's whereabouts. Luke couldn't help wondering where Jesse had gone off to. Would he return? If so, when? And when he did, would Kate fall under his charm again, acting as if nothing had ever happened? Not if she wasn't here, and that must be Kate's purpose in leaving.

Luke sighed as he lighted from the buggy and led the horses inside the makeshift barn. Women were funny when it came to men, or at least he had found it to be so. He remembered how he'd felt about Emily after first coming to Oregon. She was kind and gentle, and her gentleness spoke to him. She would have been the perfect mate for a man in the ministry, but Emily loved another: Ben. Just as Kate loved another. Yes, there was something about those Galloway brothers, some trait that Luke did not possess. Was it their commanding height? Maybe Luke would never know.

Luke had always been short. He remembered being teased when he first went to school.

"You're sure a pee-wee," his teacher had said.

"Short, but mighty," he'd declared even then. It was his father who told him: "Stand tall. Act like a man, and you will be counted."

Luke had taken that advice. Height wasn't everything. There were other things one could do to be noticed. And so he'd become studious, working hard in school and later college, making top grades. He had graduated as valedictorian, and later magna cum laude from the university. It was his diligence that made him attractive to Rachel, his wife.

Oh, how long ago that seemed now. Dear, sweet Rachel. He had loved her so, and grieved so when she died in his arms. Then when their child died two days later, it was almost more than he could bear. But God's Word had encouraged and lifted him up, and he managed to survive.

Kate was so different from Rachel. She couldn't have been more opposite if she tried. Kate was tall and regal, where Rachel had been short and round. Rachel had had blonde hair and blue eyes; Kate, dark hair and deep brown eyes. Those eyes now haunted his every waking thought.

Lord, I don't know why You keep putting Kate in my heart if she isn't to mean anything to me. I can minister to her, and I've tried to do that, but I sure didn't bargain for this deep feeling, this feeling so totally different from what I experienced with Rachel. How can this be?

Not very often had Luke doubted God's ways. Not very often did his mind wander from what he perceived as God's voice guiding him. So, why was he questioning now? God knew something that Luke did not. Kate needed him. Yes, it was as if God said, *Kate needs you. Keep talking to her. Be there for her. Let her lean on you. Let her see that you care for her.*

Well, he had certainly done that, hadn't he? But he had gone a step too far tonight by saying he wished she might turn to him. Stupid of him, when he knew how she felt about Jesse. Luke could never give her the things Jesse had given her. Whoever Luke married would be poor, though not impoverished. He gave back to the church and its people any excess he might receive from God's bounty. Kate would not understand that.

He lit a lamp and opened his Bible, turning it to the parts that had meant much to him over the years, passages he'd read when he'd felt troubled, doubtful, seeking, or in need of an uplift. It was all there in God's precious Word. How could he ever doubt what God was leading him to do? He read in Matthew 6:33: "But seek ye first the kingdom of God, and his righteousness; and all these things shall be added unto you." He didn't know how, but things would work out, and God would reveal to him the answers. It would take time. Oh, yes, he knew about time and waiting. But he would be patient. He hadn't learned verses about patience for naught. God had taught him patience many years ago, and he would be God's patient, faithful servant.

Tomorrow was Meeting Day. Luke was thankful he had studied the Scriptures earlier and had written out his message about forgiveness on Thursday.

The night wore on as Luke read the comforting Scriptures, and he had to refill his reading lamp. Tomorrow Emily and Ben would be back to the meeting, with sweet, young Pearl. The Friends would surround them with their loving and caring ways, and their good wishes. As Luke closed the Bible, he wished that a certain other person would also be there. But, then, if she were, perhaps he would be unable to concentrate on giving the message. No, God was in control and knew exactly what He was doing. Luke just had to follow His will.

Luke went to the kitchen, poured a glass of milk, and ate one of Widow Benson's oatmeal cookies. His people were so good to him. How he loved his church, the people, and life in general. He prepared for bed.

Humming the old hymn "Standing on the Promises of God," Pastor Luke Morrison blew out the lamp and settled under the quilt his mother had made him many years ago, but his mind would not settle down. Luke thought about forgiveness. When one does not forgive, no matter what the transgression, the anger eats away inside of him. It was one of the reasons the Quakers didn't go off to war.

"How can one fight his brother?" his father had asked him when he was around twelve.

"Perhaps he cannot," Luke had answered.

"That is why we are pacifists, and have been since our beginnings. We have had to endure persecution, but God gives us strength to do so."

Luke had thought about it many times since that long ago conversation. Wars, fighting, bitterness. Of course one got hurt. It happened all the time, but one must forgive and turn to God, asking His help if one found it too difficult to do.

Kate harbored anger inside her; Luke had been sure of that long ago, on the afternoon when he sat in her kitchen with Emily at the other side of the table. Emily had asked for forgiveness for what was a sin to her—dancing with Ben. Dancing had never been Kate's problem because she believed it was not a sin.

No, dancing was not Kate's albatross. It was not what caused the light to dim for a minute in those gorgeous dark eyes. It wasn't that she wasn't happy, because she was—and she made everyone happy that she came into contact with. But on occasion the anger would explode inside her, and briefly, oh, so briefly, she would show her anger and fear. It had to come out, but how? Kate might pretend it didn't matter to her, that she had forgotten about it, but had she? Somehow, Luke did not think so.

And the scar. Luke had not noticed it when he first knew Kate. It was only one afternoon, an especially hot one, when Emily still carried her baby, that Kate had brushed her hair back from the sides of her face, and the scar had shown in the late afternoon sunshine. A tiny scar, weird in shape, and not even an inch long. It didn't look like it was caused by a knife, but what then?

Luke lay in the darkness. What would it be like to have a wife again? It seemed so long since Rachel's death. Three years now, but sometimes it seemed infinitely longer. And the child. Such love they had both felt for the child, such caring, even before seeing his little face. He would be part of their family, they hoped the first of many. But God didn't deem it best, just as he didn't allow Rachel to go on living on this earth.

Forgiveness? Oh, Luke knew about forgiveness inside and out. He had railed at God those first few months—turned his back on the church. They'd given him time off, a sabbatical, they called it, and he had tried to heal. It was a long time coming. How Luke had wished his father was still alive. Papa'd had answers for everything that happened. Reasons, suggestions, comments. Luke had missed him so much, wishing he could have been alive to know Rachel, to meet his first grandson.

Luke wondered when sleep would come tonight. Sometimes it took hours to finally close his mind down and let sleep take over. He wondered if other preachers had this problem. Perhaps if he wouldn't keep thinking about Kate, he could sleep. But he thought of her alone in her little house, thought of how she laughed, and smiled, and spoke to everyone with such love. How he'd wanted to reach out and touch her face earlier. She had been so close; he could feel her breath, and knew she could feel his. He caught the fragrance of roses, a smell that was definitely Kate. He'd noticed it the first time they met. Most of his people did not wear fragrances, just as they chose not to wear makeup and bright colors. It was an individual thing, though the older ones would not agree, just as they preferred him to speak in the true Quaker way.

"Will thee go to sleep?" he said to himself out loud. "First Day is nearly here. Thee will have red-rimmed eyes and fall asleep during prayer time."

Suddenly, Luke eyes were wide open. A gift. If Kate was leaving, he must send a small gift, some token to show he cared. But what? Then he knew what the perfect gift would be, and it was something Kate could pack into her suitcase and take along.

Luke closed his eyes again, wondering if he'd see Kate before she left. Maybe she'd put on some weight in California. He'd been meaning to speak to Emily about it, hoping she might coax Kate into eating. Finally, Luke dozed off, with Kate's smile flashing through his mind.

Kate had a fitful night in the Galloways' house. Twice she dreamed she could hear Jesse's voice, and once she felt his touch, his hand on her arm as he begged her, "Now come on, Kate, try to understand how it is. I love you. Nothing I do will ever change that."

Finally she rose and tiptoed down the stairs of the dark house. It was warm from the heat of yesterday, but she would light a small fire to boil water. Should she? She didn't want to waken the rest of the household.

She pulled back the curtain and looked out toward the east. The sun was rising, turning the entire sky into a blaze of colors. It was a gorgeous time of day, but she'd never had the time to bask in it before.

She let the curtain fall aside. The yard made her think of last night and Luke's unexpected words. It was because of him she could not sleep. Jesse's words kept floating through her mind, *He's sweet on you, Kate.* She had denied it vehemently. She admired Luke tremendously, she thought of him as her friend, someone she could turn to whenever the need arose, someone who could pray for her. But to think of him in a different way? To think about marrying him? No, it was impossible.

The fire was going and the water starting to hum when Pearl entered the kitchen.

"You were up before me, Kate."

"I couldn't sleep."

"I couldn't, either. I guess it was the heat upstairs."

Pearl wasn't as solid as she once was. She had lost weight since her brother's baby died. Her arms poked out through the arms of a flannel wrapper that was way too big. Suddenly Kate had an idea. Why hadn't she thought of it before? A dress for Pearl and a new dressing gown. She'd be so pleased—she was like Emily that way.

"I was wondering," Pearl said, after retrieving a cold biscuit from the platter, "if you might go to church today?"

Kate laughed. "I hadn't thought of it, Pearl, but perhaps I will. Yes, perhaps I will."

She went to get ready, selecting a dark navy blue poplin that was faded from use. It hung on her, but nobody would notice with her shawl wrapped around her shoulders. Yes, perhaps there was time to go to church one more time before she made the trip to California. Last night, when she couldn't sleep, she realized the trip would be a good decision: a change of scenery to help her get over her heartache. And if Jesse returned while she was gone, so be it. She'd already decided she wouldn't succumb anymore to his charming ways. It was time to get on with her life.

Yes, she thought, slipping the dress on, it was time to get on with things, and going to California would be a good start.

Chapter 13

Kate found herself looking forward to church. She didn't attend often, but it would be pleasant, especially with Emily going.

"I'm so happy you're coming," Emily said, turning around to look at Kate. "It's a beautiful morning, isn't it?"

Ben smiled, reached over, and touched his wife's hand. "Emily, my dear, you always can find something beautiful just because you are beautiful."

Watching, Kate thought of another man with Ben's same broad expanse of shoulders and wished he were here. She longed to have someone care for her in that special way. Then she thought of Luke, his ragged breathing, so close to her face, his intense, yet tender, look. But, no, she must not think about that. She shook the thoughts from her mind.

"Pearl, what is your favorite color?"

Pearl looked up, her face in deep concentration. "I like all the colors, Kate, but I suppose my favorite is yellow. Yes, yellow like the sun. It's so cheery."

"Yellow it is." She remembered she still had some yellow dotted Swiss she'd ordered once, then decided looked too young for her. It would be perfect for Pearl.

"Why do you ask?"

"Oh, I am planning something, but it's to be a surprise, so that means I can't tell you just yet."

"Kate's full of surprises," Emily said. "Remember the dress with smocking?"

"I like smocking," Pearl said. "It's so different."

Kate smiled, deciding she'd begin the new dress tomorrow after she got off work. That would give her something to do to take her mind off Jesse before leaving for California. She remembered how shocked Emily had looked, but she'd promised it wouldn't be forever and she would return once she felt whole again.

She'd decided last night, when she couldn't sleep, to sell the gold jewelry Jesse had given her to pay for the train trip south. As for making a living, she would go to the first boardinghouse she found, just as she had when arriving in Cottage Grove. She could cook, sew, clean house; there were all sorts of things Kate Russell could do, once she made up her mind.

The minute they arrived in the church yard, Emily was the center of attention. Ben, with an arm around his wife, helped her inside, with Kate and Pearl following. They sat up front where Emily always sat when she played the piano.

Kate watched Luke come out and nod to the people. He looked happy when he saw Emily and Ben in the front row, then his eyes landed on Kate and she felt her face turn crimson as he stopped and stared for a long moment.

Luke had hoped, but not expected to see Kate again before she left on her trip. His heart was warmed by the sight of her in a dark blue dress, one he'd seen before. With a feathered hat, she looked as lovely as always and he wished now he might have said more last evening. He finally tore his gaze away and looked down at his unsteady hands.

"Shall we pray?" he said, hoping to quiet the large room, and allowing himself time to gain composure. How thankful he was that meeting always began with silent prayer.

Kate prayed and sang the hymns with gusto, her hand holding tight onto Pearl's, and she listened closely as Luke spoke about forgiveness.

"Our Lord talks about judgment in Matthew chapter seven, verse three: 'And why beholdest thou the mote that is in thy brother's eye, but considerest not the beam that is in thine own eye?' My people, we must not judge, 'For with what judgment ye judge, ye shall be judged, and with what measure you mete, it shall be measured to you again,' Matthew seven, verse two."

Forgiveness? Why had she never thought of it in this way? Not to forgive was wrong, and only hurt you more. That was why she was hurt by Jesse. He'd taken her money and her heart, and she was holding the resentment inside, wondering how God could allow this to happen. Hadn't she had enough pain in her life without this, too?

The verses Luke read suddenly had meaning to Kate. Yes, she had judged. And she had held grudges. There was Pa—not her real Pa, but he had given her a roof over her head and food to eat. Her step-brothers had not liked her, but why harbor ill feelings toward them? They were young. They weren't mean for the sake of being mean. They were just boys. And the hired hand. The one who had come into her room, forced her onto the bed. . .

Kate hadn't relived the whole scene in such a long time. But it all came back. . .she felt his hands on her, his hot breath on her neck. How could she forgive that despicable act? How could God expect her to forgive that? The others, yes, but the man who had harmed her so violently, hurting her deep within? Could she ever forgive him? Kate didn't realize she was crying until Pearl offered her a handkerchief.

Dabbing at her tears, Kate looked up to see Luke staring at her. The room was silent. Was the sermon over? The closing silent prayer? How long had it been over before she realized it?

Soon they were standing, and Pearl's hand slipped inside Kate's. No words were spoken, but they didn't need to be. There was a bond here, a bond as close as she and Emily felt. God had been good to give her friends. How could she survive without them?

Kate hurried out, past the crowd, not wanting to speak to anyone, especially not Luke. Somehow she couldn't speak to him just now.

She sat in the wagon, waiting for the others to come. The rest of their Sunday would be spent quietly, praying and reading Scriptures, but Kate's would be spent at home. Alone.

"There you are," Emily called when she saw Kate in the wagon. "I wondered what had happened to you." She waited while Pearl helped her up onto the high seat.

"Wasn't that a wonderful message today?"

Kate nodded. "I agree about the forgiveness, Emily. That's why I've decided to forgive Jesse."

Pearl looked at her strangely, but wisely said nothing.

"I think Luke was looking for you, too," Emily said then.

"Well, I just don't do well with lots of people to shake hands with, people I don't know."

"Were your grandparents there?" Pearl asked Emily.

"No." Emily sat back in the seat. "I doubt that they will come back to church, or that they will ever forgive me."

"Perhaps they should have heard the message today," Pearl offered.

"Yes, perhaps they should have."

Voices were coming, and soon Ben and Luke were there.

"Kate, I couldn't let you leave without saying good morning." Luke reached up and shook Kate's hand. "Thank you for coming."

"It was a wonderful message, Pastor Luke. I have lots to think about."

"Good! Those are the words that all preachers yearn to hear."

Their eyes met and held for a long moment while Ben got into the carriage.

"I have a gift for you, but didn't realize I'd be able to present it to you in person. I'd planned on letting Emily be my messenger, and give it to you before you left for California." He removed a medium-sized package from his breast coat pocket and handed it to Kate. "I hope you like it."

Kate didn't know what to say as she looked at the crudely wrapped package. It felt like a book. She remembered another man bearing gifts and her heart sank. "Thank you, Luke. It's very thoughtful of you."

"Well, I'll let you four leave for home. I'm going to go call on a few people who are ill and couldn't come to meeting today."

Kate watched as he walked away, her mind not knowing what to think. Why had he given her a gift?

"Open it, oh, please open it," Pearl begged.

"I think you should, too," said Emily, "though I think I know what it is."

Kate thought about another time before Emily and Ben were married and how Ben had given Emily a small package. It had been a carved horse to match the first horse he'd made for her. It was such a fun time, and Emily had blushed like a schoolgirl. Kate wasn't blushing, or at least she didn't think so, though her cheeks felt hot. She removed the string and the brown wrapping paper. Inside lay a small black leather Bible.

"Oh, Kate, how perfectly beautiful." Pearl reached over and touched the cover.

"I didn't have one. I left Mama's behind at the farm. How did he know?" Kate asked.

"He knew," Emily said, "although if I recall, I might have prompted him just a bit."

"It's wonderful." Kate opened the Bible and smelled of its newness. She loved the smell of new books. "I wish I'd thanked him properly."

"I'm sure he felt thanked," Ben said. "You can always write him a letter, which you are pretty good at."

Kate smiled. "You would think of that, Ben." She knew he was referring to the letter she'd sent him in Iowa, telling him to get back to Portland as expediently as possible. She didn't want Emily to marry the preacher man when she knew Emily loved Ben. Yes, Kate thought. That's what she'd do. Write Luke a letter of appreciation from California.

Kate had a sudden disturbing thought. If God knew everything that was to happen to you—and she knew most Christians believed that—and if He had a plan for everyone's life, perhaps that's why Emily couldn't marry Luke. Perhaps it was because God wanted him to wait for Kate.

"Never!" Kate said aloud, then jumped, startled by the loudness of her own voice. She hadn't meant to speak out loud.

"Never what?" Pearl asked.

"Oh, just something I was thinking about."

Pearl didn't press for an answer, so Kate looked out the side of the carriage, then back at the book. If this was meant to be, God better give her a sign, like He had with Moses and the burning bush. She'd never believe it otherwise.

Kate opened the Bible and read the first chapter, first verse of John. "In the beginning was the Word, and the Word was with God, and the Word was God." It gave her a sense of peace, of reality. That would be an easy verse to memorize.

They were almost home now. Kate remembered how Luke had looked as he held out his gift to her. Of course this was the perfect gift from him. Nothing frivolous or expensive, such as Jesse's jewelry—the gold she would now sell.

"Kate, by the way," Emily said once they were inside and Kate had gathered her things. "I have some great news."

Kate leaned forward. "What is it?"

Her face flushed suddenly. "God has blessed us with another child."

"Oh, Emily—"

Emily giggled in an unfashionable way. "Aren't you happy for us?"

"Of course I'm happy. How could I not be? It's wonderful! What does Ben say?"

"That I will need to be very careful this time. He's asked Sarah to come, and Pearl to stay. She can go to school here."

"That's the very thing Luke and I spoke of one day."

"At least I know what to expect this time."

"Yes. And I hope you do take it easy and rest a lot every day."

Emily hugged Kate hard. "I just know this baby is going to be strong with lusty lungs."

"I won't be here for a while, but at least you'll have Pearl and Sarah."

"We'll miss you, Kate."

"I know I'm going to miss all of you, and I haven't even left yet!"

"Are you sure this is the right answer?" Emily asked suddenly. "It could be that you should wait—"

"What, and wait for Jesse to come back?"

Emily looked surprised, as if she couldn't believe Kate had actually said that. "No, I don't mean to wait for Jesse. In fact I rather hoped you'd send him on his way, should he come back and beg your forgiveness."

"And what about the message Luke spoke on forgiveness?"

"I know. There is forgiveness and then there's using one's God-given sense. Why take the chance of being hurt again? I do hope you think this over thoroughly, Kate."

Kate gathered her few things from the bedroom and walked out to where Ben waited. He'd switched to the smaller wagon.

"I'll be by first thing Friday morning. Didn't you say the train left at 7:30?"

Kate looked at Ben. He was so feeling and caring. She didn't see how she could bear to leave her dear friends. And what might she find in California?

Would there be someone who cared about her as much? And what about Luke? Not that she intended to encourage him, but she knew he genuinely cared about her. Was it right to run from the memories, from Jesse? Would she be able to forget in California?

But if she would forgive, there was nothing to run from, the need to leave no longer existed. Emily was right. Should Jesse return, Kate would not listen to his excuses, his explanations, and his promises to treat her better. She had no reason to fear seeing Jesse. Her place was here in Oregon. Here with friends and her family, for the Galloways were like her family.

Kate started to get into the wagon and stopped. "No, it's wrong."

"What?" Ben asked. "Did you forget something?"

"No, it's just that I must tell you this, and I must do it now."

Ben's eyes looked at her quizzically. "Are you all right, Kate?"

She stepped down from the seat and grabbed the reins. "I have never felt better."

"I see a sparkle in your eyes that hasn't been there for a long while."

"Yes, I know. It's because I no longer feel depressed about Jesse. I'm ready to get on with my life, and you know what? I don't need to go to California after all."

"What?" Ben's face lit up. "Do you mean it?"

"Yes. Definitely!"

Ben threw his hat in the air, then caught it. "Isn't Emily going to be happy about that! I gotta admit we were all hating to see you leave."

"I know." Kate smiled as she threw her bonnet in the air, too. "I'm just glad I realized it before I got on the train. I want to be here to help Emily, to be part of the anticipation of the new baby."

Ben took her hand and squeezed it hard. "Let's go in and tell Emily and Pearl."

Kate stuck her hat back on her head and burst into song, singing one of the hymns they had sung earlier in church, "I am persuaded that He is able. . . ," and suddenly the sun came out from behind a low layer of clouds and seemed to beam right on Kate. Was this the sign she'd asked for? Could it be something as simple as this? She smiled, as tears filled her eyes. She was God's child. She'd never been more sure of anything in her entire life.

Chapter 14

O nce Kate decided not to go to California, she felt a contentment, a peace, like nothing she'd ever felt before. It was wonderful, and she knew she had made the right decision. She found herself humming on the job once again and couldn't wait to come home to work on Pearl's dressing gown and dress. She would add a few rows of smocking on the bodice since Pearl liked it so well. The yellow would set off her fair complexion nicely.

She didn't go to the Galloways' on Saturday nights but took the streetcar on Fridays instead. If Ben or Emily wondered about it, they never said. Emily had mentioned how happy she was that Kate had not gone to California, asking one day if she was over Jesse.

"Of course," Kate said with a laugh. "Out of sight, out of mind."

"I was so fearful you'd like it better there and not come back."

"You went, and it didn't change your mind."

Emily's face glowed. "But I had Ben and a whole new life opening up."

"And I would have had you, an expected baby, Ben, Sarah, and Pearl to come back to."

"And Luke?" Emily asked in a teasing way.

"Luke?" Kate looked down at the floor. "Luke is a good friend, for certain. He's part of the reason I stayed, because he helped me to see how my thinking was all wrong."

"And was that the only reason?" Emily persisted.

"Yes, of course."

Days turned into weeks. Kate finished more baby clothes and started a dress for Sarah. Emily was doing well, not having any of the troublesome symptoms of her last pregnancy.

A slushy, wet November turned into December, and Kate wrapped her gifts. She wondered what she might make for Luke. She could hardly leave him off her list, but what would be appropriate to give a friend who was also a minister? She finally decided on a pair of woolen socks.

Luke stopped by early one Sunday afternoon. Kate was surprised to answer the knock and find him standing there. She had never gotten over the anticipation, the thinking it might be Jesse coming back, even now months later. She could tell Emily she was over Jesse, but down deep she knew she was not.

"Kate, I've missed seeing you on Saturday nights, and, well, I had really hoped you might come to church again."

The look in his eyes was not lost on Kate. She gripped the side of the door and invited him in.

"Thanks, but no. Let's just sit on the porch and talk."

"I baked bread. Are you sure it wasn't the smell that led you to my door?" she teased.

"Hmm, perhaps it was at that. I do seem to hit people's homes right as they're sitting down to eat. Last night I ate with a new family in the area."

"I'll slice the bread. How about a thick piece with butter and some of Emily's homemade green tomato preserves? These are from last year's tomatoes that wouldn't ripen because of all the rain."

"There's nothing I'd like better." Luke sat on a chair on the porch. "My Grandma Morrison used to make those and watermelon pickles. Ever had those?"

Kate nodded. "Just once."

Soon they were drinking coffee and having second slices of bread.

"Kate, I consider you one of my dearest friends."

Kate glanced up, waiting for Luke to say more. This didn't sound like the last conversation they'd had.

"I felt such relief when you decided not to go to California. And I know how relieved Emily was."

"It was a good decision, Luke."

"But you're staying away from the Galloways' house on Saturday nights and not coming to meeting?"

"I—well, something held me back, Luke."

"Oh? Is this something you'd care to talk about?"

Kate toyed with her coffee, then set the cup down. How could she explain that she felt if she went to his church it was for the wrong reasons? She still didn't understand what he meant that night in the garden, and she couldn't ask him about it, not ever. "I'm reading the Bible you gave me every day, and seeking direction for my life—"

"But, Kate, that's wonderful news."

Kate nodded. "Emily helps me understand it better."

Luke felt his hopes rise. No, he needed patience. God had said to be patient. Had the time come? Could he say something now. Dare he?

"And how are you doing otherwise?"

Kate's heart skipped a beat. She caught the implication. "I'm doing quite well, thank you, Pastor."

Pastor? Why was she calling him Pastor now?

"I'm happy to hear that, Kate."

She laughed then, the sound of her laughter filling the outdoors, and especially Luke's heart. Gone was the serious look on her face, the little frown lines between her eyebrows. He liked the dimples, the way her eyes twinkled. It made him feel good all over, and he had an unexplainable desire to stay in her presence. But not yet. There was a hesitancy about her, almost a fear.

"I've been reading the parables in the New Testament."

"Are you enjoying them?"

"As a matter of fact, I am." Her eyes met his steady gaze. "I especially like the Prodigal Son story and the Good Samaritan." Kate often thought of Jesse as the prodigal son. One day he'd come back a new person, and Ben would have to forgive him. It wasn't his son, but his brother, and brothers should be friends.

Luke's arm reached up, and Kate noticed the frayed seam on the cuff of his shirt. She thought about offering to turn it for him, but it wouldn't be proper. She jumped to her feet and came back a minute later with a bolt of pale blue dimity. "For Pearl. Can't you just see her wearing this? It's for Christmas."

Her eyes twinkled when she talked about people she loved. There was such beauty in her, such loving care and concern, that Luke wanted to take Jesse to task for hurting her as he had. How could a man like Jesse deserve a woman like Kate? He chastised himself immediately for judging Jesse. Jesse, one of God's creations, was just as precious to God as was Luke or Emily or Ben. Sometimes it was hard to remember that, however.

"Yes, it's lovely, Kate. I'm sure she'll like it very much."

Kate put the material away and came back outside. "It's awfully cold out here. You could come in—"

"I should be going."

"But you just came."

Luke settled back and put his hat back on the chair next to him. So she did want him to stay.

"Kate, when are you going to do something for yourself?"

"For myself?" She looked puzzled. "What do you mean?"

"You are always doing for others. Thinking of others. Just like this dress for Pearl."

Kate laughed again. "You're a fine one to talk, Luke. What are you doing if it isn't thinking of others? Helping others all the time."

"But that's my profession."

"And maybe it's partly mine, too." Her cheeks flushed as she realized what she had said. Giving and loving wasn't her profession. She did it because she loved her friends dearly, and it pleased her to see smiles and to receive hugs.

"You are a true server," Luke said then. "One who lives to serve and serves to live."

Kate frowned for a brief moment. "Oh, I see what you mean. I like that."

"Kate, I know this may be forward of me to ask, or perhaps a bit presumptuous, but as your friend and part-time pastor, I am going to ask anyway."

Kate braced herself, wondering what Luke was talking about. Sometimes he could be a man of mystery.

"I want to help you, be here for you to lean on if needed. I believe I mentioned that one night—"

"You did, but I don't understand how you can help me. I think it takes time and lots of prayer. And I am trying."

"I know you are, but sometimes it helps to pray with others about a need."

"I've always been a strong person." She thought about the day Mama died. She'd never let up for a minute. Then she'd had to rise above the cruelty done to her. Get over Charles's death. Oh, perhaps she had thought Jesse would change her life. She'd looked forward to belonging to Jesse, to being his helpmate, to having him to lean on. But as for needing him, she wasn't sure she did. She didn't want to think about needing anyone in that way again. When they left, it was far too painful to get on with life. She had leaned on Charles, too, for that brief time. And there had been Mrs. Harris who had helped her out in one of her worst moments.

"I am getting along quite well, Luke."

"Everyone needs someone at some time in their life, Kate."

"I know. I do know that, and I rely on my friends, so in a sense I am already leaning on you."

Luke knew he was handling this badly. Strange that he could get behind a pulpit and the words came out fine, words that people seemed to want to hear and words that he felt God put into his heart to speak out about. Yet, when it came to speaking with women, he found himself not expressing himself properly at all.

"Kate, I am here if ever you decide you need me in more ways than just your pastor."

Kate slipped out of her chair and walked across the room.

"I don't think God intends for me to be married, Luke. I seem to be getting along just fine the way it is now."

"You were ready to marry Jesse."

"Yes, Jesse had a way that commands your attention and love."

"And others do not?"

"Of course you have a way with all the people at your church. They love you dearly. You know that—"

"Sometimes a man needs more than just the people from his church."

"I guess I know what you're saying, Luke, but we're friends, and I want us always to be friends." The sudden thought of losing Luke's friendship troubled Kate. She didn't want that ever to happen.

"Kate, will you ever be ready to talk about what happened when you were a girl, the thing that has hurt you so deeply?"

Her heart froze. She couldn't talk about that ever.

Not to anyone.

"I'm sorry I mentioned it."

She had thought about talking it out before, but would it help, or would it only make the pain deep and wide and raw, like an open sore?

"It's just that—"

"You think people will judge you, think less of you?"

"Well, yes, I suppose that's it."

"There is nothing you could ever do, or have ever done, that would change my thoughts and feelings about you."

She sat down and stared into Luke's face. His intense gaze mirrored love. She'd seen it before, but hadn't understood it. Now it was as if God was revealing it to her for the first time. She swallowed hard, knowing that God loved this man, just as God loved her. He loved everyone, in spite of what they had done in their lives.

"I—don't know if I can tell you everything—" Her voice grew small and tight as she wadded a hankie in her hand. "Mama had been gone for so long. It seemed like forever, and I was so tired of the farm and all the work—the heat and the same chores day in and day out."

"Farming is like that."

"I wanted to leave, but I was barely sixteen. Pa—who I had found out wasn't my real pa—needed me to work there. He'd never let me go. I knew that. Besides, where would I go? I had no relatives that I knew of." Kate leaned back, putting her hand over her eyes as if to shield her face. "Pa had hired a new man earlier that summer. Deke was his name. I didn't like him from the first day. He seemed to watch me constantly. Pa let him come in and eat supper with us. I'd feel his eyes on me, but when I'd look up, he'd look away real quick."

"Did you mention this to your father?"

"It wouldn't have mattered if I did."

"I'm sure you're right."

Kate shook her head. "I keep thinking about the forgiveness thing and I try to forgive Deke—I know what you said is true about us all being God's children—and how we all do wrong things."

Luke leaned over and took her hand gently. "Kate, it's fine. You don't need to talk about it."

"But I do. Maybe it will make the terrible ache go away. I've prayed that I'd forget that hot afternoon—prayed I'd never see his face in my thoughts—"

"You cannot forget, Kate. You can forgive the deed, but the memories stay. You must go beyond the memory and realize it wasn't your fault."

"Pa was gone. So were Carl and John. He came in after the noon meal—into the house. . .staring at me." Kate stopped and felt the silence around her. Why was it so difficult to breathe? Why did she feel as if she was suffocating? Then she knew why. He was there, pulling her, forcing her into her bedroom and she couldn't get away. He stuffed a handkerchief into her mouth, and it smelled of sweat and grease.

Kate leaned forward and cried out, "No, don't do this. . .just go away! 'I'm never going to leave,' he told me. 'I'll always be here.' I tried to get away, and his ring caught my cheek as he pinned me down."

"Kate, it's over now. It's over, and you can set your mind free."

"But I knew, I knew that I'd never be free of him, so I took the money and Mama's mare and ran away."

"You did what you had to do to survive. God was watching over you then, Kate. He loved you. Who knows but what your guardian angel was there leading you, helping you to get away?"

Kate swallowed. "Yes. That's true. I can see it now. Why didn't Pa see me on my way into town? And there was just enough money to take me on the train—I believe God was watching out for me."

"And so the hate and anger must leave your heart. They are such destructive forces to our souls."

Kate nodded. "I know that now. When I arrived in Cottage Grove, I went to the boardinghouse and Mrs. Harris took me under her wing. It was there I met Charles, and we later married, though it took me a long time to say yes. I never told him about what happened to me."

"Kate, my poor Kate. You were so young—a victim of your circumstances. How could anyone ever hold that against you?"

"I didn't want to take the chance."

"And you had a happy marriage?"

"In some ways I suppose, but the memory of that afternoon always came flashing back whenever he touched me. . . ."

"God can heal broken hearts and memories. He is there for you to turn to when the bad memories come back."

"I turned from God for so long, Luke. After what happened, I just couldn't believe as Mama did. I was bitter, too, because she died."

"But you are seeking Him now, Kate. I've seen the hunger in your eyes, watched while Emily speaks of her God, watched when I read the Scriptures the times you have attended meeting."

"Yes, I am searching for answers—"

He looked at the mass of curls he had longed to touch for so long. He wanted to take her in his arms and hold her forever, but it wasn't right. He was her friend, someone she had finally told her secret to. He could not betray that trust now.

Kate wiped at her tears, feeling better than she had in a long time. "It's going to take time. All things take time."

"Just like your getting over Jesse."

"Yes, just like Emily getting over the loss of her baby—"

"And you losing your baby son and your wife."

Luke nodded. "Time heals all wounds."

Kate looked at Luke and smiled. She knew how she must look with her eyes all red-rimmed, but she didn't care. For the first time in a long while she wasn't worried about her dress or her hair. And she knew that Luke understood. She had no secrets from him. She wasn't sure if that was good, but he was her friend. She'd told him that earlier and hoped he would always be her friend. He was the kind of friend everyone needed.

"Let's pray for God's love to fill you and for Him to take away the memories of that day." Kate closed her eyes, her hands folded in her lap. "O God, You love each one of us. You especially love Kate, as You have since the day she was born. Fill her with happy thoughts, God. Let her know and experience Your grace, Your power, Your might."

Long after Luke had gone, Kate sat at the table, looking at the flame flickering in the oil lamp. There was such peace in her heart. She'd never had this special feeling before. Was this what it meant to belong to God, to truly belong to God? Mama had belonged—Kate had always known that—and Mama had smiled when Pa said ugly things to her. Mama, who was tired from yet another pregnancy, worked hard, trying to do the things Pa expected. She never said an unkind word or snapped back. Kate could remember all sorts of things now. Mama had loved God. She was God's child, just as she, Kate, was God's child. She'd always been and always would be. And some day she would see Mama in heaven. She had wanted to believe that before, and now she did. She truly believed that one day again she would be in Mama's presence.

Chapter 15

It was Friday, almost a week after Luke had been by, and Kate had just finished eating a simple meal of leftovers when she heard the sound of horses prancing up to her gate. It was a familiar sound—a fast trot, the sudden stopping, then a loud voice calling out, "Whoa!"

Her heart nearly stopped. She couldn't move as she heard the clink of the gate opening and shutting, the sound of heavy footsteps on her porch, and then the knock at the door. Jesse. No other man sounded quite like Jesse.

The handle moved and before Kate could get there, the door opened and Jesse was in the room, filling it with his presence. "Kate!" Before she could say a word, he'd swept her into his arms, crushing her body close to his. "Oh, how I've missed the sight of you."

The beard was thicker now, and his hair was much longer than she remembered, but the dark eyes twinkled as always, the voice the same deep tone.

"I—"

But he shushed her with his finger touching her lips. "No, let me explain." A second later he removed a money purse from his belt and peeled off six twenty dollar bills. "Here's what I borrowed, plus interest."

"You've been gambling."

His eyes glittered. "Yes, and been lucky, as you can see. I'm paying Ben back, too, and we'll still have enough to get married on, plus build a house, since that other one sold. It can be right here in Portland. Those lots in Salem weren't the best I've seen."

As always Jesse's appearance electrified her. He had a magical charm she found irresistible. And yet. . .Kate's hand went to her forehead. "This is all so sudden and unexpected. I don't know what to say." Where had her rehearsed speech gone? How many times had she said it over and over in her mind? *Jesse, I cannot love you anymore. I want you to leave.* She wanted to say those words, had thought she could when or if Jesse returned, but now that he was here, smiling at her in that boyish way of his, she found her lips sealed tight.

"There's only one thing to say," Jesse said, sweeping her close again. "Say 'yes,' my love."

"But you left."

"I had to. I'll explain why."

"No need for explanations, Jesse, but you might have left word with someone. We were all worried." Kate thought of the past several months and all the pain and heartbreak she had gone through. Now he came whirling in as if nothing had happened, as if she could just forget and go on with it.

"I know how it looks, but if you only knew how much I missed you and wanted to be with you again." He looked at her imploringly. "I could hardly wait to get back here from southern Oregon."

"Southern Oregon?" At the thought of her childhood home, her insides tightened.

"Yes. I was working in a mine. Making far more than I make working for Ben."

"You took Ben's money."

"It was owed me."

Kate thought of what Emily had said, but it was better to leave that between them. She looked away, a bitterness rising in her mouth. "I gave you up," she said finally. "I've started rebuilding my life. I've been thinking a lot about God and the plans He has for me."

"And those plans don't include me?" His eyes bored into hers, pleading with such earnestness it melted her, as it always had. Dare she believe him this time? Could Jesse have reformed?

"I'm going to make it up to you, Sweetheart. I promise."

But I don't know if I can forget, she wanted to say. She'd forgiven Jesse that day in church, but she could never forget.

"I have a ring," Jesse said then. "You want to see?" He whipped it out of his breast pocket and slipped it on before Kate could protest. "With this ring I thee wed."

Tears sprang to her eyes. Jesse's saying 'thee' seemed a mockery. She took it off. "I don't think so, Jesse."

"Oh, Sweetheart, I'm so sorry I hurt you that way. I never meant to. I wanted to get in touch, but we were so busy I didn't have time."

"Ben's getting a telephone put in."

"See? That's what I mean. If he'd had a telephone before, I'd have called and let you know what was happening."

Kate leaned against his thick chest, her heart pounding so hard she could scarcely breathe. Jesse had come back. Jesse had returned the money, plus more. Jesse loved her. He'd bought a ring to prove his love. His eyes told her he was genuinely sorry and that he truly cared. How could she doubt him? How could she not say yes to his proposal? But what would Emily and Ben say? And Luke? Was this part of God's plan for her? If not, why would He have allowed Jesse to return?

"Are you going to Ben's now?"

"Yes, soon. I'll pay the money back—though I think I earned it—and see if I can get my old job back. I promise to work hard and leave the cards alone. I know that my gambling bothers you."

Kate wanted to believe Jesse. She wanted to believe that things would work out between them, yet doubt crept through her veins. It was hard to push the hurt aside—hard to think about Jesse and her starting over.

"Emily's expecting another baby."

A wide grin erupted across Jesse's face. "That's wonderful news. I know how badly they felt their loss before."

"You might have stayed to help out."

"I can't handle death well. It was the same when Pa died. Nobody thought I cared because I didn't come home, but I just couldn't."

Kate didn't like death, either. She'd had more than her share to deal with, but sometimes one had to deal with the hurts and pains of life. Didn't Jesse realize that?

"Let's go over to Ben's now to tell them we're getting married," Kate suggested.

Jesse stiffened for a moment, then relaxed as he cupped Kate's chin with his big hand and lifted her face to meet his gaze. "Honey, I don't have the courage to face Ben just yet. You don't know the animosity he feels toward me, the hateful things he's said in the past."

"He said hateful things?" Kate knew how Ben felt, but didn't think he would verbalize his feelings. He was more apt to turn the other cheek, as the Bible suggested. "He's different now," she said. "He believes in forgiving and letting go."

"Not the Ben I know."

"Give him a chance," Kate said.

"I'll go tomorrow; I just can't face him tonight."

"Where will you stay then?"

"I found a boardinghouse about two miles from here. They have room for me, and it's close to you. Oh, Kate," he pulled her close again, "I wish I could stay with you, but I must think of your reputation."

"I almost went to California."

"California! Why would you go there?"

"I felt I had to get away."

"Because of me?"

"Yes. I was just so depressed, Jesse. Nothing seemed the same after you left, and I couldn't get you out of my mind and my heart."

"I'm so sorry, my darling." He touched her hair. "I never wanted to make you depressed, but I'll make it up to you."

"You can, Jesse, if you'll just be truthful and don't leave me again."

"I won't. Not ever," he promised, holding her at arm's length. "You're such a beautiful woman. How could I be so lucky to find you waiting for me? You're far more than I deserve."

Kate smiled. Jesse came up with words sweeter than any she had ever heard. She doubted that Ben, as much as he loved Emily, told her such things.

Jesse left after a cup of coffee and more hugs. "I love you, Kate. That's all you need to remember." He lifted her hand and kissed the ring and her finger. "I'll pick you up tomorrow from work."

"Are you sure?"

"I promise."

"What will you do during the day?"

"Go talk to Ben about my old job. And tell Emily how happy I am about the baby."

Kate didn't sleep well that night. She'd read Psalm 37 before going to bed, and the words haunted her. "Trust in the Lord and do good. . . . Delight thyself also in the Lord; and he shall give thee the desires of thine heart. Commit thy way unto the Lord; trust also in him; and he shall bring it to pass."

She prayed for guidance, but Jesse's face and his smile kept breaking through the prayer. He affected her as no other man ever had. Was this a wrong step she was taking? But she must give it a try. Sleep finally came, only to be interrupted by Ben's angry face, Emily's disbelieving one. . .and Luke—she couldn't determine the look on his bearded face.

Kate finally rose, though it was still dark. Today would be wonderful. Jesse would make amends with Ben. Jesse and Kate would plan their wedding, a small one since Kate had been married before. She liked thinking about having Sarah for a mother and Pearl for a sister.

She dressed into her best calico, knowing Jesse would like the full, sweeping skirt, the bright colors. It wasn't appropriate for work, but an apron would keep it clean.

A new baby. . .a wedding. . .so much going on, Kate could hardly contain her excitement. "I love Jesse," she said, whirling around the front room of her small house. "I love Jesse, and Jesse loves me."

The streetcar clanged up the road just as she got to the end of her walk. Smiling, she lifted her skirts as she got on. Yes, it was going to be a very nice day.

Chapter 16

J esse was sweeter than he'd ever been. It wasn't enough to pursue Kate with his presence; he also continued to bring her presents. More jewelry. Flowers. A book of poems. Still Kate wavered. She had not seen Emily and wanted to tell her about Jesse's plans.

Jesse didn't come on Friday. "Because I have business plans," he explained to Kate the day before. And so, at the last minute, Kate decided to take the streetcar to the Galloways' anyway. She took along her handiwork to do while visiting. It was a pair of pillowcases with an embroidered initial "G." She was using a dark green since Jesse liked dark greens and browns. It was to be a surprise.

At last the streetcar stopped in front of Ben and Emily's. Ben's wagon and horses were there, but no fancy carriage or matching team of Jesse's. Probably she had missed him. She should have waited or gone straight home after all. Kate opened the gate and hurried up the walk.

Sarah Galloway greeted her at the door with a hug. "One of my favorite people," she said. "You're looking wonderful, Kate."

"Has Jesse been here?" Kate asked.

"Jesse?" The eyes widened in surprise. "Why no, Child. Haven't seen Jesse since that one time he came out to the farm and—"

Emily was at the door then, a questioning look in her blue eyes. "Did I hear you asking about Jesse? I thought you had given up the idea that he'd be back—"

"Given up the idea!" Kate cried out. "I had, but then when he came back he said—" She looked at Sarah, back at Emily, and then at Ben who suddenly appeared in the foyer. "You've seen him and he's working for you and he paid you back," the words came out in a torrent.

"Kate, what are you talking about?"

They all stared at her as if she had gone daft.

"Jesse came on Monday and he said he was working for you again, Ben, and he paid me the money he had borrowed, plus more, and he's been picking me up from work, and. . ." her voice drifted off. It was obvious that Jesse had not been here, for they all seemed stupefied.

226

"Don't tell me—" Kate started to say, but the words couldn't escape past the knot in her throat. "Oh, no, it can't be—"

Kate came in, removed her shawl and hat, and sat down to help them eat the beef stew Sarah had made for supper. That is, she tried to eat, but her eyes kept swimming, her mind whirling with the words Jesse had spoken. The way he had looked at her and touched her and made promises. Always promises. How could she have been so trusting?

Finally she pushed her bowl aside and stood. "I can't stay. I need to go home. There must be a reasonable explanation."

"I'll take you," Ben said, pushing his chair back.

"It isn't necessary. I can go on the streetcar." The tears began crowding her eyes once again.

"I insist."

"Yes, Kate," Emily said in agreement.

Kate left the warm, cozy kitchen with Sarah and Pearl staring after her.

"Kate," Ben said, once they were on their way, "I'm sorry this happened. It makes me so angry at Jesse. He doesn't care who he hurts or when. You're too decent a person to fall prey to his lying ways."

"I should have known better," Kate said finally. "He is charming, and I do love him so—" Tears began running down her cheeks. "It's so silly of me, I know—"

"It isn't silly. I don't think so, not even for a minute."

"He didn't ask for his old job back with you?"

"No."

"He didn't pay you back the money he'd borrowed?"

Ben's jaw grew tighter. "No."

"You haven't seen him at all?"

"No, Kate. He wouldn't come around because he knows what I would say to him."

"He doesn't think. That's it."

"No, Kate, he doesn't think. He's never thought. He's also never suffered the consequences for his actions. Oh, he may get reprimanded from someone, and I'm sure he's seen plenty of tears, but nothing seems to register with him."

"He even said we could be married in the church." Kate held up the half-embroidered pillow case. "See? Here is a G, and I—thought we would have a wedding with Luke—marrying us—and—"

"Kate, please put him out of your mind. He'll keep coming back, I fear, and you've got to tell him once and for all that it's over."

Kate leaned back in the seat, wondering what she would do if he came to her door again. She couldn't believe he had lied to her like that. He had no intention of working for Ben again. That meant he must still be gambling, and if that was the case her money wouldn't be safe. When he got broke again—as inevitably would happen—he'd return and borrow it again.

"Ben," Kate said, touching his arm, "I need to give you something for safekeeping."

"All right, Kate. I'll help in any way I can. You know that."

Kate slipped out of the buggy seat and ran into the house. The money, in a different spot, was still there. She brought it out to Ben and asked him to put it away somewhere. "I don't want to lose it again."

After Ben had left, Kate sank against the door, not believing that Jesse could have lied to her like that. How could he look her straight in the eye and tell such boldfaced lies? What made him do it? If he didn't want to marry her, why didn't he just say so? Why lead her on, making her think that he really loved her, that he wanted to be married in the church? He wanted nothing to do with it; she knew that now.

Kate finally slept, but again her dreams were tortured. Jesse would appear, holding out his arms to her, but when she reached out, he'd float away, as if he were a wisp of angel's hair. In another dream he would call out, "Foolish, foolish, foolish Kate."

There was another face that night, a dark, evil face, and she realized it was the face of the man who had violated her body that long-ago summer day. Finally morning came.

Kate dragged herself from bed and went through the motions of getting ready for work. She was glad she had her job. It kept her busy, and once again she thought of what she would do with her life.

She knew that Luke would help her broken heart, that he would listen again, that he would offer his shoulder for support, but she couldn't do this to him. Not when she knew he cared. It was there in his eyes, in his face, as he looked at her. Kate felt his love, his concern, and didn't want to hurt him more than she perhaps already had.

At last the day was over, and she went to the Galloways' for chicken dinner because she couldn't bear to go home. Since she hadn't attended the dances for several months, she didn't worry about wearing her work dress. Besides, it was Emily's favorite one, powder blue with a high neckline lined with lace, and matching lace on the sleeves.

Luke's wagon was there when Kate arrived. She took a deep breath before going inside. She wasn't sure what she could say to him, or how he would react when she heard that Jesse had come around. One thing Kate knew: She could never be anything to Luke, not with her feelings for Jesse getting in the way. Besides, now that he knew about that afternoon of long ago, he couldn't possibly want her, no matter what he said. It didn't matter, he'd insisted, but Kate knew better. Luke deserved better than her.

Luke was on the other side of the door when Kate entered. He took her shawl and hat and asked her to step into the parlor. "I want to talk to you, Kate."

"You heard about Jesse."

"Yes, unfortunately."

"I believed him, Luke."

"Of course you did, Kate."

"You knew I would?"

"Yes."

"But how could you know?" She looked at him in disbelief. How could he know this about her, when she hadn't known it herself?

"Love is important to you. You love hard, and when you love someone as you love Jesse, it isn't gotten over so quickly, nor is it treated so lightly. You believed him, and he knew that you would."

"I thought I was over him. I was getting on with my life until—"

"Until he showed up and made you all sorts of promises."

Kate sat in a chair, then got up and paced back and forth. "He told me we could be married in the church."

"Yes, Jesse would say that. He says what he thinks you want to hear, never intending to keep his words. In fact, I dare say if you told him what he'd said the next day, he'd deny it, because in all honesty—and I'll give him credit for that much—he has forgotten what he told you."

"But how do you know that's true?" Kate asked. She was starting to realize that was exactly what Jesse did.

Luke sighed. "From what Ben told me. And I think he should know, since he grew up with Jesse. It's like the old saying I found in a collection of poems, 'Oh, what a tangled web we weave when first we practice to deceive.'" Luke sighed. "I've known pathological liars before, Kate, and Jesse fits the pattern."

Kate sat looking out the window, her heart not wanting to believe it had happened again. She'd been forewarned about Jesse. Why had she not heeded the advice? Why hadn't she believed Ben, one of her oldest and dearest friends? He only wanted what was best for her, as had Emily and Luke.

"I am not entertaining notions about going away this time," Kate said finally. "I'll hold my head high and get on with things. I'll be here when that baby is born and help out as much as I can."

"I'm sure Emily will be glad to hear that." Luke smiled warmly. "And then I hope the time will come when you'll start being good to yourself."

Luke didn't mention his concern for her, and Kate didn't blame him. How could he even care for her now after what she'd allowed to happen?

Dinner was wonderful, and Pearl looked especially beautiful, Kate thought. After the dishes were done and the men sat on the front porch talking and the women prepared everything for Sunday, Kate decided she needed to go home. She figured Ben would offer to take her, but it was Luke who stood and said he had to leave early, anyway.

She felt awkward as they headed for her home. She sensed he wanted to say something to her, but he remained quiet. His strong hands held the reins with a firm grip and Kate chewed on her bottom lip nervously. She wanted to break the silence, but everything had already been said. Luke had his ministry. Kate had her job. Ben and Emily would have a baby to fill their house soon with its crying.

"Kate," Luke finally spoke as he pulled up in front of her house, "I admire you, as I always have. Surely you know that."

"I've made a few unwise decisions."

"And choices. 'Tis true."

"Thank you for bringing me home, Luke."

"Will I see you tomorrow at church?"

"I—don't know."

"May I come pick you up?"

"Not tomorrow," she finally said.

"What are you going to say when Jesse returns?"

"I haven't thought about it that much." It was not true, because she had thought about it constantly. It was the one thing she'd rehearsed in her mind countless times.

"I think you'd better decide, because Jesse is coming to see you tonight."

"He is? But how—"

"How do I know?" Luke pointed over his shoulder. "He's waiting down the block."

Kate looked in the direction Luke pointed. Sure enough, she could see a shadow there, but how could Luke know it was Jesse? She couldn't make out the shapes at all.

"Do what you must," Luke said, "and be firm about it. Whatever you do, stick up for your rights. Don't kowtow to him."

Luke left, and minutes later the shape moved on up the street toward Kate. It was Jesse, driving a buggy.

"And what were you doing with the preacher man?" Though it was dark, Kate could see the fire shooting from his eyes, as he hopped out of the carriage.

"Luke brought me home from Emily and Ben's."

"Isn't that dandy! And you a betrothed woman."

Kate could scarcely believe she was hearing right. Jesse was talking about her being betrothed and then minding because the preacher brought her home? How could he have such a small mind? How could he possibly object?

"As I told you before, Jesse, Luke is a good friend."

"A friend who is sweet on you—"

"Not that it matters," Kate broke in.

"It matters to me!"

"But how could it, Jesse? You're never here when you say you are going to be, nor do you do things you say you are going to do. You were working for Ben, so you said. But it isn't true."

"So you believe my brother more than you believe me."

"That isn't fair, Jesse—"

"What do you mean it isn't fair? My brother turns your head with lies about me. This Luke loves you, and you won't admit it. You just go around believing all these horrible things about me!"

Kate stood with her mouth hanging open. She couldn't believe Jesse was saying any of this. How could he possibly act in this manner? What was wrong with him? And suddenly as she looked at the face of the man she thought she loved, she knew him for what he was. He was selfish and arrogant, only caring about his own feelings, not caring whom he hurt or whom he trod upon. Jesse got what he wanted, and heaven help anyone who got in the way.

"I think you'd better leave," Kate said through clenched teeth.

"Leave?" His hands were on her shoulders. "Leave, just like that?"

"What do you expect me to say, Jesse?"

"That you love me."

"Don't start that—"

"What do you mean, 'Don't start that'? I love you, woman. Why wouldn't I expect to hear it from you?"

"Jesse, it's over."

"After all we've been, you're going to toss it away for the likes of that sissy-pants preacher?"

Kate stood ramrod straight as anger boiled inside her. She could never remember feeling this mad. She pointed her finger toward the buggy. "Just go, Jesse. Leave me alone. I never want to see you again."

"Now, Kate, you're just a bit miffed—"

"It's more than that." And without another thought she turned and entered the house, slamming the door hard.

Later, long after the sound of the racing horses' hooves left the street in front of her house, Kate wondered how she could have said what she did. And how she could feel so relieved now. Gone was the earlier hurt, desolate feeling in the pit of her stomach. She felt good about things again, and she knew how truly beautiful life was. All her friends would rejoice with her because God had helped her make the right choice. Yes, she had a lot to be thankful for. A tremendous lot.

Chapter 17

If Kate thought Jesse was to be gotten rid of easily, she had another think coming. When she left work on Monday, the familiar carriage and team of horses was waiting at the corner.

"Kate, we need to talk."

"I have nothing to say to you, Jesse."

"I was wrong, I admit it, but I intend to change my ways."

"It's impossible, Jesse."

"And why do you say that?"

Kate was taking big, purposeful steps, while Jesse followed her with the horses prancing at a slow gait. "Go away, Jesse."

"It's that preacher man, isn't it?" Jesse's jaw was taut.

Kate stopped and glared, hands on hips. "I told you we were good friends."

"Then why won't you listen to me?"

"Because I listened one time too many."

"But I'm going to change." He gave her that little-boy look. "I'm willing to try."

"And I say it's too late. Go see your other girlfriend."

"Other girlfriend! What's that supposed to mean?"

"Only another woman would keep you away for days, would make you lie." Yet even as she was saying it, Kate knew there was another reason. Gambling. That could make one forget all sense of time and honor, according to both Luke and Ben.

"It isn't true," Jesse was saying, but Kate kept walking. "You don't know what my mother did to me when I was a kid."

"Yes, I do. She loved you and tried to bring you up in the proper way. Not to lie, not to cheat, to be an honest citizen."

"Now you sound like all the rest of them."

"Yes, thank God, I do," Kate said proudly, her head held high. "And it's about time."

Jesse finally turned the carriage around and left. A shaken Kate got on the streetcar and went home.

Home had never looked so good. The curtains she'd made last year were bright and colorful, like her heart felt inside her. Jesse wasn't the only man in the world. There'd be someone else. She could love again, eventually. She'd start going to the dances again, because she still couldn't bring herself to believing it was wrong. Dancing to her was fun, a way to meet people. She knew all the dances and especially loved some of the Scandinavian Schottisches, the round dances, the polkas, and the waltz. Yes, she would go the next weekend. If Jesse happened to be there, which was entirely possible, she'd smile, hold her head high, and refuse to dance with him. And if she had the opportunity, she'd warn all of the other young women at the dance hall.

Then it was Saturday, and Kate worked overtime to finish filling an order for Mr. Roberts. "It's good to have you humming again," Mr. Roberts said when he stopped by Kate's work station.

Kate smiled. "Yes, I guess I hum when I'm happy and content." And she was happy, as her life was in order once again, and it felt good. She didn't allow herself to think about Jesse. That chapter in her life was over.

Luke was already there, wearing a dark suit and tie, when Kate arrived for the Saturday night chicken dinner. Kate raised her eyebrows. "A suit for Saturday night?"

"Yes, I'm going somewhere afterwards. I'm taking you to the dance, Miz Katherine Russell."

"You're taking me to the dance? But—" Kate sputtered, "—you don't believe in dancing."

"Perhaps it's time I saw what is so enthralling about a dance. You know Jesus ate with sinners, so why can't I go to a dance?"

"So, now you say we're sinners?"

Luke's face grew suddenly intense. "Aren't we all, Kate? According to God's Word we are, but I wasn't singling you out because you dance, and you know it."

She smiled and looked at him. He wasn't tall or broad-shouldered. He didn't boast about his accomplishments, though she was sure he could have, if he'd wanted to. He was just a nice, thoughtful, honest man.

He was looking at her in a way that made her heart unexpectedly skip a beat. "I can't believe that you'd go to a dance."

"I want to see what you see in it."

"I haven't been in so long, it may not be as I remembered."

"I doubt that."

After dinner, a real treat with Sarah cooking and Pearl baking the traditional apple pie, Kate and Luke left for the local barn dance. Ben and Emily stared in disbelief, but said nothing.

Luke couldn't quite believe it himself as he pulled into the area for the buggies just the other side of the grange hall. It was a good thing Luke's father was no longer living, because he would have died from shock, Luke knew.

Kate was beautiful in a lavender calico with white lace on the neckline and sleeves, and Luke felt proud as he took her arm and they went inside.

Soon the music began, and Luke watched as Kate waltzed in the arms of a man Luke knew to be the owner of the mercantile store by the church.

Kate came over, all breathless, when the dance was over. "You don't need to wait for me," she said. "I can always get a ride, or even walk home. It isn't that far, you know."

"I wouldn't dream of missing seeing you dance," Luke said, his eyes twinkling, as Kate was whisked off by another partner. Soon they were polkaing across the crowded floor.

As Luke sat watching, his heart grew heavy. It was a temptation, for he wanted more than anything to know how to dance, to be the next man who walked up to Kate and whirled her off in his arms. He had wanted to hold her for such a long time now. How could he ease the aching hurt deep inside? Yet, he knew how Kate felt. She'd said more than once that they would always be good friends. That had been sufficient in the beginning, but now he wanted it to be more, much more.

When Kate came back, she sat and took deep gulps of air. "I haven't been dancing in so long, I forgot how a polka can wear you out."

"You look wonderful out there," was all he could manage to say.

"I do?" Her eyes twinkled. "And how is that?"

"The way you dance. The way you talk to people, how everyone knows you and loves you as I do."

"Oh, Luke, it's true that everyone knows me, but as for the love—"

And then her face reddened as she realized what he'd said. He'd mentioned many times his concern, but never, ever had he said he loved her. How could that be? "Luke, you really don't need to stay."

"But stay I will."

Soon Kate was in the arms of yet another man, and Luke watched carefully as they danced. It looked easy. How could he have imagined dancing to be impossible to learn? After watching for the entire dance, Luke felt he could now waltz. And if he stumbled, Kate would help him, teach him how to do the steps.

Then his father's face flashed through his mind, and he knew it could not be. What had he been thinking of anyway, coming to a dance, being tempted just so he could hold the woman he loved? He must leave. Now. Kate would have a ride, hadn't she said so before?

Luke hurried past dancers, past the punch table, and finally was outside.

A full moon seemed to single him out as he leaned against the building and gulped the fresh air. "Oh, God, how wrong I've been. I can see that now," he cried aloud. He regained his composure and walked to his buggy. "I can't have her. Why have I been fighting it? I must give her up. It's the only way. . . 'Create in me a clean heart, O God,' " Luke recited, closing his eyes. " 'And renew a right spirit within me.' "

He heard the sounds of fiddle music and of voices mingling with the warm night air, and he took another deep breath. How could he have fallen like this? How could he have thought, even for the briefest of moments, that this was all right for him, that nobody need know, that he wouldn't have to answer to God? And how could he ever make right the part about loving a woman who did not believe as he did? Paul's admonition about being unequally yoked came to mind. Kate had come a long way since he first met her, but she longed for desires of the flesh, and Luke must forget her. It was the only way—God's way.

He hitched the horses, nuzzling their manes. Both tossed their heads as if saying, "Let's go. Let's leave." Still Luke wished he could get a message to Kate. He didn't want her to worry about him. Just when he'd decided to ask the man standing in the doorway to deliver his message, he heard a voice behind him.

It was Kate. "Luke! You're leaving."

He nodded. "Yes. It was wrong for me to come, I realize that now." He smiled, but did not look at her face. "I was going to leave a message with that man over there. You said you could get a ride home—"

She touched his arm. "Yes, of course, but perhaps that isn't what I want."

"You go on back, " he pointed toward the grange hall. "Have a good time, and I'll be talking to you later."

She grabbed his arm again and implored him to look at her. "I want to leave with you. I don't want to stay."

"Nonsense! You're the most popular woman there." He wanted to say the prettiest, too, but did not.

"That may well be, Pastor Morrison, but I should know if I want to stay or not. And I say I'm ready for you to take me home, if that's all right."

Luke let the reins slip for a moment. Why didn't Kate want to stay? Why did she think she had to come with him?

"It doesn't matter to me if you stay. I mean that, Kate."

As Kate heard "Turkey in the Straw," she envisioned finding a partner and dancing to the familiar tune, but suddenly she knew—she wasn't even sure when she had realized—that she didn't want to go back in and dance. She didn't care if she stayed until the last song was played. Suddenly the reason was infinitely clear as she looked at the man sitting high on the buggy seat, the man she had met nearly two years ago, whom she had admired but had never thought of loving. Oh, dear, God, it couldn't be. Her fingers wound through the spaces in her shawl as the realization hit. She, Kate Russell, loved this man. She wanted to be part of his life, to sit across from him at the kitchen table each morning and each night, to share his bed, to hold him close. How could she have not known? How could she have thought what she had with Jesse was right and good?

Kate climbed up alongside Luke, shaking the reins. "Let's go," she said softly.

Luke breathed easier once they were on the road heading east on Foster Road. Soon they'd pass the Galloway home. It was still early. Perhaps they would be up. Should they stop? But of course every one would want to know why they left the dance early. Ben and Emily would be relieved. Sarah would look at him questioningly. As for Pearl, she'd smile that shy little smile and ask him to come in to have a cup of coffee and a piece of apple pie left over from dinner. He wanted to say something to Kate. He hoped she might start the conversation, but out of the corner of his eyes he could see her sitting with her back straighter than usual, her face pointed straight ahead. What was going on in that head of hers? Would he ever be able to talk freely with her again?

As if reading his mind, Kate cleared her throat. "I think it would be nice to stop by the Galloways' for a piece of Pearl's apple pie."

He laughed. "You were reading my mind, Kate."

She nodded, still looking straight ahead. "I believe God is directing me." A smile played at the corners of her mouth. Luke stared, saying nothing.

"I know what you're thinking, Luke."

"You couldn't possibly know."

"Yes, I could. And I'm going to tell you, but then you must tell me if I'm correct."

"All right. That sounds fair enough."

"You felt guilty about the dance. You knew you had to leave before you were tempted, and because you always listen to God's voice, you prepared to leave."

"Go on." He liked the way her chin jutted out in that determined way, but he shook the thought from his mind.

"I also know that you think we can be nothing more than friends—"

"Now, Kate—"

"No." She held her hand up. "Please let me finish. I discovered something tonight, and it would have never happened if you hadn't taken me to the dance. You see," she turned her head, hoping he would look at her, if only for a moment, "I finished the Virginia Reel and looked where you'd been sitting, and my heart nearly stopped. I—I had this feeling of loss wash over me—sort of like when Mama died—but it was different. Oh, Luke, please look at me while I'm talking to you." Tears had formed in her eyes and were spilling down her cheeks.

Luke shifted in his seat and turned ever so slightly. Their eyes met, and it was as if he saw the inner light, as if he felt God's presence right there between them saying, *See, my son, you gave up what you knew you couldn't have, and so I am giving her to you.* He took Kate's gloved hand and held it tight.

"I'm ready to hear more—"

Kate's eyes never left Luke's face as she told him how she felt, how she had felt for a long time without realizing it. "I've been seeking God's will for my life," she continued. "I've prayed, read the Scriptures, and I feel I belong to God now. I want to know Him better, want Him to guide and direct me always." She paused, listening to the night sounds. "Was it that way with you, Luke, when you first began to believe?"

Luke nodded. "It's always been that way, Kate, because I can't remember a time when I didn't feel God's love or His presence."

"And what did He tell you tonight at the dance?"

Luke gazed into Kate's eyes and went on. "That I must give you up, that it wasn't right to want something I couldn't have."

"And God told me at the same time that I was going to look just as nice wearing gray."

"Oh, Kate," was all Luke could say as he turned and touched the sides of her face, his finger tracing the tiny scar on her cheek. The horses had stopped in front of the Galloways' as if they knew that's where they were going, but neither Luke nor Kate noticed. Luke's arms went around her and pulled her close—as he'd always wanted to, as he'd dreamed about so many times before.

When they looked at the house, Luke and Kate saw it was ablaze with lights. "It's an emergency," Kate said, fear gripping her. The baby. Oh, she hoped it didn't have to do with the expected baby.

"It looks that way, doesn't it?"

They knocked on the door then walked down the hall toward the voices. Everyone was sitting around the table with a young blond-haired man drinking a cup of coffee.

"Luke! Kate!" Ben exclaimed. "Come and meet Emily's little brother, Paul."

"Paul? Is that what the emergency is?" Kate asked, feeling sudden relief.

"Yes," Emily hugged her good friend. "I knew Paul would come one day, and he arrived on the evening train from California, just minutes after you and Luke left for the dance."

A shy Pearl sat on the sidelines, her eyes watching the tall, thin young man. His hair was the color of straw, eyes a cornflower blue. When Pearl saw Kate watching her, she blushed. Kate reached over and squeezed her hand. "Pearl, you look lovely tonight." Pearl squeezed her hand back, but said nothing.

"Paul was telling about the train trip and how he'd hated to leave the homestead, but knew it was time to strike out on his own," Emily said, "especially now that Mama is living with Mary."

"That's right," Paul added. "Tom doesn't care about the place and the girls are married and have their own homes now."

"Well, I'm just glad you came," Ben said. "I can always use an apprentice."

After everyone had another cup of coffee, Kate wondered if Luke was going to say anything. She reached for his hand and pulled him out to the middle of the room. "It looks as if this is the night for surprises."

"Oh?" Every eye was on the couple.

"Luke, aren't you going to say something?"

He grinned and put an arm around her. "Why should I when you seem to be doing a good job of it?"

She blushed and looked at Emily who was big with her baby. Ben stood, looking perplexed. Sarah had a twinkle in her eye, as if she had already guessed what the surprise might be. Pearl had her hands to her face and stood watching her friends. Paul didn't know what to think, so stood staring at Kate.

"Well," Kate beamed at her future husband. "Luke is going to—that is we have agreed that Luke is going to start courting me—"

There was a thunderous applause, and then Emily was hugging her best friend. "I never dreamed it would happen, Kate. I knew how Luke felt so very long ago, but you were so infatuated with—"

"Don't say that name," Sarah Galloway said, breaking into the conversation.

Soon all arms were around Kate, drawing her close while Luke stood aside and beamed.

"The church?" Ben asked.

"Of course I'll still preach, as that is what I know."

"And I'm eager to be a preacher's wife," Kate added. "I realized tonight that dancing was no longer an important part of my life. I'm ready to be the sort of wife Luke needs."

"Oh, Kate, I can hardly believe it!" Emily cried.

"I know. Neither can I."

"And God has brought you two together as sure as there will be rain in the morning."

"He does work in mysterious ways," Luke said, lifting his arm. "We're going on to a new and bright future with God at the helm of our ship."

"Yes, God is foremost and uppermost in our lives," Kate added. "It took me a long time to realize that this is what I want."

"Love shall come again," Ben said. "For the two of you. You loved and lost, but now love has come to bless you both again."

In answer Kate beamed at Luke as he held her hand tight. "I believe this calls for a prayer," he said, looking at his bride-to-be.

And as they gathered together, and Luke offered a prayer of thanks, Kate felt his arm slip over her shoulders. She had never felt more happy or content in her life. Yes, life as Luke's wife was going to be the biggest blessing of all.

Love's Tender Path

To Aunt Pearl, and especially Sarah, my great-grandmother,
who brought her family to Oregon.

Chapter 1

Pearl Galloway stood on the station platform, body erect, wide-brimmed straw hat in hand. Her brown hair braided for the trip was in a coil at the nape of her neck, while wisps of hair framed the round, broad face.

She was going to fill the position of schoolteacher in a one-room schoolhouse in the farming community of Stayton, Oregon, nestled in the lush Willamette Valley. School did not commence until mid-October, when the harvesting was over.

Pearl had hoped for a school closer by, but a teacher was needed there, and it was time she became gainfully employed. Though she was not quite eighteen, she'd taken the mandatory two-week training, passed the test, and had been accepted.

Sarah Galloway's voice interrupted Pearl's thoughts. "Thee will be missed. If thee must know, it is all I can do to see thee leave like this. And so far away."

"Mama, fifty miles isn't far. I just wish it weren't so hot."

"Perhaps it will cool off by Monday."

The sound of the train chugging down the track made Pearl's heart skip in anticipation. *I'd rather be married,* she wanted to say, rather than going off like this. But the words were locked tight inside her. She'd lamented once to Mama about not being a boy. "Since I look like a boy, I should have been one."

"I'll hear no more from thee," Sarah had said in her commanding voice. "One does not question God, Pearl Marie. If God had wanted to give me another son, then He would have."

The Galloway's hadn't been Quakers long, but Sarah used thees and thous regularly. Buxom and broadshouldered, she fanned her face while watching the train come down the track.

The train whistle sounded again, and Pearl squeezed Sarah's hand. "Mama, how do I know I can teach? What if I fail?"

"There are no failures in the Galloway family," Sarah said. "Remember what I've always taught you: Quitters never win, and winners never quit. You are so good with children; you'll be a wonderful teacher."

"Oh, I hope so, Mama."

Ben lumbered up then. "Pearl, I'm sure going to miss you."

"And I, you." She smiled at her older brother. "Now you must give my nephew, Clifford, his piggyback rides. He looks forward to them, at least twice a day."

"I think I can handle that." Ben leaned over and hugged Pearl as the train rolled to a stop. He lifted the heavy trunk while Pearl showed her ticket to the conductor.

"Is one trunk all?" the conductor asked.

Pearl nodded. She didn't own much in the way of clothes. Four dresses, her old shoes, and the good ones which she wore now. Buttoned up past her ankles, the shiny leather shoes had been Ben's farewell present. "You can't teach without new shoes," he'd said.

Sudden tears filled her eyes. She'd never been away from Mama or her family. The one blessing was that she'd board with people she knew. John and Nina Colville, who used to attend the Friends Church in East Portland, now owned a farm near the Stayton School and had invited her to stay with them.

Pearl smoothed out the skirt of her dress. Made of navy blue lawn with sprigs of blue and lavender flowers, it was a gift from Kate Morrison. The custom used to be that Quaker young ladies only wore gray or dark colors, but times were changing, and Pearl liked the brighter materials. It was fitting she would wear this dress as she traveled on the train to her first job.

Pearl hesitated on the step, ran back down, and hugged Mama hard. Sarah had never looked so forlorn as she did now with the sun shining out of a cobalt blue sky, encompassing her in a wave of heat.

"God go with thee, little one."

Pearl giggled, straightening the flower on her mother's hat. Little one. A misnomer if ever there was one. She'd always been tall and gangly for her years, and people often thought she was older than she was.

"All aboard!" called the conductor. Pearl clambered back up the steps and turned around once more to wave at her mother. Sarah was coughing into a handkerchief, and Pearl felt a wave of uneasiness. The cough was lasting too long. Why hadn't it gone away by now?

Ben waved from a thin patch of shade by the station, where the team of horses stood waiting. Soon they'd be back home, in time for the noon meal.

Pearl looked down the road as far as possible, hoping to see a certain someone come riding up. Why hadn't Paul come to say good-bye, to wish her well? Yet she was certain he had eyes for another—a small girl with laughing blue eyes and blonde curls cascading down her back. Why would he look at plain, tall Pearl?

If she'd been pretty like Nancy Whitfield, Paul Drake might have brought her to the train station—might have said he would wait for her return—might have asked if he could court her. But he had not, and now she must carry the memory of Nancy leaning on Paul's arm in church. Nancy at one end of the aisle, while she, Pearl, sat at the opposite end, wishing with all her might she could trade places.

She found a seat by the window and waved until her mother faded into the passing scenery. Pearl withdrew her hat, placing it on the rack overhead, then removed her best go-to-meeting gloves and put them in her lap. Now she could sit back and try to ignore the stifling heat that permeated the car.

The feelings for Paul were unexpected. They'd been the best of friends since his arrival in Oregon that night a year ago. Coming on the train from California, he'd found the Galloway home and been met by his sister, Emily, who cried with joy. Soon he was just part of the family.

When had Pearl's feelings changed? When had she dared to hope he might look at her in the special way Ben had for Emily, and their friends Luke and Kate had for each other? She tried to stifle the thoughts, but Paul's face came to mind often. The year that ensued had been one Pearl would carry always in her mind and heart. Pastor Luke and Kate's marriage—Emily and Ben's baby Clifford arriving with strong body and lungs. Nobody spoke of Isobelle, the baby born a year earlier, living only a few hours. How Emily had braved it, Pearl did not know. If it had been her baby— There she went again—dreaming the impossible.

She and Paul used to talk about a lot—evenings after work when he shared what he wanted out of life. Other times when he expressed his disbelief in a higher being. When she asked why he felt this way, he smiled in that shy, boyish way and said he had never seen anything happen to make him believe. This lack of belief bothered Pearl, but she kept it inside. Nobody knew, because he attended the Friends meeting each Sunday, because not to do so would have caused ire in Ben, his brother-in-law, and consternation to Emily.

Yes, Pearl realized she had nothing to despair about. If God had intended for Paul to be her husband, He would have allowed her to find a teaching job closer. This going away was a test. Pearl would prove she was capable of being on her own, and in time she would put feelings for Paul aside. Besides, she had so much to be thankful for. If Emily could live through the death of her first baby and still love God—if Kate could have her heart broken twice by Jesse and find more love in her heart for Pastor Luke, Pearl had had nothing to face by comparison.

Forget about Paul..., forget about Paul..., forget about Paul..., the wheels seemed to say as they clacked over the miles.

" 'Count Thy Blessings,' " she hummed under her breath. " 'Count thy many blessings, see what God hath done.' "

"I like that hymn," a voice said suddenly from across the aisle.

Pearl turned and stared at an older woman with kind gray eyes. "Pardon me, but was I humming aloud?"

The woman nodded. "Yes, you were. 'Count Your Blessings' is what we all must do. Seems we tend to forget how good God is and how He blesses us in so many wonderful ways."

Pearl's face flushed. "Yes, I find it to be so."

"You've certainly made this hot, windless morning much better, believe me."

Pearl leaned back and smiled. Yes, she was a child of God in every way. How dare she sit here feeling sorry for herself? She had a family who loved her. She also had a position to fill—children who needed to learn. She hoped they would be eager as she had been when she first arrived in Portland.

"And where might you be going?" the lady asked.

"To Stayton—to teach school."

"You'll be one fine teacher," the lady said. "Anyone can tell by just looking at you."

Pearl beamed. "Thank you for those kind words."

Her traveling companion was going farther, to Eugene, but the two chatted about Oregon, the land, and the way the area was growing, and soon the train pulled into the Stayton station and Pearl leaned over and hugged her new friend. "May God go with thee on the rest of thy journey."

"And also with you, child."

Soon Pearl's trunk was taken off, and the train pulled out of the station, leaving her on the deserted platform. A feeling of fear engulfed her as she stood, looking around.

Where was the man from the school board? He had promised to meet her train and would drive her to Stayton. Pearl fanned her face with her hat and tried to ignore the way her new dress stuck to her back.

A sound of thundering horses hit the hot, still air, and Pearl turned to see a man dressed in a suit and top hat alight from the carriage. He tipped his hat. "Miss Pearl Galloway? I'm Judson Rome, head of the Marion County School Board." He stood over Pearl, a fixed smile on his face. "Welcome to Stayton!"

Pearl held out a gloved hand. "I'm happy to be here, Sir."

He shook her hand. "Sir won't be necessary. It's quite acceptable to call me Judson."

"Yes, Sir, Judson," Pearl murmured.

He was tall with a determined stance, but it was the dark brown eyes with their sternness that made Pearl realize this man might be difficult to please. A sense of foreboding hit the pit of her stomach. He seemed to be sizing her up as he lifted the trunk into the back of the buggy. She couldn't tell if he approved or not; his mouth remained tight-lipped.

"We have a wonderful little school with sixteen pupils expected, as I told you in the letter—including three of mine."

Pearl twisted the handle of her valise. "I'm eager to get started, Sir. . . Judson. I understand the ride will be long."

"Yes, and unfortunately, a dry, hot one. I have brought a jug of water along."

Pearl breathed in deeply of the fresh countryside air. Newly harvested bales of hay filled pastures, and an occasional barn and farmhouse was visible from the road. She'd forgotten how much she missed farmlands after living in the city the past three years.

"It's beautiful here," she said, holding on to her hat as the horses trotted over the rough dirt road.

"I'm glad you like it."

"Can you tell me about some of the students?"

He smiled, revealing a row of even, white teeth. "My children have no mother, so they may cling to you at first, but you are not to allow it."

"No mother?"

He stared straight ahead, giving the reins a severe crack. "My wife died a year ago. It was the flu. Several died in our little community."

"I'm so sorry—," Pearl reached out, but drew her hand back. "It must have been painful for you."

He nodded, but did not look her way for a long moment. "It was. I'm looking for a mother for my children. They *do* need a mother, and I a wife."

Pearl trembled unexpectedly. As if reading her thoughts, Judson changed the subject.

"You will teach arithmetic, English, reading, and writing."

"I am prepared, Mr. Rome. . . Judson."

"We want only truths taught. Facts the students can use in their lives."

Pearl nodded again. "I understand."

"Did I hear right that you are acquainted with the Colvilles—where you'll be boarding?"

"Yes, Sir. They are Friends, as I am, and used to attend the Friends Church in East Portland. Fine people."

"I have heard they are, but I don't go along with the teachings of the Quakers."

Pearl swallowed hard. She knew people didn't understand the persuasion of the Friends, and she didn't care to discuss the reasons why. It was often best to say nothing.

"I am a Christian," he said as if that answered the question sufficiently.

"Well, we all worship one God," Pearl said then, hoping the trip was soon to be over, feeling suddenly uncomfortable without quite knowing why.

"I'll pick you up each morning and deliver you to the school, Miss Galloway."

"Oh." She didn't know what to say to that.

"The Colvilles have one small wagon, and that isn't suitable for a teacher to be transported. As you can see, my carriage is large. My sons will drive their own buggy to school each day, but I shall have Mary Alice ride with us. If not, people might talk."

"That is very kind of you, Sir. Judson." *But I don't want to be indebted,* thought Pearl. How can I possibly let this man pick me up and take me home each day? She glanced at his profile, the chin set in a formal manner, and shivered again. No, she couldn't allow this to happen.

"Mr. Rome, that is, Judson, I am used to a hay wagon; it's all we had on the Iowa farm I grew up on. I won't mind taking that to school."

His jaw tightened even more. "I want our schoolteacher to have only the best. Believe me, it's all I can do to deliver you to this crude place these people call home. I wanted you to live in my house, but people would talk, without there being a chaperone, and as luck would have it, my housekeeper quit last week."

Pearl straightened imaginary wrinkles in her dress and wished the ride was nearly over. "I will be fine at the Colvilles'—no matter how crude the dwelling, and I'd be only too happy to take their wagon to school."

"Are you always so insistent, so determined in getting your own way?" His tone was almost surly.

Pearl raised her chin. "Sir, more than anything I want to be a good teacher."

"Yes, ahem. I suppose you know we have rules which you are to adhere to in the strictest of fashion."

"I'm sure there are rules, and I can assure you I will fulfill them to the best of my ability."

He handed her a slip of paper. "These were made in the year 1875, but they apply today as well."

Pearl unfolded the sheet of paper:

RULES FOR TEACHERS

Drawn up by the school board for the good of all, including teachers and pupils. All teachers being hired by this board will read and sign accordingly.

1. Teachers each day will fill lamps, trim the wicks, and clean

chimneys, if applicable.

2. Each morning the teacher will bring a bucket of water and a scuttle of coal or load of wood for the day's session.

3. Women teachers who marry or engage in unseemly conduct will be dismissed.

4. Men teachers may take one evening each week for courting purposes, or two evenings a week if they attend church regularly.

5. After ten hours in school, teachers may spend the remaining time reading the Bible or any other good books.

6. Every teacher should lay aside from each pay a goodly sum of his earnings for his benefit during his declining years so that he will not become a burden on society.

There was a line for her signature and the date.

Pearl read each rule twice, then took a deep breath. "There should be no problem as far as I can see," she finally said.

"Good. I'm glad we're in agreement on something, Miss Galloway."

I want to make a rule of my own, Pearl wanted to say. *Teachers will be responsible for their way to and from school.* But she said nothing, and they rode the rest of the way in silence.

Later, when Judson Rome pulled into the Colvilles' dirt yard, he jumped down and helped Pearl alight from the buggy, and carried her trunk to the front door.

"Thank you," Pearl murmured. She looked around and saw there were no flowers. No paint on the small house, but a curl of fire circled from the chimney, and Pearl relaxed. Someone was home, at least.

"I will pick you up Monday morning at seven o'clock sharp!"

And Pearl, realizing she would have to concede, at least in the beginning, retorted, "And I shall be ready at 6:55 sharp!"

The door flew open, and soon Pearl was enveloped in Nina Colville's arms. "Oh, my dear girl, just look at thee. Thee is all growed up!"

Pearl stood back and stared at the friend she hadn't seen in over a year. There was a glow about her she hadn't remembered, and Pearl's heart pounded in thankfulness.

"So much has happened since we last saw each other." Nina poked a wisp of hair back into a loosely made bun. "We're finally starting our family. A spring baby, right along with the planting of the crops."

"Nina! What wonderful news! And perhaps I can help."

"Oh, Pearl, that would be wonderful. We'll be like sisters."

Pearl stared after the retreating buggy. Judson Rome hadn't even tipped his hat to Nina, nor had he said good day to Pearl. He was a most disconcerting, rude man.

"Did thee have a pleasant train ride?"

Pearl nodded. "But not as nice as the ride out through the hay fields. I do love the country."

"Thee will like teaching here then. John is still working, but should be in for dinner shortly. He can bring thy trunk in then."

Pearl was led to a makeshift bedroom in one corner of the square little house, with a curtain partition. She'd taken her faded brown muslin dress out of the trunk so she could change. Since there was no closet, the trunk would go under the bed.

She sat on the bed, a twinge of homesickness sweeping over her. Already she missed Emily, Ben's booming voice, Mama's smile, and Clifford's chortle. And Paul. She didn't want to think about him, but there it was. In her mind. In her heart. And though he denied God's existence, there was room for questioning, room for growth.

But she must stop thinking about home and go visit with Nina. There were lots of things to talk about.

Chapter 2

That first night in her new home, Pearl opened her Bible with trembling fingers. Whenever things were going wrong, she always found solace in God's Word, especially the Psalms.

The day swam before her eyes as she recalled the long train trip and what seemed like an even longer buggy ride with Mr. Judson Rome. She felt disappointment, not quite knowing why. His refusal to even speak to Nina Colville because she was one of those Quakers made her realize he was worldly and lacked common courtesy. Courtesy was of utmost importance to Pearl.

Pearl began reading Psalm 30:5: "Weeping may endure for a night, but joy cometh in the morning."

After reading a few more verses, Pearl prayed for strength, wisdom, and knowledge for the morrow. To be a good teacher mattered more than anything. She could not fail the children. She was here to teach, and teach she would. The rudeness of one man, even if he was head of the school board, wouldn't change how she felt.

Paul's face came to mind as she slipped under the light cover. The heavy quilt would be needed later, but not now with the house still holding the afternoon heat. If things had been different, Paul might have considered her as more than a friend or sister, but it wasn't meant to be. By all indications, she was to be a teacher. That was where her talents lay and where she was needed, and Pearl needed to be needed. Tomorrow she would prove her mettle.

Morning came, and Pearl was more than ready. A low layer of clouds made everything look dismal. She shivered as she slipped into the sunny yellow dotted Swiss, the first dress Kate had made for her. If anything could cheer her up, this would. It fit nicely and was her second-best dress. Paul had commented once that she looked downright pretty in it. It was the only compliment he'd ever given her, and she'd kept it close to her heart, treasuring the words from the man she cared about so deeply.

She dreaded the thought of riding with Mr. Rome and realized this bothered her far more than the gray day. How far was the school? What would they talk about? He had said very little about his own children, though

251

Pearl had tried coaxing some answers out of him. She wanted to know as much as she could about her charges. He had mentioned that his daughter Mary Alice looked exactly like her mother.

The teakettle whistled on back of the wood stove and made the morning chill disappear as Pearl entered the middle room which served as a kitchen/dining area and front room.

"Good mornin', Nina," she called.

Nina turned and smiled. "Since this is thy first day, I thought we'd celebrate by having biscuits to go with our oatmeal."

Pearl washed up, nodding. "I'm just a mite scared."

"I know I'd be," said Nina, bringing the pan of biscuits to the table. "Let's pray before thee leaves."

Pearl had thought of it already, knowing it would soothe her being.

After requesting God's help to watch over Pearl and to bless each child that came, Pearl finished her oatmeal just as a noise sounded out front.

"Why, he's early, if that's Mr. Rome," Pearl said. "I wanted to help with these dishes."

"Don't thee worry one minute about them dishes. I don't mind. Thee just go along now and remember: Hold thy head high and keep a smile on thy face."

The knock sounded as Pearl put a wrap around her shoulders. Fall mornings were cool and crisp, and she knew it would be windy as Judson Rome drove his team hard.

"If'n you are ready, let's go," came the gruff voice when Nina opened the door.

"Won't you come in, Mr. Rome?" Nina offered.

"No need for that since I see Miss Galloway is ready."

Pearl took a deep breath, partaking of the beauty of early morning. She would smile and not let Mr. Judson Rome ruin this morning. It was then she noticed the absence of his child.

"And where is your daughter?" Pearl had so hoped to meet at least one child before the school day began.

"She wasn't ready. She's coming with the boys."

"Oh." *So much for being chaperoned,* Pearl thought.

Judson talked as the horses made their way along the well-worn path. Pearl listened, but her heart was on what she would do on her first day of teaching. She did so want to be a good teacher. She also hoped the children would like her. She had a sudden tickle in her throat, but she didn't cough.

The horses turned and suddenly stopped in front of a one-room building. The rough-hewn logs were new and Pearl remembered hearing this would be the first year for the school. Before Mr. Judson Rome could come around to assist her, she'd hopped down, holding her skirt high with her right hand, her left holding onto her satchel. She marched into the room and gasped. It was perfectly wonderful. Desks had been hewn out of logs, and the floor was made of wooden planks—she'd half expected to find a dirt floor. A blackboard covered one wall, and a flag hung from a pole in the corner.

Judson barreled in behind her. "I am not used to seeing a woman get out of a buggy on her own."

Pearl didn't respond as she went about displaying her books—the spelling, the reader, the arithmetic. There was chalk, a thick tablet, and pencils. She didn't know if the children would have their own supplies and had brought extra paper for this first important day.

"I see you approve of our new school."

Pearl clasped her hands. "It's more than I dreamed about."

Judson Rome nodded. "And if it weren't for me, you wouldn't be here."

Smiling, Pearl held out her hand. "Thank you for giving me my first job as teacher."

"I shall return to fetch you later."

"And your daughter will accompany us?"

He didn't answer, but turned and stomped out the door. It was a temporary truce.

Pearl had considered the possibility of walking the three miles to the schoolhouse. She could do it in less than an hour and somehow knew it would be far more pleasant to do so than to rely on Mr. Judson Rome to fetch her each day. But her mind was diverted with the arrival of the first few children. She asked each name as they came shyly in.

Mr. Rome's children were the last to arrive. Pearl knew it had to be them, as they were the only ones who had a team of horses and a wagon to bring to school. This she'd learned from the girls who sat in front.

The team was driven hard, and Pearl noticed the small figure hunched over in the back. They had probably frightened their little sister deliberately. All the more reason she should ride with us each day, Pearl thought.

"Do come in," she called brightly. "School's about to begin, so find a desk and tell me your names."

The room had filled with warmth, thanks to the fire Pearl started in the small pot-bellied stove. That was one thing she had learned when she was young: building fires. A lot of things had depended on her, back on the Iowa farm.

The boys shuffled to the back of the room while Mary Alice chose a seat next to Cora Gentry. The twins removed their coats, then came back to hang them on the nails on the north wall, tracking large clumps of mud across the new floor. Pearl winced. She could hardly ask them to remove their shoes. Tomorrow she'd bring a broom for sweeping.

Pearl went around the room twice, putting names to faces. Sixteen pupils was a goodly number. While the younger ones learned the alphabet, she'd listen to the older ones read and work on arithmetic.

After the Pledge of Allegiance was recited, Pearl read the hundredth Psalm from her Bible. Just touching her well-worn Bible gave her a small amount of comfort.

> *Make a joyful noise unto the Lord, all ye lands.*
> *Serve the Lord with gladness:*
> *Come before his presence with singing.*

A whisper sounded from the back of the room, but they were otherwise quiet for the reading of God's Word.

Pearl passed out sheets of paper. A snicker sounded, and she knew it was one of the Rome boys. Thomas and Timothy. Tall, yet skinny, with dark hair that needed a good combing, they were identical twins and she wondered how she'd ever keep them apart. She was also certain they had traded seats when her back was turned. She decided to ignore it for now.

"I want everyone to write a story or draw a picture this morning—"

"I can't write," interrupted Tim, or was it Tom?

"It's to be in essay form," Pearl began, ignoring his comment as she handed out pencils and paper. "Write what you like about school. Or perhaps you want to tell me what you did this summer."

"I'd like it better if we had a pretty teacher," said Carl, the boy at the last desk. His face was dirty, his clothes soiled and ragged. He was bigger than the twins and wore a defiant look.

The words stung, but Pearl thought of the adage and recited it.

" 'If wishes were horses, beggars would ride.' "

Carl shuffled his feet. "That's a dumb saying."

"Please, start writing."

The younger children who could not write were to draw a picture. They would work on writing numbers and letters soon. There was more commotion in the back.

"I want to see you writing. Now." Pearl walked between the desks. "If you don't do it now, you will stay after school to finish."

The boys groaned, then Thomas spoke up. "I don't ever have to stay after school. My father won't hear of it."

"Then I will think of something you can do here. I expect you to do the lessons. You cannot be excused just because your father is head of the school board."

His face turned bright red. Pearl had not been exposed to hatred, but she saw it flash in his eyes. She shivered. She must outsmart him and the others who stared at her in a daring way, but how? It was imperative to maintain control. To lose the upper hand meant that everything would fall apart.

Pearl admired some of the drawings, then looked at Mary Alice's full-page essay. She seemed so sweet, so wanting to please, but there was a sad look on her face, and Pearl couldn't imagine how it must be to lose one's mother.

"Essays are dumb," Carl said grumbling. "I definitely don't like this lesson."

"Teachers are stupid," Timothy added. "And ugly," another voice said under his breath. "Why do you suppose she isn't married?" hissed a third. Pearl heard the stinging words, but pretended she had not. It was better to ignore some things. Soon it quieted down, but she sensed she hadn't heard the end of it.

Pearl let the students take a longer recess, watching the boys play tag while the girls played hopscotch. She knew they all needed the exercise, but especially the older boys who were used to working in the fields, not sitting at a desk all day. Then it was math and reading in the afternoon.

As the afternoon sun came in the west window, she allowed each to get a drink of water, though the boys didn't want to settle down after that. Pearl felt a sinking sensation. There was trouble ahead; she sensed it with her very being. Discipline could be a major problem. What would she do? How could she make the older ones understand the importance of learning? She thought of the books her teacher had read each day. Every student had looked forward to that time. Could she try that here? But what of Mr. Rome's admoniton that there would be no reading of books?

Pearl was thankful when she heard the horses clip-clopping outside and glanced at her watch. Three-thirty. Her first day of school was over. And, somehow, she had lived through it. One day down and forty school days to go until the Christmas holidays, when she could go home. Home. How far away it seemed. How long ago it seemed. Yet she knew she would make it, for God was on her side. He would help her through.

Chapter 3

Judson Rome assisted Pearl up front while Mary Alice climbed into the back of the buggy.

"I trust the day went well."

Pearl wasn't sure what Mr. Rome wanted to hear. The Rome twins had continued to test her. Big boys of eleven, they had to be told twice to open their books, twice to get their feet under the desk and not to talk unless spoken to. Two other boys, John Mac and Carl, were even bigger, with louder mouths. The smaller children had been a joy, especially Mary Alice Rome. Pearl had watched her as she bent over her work and painstakingly wrote her alphabet, then her numbers. She so wanted to please. If only the boys cooperated half as well.

"I know everyone's name," Pearl finally said.

Mary Alice chatted about her essay and how she could now add and subtract. Pearl smiled. Maybe the boys didn't like her, but Mary Alice did, and it helped her feelings of despair.

"And how did your brothers do?" Judson asked.

"They don't like writing," she said, her voice dropping.

Pearl glanced at Judson sideways, hoping he would let the matter drop. She just wanted to go home, get into her comfortable muslin, and talk to Nina while they prepared dinner.

At last Judson pulled into the yard, and Pearl lighted from the buggy and hurried inside, stopping long enough to wave once more at Mary Alice.

"Dinner will be ready in thirty minutes," called Nina.

"I'll help in a bit," Pearl called back from her bedroom space, slipping the yellow dress down past her narrow hips.

"No need. Not tonight. After one look at thee, I know thee needs complete silence and rest."

"Do you think I'll be able to teach the children?" Pearl asked a few minutes later, as she set a plate of sliced bread on the table.

"Of course thee will." Nina smiled as she looked at Pearl. "Here I am just one year ahead of thee, but I feel so much older."

"That's because you're married."

"And going to have a baby," Nina added.

John came in and washed up at the basin. He was quiet, but a good man. One knew that after seeing his broad face and the look of compassion in his eyes. Pearl was lucky to be here in this home where her friends served God and loved Him above all.

The meal was pleasant, but Pearl kept thinking of how it would be back at Ben's. Emily waiting with the food keeping hot in the warmer on top of the new stove Ben had ordered from the Sears & Roebuck Catalogue. Sarah, setting the table or rocking baby Clifford should he be fussy. The sounds of the horses drawing up out front, then around to the side where Ben would give them their hay for the night. And Paul. Washing up out back, coming in filling the doorway with his broad shoulders, the smile on his face as he seemed to seek her out. Of course it was her imagination, since Paul liked everyone, and if he had eyes for someone, it was Nancy Whitfield. How could Pearl even dare think that a man as handsome as Paul could look at plain, tall Pearl?

"Why is thee smiling?" Nina asked as she passed the bowl of mashed potatoes.

"Oh. Was I?" Pearl felt her cheeks flush. "I expect I was just thinking about home and how many there'd be around the table."

She quickly added that though she missed her family, she was as proud and happy to be here in this home, eating with these friends who had made room for her.

"Thee has a right nice family, all right," Nina said. "I miss all our friends in Portland." Then seeing the look on her husband's face, she added, "But God has been good to us here. The land is good for growing, and we're going to add on another ten acres soon."

John wiped his mouth with his napkin. "Yes, God has certainly attended to our needs."

Pearl wondered if God would hear her prayer tonight when she asked for help with school.

"Hear thee has some big, mean boys in the schoolroom," John said then.

Pearl nodded and looked at her hands. They were knotting in her lap. "They don't want to be there. Boys that age would rather be out in the fields, working."

John pushed back his chair. "I didn't go beyond sixth grade, Miss Pearl. I wonder if we're doing the right thing—pushing this education thing on our young boys. Seems it might be okay for the womenfolk, but boys need to be busy at hard labor."

Pearl nodded but knew she had to say her feelings on the subject, just as she'd spoken freely and openly with Judson Rome.

"That might be true, John, but doesn't thee ever wish for more learning? Don't you wish you had stayed in school longer?"

John hesitated, his hand on his hat as he stood by the door. "No, can't rightly say that I do. I like things just the way they are. And now if you ladies will excuse me, I got to see to my chores."

Long after the dishes were done, bread mixed and put to rise on the back of the stove, and after John had come back inside, Pearl walked out across the barren front yard. It needed some color, not just plain, brown dirt, hard-packed from summer's heat and from the wagon rolling over it. She missed the green grass, the roses Emily grew in front of the house, the other flowers that came up by the porch. If only she had some flower seeds. Why hadn't she thought of that before leaving Portland?

Pearl's long, gray skirt swept across the parched ground as she gazed into the sky. Soon it would be dark and clear. She thought of the numerous times she and Paul had watched as dusk came, then the growing darkness and the sky overflowing with stars. She remembered the time they had tried to count the stars—an impossible task. Later they had eaten pieces of Pearl's apple pie and had tall glasses of water. Then Paul had left to go out back where he slept, and she had climbed the stairs to the room she shared with Sarah.

A knot rose in her throat. How dearly she loved her mother. How much she wanted to go to her now and tell her about the boys, ask her advice in how to handle them. Maybe she wasn't old enough to teach. Maybe she wasn't meant to be a teacher. How did one ever really know? How could she still her beating heart when she thought of Paul? How could she know what God intended for her to do with her life? Was it right to pray for a husband, a family, when that might not be God's intent for her? "Thy will be done, Lord. Thy will be done," she prayed aloud.

Pearl walked to the end of the pasture and laughed when the mare, Missy, trotted over. She patted her side, then her head. "Are you as lonely as I am?" she said, nuzzling her close.

She'd always preferred familiar things, had dreaded leaving the farm in Iowa when she and Sarah had come out to Oregon to live with Ben. Their first house in Oregon City had had several acres, and Pearl had planted a garden. But that spring was wetter than usual, and the seeds had rotted.

"It isn't like Iowa," Ben explained when Pearl had all but cried over her ruined beans and tomatoes. "Spring comes much later here, but you can harvest into fall. Things don't die on the vine as they did back home."

Pearl planted seeds again, and they harvested a few onions, carrots, and beans, then she and Sarah moved to the big house on Foster Road—the house Ben built for Emily. And it was good they had done so as Sarah became more ill with each passing month. She couldn't be left alone when Pearl went to help Emily out before Baby Isobelle was born. Doctors were closer in Portland, too, so Sarah could get medicine for the cough that lingered on.

It was growing late, and Pearl wanted to go over her lessons before bedtime. After one more call to Missy, she turned and walked back to the house. Just as she rounded the corner, she saw the familiar team of horses trotting up the road. Her heart sank. Judson Rome. What was he doing here?

Pearl tucked a few loose strands of hair behind her ear, knowing she should look her best at all times. Then she held her breath as Judson hopped down and strode over.

Dressed in a white shirt and dark tie, he had slicked his hair back from the sides of his face. Smiling, he approached her.

"I've come calling on you, Miss Galloway. I know it isn't proper to be courted without the presence of a chaperone, but the Colvilles are nearby. Keep in mind," and he licked his lips, "that I'm the chairman of the school board, so whatever I say goes."

Pearl looked skyward and asked for help. "Perhaps you've come calling on me, Mr. Rome, but I didn't hear myself saying it was okay."

"Well, I just assumed—"

"Mr. Rome, I came here to teach, not to get married. You know that one cannot be married and still be a teacher." She shot him a quizzical look. "I do believe you remember the set of rules you gave me the day I arrived?"

Judson bristled. "Yes, well, that's my point exactly. My children need a mother far more than this community needs a teacher. I expect you need to be occupied, plus have enough funds to take care of yourself, so my solution is the best one for both of us!"

Pearl felt caught. Trapped. What could she say next? How could she even consider being called on by this man when she found him so disreputable? So lacking in manners and simple courtesy?

"If and when I should want to be called on, Mr. Rome, I think I'll be the one deciding who that might be. Thank you for stopping by."

He sputtered, exclaiming he'd see her in the morning, as she hurried off toward the house. So that was the real reason she was asked to come. It wasn't to teach, but to marry Mr. Judson Rome, to provide a home for him, to cook for the family, and to mother his children. She could have taken Mary Alice under her wing in a moment, but not the twins. They needed discipline, and she knew she wasn't capable of handling them. They also needed a father who cared, but somehow she thought that Judson Rome cared for nobody but himself.

Pearl watched while the team of horses left in a cloud of dust, then headed into to the house.

Nina was setting out bowls for the next morning's breakfast and glanced up with a puzzled look.

"I see Mr. Rome came calling on thee."

"He did."

"And what did thee talk about?"

"That I came to teach, not to be courted."

"Thee probably shouldn't have refused Judson," Nina said as she poured Pearl a cup of coffee.

"I know." Pearl set the cup down. "I don't know why I said what I did, but I honestly cannot bear to think of him calling on me."

"He has a lot of influence in this town."

"I realize that, Nina. Oh, how I realize it."

"He was the one who said we needed a schoolteacher."

"Yes, he told me." Pearl shivered and drew her shawl closer.

"He could see to it that thee was replaced by another teacher."

"And you think he will?"

Nina nodded. "I think thee needs to pray about it."

"Then let's pray that God's will be done and let it rest at that."

Later Pearl set out her dark calico and the lessons for tomorrow. She lit the lamp and sat at the table, penning a note to Emily.

> *Dear Emily, and to anyone else who might be interested,*
>
> *I arrived. The schoolhouse is new. There's a beautiful little stove in it.*
>
> *I have sixteen pupils, and so far Mary Alice is my favorite one, though I realize that teachers should not have pets.*
>
> *I miss everyone there. I just wish I could come home to see you all. Baby Clifford. I want to hold him close and nuzzle his soft cheek next to mine. Emily, to just chat with you. Mama, to ask advice, to hear tell that I've made the right decision by coming here. Ben who is such a dear brother, and Paul who likes to gaze at the stars on a warm summer evening.*

She signed off, wondering if it was all right that she'd included Paul. Would he even read the letter? Surely he didn't care, but how could she talk about everyone else and leave him out?

She blew out the light and crawled under the sheet. It was too warm for covers, but before dawn, she'd pull the heavy quilt up under her chin. By morning it would be cool, and she would ride to school with the sun just coming up over the eastern hill, filling the sky with its brilliance.

Pearl prayed for wisdom, and several verses came to mind: "God is love." "God cares for you." She believed it. She held God's Word tight to her chest. He knew what was best for her. Tomorrow was another day, and that thought made her remember another favorite Psalm: "Trust in the Lord thy God with all thy heart, soul, and strength, and he shall direct thy paths."

Pearl thought of Paul and how he had not accepted God as his maker, his redeemer, but Paul was God's creation. He would always be God's creation. Nothing Paul did or said, or didn't do or say, could change things. Still, Pearl thought Paul did care, did believe in God; he just didn't know it yet.

When sleep didn't come, she remembered one hot summer afternoon, the day of the water fight. . . .

The evening meal had been prepared and two of Pearl's apple pies lay cooling on the counter. Pearl had also fed the chickens, changed Clifford's diaper and rocked him to sleep, all the while telling him he was a very special baby, even if he was a trifle spoiled. He was teething and crankier than usual. Emily and Sarah were taking naps. Paul would have gone with Ben to work on one of the new homes across the river, but he was learning to plaster and had stayed home to perfect his craft. He'd chosen a wall just outside the kitchen steps to practice on.

First Paul mixed the plaster until it was the right consistency, then he took the trowel and smeared a large amount on the wall, using long, swirling motions. He'd stand back, survey his work, then smile if he was pleased. If not, he'd take it off, dumping it back into the trough, add a little water or cement, and start all over again. Ben had said this was the best way to learn.

Just as Paul started to throw the mixture back in, Pearl came around the corner. Startled, he slipped and fell into the trough. It was his look of surprise that made Pearl laugh more than anything. She knew she shouldn't laugh, but she couldn't help it.

"If you aren't a sight, Paul Drake!" she screeched.

At first Paul glared, but the more Pearl laughed, the more he saw humor in the situation. Besides, one could hardly keep a straight face when Pearl laughed.

"It isn't funny," he said wiping the white, wet stuff from his leg and foot.

"I wish I had a camera," she said between laughs.

"Well, I'm glad you don't." He turned and walked over to a bucket of water and dipped his hand in.

She stood at the corner of the house, watching and attempting to stifle her giggles as he began washing off the plaster. Suddenly, he threw a whole dipper of water on her, and another. Soon the front of the old navy blue calico was soaked, her hair had slipped out of the ribbon and hung in wet streaks about her face. Pearl stared in disbelief.

"Pearl—Gem—I don't know what came over me—" he began.

In answer, she laughed as she shook her dress out. "Just you wait," she cried, laughing even harder. Then she threw a dipperful on him and chased him around the side of the house.

He caught her hands and held her so she couldn't move. Suddenly, Pearl stopped struggling and stared. As their eyes locked, her heart beat faster. It was almost as if the world stood still, and Pearl was to wonder later what might have happened if Emily hadn't called out then.

She stood in the doorway, holding Clifford close. "I heard laughter and wondered—" She looked from Pearl to Paul, and then started laughing. The baby who had not yet learned to laugh looked at his mother and then his tiny voice joined in the melee.

"His first laugh!" Pearl cried out. And then she flipped water from her fingers onto his face. He laughed even harder.

"If you two don't look a sight! You'd better both get washed up."

Pearl's shoes squeaked as she went up the stairs. She changed into her oldest muslin, pulled her hair back into a knot, foregoing her usual braid. She tried to put Paul out of her mind, the way he had looked at her, but the thought kept coming back, even later as she mashed potatoes for dinner.

Nobody spoke of the plaster incident again, but Pearl knew she would never forget that afternoon and the way they had looked at each other.

The sound of the wind whistling around the sides of the small house finally drew Pearl into a dreamless sleep. . . .

Chapter 4

In the two weeks that followed, Judson Rome persisted in his quest to court Pearl. He'd asked her to go buggy riding, to accompany him to a barn dance, and to attend his church. Pearl had declined all offers. She knew there would be no turning back if she once said yes. But Judson was stubborn and not one to give up easily.

"Every woman has something she will say yes to," he said one afternoon after school as they drove over the road to the Colvilles'.

"I prefer teaching," Pearl said for what she knew must be the hundredth time.

"We shall see."

"He seems to think it makes everything all right because he owns a vast acreage and large house, that I should be happy to agree to his proposal of marriage," Pearl lamented to Nina as she tore off the outer wrappings of a package that had arrived from Portland. She could hardly wait to see what Emily had sent.

"Perhaps he will continue in an effort to wear thee down. Or, he might find a way to rid thee of thy teaching position. And the boys have been difficult," Nina added.

Pearl nodded as she withdrew the contents from the cardboard box. "Believe me, I have considered the proposal, but wish it were from a different person."

Pencils, paper, string, glue, and best of all three books. One was *The Night Before Christmas* by Clement C. Moore, and the other two were *Robinson Crusoe* and *Gulliver's Travels.*

Pearl clutched the books close to her bosom. "*Robinson Crusoe* is the first book I shall read. It's the one thing that might keep the older boys interested in coming to school."

"And the paints?" Nina asked.

"Later, for Christmas."

Pearl would teach math in the morning, read a chapter, followed by English and recess. Afternoons they'd practice penmanship, something the boys detested. Pearl also planned a brief history lesson starting today.

Judson Rome arrived the following morning, after insisting that it was only proper that he continue to take her to and from school. Pearl continued dreading the trip, but it did no good, so she prayed for patience with this man. He held his hand out to assist her, and she took it grudgingly.

"What's in the box?" he asked, his eyes narrowing.

"School supplies."

"Did we not furnish you with paper and pencils?"

"Yes, but this is extra. Drawing paper and paints and—" She hesitated, realizing she dare not mention the reading books.

Besides, they were good reading books. Hadn't her teacher read them to her at school in Portland?

"Don't take up time with frivolous pursuits," Judson said then.

"It is for days when it rains too much to go outside."

"The children need to go outside." He watched her, but Pearl wouldn't look his way. "Rain never hurt anyone."

"A fine morning it is," Pearl declared, in an effort to change the subject. Actually, it would be a fine morning once she arrived at school. Though fall mornings were cool, and often rainy, the sun was beaming today and its warmth filled Pearl with promise. Promise of a better day than what yesterday had been. If only she could reach the boys by reading *Robinson Crusoe*.

"I've seen better," Judson finally grumped. "Why are you so cheerful?"

Pearl smiled. "I'm always cheerful in the morning, thanking the Lord for yet another day to celebrate life."

Judson grunted again. "Don't start preaching. I've had enough preaching to last a lifetime."

Seems not much of it rubbed off on you, Pearl longed to say, but she saw no need to get Judson's anger riled up and ruin her perfect day. There'd be time for that later when the boys arrived all full of pep and arguments.

"I been meaning to talk to you about something, Miss Galloway. Mary Alice tells me the boys have been giving you a hard time."

"Yes, there are four of them who have a problem settling down."

A sudden scowl crossed his broad face. "My boys can be a bit rambunctious at times—"

"Calling the teacher names goes beyond being rambunctious," Pearl cut in. "I would like—with your permission of course—to keep them after school. They can write extra sentences or read a chapter in the history book—"

"Absolutely not! You'll not single out my sons just because you don't have control of the class."

"And I might have control if I was allowed some means of discipline."

"They're good boys," Judson retorted. "A gentle reminder should work nicely."

"Gentle?" Pearl cried. "Those boys don't know the meaning of the word." She half expected Mary Alice to comment from the backseat, but she knew when to keep quiet, and this was one of those times. What the boys needed was a sound thrashing. Pearl, being a Quaker, was opposed to violence, yet wondered if there couldn't be an exception to the rule.

"Ignore their capers," Judson said then. "The more air you give a flame, the higher it goes."

Pearl had one last thing to try and she'd begin today. Surely they would obey as they would want her to keep reading the story.

If she didn't receive respect soon, she would have to quit, though she never considered herself a quitter. She thought of Mama's saying again: "Quitters never win, and winners never quit."

She prayed nightly and knew Emily, Ben, and Sarah prayed, as well as Nina and John, but she had to find the answers herself, and these books were the answer.

"If a teacher doesn't have control of her class, perhaps there is something wrong with her method of teaching," Judson said then, a smirk on his face.

Pearl stared straight ahead, saying nothing.

"I hope you won't expect a good recommendation, in the event you quit."

"Not that I would expect one at all."

"I trust you'll continue on until Christmas break—maybe winter break?"

"Of course." Pearl realized now what he was doing—setting her up for failure so she'd be forced into quitting then agreeing to marry him. He thought she'd be too ashamed to return home to admit her failure.

Judson didn't help her down from the buggy, which Pearl was thankful for. She adjusted her bonnet and stepped over a huge mud puddle by the front door and entered the building. One student had arrived. It was Cora Gentry.

"Cora, did you come alone?"

"Yes, Miss Galloway."

"Why didn't you wait for your brother?"

Her small face looked so serious.

"Cora, what is it? You're absolutely trembling."

"It's the boys. I had to come early to tell you."

"The boys?" She removed her bonnet and hung it on a nail in the corner. Her gloves were placed on the shelf below the hat. She turned to look at the pinched face of her next-to-youngest pupil. "What boys are you referring to?" Pearl walked over to Cora and held the small, trembling hands.

"They were a-talking yesterday, Miss Galloway. I overheard them when they thought I was playing during recess."

"And what did you hear?"

"They are going to put a snake in the desk drawer when we're out for recess. They want to scare you off."

Pearl shuddered for the second time that morning. A snake. Of all God's creatures, she feared snakes the most. Did the boys know that, or were they making a good guess?

She looked at Cora and wanted to take the child into her arms. She decided to do that very thing, favoritism or not. Cora, like Mary Alice, had no mother. Her brother, Carl, just like the twins, demanded attention and got it by naughty behavior.

"Cora, it was a brave thing you did, coming to tell me this. I'll figure out a way to surprise them back."

The thin shoulders seemed to rise under the thin cotton dress as she smiled. "I like you, Miss Galloway. Better than anyone I know."

"And I like you very much, too."

"You won't tell on me, will you?"

Pearl held her tighter. "Of course I won't, Cora. I'm good at keeping secrets."

Cora smiled and hugged Pearl back. "I wish you were my mother," she said before sitting back down.

Pearl felt her heart pound. If only she could reach the boys. Well, today she would try it. Since she was probably quitting at the end of the term anyway, why not go ahead and start reading *Robinson Crusoe*. If the boys weren't interested in a shipwrecked sailor on a deserted island, she doubted they'd ever be interested in reading or literature of any kind.

The sounds of horses drew up outside and soon the schoolhouse was full of boys and voices and talking. Pearl let them talk as they shuffled to their seats. It was ten minutes before class began. She'd ask Cora to lead the flag salute this morning.

Later as Pearl looked out over the desks and a few leering faces, she decided to go with her plan. After Scripture, she would begin chapter one of *Robinson Crusoe*. Then, when she had them hooked, she would say it was time to write their numbers. Two more pages would be read if all work was completed and handed in.

The book was welcomed. There were no disturbing voices or feet shuffling as even the older boys leaned on their hands and listened. Once in a while Pearl would stop and ask a question about what they would do in that situation. Nobody seemed to know and they would beg her to read on so they could find out. When she reached the end of the first chapter, she found the bookmark and closed the book. At first there was silence, then every one began talking at once.

"You can't stop there," Timothy said, being the first to speak out. "We have to know what he did."

"We have other things we must do."

"But we gotta know what happens," Timothy insisted.

"There will be more chapters later on if you do your work promptly."

There were groans, but the boys took out their tablets and pens.

After recess, Pearl watched out of the corner of her eye from the edge of the play area. She thought she saw two boys slip back into the school building, but she couldn't be positive.

When she rang the small silver bell to mark the end of recess, Pearl was ready and waiting. After everyone found their seats, she asked them to open their reading books.

"Kenny," she called out, "my desk drawer seems to be sticking. Could you come open it for me?"

Kenny, a second-grader, not in on the trick, shuffled up to the front of the class. He had trouble learning, but he showed Pearl respect.

"No! Wait!" Thomas called from the back of the room. "I'll do it!"

"I think Kenny is capable," Pearl said.

"But I'm more capable," Thomas insisted, making his way to the front of the room.

"Very well, then." Pearl stood back and closed her eyes, not wanting to see a snake in any shape or form, no matter who had it or what it was doing.

Thomas opened the drawer and Pearl saw movement out of the corner of her eye. She held her mouth closed tightly, willing herself not to scream.

Thomas shook his head, as if bewildered, and held the snake in his large hand. "Miss Galloway, there seems to be a snake here. I wonder how on earth it got here?"

Pearl gasped, then smiled. "My goodness, yes, I wonder how."

Thomas disappeared out the door and Pearl heard some muted whispers from the back of the room. Well, they would plan on something else. She was sure she hadn't heard the end of the snake incident.

And Cora, rewarded for her role of snitching, arrived the next morning with a welt on her leg and red-rimmed eyes. Since everyone had arrived, Pearl could not ask what had happened, but she suspected Carl had given her a whipping. How dare he! How could she make sure her students were not beaten by older siblings?

That afternoon Judson Rome asked about the snake incident. "I hear tell you had a snake in the schoolroom yesterday."

"Yes, well, it got in the desk drawer somehow, but I think the problem's been resolved."

"Resolved? And how could that be?"

"The offending pupils who had something to do with that are going to chop some wood for the stove so they'll have heat come winter."

Judson looked puzzled. "And you know who these offending pupils are?"

Pearl smiled and looked straight ahead. "I do."

"It ain't either of my boys."

Pearl still wouldn't look him in the eye. "That's for me to know and for you to find out, Mr. Rome."

"You ain't saying, because you don't know."

"Oh, I know all right. Never fear about that—"

"Someone snitched then."

"You might call it that."

"That isn't fair play to tattle like that, and you know it."

"Nor is it fair to try to harm the schoolteacher."

Judson hit the reins and his team reared. "Like I said before, perhaps you aren't fit to teach school, Miss Galloway."

And, perhaps you, Sir, aren't fit to be a father, Pearl longed to say, but kept the words tight inside her. Judson Rome appeared on the outside to be a law-abiding, God-fearing citizen of his community, but he was a bully. Mean. Conniving. He stepped on toes, and if he didn't get his way, he'd retaliate in some way. Either everyone did not know what he was doing, or they chose to look the other way in case they might be the target for his abuse. She did not want to be part of such actions and might even tell him so one day.

In the meantime, she was doing the one thing he had forbidden her to do: read a book to her students. The boys did not tell on her because they were too interested in the story and wanted to find out what happened. Yes, she had a hold on them, at least for now. After *Robinson Crusoe*, she would read another. Emily's bookshelves hosted several volumes. She might write to see if Emily could send her Elsie Dinsmore books. She knew Mary Alice and Cora would like to read them. All her pupils could read well now, and Pearl was proud of her first class, even if there were other problems. Nothing ever ran completely smoothly. Life just wasn't that way.

Chapter 5

Paul Michael Drake stood at the mirror, trimming the beginning of a beard. It was straggly at best and thin in spots, and he wondered why he kept trying to grow it. His hair, the color of sand, was thick and long. It was time for a cut, but there was no rush. Nobody to impress now that Pearl was gone. Blue eyes stared back at him from the mirror, and he wondered what Pearl was doing this very minute.

Paul had never realized he would miss Pearl so much. She was just one of the family. They were just friends and one missed his friends, but his feelings went deeper than that. The first inkling he'd had was after a water fight one afternoon. She'd looked into his eyes with such intensity, it had unnerved him. Now he found himself thinking about her constantly, wondering what she'd say about this, think about that. He hadn't shared his thoughts with anyone, though he expected Ben knew—after their conversation yesterday on the way home from work.

"Sure seems quiet with Pearl gone, doesn't it," Ben had said.

It wasn't a question, but more of a statement.

Paul nodded. "And it isn't that she talks that much."

"No," Ben said in agreement. "Pearl's always been quiet. Well, perhaps not as quiet as Emily, but quieter than the rest of us. Of course then there's Jesse. Jesse can out-talk every one of us Galloways."

Paul turned and stared at his brother-in-law. Ben rarely spoke of Jesse, and Emily all but refused to allow his name to be mentioned in her presence. He knew that Jesse, the oldest of the Galloways, had broken many hearts, but it was Kate's heart that Emily remembered, for Kate had nearly married Jesse, but he had run off, and nobody had heard from him now for well over a year.

"I knew someone in California like that," Paul said. "He worked for us one summer. That's after Pa died, and Ma needed some stuff done around the place. He said he could do anything she needed fixing and wouldn't charge much."

Ben let the reins go slack. "So? Did he do what he said he could do?"

"Nope! Ran off with the shed half built. We all had to finish the job and Ma was right out there, pounding nails, too."

"Jesse never did anything like hold a hammer," Ben said. "He's a genteel man. One who can't get his hands dirty."

"Never held a hammer?" Paul repeated.

"Don't rightly think so."

Paul eased back against the seat. "Strange how some people see things differently. How they don't see things like the rest of us do. Like being honest."

"Or worshiping God," Ben said.

Paul looked away. He didn't like to get on the subject of God. It wasn't that he didn't believe, because maybe he did, just a bit. But he couldn't say he rightfully belonged to God, either. Not like the others spoke of. Maybe he just had to be shown, to see proof. Yes, that was it. He needed proof.

"I don't exactly worship God, Ben, but I'm a good person, or at least I like to think so."

Ben nodded. "Yeah. A lot of people think that works is what makes you belong, but it isn't. It's faith and believing."

"Well, then, guess I am just a plain ole heathen." He turned and caught Ben's arm. "Not that you have to go tellin' Emily that. Don't know what she'd do to me if she heard how I felt about religion and God and such."

Ben smiled. "Your secret's safe with me, Paul. I think you're just one of those people who don't exactly believe, but don't rightly disbelieve, either."

"I think it's important to Pearl, too." The minute Paul had said the words, he wondered why he had even thought of her. It made him sound as if he had serious thoughts about Pearl, and he didn't. Or he didn't think he did. Not exactly, that is.

Or did he?

Long after the two men arrived home, greeted Sarah and Emily, and after Paul played with his nephew and they sat down to dinner, thoughts of Pearl kept hitting him. He didn't want to think about her. He knew she didn't think of him as anything more than a brother. But her face kept getting in the way. It got in the way of his gazing at the jet black sky and intruded on his thoughts when he went to bed and lay propped up with arms under his head. He wondered how Pearl was faring this very moment. Wondered how she was getting along in a strange place, teaching children. At least she had friends to board with. Yet, he found himself counting the days until Christmas when he knew she'd be home. Even if only for a month or so, she'd be here and they'd talk.

Nancy Whitfield came to mind. Pretty and tiny, Nancy had golden curls and a pair of the bluest eyes he'd ever seen. Her smile always seemed directed at him, but try as he might, he couldn't seem to smile back.

She sat across the aisle during church, talked to him after the meeting, asked for a ride once when her father had to leave early. He remembered taking her; he had an old team of horses and a rickety wagon, but she didn't seem to notice, or if she did, she didn't mind.

"I just think our church is so special, don't you, Paul?"

Then without waiting for an answer, she bubbled on, "And I like our new minister."

Pastor Luke Morrison and his wife, Kate, had started a new church down south in the valley, and Paul missed his friends.

"I don't think anyone could ever take Pastor Luke's place," Paul started to say, but Nancy cut him right off and went trilling off on how the area was growing, how she hoped to move, to have a home someday a bit closer to town.

"Don't you just love it in Oregon? So much is happening. I mean it's better than California—" And again before he could answer, she was talking about California and how people were going there because of the weather and growing seasons, but how much better Oregon was in spite of the rain.

"Do you agree? Paul?" She raised puzzled eyes in his direction.

"Agree?" he said, when he realized she was waiting for his answer. "What am I supposed to agree to? That California is not a good place to live, or that Oregon is growing, or that you prefer living in town to the country?" Or had she said something else that he'd missed entirely? He wasn't good with small talk, and sometimes he just liked the silence. In fact, preferred it.

Her face flushed bright red. "Oh! I've done it again, haven't I?" And then before he could answer, she went on exclaiming how her own mother said she never let people get a word in edgewise.

"And that's true, isn't it, Paul? Oh, you needn't answer, for I know it is. I truly do."

Paul felt relief when the Whitfield farm came into sight.

"Won't you come in for a glass of buttermilk and some cookies? I made them yesterday—they have oats and raisins and walnuts. They're called Poor Man's Cookies, though heavens know we're not poor!"

Paul shook his head. "Thanks, but I have to get back to help Ben."

"What? Work on the Lord's Day? Surely you can't mean you work on Sunday." He knew he would be in for another long dissertation so he excused himself, tipped his hat, and turned the horse around before she could say anything more. Or at least say anything he could hear.

"Pearl wasn't like that at all." He was talking to the wind, and occasionally the horse turned his head just a little as if he was listening.

"You heard me," Paul said. "Pearl gives a guy a chance to answer. She gives the air a minute to settle down and around a person. Nancy keeps it moving, shuffling it up with her endless chatter."

Paul hit the reins, and the horse started off in a gallop. No, there wasn't work to be done. He had said that, not thinking how it might sound to

Nancy. The only work they would do was sit and read in the parlour or sit on the front porch and watch the traffic go by. Not that much happened on Sundays. He might play with Clifford, or rock him to sleep if Emily needed a moment's rest or Sarah was too ill to help out.

The rest of the journey was spent thinking about Pearl, remembering how she'd made him a special apple tart to take to work. She packed his sandwiches, putting in an extra one on days when she knew he had extra work. She was one of the nicest, sweetest girls he had ever known. But, no, he knew she thought of him as a brother. Pearl wanted to teach school, besides. And when you taught, you definitely could not marry or have a family. The schoolchildren were a teacher's family. No, Pearl would not think of him twice as a possible husband. And it was just as well. Paul couldn't believe as she did. Pearl would need a religious person, just as Ben was suitable for Emily. And Kate for Luke. Though Paul had heard that Kate had not always believed. Sudden inspiration hit. Perhaps he needed to talk to Kate. It just might be a good idea.

It was late, very dark, and the night's chill had settled around the porch when Paul finally tiptoed off to bed. But try as he might, his thoughts were on Pearl with the shy smile, the brown hair she wore in long, coiled braids, the way her tall body looked when she was dressed up for church, the way she had looked the morning before leaving on the train.

He'd wanted to take her to the station, but Ben had offered, and Sarah went along to wish her youngest child blessings and to send her off with a hearty farewell.

Before they left, Paul had wanted to reach up and give Pearl a light kiss on the cheek. Surely she wouldn't have minded, but it was probably just as well that he had not done so.

Paul thought of other things that night. His family. The way they followed the crops from spring to fall. Winter found them farther south where vegetables grew abundantly in the middle of winter. Actually, winter never came to the Imperial Valley.

He never liked the moving and remembered Pa, more than once, standing at the end of his row, glaring, threatening him if he stopped for even a moment to glance around. You had to keep busy. The more you picked, the more money you made and the nicer house the family could buy when they moved farther north.

Paul had gone to school through sixth grade. His father took him out then because he was lean and tall for his age, and broad-shouldered. People thought he was much older than he was.

"You don't need to go to school, anyway. Larnin's for sissies."

It was for that reason Paul felt he was no match for Pearl. She had taken the test enabling her to teach elementary children. She was smart. She knew a lot of things Paul didn't know. Of course he could stucco the whole outside of a house, plaster the rooms inside, and as she told him more than once, she had no idea of how to do that.

"You are smart in your own way, Paul," Pearl had said one night when they sat on the porch steps watching a sky full of stars. "Each of us is smart in his own way."

Pearl never said an unkind thing about anyone. She refused to say anything about Jesse even. "There's good in all people. We just have to look harder for it in some," she'd said.

Paul wished he could believe that. He wished he could carve out of wood as Ben did. Then he'd carve an animal for Pearl and give it to her at Christmas when she came home. But he couldn't. He'd tried. He thought about the books Emily read. He'd tried to read some, but most of the words were complicated. At least Emily had finished school. He should tell Emily that sometime when she mentioned how much she missed growing up with her family.

He picked up the small notebook Emily had given him. It was supposed to be for writing down his thoughts. Well, he couldn't do that. What thoughts?

Pearl had sent him a short note when she wrote Emily to ask for school supplies. Paul unfolded the page and stared at the handwriting.

My Friend Paul:
> *How are you? Did you finish the Creighton house in Moreland? Do you give Clifford a hug each morning and each night for me? Please know that my thoughts and prayers are with you.*
> *I count the days until Christmas. . . .*

> > *As Ever,*
> > *Gem*

Paul read the letter twice, then refolded it and stuck it under his pillow. He liked keeping it there. It was as if Pearl were close by, part of him, feeling his heartbeat as he slept. . . .

Paul opened the small tablet and picked up a pencil and wrote her name at the top of the page.

Pearl:
> *I miss you, I do.*
> *I wonder if you miss me half as much.*

Christmas will be here soon, and I wish you could stay and not go back to teach. . . .

It didn't say much, but he'd give it to her at Christmas. Knowing Pearl, she'd appreciate it.

He wrote a few more lines, but they sounded silly. He scribbled through the words. The only thing he could do was plaster a house. A sudden thought hit. What if he designed one? A special house with Pearl in mind. It would need a big kitchen because she liked to cook and bake. He'd order one of those new stoves from the Sears catalogue. It would be all shiny with lots of chrome, so you could see your face in it. And he'd rent one of those new-fangled irons from PGE. If you liked it, after a month's trial, you could buy it for four dollars. Wouldn't Pearl like ironing her dresses with a spanking new electric iron?

Paul closed the tablet, slipped it under the mattress, and rolled over on his side. He'd finish the letter later. No use in dreaming up things like new houses and irons. Someday there might be someone for him. Nancy Whitfield would like to think so. At least he wouldn't have to wonder about what to say next. But he couldn't begin imagining building a home for Nancy. It would never be nice enough for her. He just knew it wouldn't be. Pearl would like anything he did. Why and how did he know that?

He tried to sleep, but it was impossible. Finally, he turned on the small bed lamp again and reached for the small book on the nightstand.

Sarah had given him a Bible, insisting that everyone needed one for his very own. Paul had tried to understand the words, but some made no sense. Then he remembered what Luke had said in a sermon just before leaving Portland.

"Those of you who are new Christians need to read John and Romans. Read the Psalms and Proverbs for enlightenment." Luke had read the most important law of all from Deuteronomy: " 'And thou shalt love the LORD thy God with all thine heart, and with all thy soul, and with all thy might.' " And the second important one came from Matthew: " 'Thou shalt love thy neighbour as thyself.' "

Paul read the underlined words. They were good laws. He knew he could and would obey these two commandments, though he did not understand their full implication. Who was his neighbor? As for love, just what sort of love did it mean? He mulled it over, closed the book, and blew out the lantern.

"God, if You are there, tell me what I should do. Can Gem be part of my life, or am I going against Your wishes?"

Chapter 6

Thanksgiving came, and Judson invited Pearl to spend the holiday at his house. He had a new housekeeper who would do the cooking, but she politely declined and ate turkey with Nina and John and their friends from church. She missed her family and now counted the days until school would be out for the winter break.

That Saturday Pearl began knitting socks for Christmas. Emily had sent yarn in the earlier box. She also was working on a cross-stitch pattern for Nina and John. It was a surprise. When she wasn't knitting or preparing lessons, she wrote letters. Paul had written twice now. His last letter mentioned Nancy Whitfield, and Pearl's eyes unexpectedly filled with tears. She wrote back immediately:

> *Paul:*
>
> *I hope thee and Nancy will be most happy together. She is a beautiful young woman and loves the Lord very much.*
>
> *School keeps me busy. The boys are so good now. I get the wood box filled up without asking, the water is brought in from the well, and Thomas insists on hanging my wraps on the nail by the door. Such a change!*
>
> *Please hug baby Clifford for me. And write again.*
>
> > *Your friend,*
> > *Gem*

Two weeks later Pearl received another box of paper, watercolors, and brushes. She knew what they would do with the new paints—an activity all would enjoy.

Again, Judson wanted to know what was in the box, but she declined to answer.

Once the lessons were out of the way, she passed out paper and scissors for the snowflakes. "And when we finish these, we'll cut strips, paint them red and green, and have paper chains to put on your trees."

"We never have a tree," Cora said.

"Well, perhaps this year you might. If you don't, you can hang the chains on the walls."

Pearl remembered the story of Emily's first Christmas with a tree and how excited she had been. She'd want one now for Clifford's first Christmas.

When the chains and snowflakes were finished, Pearl brought out the plate of taffy. She and Nina had pulled taffy, then cut it into squares and put it on one of Nina's pretty blue plates.

"After singing Christmas carols, we'll have taffy and if there's enough time I have a new story to read."

"A Christmas story?" asked Mary Alice.

"Yes, a poem, actually. It's not as beautiful as the story of Jesus' birth, but you will enjoy it, I'm sure."

"I don't want school to end," John Mac said. "I like the stories."

"Perhaps you'd like to borrow one of my books," Pearl offered.

John Mac suddenly scowled. "Pa wouldn't let me read. He says it is girl's stuff."

"I see."

"We used to think that," Timothy said then.

"Because we didn't want to study," said Thomas.

"Yeah," Carl added, "but we know it's a good idea to learn numbers and to be able to read. Just last week I read a letter for Pa, one he got from the governor of Oregon!"

"My goodness, that is wonderful," Pearl said, eager to hear what the governor had to say. "Was it good news?"

Carl whipped the letter out of his back pocket. "It was." He looked thoughtful. "My father caught a runaway horse and saved a girl's life. The governor has invited him to a special ceremony at the capitol building next Saturday to get an award."

"Carl, this is wonderful news."

"Pa said I could read the letter," Carl said, unfolding the sheet of paper. "If you want me to."

"By all means."

Carl read the words haltingly and only once did Pearl have to help, with the word *accommodations*.

"What's that long word mean?" Thomas asked, breaking in.

"It means that Carl's father will be put up, so he doesn't need to worry about going home that same night."

"I'm sure your father will enjoy going to our state's capital and collecting his award," Pearl said. "That is quite an honor."

Pearl unwrapped the dish of taffy and the kids oohed and ahhed.

"Treats after we sing and have our Christmas story."

Pearl had finished the last stanza, " 'Happy Christmas to all and to all a good night,' " when the door burst open.

Judson Rome stood in the doorway, eyes blazing. The children gasped.

"Miss Galloway! I've been standing outside, listening. You just now read one of those make-believe stories! And partying to boot!"

Pearl's face flushed. The room was a shambles with paper chains and snowflakes littering the desks and floors. She finally found her voice. "It's true that we're having a party, but the pupils finished their work, and it is almost Christmas."

The room was so silent Pearl could almost hear her heart beat.

"Christmas is no different from any other day! I remember specifically stating that you teach the basics. This—" and he grabbed *The Night Before Christmas* and flung it across the room—"is hardly the basics."

Pearl had never been so mortified in her entire life. For a long moment she could do nothing but stand and stare. Finally she gathered her composure, walked across the room, and picked up the slim volume. She examined the spine, ran her fingers over the words she loved so well, and closed it gently.

She remembered the lessons she'd given the children on how to care for a book. Never bend it back. Always lay it in a flat place. Wash your hands before handling one, and absolutely never, ever throw it on the floor. The children, eyes wide, waited to see what would happen next.

Pearl stood straight and stared at her accuser. "Mr. Rome, one can throw books and burn books, but they can never get rid of the precious words written therein. Those we keep in our hearts."

Stunned, as if not knowing what to say, he sputtered. "The school board will have to vote on the matter, of course, but I'm afraid we have no choice but to let you go and begin our search for another teacher."

"But, Pa," Mary Alice's voice broke in. "We like Miss Galloway."

"Yes, Pa," Timothy said.

"Obviously," Judson Rome snapped, "since all you do is have fun." He picked up a chain and tore it in half. "Such frivolity! This is not what school is about. You'll be hearing from me!" Without another word, he spun on his heel and slammed out the door, shaking the windows.

There was only one more day until winter break. Pearl would still go home, as planned, then wait to hear from Judson Rome.

"My father wants to marry you," Mary Alice said during recess. "I heard him say that."

"I know, Mary Alice. If you and your brothers were all that came with the bargain, I would have accepted gladly. However, I cannot marry a man who does not like words and books and fun. I simply could not bear it."

"My mother always agreed with Papa."

"And your mother was a saint." Pearl reached over and ran fingers through the snarled curls. What she wouldn't give to mother this child. If only she could take her home. Emily would love her as her own, as would Ben and Sarah and every one else. She shook the thoughts from her mind.

Recess was over, and every one came back in, blowing steamy breaths into the room. It was cold enough to snow, Pearl thought.

"Please read *The Night Before Christmas* again," they begged.

She held the book, noting the wrinkled corners. What was the harm? She no longer had a position here; she might as well read, give them some enjoyment. Heaven only knew when they might have a teacher again.

"I will read after you do one page of numbers." She passed out the arithmetic: addition for the younger ones, multiplication for the older students.

As they worked, Pearl thought about the possibility of not returning to Stayton School. She recalled one of Sarah's favorite sayings: "Things always work out for the best."

John Mac looked up from his numbers, holding his page high. "I'm all done!"

"Good, John Mac. Give everyone else a chance to finish."

"Are you really going to leave?"

"I don't know. It depends on what decision the school board makes." Pearl looked out over her classroom. "Whatever happens, I want you to remember what you have learned. I want you to do your work and cooperate with the new teacher." A funny feeling started in the pit of her stomach as Pearl realized how much she had grown to love the children.

Pearl was silent when Judson Rome came to pick her up after school.

"Perhaps I was wrong," he said as he helped her into the buggy. "I may want you to stay, Miss Galloway."

Pearl bristled inside. "Say what you will, Mr. Rome, but I may not want to return after my winter break."

"Confound it!" He hit the reins hard. "I don't understand you!"

"Nor I you."

Sudden clouds scudded across the sky then, and Pearl wondered if it meant snow. Snow didn't come often to these parts, nothing like it had in Iowa, but it did fall in November sometimes and definitely December. January was usually the worst month for snow, according to Emily, who had lived in Oregon longer than anyone else in the family. She told of the long winter when the snow lasted a week, and then ice came and stayed another week.

"There will be just one more day of school," Judson said then. "That's in the contract."

"I may go early," Pearl said. "The train leaves at three o'clock and I'd like to be on it."

Judson Rome frowned. "I can't give you full pay."

"Do as you must, Mr. Rome."

At last they were at the Colvilles' just as the first snowflake fell.

"It's snowing!" Mary Alice cried, coming out of her quiet lethargy.

Pearl hugged the small child, knowing she'd always remember the way her face lit up at the sight of snow.

"I will see you in the morning, Miss Galloway."

Pearl paused. "I really prefer that John take me to school tomorrow, if you don't mind."

Judson Rome sputtered in that way he had when someone dared to cross or question him. "We shall see," he called out as Pearl hurried across the yard.

A warm fire blazed in the fireplace, and Nina looked up expectantly when Pearl entered the cozy house. She hung her wraps on the nail beside the door.

"Thee looks angry."

"I am."

"I have some lemon tea. Perhaps that will help thy disposition."

"Perhaps, but don't count on it." Pearl sank into the nearest chair. "I think I've lost my teaching position, Nina."

"No. What is thee saying, Pearl?"

"Judson Rome does not like my method of teaching. He wants to find another teacher." She took the cup of tea and felt its warmth. "I was never what he expected."

"But thee is a good teacher."

"I know, but Judson wanted someone to marry, and I wouldn't go along with the plan."

"He may change his mind before tomorrow."

"It won't do any good."

"Thee means—"

"Yes, Nina. I'm sorry, because I enjoyed being here. I wanted to help with the baby. Wanted to plant flowers around the house, make new curtains. . . ."

Pearl thought of the cross-stitch pattern she was embroidering to decorate the kitchen wall. It wasn't finished, but maybe she could complete it tonight.

The wind howled around the small house and Nina looked concerned. "I thought John would be home by now."

"Perhaps I should go after him," Pearl offered.

"He's got the wagon and old Ned. He will be all right. He grew up in the Midwest where snow is nothing. He probably thinks he can work a few hours longer."

As the snow flurries grew thicker, Pearl worried along with Nina. If anyone was to go, it should be her, not Nina. Nina had a baby to watch out for. She didn't need to be out in this kind of weather or get chilled.

"I really think I should go—"

"No." Nina held her arm. "He'll be here soon. I know it."

Beans bubbled on the back of the stove, their good smell filling the small cabin as Pearl gathered her belongings.

Tomorrow she would board the train to Portland. John would take her, not Judson Rome. She'd had all of him she could take. Of course if a heavy snow fell, they might not get to the station. The thought of staying one more night, one more day, made Pearl sad. Now that Judson Rome had forced the issue, she longed to be back with her loved ones, longed to see Paul's face again, longed to hug Mama and Emily and Ben.

Pearl thought of Emily's last letter. She said she was worried about Paul. He seemed unhappy. "Not his usual cheerful self," she said. Pearl laughed after reading that part. She felt languid a lot. Tired. Out of sorts. She wondered if her coming home would have any bearing on her feeling, or Paul's.

She smoothed her brown muslin and placed it in the trunk as the clock struck six. It was then she heard the horses outside and Nina calling out, "I thought you were never coming home."

There was silence, then John's robust laugh. "Me, an old farm boy from North Dakota would get lost in the snow? This snow is nothing by comparison."

They laughed, and Pearl came and joined in the fun. She was going to miss her friends. They truly loved one another, and she would miss their company, the little house, and Nina's good cooking.

At last they sat, and John asked for the Lord's blessing on the food, on this the last night Pearl would be there.

"It'll all be melted by morning," John said when Pearl voiced her concern. "Snow doesn't last here like it does elsewhere."

That night Pearl hummed a song as she finished packing the trunk. Tomorrow—if the snow had melted—the children would come, pick up their papers, and she her supplies, then she'd head for the train station and soon would be on her way home—back to Portland. Would she return? Only God knew.

Pearl opened her Bible and read from James: "If any of you lack wisdom, let him ask of God, that giveth to all men liberally, and upbraideth not; and it shall be given him."

Pearl closed her Bible. Had God led her here not only to teach children, but to be a wife, a mother to three motherless children? She knew some married for convenience' sake, but could she do that? Perhaps if Paul wasn't in her heart and mind, she might look at Judson differently. Perhaps if all hopes were dashed where Paul was concerned—if he became betrothed to Nancy Whitfield, she might reconsider. But for now, she could think of nothing more offensive.

She closed her eyes and prayed for the snow to stop.

OLD-TIME TAFFY

1 cup sugar

1 cup dark corn syrup

2 tablespoons water

1 tablespoon apple cider vinegar

Butter, the size of a peanut

Place ingredients in a pan; bring to a boil. Boil until it forms a hard ball in a cup of cold water. Then add 1/2 teaspoon soda; stir well.

Pour on buttered pan and when cooled, pull until shiny and ready to cut. Takes two or more to make. Try it!

This is the recipe Pearl made and took to school for the Christmas party.

Chapter 7

Just as John predicted, the snow had melted by morning. Rivers of mud ran across the dirt road in front of the house and the only indication that snow had been there was a small drift not quite melted against the north side of the barn.

It would be a short day, and Pearl knew her pay would be less than previously agreed on. John would take her to school, help her pack her things, then drive her to the train station. The children would come for that morning, pick up their belongings, and say good-bye.

Nina prepared a breakfast of bacon, eggs, baking powder biscuits, and her best cherry preserves. She hugged Pearl close and dabbed at her tears. "I wish things had worked out, but thee did the right thing."

"I did?"

"Yes. Everyone knows that Judson Rome is used to having his way and if he doesn't, he makes things a mite uncomfortable. No godly man could act that way, and thee needs a godly man, Pearl. There's someone there for thee. Just be patient."

Yes, there is someone for me, but is it Paul? He's not exactly a godly man. Soon she was hugging her dear friend. "We'll see each other again someday," Pearl said. "I promise."

After more tears and hugs, John placed the trunk on the wagon.

They started out only to find Judson Rome waiting at the end of the road.

"What—?" Pearl's heart nearly stopped when she saw the fancy wagon and the pair of Morgans.

Judson hopped down and held out his hand. "I came to take Miss Galloway to school."

John said nothing, but looked at Pearl, as if he expected her to decide.

"It won't be necessary," Pearl said, trying not to spit the words out. "John will take me, then come back at noon to take me to the train station."

"That's what I wanted to talk about."

It was then Pearl noticed Mary Alice in the back of the buggy, and she was crying.

He jerked a thumb in his child's direction. "She don't want you to leave."

Pearl wanted to take the small child in her arms, tell her everything would be all right, that she'd like the next teacher just as well. "We discussed it yesterday. Everything's settled."

"But it isn't settled." Judson motioned for John to go back home. "We need to talk."

"There's nothing to say. Please stay, John," Pearl said.

"I want you to marry me," Judson said then. "No courting. Just marrying. Now. Tomorrow. Or within a week."

Pearl gripped the seat of the wagon. "But, I can't. I have said that many times over."

"Can't?" He cocked his head. "And why ever not?"

"Oh, please Miss Galloway, be my mommy," the small voice pleaded from the backseat. "I want you to be my mommy forever and ever."

"She's been crying all morning."

For the first time, Pearl saw a tender side of Judson Rome. He was worried about his little girl, and that touched her. She tried to steady her hands in her lap. How easy it would be to say yes to the proposal. She could have her own home, a ready-made family, and never have to worry about money or a roof over her head. Was this what God wanted her to do? Was this how He had answered her prayers?

Surely not. She knew Judson did not love God. Nor did he love her. He was asking her for selfish reasons. How could she marry under these circumstances?

In the end she had gone with him, just so she could console Mary Alice.

A fire was built and the Rome twins stood beaming.

"We came early so it would be warm."

"I appreciate that. Thank you."

Pearl was beginning to realize how much she would hate leaving the Stayton School. She loved all the pupils, especially the younger ones.

"Pa said you might marry him," Thomas said then. "Is that true?"

"I cannot." Pearl removed her wraps and warmed her hands by the stove. "Please do not ask why."

Judson Rome assured her the school board had someone in mind, and the new teacher would arrive in January.

Soon the others came and crowded around. There were gifts of marbles, raisins, a cookie, pictures, and letters. Pearl looked at each face and smiled. She might not have been here long, but she loved each one of them.

"Don't open my present until you're on the train," Mary Alice said. She held out an envelope with *Teacher* written on it.

Pearl nodded and pulled the small girl close. "And you keep learning your letters and numbers, and I know you'll like the new teacher."

Cora hung back, a look of sorrow on the small, pinched face.

"Cora, what is it?"

Tears filled her eyes. "I have nothing for you, Teacher. I have no presents at my house."

"Oh, Cora, I don't need anything. Just your smile is enough to make my whole day bright."

Cora beamed, along with several others who had obviously not thought of bringing something for teacher's last day.

"Who's going to read to us now?" Thomas asked.

"Your new teacher will bring different books."

"We're sorry you're going," John Mac said then.

"And I am sorry to go, but perhaps I can come visit again one day."

All agreed that would be a good idea.

They recited the Pledge of Allegiance, and Pearl read the story about the three kings bearing gifts for the Savior, from the book of Matthew.

"We want to sing," Timothy said.

They sang several songs, and Pearl finished the morning with another reading of *The Night Before Christmas*.

It was time to go. She heard the horses outside and half expected it to be Judson Rome. But John sat on the seat, nodding when she opened the door. One more hug all around and she walked to the wagon and looked back just once at the small log school and the waving hands. A lump came to her throat.

John helped her into the wagon. "Thee has been a good teacher. Don't forget this moment."

Pearl smiled. "Yes. I know I am a teacher, and that means more than marrying and having a family."

The trip to the train station was spent in silence as once more Pearl took in the countryside, the barren fields, long since yielding their annual harvest. A farmhouse rose on the horizon now and then, and she remembered the children she'd taught, hoping the new teacher would be a godly person and would love all of them.

At last they arrived—and none too soon as the train chugged into sight.

"Here," Pearl said, "a present for you and Nina. Just a way of thanking you both for being so loving and kind. I didn't want to give it to you sooner because Nina would have felt bad that she didn't have a going-away gift for me."

It was the cross Pearl had cross-stitched in the evening when she couldn't sleep. She could visualize it now, up over the table in the small house. "I know God will bless thee, and soon a new one will join thy lives."

John looked pleased as he bent over and hugged Pearl. "Nina sent thee a lunch," John said. "Leftover chicken, biscuits, and some of her special watermelon pickles."

"Thou hast been so good to me. How can I ever repay thee?"

John tipped his hat. "No need, Pearl. Thee made us plumb happy, and I truly mean it."

Soon Pearl was on the train and found a seat at the rear of the car. *Going home, going home, going home,* the wheels clacked this time. And going home she was. Soon she'd be in the comfortable house Ben had built. Soon she'd hear the streetcars clanging down the street. Gone would be the smell of grasses blowing in the breeze, the flat land where few trees dotted the landscape. She was returning to the city, to her friends, and to the small Friends meeting she knew so well. And Paul. Somehow her heart and mind couldn't stop thinking about him. If it was meant to be, it would come to pass, but somehow she didn't think that was what God had intended for her life. She'd find out soon. He would point her in the right direction soon. Perhaps there would be more pupils to teach. At the thought of her pupils, she thought of Mary Alice's present. She'd tucked it into her valise, remembering the admonition to read it on the train.

She removed the string and laughed at the picture the child had drawn. Pearl had on her yellow dotted Swiss and stood in front of the classroom. The desk was off to the side, and out of the top drawer a snake was slipping.

Pearl laughed as she clutched the picture close. It had been a dreadful moment, but a fun one for her pupils. She would certainly be prepared for snakes in the future, she decided, should she teach again.

The wheels clacked on: *going home, going home, going home,* lulling her to sleep.

Chapter 8

As the train pulled into the station, Pearl patted her hair into place, grabbed her bonnet and gloves, and tried to control her excitement. What if Paul had come to fetch her? What would she say? Would her expression tell how she felt?

It wasn't Paul, but a smiling, waving Ben, and she found she was just as excited. Pearl jumped down and into her brother's arms, suddenly wanting to ask about everything and everybody.

"Oh, I've never been so glad to see anyone in my whole life." She grew somber for a moment, remembering she hadn't yet told anyone that she was fired from her very first job.

"You look wonderful, little sister. That valley air must agree with you."

Pearl let her bonnet slip down her back and nodded. "I love the farming community, as you know, and the children are special, but it's good to be home!"

Ben hoisted the trunk onto the back of the wagon and started to help Pearl, then stopped. "Oh, yes, that's right. You're an independent woman now, right?"

Pearl giggled. "I suppose you might think that." She handed him the envelope Judson Rome had given her that morning. "This is for you, Ben. To help pay for me and Mama."

Ben shoved the envelope back. "I'm not taking your money. Keep it. You'll need it one day. Wait and see."

Soon they were heading for home and though she wanted to hear about Paul, she just couldn't bring herself to ask.

"And how's that little nephew of mine?"

"Growing like a weed."

"And everyone else?"

"I'm worried about Mama, if you must know." Ben's smile faded. "Still coughing. More now."

"I can't bear to think of anything happening to Mama."

"We're making her rest more these days."

"And how's work going?"

Ben smiled again. "Getting more jobs than I can handle, but I praise

286

God for the work."

"Yes, I should think so."

"But it's Paul whom you really want to know about."

Pearl's face flushed. "I never said—"

"Sis, you didn't have to."

"Well, then. . ." She was careful to look straight ahead. "How is he?"

"He's working across town; boarding with another fellow."

Pearl felt her hopes dashed for the second time that day. That meant she wouldn't see him tonight. Maybe she'd never see him again. Her heart suddenly stood still. He was one of the reasons she couldn't wait to get back, and now he wouldn't be there. She wanted to ask about Nancy Whitfield, but knew she'd find out soon enough. As if Ben were reading her mind, he spoke about Nancy.

"You know that woman who sits by Paul at meeting?"

"Nancy Whitfield?"

"Yes, I believe that is her name."

"I know of her."

"She isn't the sort for Paul—" Ben turned and gazed a long moment before his half grin erupted into a wide smile. "Not that you'd be caring or anything."

Pearl hit his arm. "You're teasing me."

"And why shouldn't I when it's so much fun?"

Pearl longed to say what was on her heart, her mind, but the words stayed locked inside. It would sound ludicrous to admit she cared even a tiny bit for Paul. She knew she'd never stand a chance, not when there was a beautiful woman who loved him. Why couldn't she put him out of her mind once and for all?

"So, you'll be here two weeks, then back on the train?"

"I'm not going back—"

"Not going back?"

"I don't know how to tell you this, Ben—" She braced herself, wanting to put it correctly, so all the fault did not lay with Judson Rome. "The man who hired me for the position—"

"Yes, go on." Ben was all serious now.

"He—well, he didn't like my teaching methods. Said I had no control over the older boys."

"And why didn't you? I can't imagine you not cracking the whip when you can run ole Tess, the mule. You got her to move when nobody else could."

Pearl smiled at the almost forgotten memory of the mule in Iowa. "Yes, I 'spect that's true, but animals are far different from men." Her voice trailed off.

"Do go on."

"I was let go because I read one of the books Emily sent."

"One of those wild tales?"

"*Robinson Crusoe* is not wild, but it is fiction, and I knew from the first day that Mr. Rome wanted nothing but the truth read in school."

"And you broke a rule."

Pearl took a deep breath. "I was justified."

"How?"

"The older boys wouldn't do their schoolwork, so I hit on the idea of reading once they did their numbers and English. It worked."

"What else happened that you're so carefully trying to hide from me? Remember, you can tell me when you can't go to anyone else."

Pearl twisted her hands in her lap. "He—that is Mr. Rome—wanted to court me. He needed a mother for his children. I wasn't interested—" Her hand touched his sleeve. "Oh, Ben, he is not a kind person. I could never let myself even think of having such an uncouth man court me."

"He isn't a believer?"

"He says he believes in God, but he said such unkind remarks about the Friends."

"We have heard these things before."

"I know, but it would have been difficult for me to return, so his saying I wasn't suitable for the job was almost a blessing, except—" Sudden tears filled the pale blue eyes. "I have a dark spot on my record now."

"Nonsense!"

"It's true."

"You'll have no trouble finding a position, Pearl."

The rest of the ride was spent in gay camaraderie as Ben continued to fill Pearl in on all the happenings of Portland.

The day was gray, but at least it wasn't raining as Pearl looked around, noticing there were more buggies on the road, an occasional car, and of course the streetcar that clanged down Foster.

Soon the familiar and much-loved house came into sight. Pearl hopped down and ran up the walk and into the house. "Where is everyone?" she cried out.

"In the kitchen, preparing dinner," came Emily's answer as she rushed to Pearl, drying her hands on a tea towel. "Lands, but you are a sight for sore eyes."

The house was festive as Pearl knew it would be. The smell of cinnamon and sugar filled the air. "Cut-out cookies?" Pearl exclaimed, looking at the cookies lined up in a row.

She heard a chortle and turned to see baby Clifford and her mother.

"Mama! I missed you so."

She hugged her mother with Clifford getting squeezed in the middle. "I never thought the holidays would come."

"Is thee remembering the reason for celebrating?"

Pearl flushed for a moment. "Perhaps not, Mama. But God is near, He has been with me this whole time. Helping and guiding me."

"Oh, sister, I thought of thee so many times, prayed for thee, too," Emily said.

Pearl could hardly believe she was home again with those she loved and who loved her. The picture was complete with the exception of Paul. She had so hoped to see Paul.

Pearl removed her hat and set it on the top shelf in the entryway, straightened the wrinkles in her dress, and poked some loose hair back into the knot at the nape of her neck. "It's so Christmasy—this house filled with love."

"We treasured your letters," Sarah said, easing into a chair. "I've been kind of weary with this cough hanging on—can't sleep nights. I would read and reread thy letters."

"Oh, Mama, I thought of thee and remembered what thee told me about not giving up, about praying for strength, and it worked."

Pearl thought about the happy faces, the hands waving as she left the small school that last day. Even the twins had given her a good-bye.

"I have gifts," she said aloud then. "From my students. I'll bring them out later."

"We want to hear all about it," Emily said. "Letters are fine, but don't take the place of face-to-face good ole talking."

Pearl slipped a cookie off the end of a row. The sugar melted in her mouth as she bit off the top of the star.

"We made taffy. I took it to school so we could have a party. Then Mr. Rome was angry because we were 'partying,' as he put it."

"Forget Mr. Rome," Ben said. He'd been standing there and now held baby Clifford. "Thy nephew has missed thee." He held the squirming body out.

"My, but thee has grown," Pearl said. "And heavy, too."

She held the soft face next to her own and laughed when he reached for the comb in her hair.

"No, no—" It didn't keep him from reaching. "Thou must learn some manners, I see," Pearl said with a chuckle.

There was a mischievous gleam in his eye, and she knew he was going to be a stubborn, determined man someday. Probably give some teacher fits, just as Timothy and Thomas had given her.

Then she realized he smelled the cookie she'd just eaten. "Ah, that's what thee wants! A cookie. Can I, Emily? Just a tiny, teensy nibble?"

Emily nodded and handed Pearl a bell. "Just one now, mind thee. I fear he may have a sweet tooth."

And so Pearl enjoyed her second cookie, almost the whole cookie. Clifford's eyes sparkled even more as he chewed away.

"Come. It is time for this boy's bedtime." Emily reached for her son, her second born. She held him close, though he struggled to go back to his Auntie Pearl.

"Nah, nah, thee needs no more sweets!"

Pearl took the coffee Sarah handed her with the words "You must need coffee to wash down the sweets. Did thee eat lunch?"

Pearl nodded. "Nina packed me a wonderful lunch."

Pearl placed an apron over her middle and offered to finish the rolls for tomorrow's dinner. "I haven't had much chance to cook as Nina did everything. With being a working woman, my time was consumed with teaching and preparing to teach."

"Did the books come in handy that Emily sent?" Sarah asked.

"Oh, very." *I might still have the job if I hadn't read to the children,* Pearl thought, knowing there'd be time to explain it later.

The rolls were set to rise, and the kitchen was quiet as Pearl slipped into a chair and took in the walls of the huge kitchen. Such a difference from the small home at the Colvilles'. And how she had missed the conveniences.

She thought of the running water, the indoor bathroom Ben had put in right after he and Emily married. The phone put in last year, and the electric iron. Emily hadn't thought she'd like it, but Ben said it was such a good price and they were making history by taking part on a trial basis. Pearl liked the iron and had sorely missed it when staying at the Colvilles'. She remembered Mama's comment, however.

"What's this world a-comin' to anyhow? Too many new-fangled things, if thee asks me."

"Well, Mama, times change, and I guess we must go along with those changes," Ben had said, trying to reassure her. "One thing that will never change is our growing need for God and His ways." And everyone had "Amened" that.

"We'll have singing tonight around the piano," Emily announced. "I'll take requests."

Pearl had forgotten how much she missed the piano music. It had been so much a part of her life the past two years.

She remembered then the wristlet of bells John Mac had given her. It would be the perfect gift for Clifford. He'd love the noise the bells made, the sweet sound.

Pearl waltzed around the room, throwing her arms out. "I can't believe I am here. God is so good. God has brought me home!"

The evening meal, a thick beef stew, was soon on the table, and Pearl was happy there were big slabs of cornbread to go with it

And for dessert, one of Emily's pies made from pie plant; one of Pearl's favorites.

"Seems you were expecting company," she said when Emily handed her a large piece of the pie.

"Of course. You are company, Pearl Galloway, and don't ever forget it."

Soon Pearl talked about the children, how much she liked teaching, telling about little Mary Alice who needed a mother, about the others who learned their numbers and alphabet easily. "If it weren't for the boys. They were so rowdy at first. I think Judson—Mr. Rome put his sons up to heckling me. I really do."

"Pearl's out of a job—" Ben began explaining.

And then Pearl's face crumpled up as tears spilled forth. "I tried so hard."

"There, there." Emily held her close, offering her best white linen hankie. "Tears are cleansing and thee knows that we believe that God doesn't close a door, but what He opens a window somewhere else. There's something more important for you to be doing. We just need to find out what it is."

Pearl washed dishes while Emily dried.

"I've been worried about you," Emily said.

"Worried? Because of my lack of a job?"

Emily's fingers held Pearl's wrist. "No, Sister. You know you will always have a home here with us. That is why Ben built the house so large."

"What, then, is your worry?"

"Your face, Pearl. You have a worried look when you think nobody is looking. Your eyes look lost. Sad, somehow. Thee doesn't think I can tell about such things, but I can."

"If I had married Judson Rome, I would have had a nice home, children to love, but it didn't feel right. How could I love man who isn't right with God?"

"I know. I understand."

And how can I keep loving a man who doesn't know God at all? Pearl wanted to say, but she kept the thoughts locked tight inside her. *Some day it might come out, but not now. Not yet.*

"Thee has plenty of time for marriage and a family," Emily said. "Remember I was twenty-four when I met Ben."

"I remember hearing."

"I had doubts, but God directed my paths, just as He will yours."

Pearl nodded and changed the subject. "And how are Kate and Pastor Luke?"

"Fine as ever. They'll be here for dinner tomorrow night."

Pearl dried her tears. "I can hardly wait to see them."

After dishes, everyone retired to the front room where Emily sat down in front of the piano.

"I dreamed of this night so many times," Pearl said, clasping her hands in front of her. "Emily playing, us singing, baby Clifford clapping his hands."

"Now, what shall I play? Any special requests?" Emily asked.

Pearl reached over and hugged Emily. "I love you, sister. So very, very much."

"And thou art loved in return more than you will ever know."

"Play 'Have Thine Own Way, Lord,' " said Pearl. "I kept humming that on the train."

"And I'll add 'Standing on the Promises,' then we'll sing Christmas carols."

Pearl sat in the front room and watched Emily's hands fly over the keys. She sang heartily, and soon Ben added his voice. Sarah could not sing; it made her cough.

"What is better than standing on the promises of God?" Ben said when the hymn was finished.

"Indeed, what more?" echoed Sarah.

"And now some carols, since the Lord's birthday is so close," Emily said.

"There is nothing more beautiful than Christmas carols. I wish we could sing them all year long."

"I suppose we could," Emily said. "Who is to say what we can and cannot sing?"

Sarah nodded. "The carols bring such deep peace to my heart. Such wonderful knowledge that our Lord reigns."

Pearl didn't add to the conversation. Instead her mind was fleeing again, thinking of a certain tall young man, remembering the first time she'd laid eyes on him in this very house, on a night much warmer than this with everyone around laughing and talking. Paul's absence left a big chunk missing from the picture. How could she make her heart content once again? Pearl knew that Paul would have been here if he cared in the same way that she did for him. "Sometimes things are not as we would wish them to be," she remembered Sarah saying. That is what she must fall back on in the days and weeks ahead.

Sarah coughed and held Clifford out toward Pearl. He was more than she could handle, especially when she started coughing. He reared up on his feet, as if wanting to fly. Pearl leaned over and gathered him in her arms. He patted her face as tears filled her eyes.

"The tree will go in the same corner as last year," Ben said. "I'll cut it down tomorrow morning."

"And we'll cover it with tinsel," Emily added. "It's the latest thing to decorate trees."

"Tomorrow we'll make more cookies and fudge and a fruitcake," Sarah pronounced.

Pearl had much to be thankful for, yet she couldn't help missing the face of a certain young man. Would he be home for Christmas? For meeting? Oh, she hoped so. Even if there wasn't a special gift for him, she knew she could make him a special treat and wrap it as a present.

"Hark the Herald Angels sing," Ben sang.

"Glory to the Newborn King." Emily joined in the singing, her fingers racing up and down the keys.

"Glory to the Newborn King!" a voice rang out, repeating the last refrain of the chorus.

"Paul!" Emily turned and smiled at her little brother. "I thought we wouldn't see you until tomorrow."

"What? And miss my best friend and sister?"

Pearl's eyes lit up, her face beaming, and without a second thought, she ran across the room and hugged him.

"It's good to have you back, Gem," he said, touching the top of her head but for a brief moment.

Pearl broke away and met his gaze. Sister, he had said. Friend. How could she expect more?

"It's wonderful to be home," she said, her gaze meeting his. "I missed all of you so much."

"Well, let's get back to the singing," Paul said. "I'm just getting wound up."

"How about 'Joy to the World'?" Emily said.

Later they sat around having second and third cups of coffee, finishing off the pie plant and sugar cookies made that morning.

"I'll make more," Emily said. "Eat away."

"Goodness, isn't it past this young man's bedtime?" Sarah asked, again holding her wriggling grandson.

"Oh, Mama, he's just wanting to be part of the festivities," Ben said. "Here. I'll take him from thee."

As if in answer, Clifford reached up and patted his father's face.

"What do you think of the nephew?" Paul asked then. "Hasn't he grown?"

"A bunch," Pearl said.

Pearl never wanted the night to end. She wanted to talk to Paul. She wanted to go out and see if the stars were out. She wanted to hear about Nancy Whitfield, see if there were any special future plans. But she said none of these things.

"I have something for you," Paul said then. "I found it in an old house we bought to fix up."

"Something for me?" Pearl repeated, wondering what it could possibly be.

"It's tattered, but you'll like it."

Tattered? Pearl wondered what could be tattered. Paul held out a small book. With worn, brown cover, its pages musty smelling and torn, she read the title: *Black Beauty*.

"It's about a horse. Do you think you'll read it?"

"It's beautiful," Pearl answered. "Of course I'll read it. And Emily will, too. I'll treasure it always and forever." She glanced up, thinking he was taller than she remembered. Taller than she was.

He laughed. "That's my Pearl. Always happy. Always smiling."

Ben scooted his chair back. "It's time for bed. We've got a full day ahead of us."

Paul grasped Pearl's hand for a moment. "I'm glad to see you looking so well."

Pearl felt her face flush as she finally looked away. "You're even taller than I remember," she murmured.

Everyone left the room, but Pearl stood in the doorway, watching as Paul moved toward the back door and thinking of how his eyes had met hers.

He hesitated, then turned around. "It's good that you're home." His gaze lingered, and Pearl felt her face flush. "I'm glad my job is over so I can move back home, too."

Finally she climbed the stairs to the bedroom she shared with her mother. *My Pearl*, he'd said. Of course that didn't mean anything, but she liked the way it sounded, the way he had looked at her, the special book he'd kept for her.

If it were summer, she might have sat on the porch for a while and counted the stars with Paul. If tomorrow weren't Christmas Eve, she might have stayed up and read *Black Beauty*. But she could not do either. It had been a full day, and she needed her rest.

Chapter 9

Sarah was coughing into her pillow when Pearl entered the bedroom. "Mama." Pearl leaned over and rubbed her mother's back. "Thy cough seems worse."

"I'll be okay." She reached out and took Pearl's hand and held it against her cheek. "It's good to have you back home, daughter. I been a-laying here a-thinkin' about you and how beautiful you've become."

Pearl felt color rise to her cheeks. "Mama, you know I have never been beautiful, not one single day of my life."

"No, child, you have a radiance that catches the eye."

I wish it would catch a certain gentleman's eye, Pearl wanted to say, but of course she didn't.

"We missed thee terrible while thee was gone," Sarah went on.

"And I missed you and all the others," Pearl said, putting an arm around her mother's broad shoulders.

"Thou must go after what thee needs," Sarah said, as she crawled under a comforter.

"Mama, whatever do you mean?"

Pearl fussed with the sheet, tucking it in. Her mother had always been wise. Perceptive. Had she meant what Pearl thought she did? Could she possibly know how she felt about Paul?

"God can't answer a prayer if thy request isn't made." Sarah squeezed Pearl's hand again. "It's time to start asking, my child. 'Ask and it shall be given you; seek and ye shall find.' "

Pearl eased out of her best dress and hung it over a chair.

"There is one prayer I used to say many times over—"

"What was that, Mama?"

"That I might see my children again before I die."

Pearl thought of the others. Mama had Ben and her. Jesse had come and gone, but she knew Mama missed Anna who had stayed behind in Iowa to be a nurse. Clara lived in far-off Connecticut. And Lulu was in California.

"I wonder if Albert is in Washington still—on the coast, I believe Ben said?"

Sarah nodded. "He doesn't write. The girls do write sometimes. They are busy. Happy. I should be happy, too."

Pearl wondered now, as she often had wondered, why she was so tall and manly looking. Mama was tall, but not as tall as Pearl. Anna was tall, as were Clara and Lulu, but Pearl was the tallest and had the broadest shoulders. In spite of Sarah's words, Pearl felt big and bulky and downright ugly. She dismissed the idea from her mind immediately. No sense in dwelling on it, she reminded herself.

"Mama, do you want me to read from the Bible?"

Sarah nodded. "I love to hear thy voice, Pearl. It has such a wonderful quality to it. Lilting. Expectant."

The worn Bible automatically opened to Proverbs, and Pearl found one of her favorite passages.

> *Trust in the Lord with all thine heart;*
> *and lean not unto thine own understanding.*
> *In all thy ways acknowledge him,*
> *and he shall direct thy paths.*
> *Be not wise in thine own eyes:*
> *fear the Lord, and depart from evil.*

"He knows what is good for me, for us," Pearl said. Sarah's eyes were closed, but she wasn't asleep yet. "When I think of how many times you have read Scripture to me—"

Sarah's ragged breathing filled the room. Pearl knotted her hands. She wouldn't think about it. Mama was invincible. She would always be there.

Pearl turned off the lamp and sat in the darkness, listening to Mama breathe. She wanted to talk more, wanted to ask what was meant about "going after what thee needs." Did Sarah know about the young and beautiful Nancy Whitfield? Did Sarah really know what was inside Pearl's heart, how she felt? Mama was wise. Mama knew things just by looking and listening. Yes, Mama must know or she wouldn't have said what she did. Was there a chance that Paul might someday love her? Was there a chance that he might find God and make Him real in his life?

Pearl thought of Judson Rome. He wanted a marriage of convenience, and even if he didn't love her, she could have accepted that. But not loving God with all his heart and soul bothered her more. She was glad to be gone, though she'd always worry about the children. What was to become of Mary Alice? Thomas and Timothy? And John Mac? Cora and the others? Would the new teacher love them?

Clifford's hearty cry interrupted Pearl's thoughts. Strange for him to be getting up at this time of night. He was sleeping straight through now, Emily said. Pearl reached for a robe and slipped it around her shoulders before tiptoeing down the steps to the nursery.

Emily had not come. Had she not heard him? Pearl opened the nursery door and there he was standing up in his cradle.

"Goodness, gracious, if you're not careful, you're going to fall right out on your head." She leaned over and picked him up.

He laughed and patted her face.

"You missed me, didn't you?" She held him tight against her cheek. "I know I missed you. Yes, even your crying."

She changed his diaper and gown and wrapped him in the blanket. Maybe if she rocked him for a while, he'd go back to sleep. There was a rattling in his chest, but it was cold season. The winter winds had whipped up from the east and seemed to engulf the house. Pearl started humming a tune she especially liked.

" 'Have thine own way, Lord, have thine own way.' "

"I expect if anyone gets his own way around here, it's young Clifford." Ben stepped into the room. "I wondered why he shut up so quickly."

"He just wanted his auntie to rock him."

"Can I get you anything?" Ben asked.

"Brother, do you remember anything at all about Grandpa and Grandma Galloway? Or Mama's parents?"

"Sprouse," Ben said then. "Her maiden name was Sprouse. And no, I don't know anything about either of them." He sat across from Pearl. "Why does thee ask?"

"Just wondering why I am so tall." She wanted to say "and ugly," but knew Ben would admonish her just as Sarah did. They both thought she was pretty, but that was because they were family and loved her.

"Saw a photo once," Ben said then. "Ma probably has it somewhere in her treasure box."

"Of her parents?"

"Yes," Ben said. "Seems her father was tall and her mother, too. It's an asset to be tall," Ben said then, as if reading Pearl's mind. "Lots of people wish they were tall."

Clifford started jabbering as if he wanted to add his opinion to the discussion. Ben got up, leaned over, and took the smiling baby from Pearl. "And you, young man need to get back to bed. It is not morning."

"Emily didn't hear him?"

Ben frowned. "She did, but I told her to rest. She's having some problems again—I hope she'll be okay."

"Problems?" Pearl asked.

"I don't think she's fully recovered from Clifford's birth." Ben held his small son close. "I just thank God every day for such a healthy, robust child."

"I'll get up with him at night," Pearl offered.

Ben touched her shoulder. "Thanks, Pearl. You're such a help and blessing to us all. We'll manage just fine now that you're back home again."

Soon Clifford was back in bed, with Ben commanding him to be quiet in the authoritative voice fathers often have.

"I'll wait until he's asleep," Pearl said.

"Sometimes when he stays fussy, I put him in the buggy and rock him over a log."

"Over a log?"

"Yes. Seems he likes the bumpy part. Calms him down and makes him sleep."

"Well, I can try it," Pearl said, but he had already closed his eyes and was sound asleep. Pearl crept back up the stairs, thankful once again to be home where she belonged.

The night was chilly, but Paul didn't seem to notice as he made his way to his room at one end of the shed. He had a lantern to see by. Not that he needed to see. His heart pounded, and he wondered if he'd be able to sleep at all this night. This Christmas Adam.

He chuckled when he thought about Christmas Adam. It was something he and Pearl talked about last year.

"If December twenty-fourth is Christmas Eve, then the twenty-third should be Christmas Adam," she had said, laughing. "Didn't Adam come before Eve?"

Paul had agreed that her reasoning was sound. "So? What do we do? How do we celebrate?"

"We must prepare our hearts for the Lord's birth."

Paul remembered how he had changed the subject. He didn't want to talk about God—not then. Not now. He just couldn't believe as they all did. He was still seeking answers, searching for truths.

Searching. Seeking. He lay on his bed and stared at the rough walls of the shed. One thing he knew was how he felt about Pearl. He'd admonished himself many times in the two months she'd been gone, saying he didn't care for her in that way. She was his sister-in-law. They enjoyed each other's company. That had to be enough. Yet there was something in her eyes. The way she met his gaze and didn't look away. He had seen it before. He had wondered about it. Could she possibly care for him?

Nancy Whitfield had that look when she talked to him, but try as he might, he felt nothing but friendship while in her presence. His heart didn't beat faster, nor did his palms feel sweaty as they had tonight.

Pearl's voice. Her laugh. The way she walked. And held baby Clifford. He wanted to see her holding their child in that same loving way.

He rolled over and pounded the floor. Pearl didn't seem to be the marrying type. He had to forget her and concentrate on his work.

He lit the lamp and pulled a box out from under the bed. Inside lay the design for the house he wanted to build. He picked up the tablet and sketched the scene from tonight. Clifford with his hands flying, the bells jingling. . . . Ben standing beside Emily at the piano, his voice filling the room. . . . Sarah, her gray head held high as she listened and watched and tried to stifle her coughing. . . . Emily's fingers running up and down the keyboard of the magnificent piano that only she could play. . . . Then Pearl. His beloved Pearl. Talking. . .laughing. . .singing. . . . Her gaze as it rested on his face. The hair, thick and brown with a silver comb in the side. . . .

Paul set the sketch aside and wrote some words on the next page. It was a poem of sorts. It was one way he could get his thoughts down. He'd mentioned it to Emily shortly after she'd given him the sketchbook.

"Men don't write poems, Sis."

Her hand rested on his shoulder. "Oh, yes, they do, Paul. They write poems and books and stories, and they are all so beautiful."

Could he be a plasterer and an artist? A poet? Was that what God would have him do?

He pushed the box under the bed and lay on his back, wondering how God had crept into his thoughts like that. He had underlined a verse in the Bible, "He will direct thy paths," and wondered if God could be directing him. If God cared, as Emily and the others claimed, He would have the answers. Paul just had to figure out what they were. And he guessed one of the ways would be through talking. Prayer. That's what they called prayer.

Paul thought of the long moments of silent prayer at Meeting Day. He always found his mind wandering off on the next day's job, or later on he'd think of Pearl at the other end of the aisle. And Nancy would come sit beside him, as if she belonged there. He didn't want her there. He couldn't think of her in the way she thought of him. One couldn't court one lady if his thoughts were on another, could he?

"God," Paul said aloud "show me how to pray. I want to talk to You about a few things." Then he smiled. "Actually, I think I already have. Amen."

"Happy Christmas Adam," he said, rolling over and giving his pillow a hard jab.

Chapter 10

Breakfast was a flurry of cooking, baking, and making pots of coffee. Ben and Paul had gone after the tree. Ben had seen one of the right size on a lot he owned, and they would be back with the Douglas fir in a few minutes.

Pearl clasped her hands in delight when she saw and smelled the huge tree. Clifford clapped.

"You're such a mimic," Emily said, looking at her small son and remembering how lonely last year had been with no baby to share their joy.

"He should put the first decoration on the tree," Pearl said. "And I have just the thing."

She went to her trunk and brought out the chains and snowflakes. The colorful paper chains could be draped around the tree while the snowflakes could be pinned onto the branches.

"These are gifts from my class."

"I just bet those students will be happy to have you back," Paul said. Pearl grimaced. Paul didn't know. He hadn't been here when they had discussed it, and the two of them hadn't had a chance to talk.

"She isn't going back," Ben said.

"But why ever not?"

"I was not suitable, according to Judson Rome, head of the Marion School Board."

"He brought Pearl there under false pretenses," Ben added.

Pearl couldn't quite look at Paul. What must he be thinking about her? That she couldn't finish a task she'd started?

"He wanted a wife, a mother for his children," Ben continued. "Pearl could not concede to marry a man who does not serve God."

Now it was Paul's turn to grimace. Of course Pearl would only marry a godly man, should she choose to marry one day. That definitely meant he did not have a chance. What had made him think there was a certain look in her eyes?

Since he was the tallest, Paul put a golden star at the top. This time Clifford clapped his hands first.

"The star of Bethlehem," Sarah said. "It's there to guide us, just as it guided the shepherds of long ago."

Pearl wrapped her chains around the tree and added a few snowflakes. The strings of popcorn and cranberries were Sarah's contribution, since it was something she could do while sitting.

Emily brought out the tinsel. "This is supposed to look like rain."

"Rain!" Ben sputtered. "We get enough rain here. We don't need to make the false stuff to help us remember."

Everyone laughed and agreed. Still Emily wanted the shiny tinsel to adorn the tree, the baby's very first tree. She had to hold Clifford, as he wanted to crawl over and get into the tree.

"I can just see him pulling the whole tree down," Ben said.

"Yes, thee is right," Emily said. "He must be watched very closely."

"It's a gorgeous tree," Pearl said after the tinsel was added. "The most beautiful one I've ever seen."

Paul stood close, wanting to say something, but he couldn't even answer an affirmative. It was beautiful, but not as beautiful as the woman who had just decorated it.

"We have to work!" Ben said then. "Thou knowest what it says in Proverbs chapter six, verse six: 'Go to the ant, thou sluggard; consider her ways, and be wise.'"

" 'And an idle soul shall suffer hunger,' " Emily added, quoting the second part of Proverbs 19:15.

Ben grinned. "C'mon, Paul, help me finish the roof on the lean-to."

"And we will finish our baking," said Emily, heading to the kitchen.

Sarah sat at the table, peeling apples, while Pearl rolled out enough dough for three apple pies. She knew apple was Paul's favorite. She might even make him an extra tart if there were scraps left.

"I can hardly wait to see Luke and Kate," Pearl said, breaking the silence.

"Thee hasn't seen them since thee went away to teach school."

"I'll change into my best dress, the one Kate made, before they arrive."

Paul didn't come in for the noon meal, and Pearl wondered what he was doing in the shed. She heard pounding and knew it must be a Christmas gift.

The food was prepared, gifts wrapped and under the tree, and a roast chicken and ham filled the kitchen with delicious smells. The Galloways adhered to the rule of no working on Sunday, and tomorrow—Christmas—was on Sunday this year. There would be plenty of leftovers for the morrow. Ben had bought oranges at the farmer's market downtown, and they sat in a bowl on top of the piano, next to the blue candles Emily had placed there yesterday.

The table was set with Emily's bright red tablecloth. Everyone had washed up and dressed in their finest. Pearl wore the sprigged calico and brushed her hair out, then braided it in one long braid which she left cascading down her back. It was her dress-up hairdo.

She helped Sarah into a dark percale she saved for Sunday meeting day, and together they went downstairs. "I love thee, Mama."

"And I, thee, child."

"I've been thinking about what thou said last night. I think Ben should try to reach everyone. Maybe we can have a big family reunion."

"It's too far for all to come." Sarah coughed into her handkerchief.

Pearl tried to steady herself as she helped Sarah down the final step. "I'll see what Ben thinks." *And he'd better not wait if they are to arrive in time,* she thought.

Kate and Luke arrived at five sharp. Pearl heard the horses draw up out front and opened the door and ran out without waiting to put a wrap on.

"Kate! Luke!" she cried, hugging first one, then the other. "Merry Christmas!"

"And Merry Christmas to thee, too," Kate said. "It's wonderful to see thee again!"

Luke nodded. "Thou art just as pretty as ever, I see. And excitable, too."

Pearl felt her cheeks flush. "Excitable is right, but the pretty is not."

"Have ye not heard 'Beauty is in the eye of the beholder'?" Luke asked. His eyes twinkled. "Or as a man once said, 'Give me beauty in the inward soul.' I believe his name was Plato."

"Oh, thou and thy history lesson," Kate said, hugging her husband.

"Come in, come in!" Ben stood in the doorway, beckoning the Morrisons in.

Kate wore a full-skirted scarlet dress with lace at the collar and cuffs. Tiny jewel buttons decorated the bodice.

Her cheeks were pink from the long ride, and she discarded her heavy cloak and wide-brimmed hat. Combs decorated the dark hair. She would always be beautiful, Pearl thought as she felt a sudden tightness in her chest.

"I see thou art lovely as always," Ben said, kissing Kate's cheek.

"And an early Merry Christmas to the Galloways!" Luke said, coming in and hugging Sarah.

Clifford, up from his nap, jumped up and down in a chair Ben had made for him. It kept him out of trouble, yet he could bounce.

"I thought we would never arrive," Kate said, "but we had fun singing songs and reciting Bible verses from memory. The sky is full of stars!"

Luke looked at his wife adoringly. "Kate makes an adventure out of everything, and that is why God loves her so."

"And us, too," said Ben.

Soon the eight sat around the huge oak table and filled their plates with Emily's good cooking. Then Luke asked the blessing:

"God, our father, we thank Thee for this special occasion—that of Thy Son's birth. We thank Thee for friends. For warm, comfortable homes. For family. For blessings not yet received, and for this food prepared for us as we celebrate and remember Thee."

"Hear ye! Let's eat!" declared Ben.

Pearl could hardly swallow. So much had happened in the day since she'd come home. She stared at the gravy, then glanced up. Paul was watching her. She waved her fork at him and smiled.

"We are wanting to hear all about thy teaching job and thy pupils," Luke said.

"I shall tell thee all about it later," Pearl said. "Over pie and coffee."

"After we open the gifts," Emily added.

New mittens came from Emily, while Sarah's gift was stocking caps for all. Pearl was glad she'd knitted stockings. Ben's gift was books for the three younger women: Emily, Pearl, and Kate.

"If I was handy with knitting needles, I would have made my gifts," Ben said. "Not enough time for whittling gifts these days."

"I love books," Pearl said, holding hers close.

Emily looked at her book of poems and read the inscription from Ben. "To my Emily, the light of my life."

Pearl's *Uncle Tom's Cabin* was inscribed: "To Pearl, the best sister in the world."

Kate's book was poetry, and Sarah had a new Bible, all leather covered and soft, just the right size for her arthritic hands to hold.

Baby Clifford had a jaunty new little cap in brown corduroy. "I couldn't resist," said Ben.

Pearl watched while everyone opened their stockings.

"Thy knitting is much tighter, I see," said Sarah, holding a sock up.

"I'm glad thee likes it." She saw Paul leave the room and wondered where he was going. He had not opened the gift from her, though she knew he could tell it was a pair of socks. She wished now she'd thought of something different. A surprise.

Clifford was enjoying the noise the paper made when he tore it. Everyone watched him and didn't notice Paul until he came into the room holding a framed picture out for all to see.

"My gift for this family," he said.

All crowded around to see the fine pencil sketch—a gathering around the piano as everyone sang carols.

"Oh, Paul, it is lovely!" Emily looked as if she was about to cry. All agreed.

"And the frame?" Ben asked.

"That's what I was making today."

Pearl said nothing as she stared at the picture, looking at each one's face. But it was her face she looked at the longest. Paul had made her beautiful. Her eyes. Her face. This didn't look like her, did it?

"I have another smaller one for you, Gem," he said, holding out a small sketch.

Pearl looked at it, then held it out for all to see. "Paul—it's wonderful. I adore it."

And, again, she noticed that she looked almost pretty.

"I'd say thee captured our Pearl's face quite well," Luke said then.

"And I say we need to sing songs!" Pearl said, not wanting her loved ones to keep staring at her.

"There's another gift," Paul said, "a poem I wrote to you. It was a long time ago, but I was afraid to give it to you before."

"Thou hast given me enough, but I'd be honored to own one of thy poems along with the drawing."

"I do miss thy playing, Emily," Luke said. "We have found no one yet to play the piano in our small gathering of souls."

It was because of the new church that Luke and Kate would stay only for the evening. They would rise early to prepare for the first Christmas service at noon in their small, crude church.

Kate stood and raised her arm. She liked secrets and had waited to share the good news.

"We will be parents come summer," she announced, grabbing Luke's arm before sitting down.

"I knew it," Sarah said. "Thee had a glow, as mothers-to-be often have. A sweater I've been knitting is already too small for our robust Clifford."

"Sarah, how wonderful."

"Seems we have much to be thankful for as the old year draws to a close," Ben said. "We'll pray for a healthy child."

"I'll say Amen, Brother," Luke said.

Pearl knew Luke's heart must still ache for the small child lost, along with his first wife, a few years ago in Ohio. His son was in heaven with Isobelle, Ben and Emily's newborn who had died.

Surely God would bless this child of Kate and Luke's.

Later after wrappings were cleared up, Luke and Kate packed the buggy for their return trip.

"You take care," everyone shouted as the Morrisons left. Amid waving hands and choruses of "good-bye until next trip," they started off.

"And Merry Christmas!" Pearl added.

Soon they were back inside and bedding down for the night. Pearl found her presents under the tree, where she'd placed them. The sketch from Paul was so beautiful. She touched the lines, the eyes, with the crinkles at the end. It was something she would treasure always.

"Do you really like it?" Paul stood behind her.

Pearl's face beamed. "It's my best gift," she said, her gaze meeting his. "I never knew you were an artist."

"I'm not."

"Oh, yes, you are, Paul. This picture and the other one is wonderful. You captured each one's expression so well. Except. . ." she paused.

"Except?"

"I think—" But she couldn't say it.

"You think yours is not a good likeness—"

"I never said that."

"But you think it, Gem. I can tell."

"Thou made me pretty," she said finally.

"Because you are," Paul said. "Everyone thinks it, but you."

Pearl looked away. Could it be true? Did she look pretty to others?

"I thank you for thy gift and for the compliment. Merry Christmas, Paul."

"Merry Christmas, Pearl."

He turned and walked out of the house while Pearl sat in the darkness, cherishing this moment. If she lived to be a hundred, she would never forget this Christmas Eve, this wonderful, precious day.

Chapter 11

As it turned 1911, William Howard Taft was still president. Not that it mattered to the family on Foster Road. The new year brought little change to the Galloway household.

Ben worked hard building houses, rain or not. Paul's work was mostly indoors, and he kept busy. Emily was sick mornings, and Pearl knew she must be in the family way again. She seemed more tired now. Sarah's cough was worse, and the doctor said if she could go where the sun came out every day, if she could find warmth, she would get better, but Sarah wanted to stay in Portland with her family.

Pearl did not seek another teaching position. She was needed at home. Clifford was too much for Mama to handle, and Emily was sick each morning. It was up to Pearl to cook, to put the house in order. Ben insisted she not try to find work. At least not yet.

Letters about Sarah's condition had been written to all but Jesse. So far nobody had answered except Clara: "I want to come visit you, Mama, but the doctor says I cannot travel. You will have another grandchild in a few months. I love you. God bless."

Sarah slept much of the day, though she was often restless.

Pearl now slept downstairs, where she could be close to Clifford. Her heart and mind thought of what might be, but for now she was too busy working and praying for more sun so Mama could go out and sit in the sunshine.

January turned to February, then March came. It seemed as if many months had passed since she had taught at the Stayton School. She knew school would be out soon so the older ones could help plant crops. She wondered about Mary Alice, Cora, John Mac, and the twins. Any day now they might hear that Nina had delivered her baby.

It was on Saturday that Luke suddenly showed up at the Galloways'.

"Kate, is she all right?" Pearl asked. She'd stopped ironing a dress when the knock sounded.

"Kate is fine."

"What is it then?" Pearl knew by the look on his face that something had happened.

"I just received word that Harrison Drake has had a stroke. And Beulah—bless her heart—is not doing well, either. She has the cough—similar to Sarah's. It may be tuberculosis, though she has not seen a doctor recently."

"A stroke! Oh, no. I must tell Emily."

"I will do that, Pearl."

Luke set his hat on the table in the foyer, and Pearl followed him to the bedroom where Emily was resting. She looked up from her diary.

"Luke!"

"Emily, I had to come tell thee, as I did not know what to do."

"What is it? Ben?"

"It's your grandparents. Both are gravely ill, and though Harrison was taking care of Beulah, he's had a stroke and is bedridden. A neighbor had been coming in once a day, but she can no longer do this. Does thee know of anyone who could go? See that they are taken care of?"

"Anna," Pearl said. "My sister Anna is a nurse, but she's in Iowa."

"I should go." Emily stood, then held onto the bedpost to keep from falling.

"No!" Pearl cried, reaching out to steady her. "You are not strong enough."

"The sickness is better. Someone must help, and it should be me."

"No," Pearl almost shouted. "If it's anyone, it will be me."

"Pearl, you can't mean this. You're not a nurse, and why should this be your burden?"

"Because we're family, and families help each other. I'm the strongest and most suited to go."

Emily nodded, not even sure her grandparents would accept her help. They had yet to forgive her for marrying Ben, a non-Quaker, and for being ungrateful and deserting them.

"It is true," Luke said in agreement. "Pearl should go. At least for now. Save your strength, Emily."

"I know it's right for me," Pearl said suddenly with complete conviction. "I am not teaching now and just get in the way around here. I thought about applying at the candy factory where Kate and Emily used to work, but if I'm needed there, that is what I should do."

In the end Emily agreed. She pulled Pearl close. She loved Pearl more than she could have ever loved a sister. How could she do this so readily, so easily?

"I don't know a lot about nursing, but I should certainly be able to build a fire, cook the meals, and bring in water and medicine for the patient."

"You'll do a fine job," Luke said. "And God will bless thee for doing this far more than you can imagine. God has a wonderful life ahead for you. You are a true server if ever I saw one."

Pearl knew she would miss seeing Paul every night when he got off work—miss his smile, their conversations. But she was needed elsewhere, and it was something she felt led to do.

She packed a bag and left with Luke that afternoon.

"It will seem primitive," Luke warned, helping her into the buggy.

"No worse than our house in Iowa," she said, her chin jutting out.

"Art thou doing this for another reason, one you want to talk about?"

She stood, staring at Luke, wondering why he would ask such a question.

"Very well, Luke. I will talk to thee, though I could tell no other. Not even Emily."

"Your words are safe with me, my friend."

"It is Paul."

"Paul?"

Pearl knotted the linen handkerchief. "I find myself being drawn to him, and can't get him out of my heart. I know it is not good. Paul doesn't serve God, and—"

"Pearl, you cannot sit in judgment for any of God's children."

"But we have talked many times. He says he cannot believe. I fear he may end up like Jesse."

Luke looked pensive. "Some of this might be true, but I think he believes more than he realizes." Luke had seen a noticeable change in the young man and was confident it was only a matter of time before he, too, would seek God as his Savior. But could he say this to Pearl? What if Paul didn't feel as she did? It could do far more harm if he were to give her hope and it turned out to be false. No, he could not tell her this, yet he thought of the Christmas drawing, remembering the look Paul had captured.

He had made Pearl beautiful, made his love come through.

"Remember where it says that God cares for thee, that God will always take care of thee?"

Pearl nodded. "I believe that."

"I think the time is coming when you will have your answer, my child. But I need to say something about Paul. Never, ever would he be like Jesse. I know him well enough to know what is in his heart, and he is not the type of man to consort to several women. When Paul finds the woman he loves, he will be true to her to the end."

Pearl felt her cheeks redden, and she didn't know why. Paul had never indicated his feelings, yet a tiny shred of hope spread through her. She stared back at Luke's kind, thoughtful face, thankful she could talk to him.

"Kate did not believe for a long while. I loved her in silence, Pearl. I, like you, knew it was wrong, but God in His infinite glory made the change in Kate. Without killing her beautiful spirit, she came to believe God's plan for her life. No man could ask for more."

Pearl sat and pondered what Luke said. She knew Kate had given up dancing and didn't mind it. Perhaps he was right. Maybe Paul would come to believe one day, too. She had to believe it.

The horses had stopped and Pearl got her first glimpse of the Drake homestead. The old house was in need of a fresh coat of paint. Pearl wondered if it had ever seen paint.

"Let me tell thee about the Drakes," Luke began. "Before you go in, you must understand that Beulah has a strong mind, a determined one. Bless her heart, she has never known how to be kind."

"I know this from things Emily has said. I believe I can handle that." She thought about Judson Rome. His overbearing ways had cost her the teaching job. Beulah Drake couldn't be worse.

"Pearl, it is wonderful for thee to do this. I have no way of knowing how long it will be before Beulah is back on her feet—or Mr. Drake."

Pearl squared her shoulders. "Well, I think we'd better go inside and see just exactly what my duties will be."

Luke nodded, and the two walked up the overgrown path. He hesitated just a moment before lifting his hand and knocking on the heavy wooden door.

"Just say a prayer that I will meet Mrs. Drake's standards."

"That I will," Luke said. "That we all will."

The door opened, and a woman stood there, crying.

"Are you the person coming to help?"

Pearl stepped forward. "I am."

"Well, bless you, honey. I hope you have more fortitude than I do."

And without another word, she grabbed her coat and hurried up the path.

"Yes," Luke said, touching Pearl's arm. "Thee will need all the prayers we can muster. And I must go in first to see Sister Beulah."

Pearl followed Luke down the hall, noticing its cobwebs and unkempt appearance. The house looked as if it could stand a good spring cleaning, and she figured she had come none too soon.

Chapter 12

Pearl's days became a blur as she cared for the Drakes. Mr. Drake was no problem, though she had to feed him, and most of the food dribbled down his chin into his neck.

Mrs. Drake, however, had a sharp tongue, and Pearl soon realized it was best to ignore her. She was sick, and people were not at their best when sick. Not that Beulah had ever been at her best.

But it was the grueling housework that wore her to a frazzle. Though not used to carrying water, she carried several buckets those first few days because everything had to be washed and cleaned.

She washed all the dishes in the cupboards and the curtains and the floors. She pounded the front-room rug and shook the small rugs until she could shake no more.

Soon the kitchen sparkled with clean cabinets, floors, and walls. Then everything was dusted, and even the parlor was cleaned thoroughly.

"What is thee doing?" Beulah asked each day when Pearl wasn't sitting beside her. Pearl felt she must make excuses because she could hardly say, "I was cleaning your dirty house."

Pearl read a lot to the Drakes. She read the Bible aloud to Mr. Drake, but he didn't seem to know if she was there or not. When the doctor came, he explained to Pearl that Mr. Drake knew more than he let on. That he could hear and assimilate; he just couldn't answer. He also said it was good to continue reading and talking to him—that it might help him to get well sooner.

So Pearl had continued. When she fed him the clear broth and most of it dribbled out and down onto his napkin, she smiled and patted his hand. "It's okay, Mr. Drake. Some of it's getting inside you." She had to laugh, as it was like trying to feed Clifford when he was smaller. He would spit out more than he kept inside his tiny mouth. Mr. Drake certainly didn't spit, but he had no control over his lips.

Pearl felt sorry for him. She remembered Emily saying how kind and wonderful he had always been. Now the eyes stared blankly ahead. She wished she knew what else to do for him, but since there was nothing, she kept him as warm and comfortable as possible.

Mrs. Drake, as Pearl thought of her, since she could never call her by her first name, was another matter. She seemed to like being critical, cross, and crotchety. She wondered if she had been this bad when Emily lived here and somehow thought she probably had. She wanted so much to be up and about, taking care of her house and especially the kitchen. She complained when Pearl brought cool soup. She didn't like strong coffee, weak tea, and the baking powder biscuits were far from flaky. The only thing Pearl had ever made that she liked was apple pie.

Pearl had to smile when she thought about apple pie. Paul always liked her pie. Once when she had made pie plant pie, he had eaten it, but didn't ask for seconds. When she asked why not, he smiled. "Because I prefer your apple pie."

It was good that Pearl knew what to bake to make him happy. She could hardly wait to go back home and to work in the sunny, yellow kitchen. The kitchen here, in spite of her cleaning it, was dark and dreary.

Pearl sighed. Of course she had no idea when she could go home again. Mrs. Drake could go on forever with this coughing condition, and stroke victims, though bedridden, often lived a long time, according to the doctor. It was not a bright prospect. Still, she was glad she could do it.

The little bell tinkled then, and Pearl rushed to see what Mrs. Drake wanted.

"My photo album," the older woman said. "It's in the parlor. I must have it immediately."

"Of course." Pearl didn't know where in the parlor, but knew she could find it.

It was heavy and very old. It smelled musty, too, as she lifted it and carried it to the bedroom.

"I want to show you what my parents looked like. I also wanted to know if you would give this to Emily and Paul."

"Emily and Paul?" It was the first Pearl realized that Mrs. Drake knew who she was.

"Come now. Don't think I'm a simpleton. Of course you belong to Benjamin. One look at your face and the broad shoulders and I knew who you were, where you came from."

Pearl sputtered. "Why did you let me stay then since you dislike my brother so?"

Mrs. Drake's eyes widened as she was about to snap back, but it was as if she thought better of it and closed her mouth. She opened the album and pointed to a couple sitting on a small settee.

"I do not dislike Benjamin. He just isn't right for Emily."

"He loves Emily," Pearl countered. She did not want to hear cross words where her beloved brother was concerned.

"That may very well be, but he was not raised a Quaker."

"He loves the church and the people and worships and loves God," Pearl said, again coming to her brother's defense.

"Humph! There's no point in discussing this further."

Pearl longed to discuss it. She longed to tell Mrs. Drake how wrong she had been, how wrong she was now not to want to see Emily again, not to want to see the baby Clifford. How could she treat Emily with such disdain?

"Would you like a cup of tea? It's nigh on to four."

"After I finish showing you this."

Mrs. Drake identified several photos, then closed the heavy book. "These are photos that belong to Emily and Paul. They are of their paternal side. I want them to be taken and valued."

Pearl held the book close. "I know Emily will like having them, Mrs. Drake."

"Very well. Don't get maudlin on me. Go fetch the tea. And you'd better check on Mr. Drake. I have a feeling about him."

Pearl went to the other bedroom first. He had moved. She knew it. He was still lying on his back, his gaze fixed on the ceiling, but he was looking toward the window, toward the winter sunshine streaming in through the window. She was sure he had moved, even if only a few inches.

"And it's the sunshine you're a-wanting to see?" Pearl asked. She pulled the curtains back just a bit so he could see into the yard. Perhaps this meant he was going to be all right after all. She leaned over and straightened his pillow just a bit, then folded the top sheet down over the layer of quilts. His sudden grunting sound made her jump.

"Mr. Drake, you're trying to tell me something. Oh, what is it? If only I knew what it was."

Pearl thought about opening the window, but knew it was too cold. Still, a bit of fresh air might be invigorating for him.

She went over and pulled up until just a small bit of air filled the room. She looked back. "There now! Is that what you wanted?"

His expression did not change, nor did he move or make any more noise.

Pearl looked out the window. An evergreen tree filled the corner and a smell of pine hit her nose. Spring was definitely in the air.

"I am going to make some tea. I'll be back with a cup after I take Mrs. Drake hers."

There. Again, she thought she detected a small bit of movement.

Pearl hummed as she poured the water that was still hot on the back of the big old-fashioned cook stove. A bit of sugar for Mrs. Drake, but plain for Mr. Drake. Doctor's orders.

"Is he all right? My husband?" Beulah asked when Pearl came in with the tray and two cups. "I heard you talking to him."

"He moved."

"Moved?"

"Yes. He turned toward the window so I opened the curtain a bit more."

"But that's impossible."

"He did. I'm sure of it."

"We'll tell the doctor when he comes."

Beulah stirred her tea and watched as Pearl left with the other cup.

She helped lift Mr. Drake's head, raising the cup to his lips. Did she only imagine it, or had he actually swallowed more than usual? "There now, you're not as messy today." She smiled, bent down, and kissed his lined forehead. It was cool, almost clammy, as always. Pearl thought of Emily and what she might do if she came to visit. What if she came to see her grandfather, but stayed out of Beulah's room?

"Mr. Drake, I know Emily wants to come to see you. She wants to express her concern for you—play some of the hymns you love, sit and talk to you. I wonder—would it be okay if I were to bring her with me next week?"

Pearl looked, but the face seemed expressionless. If only he could communicate. There had to be a way. She couldn't help but think that Emily's presence would make him feel better. Might make him want to try to talk again. It was worth a try in spite of how Mrs. Drake felt.

Pearl left the room but closed the window and drew the curtains. The sunshine had left, and soon it would be dark out. Tonight they would have leftover soup from yesterday. And sugar cookies for dessert.

She hummed as she stirred up biscuit dough and put the pot of potato soup on the stove. Thoughts of Paul flashed across her mind again. How she missed seeing him. How she wanted to go back to how things had been before. Evenings spent on the front porch while they watched the sun disappear over the hill, then waited for the glorious reds, golds, and oranges of a sunset to fill the entire sky. Or watching the stars as they filled every bit of inky darkness. Sometimes Clifford, all bundled up, sat between them. Pearl had to laugh. It was as if the baby was their chaperone. Not that they needed one. They were friends, like brother and sister. Didn't everyone know that? Or could some read her mind—know what she was thinking—realize that her heart was shattering. If only she could speak her mind, but she couldn't be bold as Nancy Whitfield was. Never could she speak her heart to Paul. If anyone did any speaking, it would have to be Paul himself, and of course she knew that would never happen.

After the Drakes were tucked into bed, Pearl sat beside the fire in the dining area and tucked her long legs under her. She had brought some of Emily's books, so now was the time when she would read another chapter from Elsie Dinsmore. She'd read *Black Beauty* twice now and the poem Paul had given her at Christmas many times over.

A new, large library was to be built downtown, across the river. Emily said there would be many books to choose from, and they didn't have to buy; they would be for all to read and enjoy.

The house was quiet, and Pearl missed the sounds of family bustling around, the cries and peals of laughter from baby Clifford. She missed seeing Emily write in her journal, seeing Mama sit beside the fire, her hands busy with knitting needles. It was probably a sweater she knitted for the baby. Or perhaps new mittens for Emily—or maybe Ben or Paul.

Finally Pearl took the light and climbed the attic stairs to the bedroom where Emily had once slept. It was sparsely furnished, but the bed was comfortable, and the small braided rug was the very one Emily had kneeled on to say her prayers. Pearl bent down now and asked for God to heal Mr. Drake. Asked that Mrs. Drake might ask for Emily, that she'd want to meet her great-grandchild. Pearl was glad about the photo album, but more than anything, she wanted Beulah Drake to give it to Emily.

"Help me to understand, O Lord, Thy will for my life, also. If it is to be that I will teach here in Portland, or if it is Thy will that I will take care of those who cannot help themselves, I will accept this. I will try to make others happy, for I know, in so doing, I in turn will be happy. Just serving Thee makes me happy. Thy will be done. Amen."

Pearl took out a small volume she kept under her pillow. It was a diary. Emily had suggested she write down her thoughts, and so she had tried to do so. She couldn't write for long periods of time as Emily did, but some thoughts came into her mind. Tonight seemed to be one of those times.

My life is full. I am reasonably happy. Just thinking of Paul makes me happy. Seeing his smile erupt across his broad face gives me much pleasure.

I know if there is ever to be anyone for me to love, to marry, to have children with, it is Paul. But perhaps that is not to be my lot in life.

> *As I take up my pen to write*
> *On this, yet another dark, cold night,*
> *I think of things that have been and will be.*
> *I think of laughter, smiles, tears, and joy for me.*
> *I think of Mary Alice this day*
> *And hope she is loved and cherished.*

Pearl closed the small book and lay back on the pillow. She wondered about the Rome children, especially Mary Alice. What she wouldn't do to bring Mary Alice here to live. Who was to help her to know what it was like being a woman? Who would be there to comb and braid her hair, to listen to her numbers and as she read pages from her reading book? She knew Judson Rome had no interest in what his children did. Perhaps the new teacher would become their mother. Perhaps she, Pearl, was silly to even think of such things, much less worry about them. There wasn't anything she could do. Then a thought hit. She could write to them. She would borrow paper from Mrs. Drake and have a letter ready to go on Monday morning. Yes, she must know how everything was in Stayton. She must let them know how much she missed them. And she might even write to the new teacher, whomever she was, and tell her that her prayers were with her, that she would find happiness there and please the school board.

Pearl closed her diary and blew out the flame. Tomorrow would be another busy day with carrying water, building a fire, and making tea. Lots of tea.

Chapter 13

One morning two weeks later, after Mrs. Drake refused the oatmeal Pearl brought, Pearl took it away without a word.

"I prefer the green glass bowls," Beulah said, then started coughing.

Pearl took the tray back to the kitchen and transferred the cereal to a green bowl. Soon she returned to the bedroom with a daffodil in a small vase. Perhaps a touch of spring would raise the woman's spirits.

Beulah took one look at the flower and frowned. "I don't need a daffodil on my tray."

"Very well." Pearl removed the daffodil and stuck the vase on the dresser.

"Does anything bother you?" Beulah asked.

Pearl turned and looked at the older woman. "Yes, many things, but I pray about them and soon the bother passes."

"Thee is a special person," Beulah said then. "Most people can't stand me."

Pearl smiled. "I just think of thee as one of my pupils at school where I taught. He didn't like me. He said nasty things about me, but I won him over. I read to him."

Beulah's face lit up. "I don't know if I like being compared to a naughty child, but I like the reading part."

"Oh. Would thee like me to read?"

"Yes, please."

Pearl sat, facing Beulah Drake. The once bright eyes were dull, lifeless. The doctor had come, at Ben's insistence, and said she wouldn't last another month. Pearl had walked him to the door.

"It's tuberculosis. Though some say a cure is possible, I've not seen it happen in any of the cases I'm familiar with."

Pearl thought of Mama. Had he given the same prognosis for her?

Somehow she didn't want to ask, didn't want to know. Mama had to live a good many more years.

"Is it contagious?" Pearl asked then.

"We cannot be sure. Again, some studies indicate one might catch it, but it depends on the immune system and whether it can be fought."

Pearl was suddenly thankful for her strong constitution, her height and large-boned frame.

Pearl took the well-worn Bible in her hand. "Does thee have a favorite passage?"

The head nodded. "Please read from 1 Corinthians," her voice went low. "I believe it's chapter 13."

Pearl's voice filled the otherwise still room, pausing in the right places.

" 'If I have not charity, I am become as sounding brass. . . .' " She paused, then read on. " '. . .the greatest of these is charity.' "

Beulah reached out. "Read that passage once again, child."

Pearl read the chapter twice and when she had finished she noticed a tear had slipped down the lined, pale cheek.

"I find that chapter especially gratifying," Pearl said, not knowing what else to do. Should she offer her a handkerchief, or pretend she didn't see the tears? Beulah was proud; far be it from Pearl to offend in any way.

Beulah sniffed and Pearl moved closer. "Perhaps a cup of tea would be refreshing."

"Thee knows my granddaughter, Emily."

"Yes, I know. . .her."

"Emily planted those daffodil bulbs. She liked flowers and Christmas trees, singing and playing the organ. This house has not heard music since she left."

"Emily has a piano now."

Beulah's eyebrows raised. "I'm sure she must be pleased about that."

"Yes, she is."

"People do not understand how it was with Emily."

"Perhaps not." Pearl always answered, because if she didn't, Beulah would demand a comment.

"She came to us at age ten. . . ." She began coughing and, once started, had a problem stopping.

Pearl leaned forward. "Take thy time, Mrs. Drake."

"She was the oldest of eight at the time."

"A large family."

"They—that is my son—worked the fields. Traveled from place to place, picking crops." Beulah coughed again, and Pearl leaned over and fluffed the pillows, holding her head as she rose to try to get rid of the phlegm in her throat.

Finally she had stopped. Her fingers clutched the top of the quilt. "My son could have worked elsewhere, but I'm sorry to say, he let his family work. And they worked many hours, especially during the summer months."

Pearl swallowed hard. She had never heard this much from Emily. In fact, she wasn't sure Emily even knew about it. If so, she'd never said.

"I—offered to take Emily because she was a mite sickly."

"She was?"

"Oh, yes. She fainted out in the fields, and once they had to take her to the hospital, so my son asked if she could come here. Live with us."

"And that was many years ago?"

Beulah raised a hand to her forehead, looking as if she was in pain. "I think it must have been nigh on to eighteen years ago now. If thee must know the truth, I cannot remember exactly."

"Emily spoke of missing her mother."

"Yes, she often asked to go on the train to visit—"

"And she did go—before she married Ben."

"That is good to know."

"Do you want to make amends?" Pearl asked. She knew if it was going to happen, the time was short and it should be done as soon as possible. She also knew that Emily longed more than anything to see her grandparents again, to know that all was forgiven. Perhaps not forgotten, but truly forgiven.

Beulah nodded; her hands gripped the binding on the sheet. She looked away then, as if fighting back tears. "I never told her how much I cared for her. And I want to see her baby. I hear she has one."

"I can fetch her here."

Pearl wished the grandfather was better, but since the stroke, he knew nobody and lay lifeless and listless in his bed, not even acknowledging Pearl when she fed him. Pearl knew, too, that it was Emily he loved so much.

Pearl rose. "I will see what I can do. Another person is coming tomorrow to take care of things. I will speak to your Emily."

Beulah clutched her hand. "You are a nice person."

Pearl couldn't believe it as she took the dinner dishes to the kitchen. Beulah wanted to see Emily and the baby. Of course she hadn't mentioned Ben, but Ben would understand. He was good about things like that. He would want this for Emily, knowing how happy it would make her. And baby Clifford. His fat little cheeks and rosebud mouth would please any great-grandparent. He laughed a lot, was a noisy child, and if anyone could bring a smile to Beulah's face, it would be him. And perhaps the grandfather would even take note. It was something to hope for.

As she washed and rinsed the dishes, Pearl wondered how Paul was, what he was doing this very moment. Tomorrow she'd see him in church. She could hardly wait. It was difficult when she saw him only once a week, but perhaps it was better that way. Her heart remembered, and her mind was full of memories—his smile, the laugh, the way he called her "Gem," and the way he smelled and looked after working all day. Dirty, unkempt, but she loved it anyway. Would the day ever come when he might know how she felt? Was there a chance? Pearl dried her hands and went down the hall to the grandfather's bedroom. He lay still, staring up at the ceiling.

"Hello, Mr. Drake. Did you know your granddaughter Emily is coming to visit tomorrow?" Pearl smiled. "Well, I can't say absolutely, but I think it will happen. I know she wants to see you—"

She stopped. Did his left hand flutter just a bit? Wouldn't that be something if Emily could bring a few happy moments back into the old man's life? Pearl tucked the covers in and adjusted his pillow. "Thee rest well tonight. If thou needs me during the night, call out if thou can."

Pearl checked once more on Beulah. The heavy quilt rose up and down in rhythmic tones, the labored breathing filling the room. Pearl leaned over and said a quick prayer. "And if it pleases Thee, Lord, help this to work out well in the morning."

Pearl tiptoed up the steep stairway, lamp in hand. Though most people now had electricity in their homes, the Drakes clung to the old ways. They still pumped their water from a well and used kerosene lamps. It was dark and cold in the small bedroom. She went to her knees and prayed for God's will to be done. So much had happened. Emily had left, without notice, because she knew she could not stay if she were to marry Ben, a non-Quaker, but a God-fearing man, nevertheless. And her grandmother had forbidden her to ever come back again, disowning her. But Emily felt God led her to Ben. And she left, not looking back once.

"O God, You know how Emily tried to make peace. She invited her grandparents to the wedding, but they refused. Just as they refused to come when she was expecting a baby. And that baby died, and now there is Clifford. Oh, please let it all end happily. Amen."

Chapter 14

Pearl waited for the horses to come fetch her for Seventh Day Meeting. A nurse, someone Ben had hired, had come to stay with the Drakes on Sunday. Pearl showed her where everything was and gave her instructions about which cup Beulah preferred to drink out of, and passed on other little hints.

Pearl slipped on her best gray muslin, tied her braids into a thick knot, and glanced at her face in the mirror in Emily's old room.

"O God, I may not be the most beautiful woman, but Emily and Mama say that looks don't count; it's what's in the heart that does, and I thank You for my blessings."

She heard the sound of horses hooves coming up the lane and hurried down the steps and opened the door just as a knock sounded.

Paul stood, grinning as he held out his arm to Pearl. "I understand you are in need of a ride this morning, and Ben suggested I could pick you up for church. That is, if you don't mind."

"Oh!" Pearl was so surprised words couldn't escape past the lump in her throat. "I—expected Ben—I thought you were off working on a new house—"

"Well, I can see you are not pleased to see me, but I think thee will be happy to ride behind my new team of horses."

"Oh, Paul, you didn't!" Pearl clasped her hands as she ran out to look at the new team. "They're absolutely beautiful!"

"Pandy and Mandy," he said. "Bought 'em yesterday."

"Oh," Pearl said again. "I would adore riding to church behind such a gorgeous team!"

Paul helped her up into the carriage, and Pearl smoothed her skirt down and adjusted her bonnet. Her heart thudded against her rib cage and she wondered if it would ever slow down. He lifted the reins, and they were off.

Pearl felt a bit awkward sitting next to Paul, then remembered the news and knew she must tell him. Especially since they were his grandparents, too.

"Grandma Drake wants to see Emily and baby Clifford."

"Pearl, are you sure?" Paul let the reins slip for a minute. "Is this true?"

"We talked for at least an hour, and she—I could hardly believe it—she was crying."

"Oh, Gem, this is wonderful. This is what Emily has been praying about."

"I know." Pearl smiled. She liked it when Paul called her by the nickname. It had come out so easily, almost as if he had been rehearsing it. She felt comfortable. At last. It was like the old times. Times when they had talked on the porch, counted the stars, eaten apple pie together. They had been friends then, and maybe that's all they would ever be, but it would be enough. Pearl could manage it somehow.

"What're you grinnin' about?" Paul asked suddenly, poking her in the ribs.

"Just thinking about how things are working out and it's just like in the Bible. 'All things work together for good to them that love God.'"

Paul's face clouded over for a brief moment. "I guess that's right, Gem, but I don't know if it applies to everyone."

"Of course it does, Paul Michael Drake."

He laughed. "You get the cutest look on your face when you get riled up."

Pearl felt her face flush. "I'm not riled up."

"Are, too."

"I should know if I am or not." She tightened the strings of her bonnet and knew she was acting like a little girl, not the adult woman she wanted to be. The woman God intended for her to be.

"I should think you'd believe in God considering all the things He's done for you."

"Such as?"

"Bringing you here to Oregon, giving you a fine job, a house to live in, food to eat. What more could any one person want?"

"A woman to have his children?"

Pearl's face colored more than before. "I—well—that is—maybe you have a point." She looked away, not wanting Paul to see the color of her cheeks, the way her eyes had misted over. He must never know how she really felt— he would really laugh then.

"Are you going to go back to teaching?" he asked then.

"I have considered it."

"And?"

"I'm not sure if that's what I should do."

"Go where your heart leads you. Isn't that what Luke would say?"

He ran a hand through his thick, sandy hair. Pearl wanted to reach up and touch the one lock that kept falling onto his forehead.

She nodded. "I guess that's what I'm having a problem about."

She avoided Paul's gaze. "The man I marry someday must love God with all his heart and soul."

Paul was silent for a long moment. "I hope you find what you're looking for, Pearl."

The light banter of minutes before was now punctuated by silence, and Pearl wanted to take her words back. Why couldn't Paul understand God was the Master of the universe, that He was in control of every facet of a person's life? Why did he struggle so? Why didn't he just try harder to understand the principles of faith, to trust that things would work out?

"Looks like we're here," Paul said, commanding his horses to a halt. Pearl didn't wait to be helped, but gathered her skirts and jumped down. "Thank you very much for the ride." She hesitated. "I'm glad you came to pick me up this morning." Before Paul could answer, she hurried inside, eager to tell Emily the wonderful news.

Ben, Emily, and baby Clifford were already in church. Pearl nearly raced down the aisle to the pew.

"Where's Mama?" she asked, nearly forgetting her message when she failed to see her mother sitting next to Ben.

"Mama's not good this morning," Ben said.

Pearl felt the tightness return as it did lately when she thought about her mother. "I should go see her this afternoon." Then she remembered her mission.

"Emily, you must come to the Drakes' this afternoon after church."

Emily stared at her sister-in-law. "What are you saying?"

"Mrs. Drake has asked for you. She told me lots of things and how she cared about you—always had—and—"

"When should Emily go?" Ben interrupted.

"She said it was time to forgive, that her time is running out."

"Oh, Ben." Emily turned to look at her husband, and her mouth quivered. "Have my prayers been answered?"

"Rather looks that way."

Pearl sat, offering to hold the baby. She'd missed him so terribly during the months she lived in Stayton and even more so now that she'd been staying with the Drakes. She held his face next to her own, repeating the prayer she'd offered to God many times before. "O God, if is Thy will, please let me have a child someday. And if it isn't asking too much, let it be Paul's child."

The service started, but Pearl was much too excited to concentrate. Besides, Paul sat in back of her and she could feel him watching her every move. She decided from now on she'd sit behind him.

Chapter 15

Pearl held baby Clifford as she and Emily stood on the front porch of the Drake home. Paul had brought them over from meeting and was tying the team to a post while Ben went home to see how Sarah was.

Emily grasped her hand for a long moment. "I don't know what to do, Pearl. It's been so long since I walked in this door."

"She's expecting you. Just go in and give her one of your best smiles and say—well—say hello. The rest is up to your grandmother."

Emily nodded. "You're right. I'll act as if I'd never been gone."

The door opened and the nurse peered out. "You must be Emily."

Emily stepped forward, her hands gripping the sides of her coat. "Yes, I am. Is my—grandmother ready to receive company?"

The nurse smiled. "Mrs. Drake has been expecting you. As for the mister, he just stares at the wall or ceiling. Won't be no recognition in those eyes."

Emily tried to stifle the pain deep inside her chest. She wanted this to be over. Clifford let out a noise, and Pearl held a finger to his mouth. "Sh-h, baby boy."

"Here, let me take him." Emily reached for her robust six-month-old. "Please don't cry, my son."

The nurse led them down the hall, not that she had to lead the way for either one. Pearl entered the room first and Beulah turned slightly. "Has she come? I thought I heard a baby's cry."

"Thee did, Grandmother." Emily entered the room and turned the baby around to face his great-grandmother. "This is my son, Clifford. I wish you could hold him, but he's a handful."

It was dark inside, as the light bothered Beulah's eyes. "Thee can come closer."

Emily moved to the head of the bed and held out her son. Clifford laughed and pulled at the nightcap Beulah wore.

"My, but thee's a fine, strapping young boy!"

"That he is, Grandmother."

"And thee. Look at thee. A sight for sore eyes. Never thought I'd see thee again, child."

Emily handed Clifford to Pearl, leaned over the bed, and kissed her grandmother's cheek. Tears shone in both eyes. "Nor I thee."

"Come. Sit. Tell me about thy life. We've got some catching up to do."

Was that it? Pearl wondered. No words saying she was sorry? Of course Beulah Drake was a proud woman, and even in her sickness she would hold her head as high as possible.

"We lost our Isobelle."

"Yes, I heard."

"We decided—Ben and I—to try for another child. And here he is."

The squirming child tried to be free.

"I think he might be hungry," Emily said then. "That might calm him down enough to take a nap."

"Is Benjamin here?"

Emily's eyes widened. "Oh, Grandmother, I did not think thee wanted to see Ben."

"Humph! He's thy husband, and thee does love him and are making a home for him?"

"Of course."

"Then I want to see him."

Emily looked shocked, then a slight smile turned up at the corner of her mouth. "Thee will see him. I will send Paul after him."

"I will tell Paul to fetch Ben," Pearl said. "I may ride with him as I'm worried about Mama."

"Yes, go," Beulah said. "I have plenty of care now."

Clifford's chatter and the women's voices filled the house as Pearl slipped out the front door.

"I was wrong not to forgive thee, Child," Beulah whispered, then the rasping cough began again. "Thee followed thy heart, and God has given thee a good man, a righteous husband."

"Oh, Grandmother." Tears squeezed out of Emily's eyes, falling down on top of Clifford's head. How long she had waited to hear those very words, prayed for forgiveness and that she could see her grandparents once more before they died.

The calloused hand gripped the small, thin one. "Thee always has been a puny little thing."

Emily smiled through her tears. "And thee has been strong and stout and can I say a bit feisty?"

"Determined." Grandma Beulah nodded. The gray hair fanned across the pillow, and Emily reached out and touched it.

"I love thee," she whispered.

"And I love thee."

The two women sat in silence as the sun poked through the windows, lighting the two figures who sat close together, neither speaking because words were no longer necessary.

"Thee needs to play the organ," Beulah said, breaking the silence. "I need to hear thee play once again."

"Soon as I have fed Clifford."

Clifford nursed and minutes later his head bobbed in complete relaxation.

"Here. I shall make a bed for him on the floor, then see Grandfather before playing."

"A spot of tea before thou goes," Beulah said then.

Emily brought the tea, went to her grandfather's room, and held his hand for the longest moment. No movement, no recognition, though she spoke his name several times.

She left the room, tears coursing down her cheeks again as she went to the parlor where the old organ sat in a corner.

She would play everything she knew. She would once again fill this house with music and song. And she might even sing along, too.

Paul saw Pearl approach and hopped down from the buggy. "Is something wrong?"

"Oh, no." Pearl tried to calm the tremor in her voice. "Everything—oh, Paul, everything is very fine."

"Oh, thank goodness. I was worried."

Pearl looked at this lean face, the eyes that went from troubled to light. How she loved those eyes, the steady gaze, the man standing before her, but she could not speak her heart, her mind.

"You are to go after Ben. Your grandmother wishes to see him."

"Now?"

Pearl nodded and pushed a pin back into the braid at the nape of her neck. "Yes. Now."

"That looks as if it pleases you very much."

"It pleases Emily, and what pleases my dear sister-in-law pleases me."

Paul looked with longing for only a moment, then climbed into he buggy. "Do you want to come with me?"

"Yes," she replied without a moment's hesitation. She felt her face burning under his strong gaze.

"Your coming will make the trip more pleasant. Unless you need to stay to take care of Clifford."

"No," Pearl answered a bit too quickly. "Emily will put him down for a nap—after he has his milk."

"Then let's go." Paul hopped down again, gave his arm to Pearl, and helped her into the high seat beside him. She was tall and broad-shouldered, but she was also graceful and the smile she wore on her face constantly pleased him.

"Thy grandfather stays the same," Pearl said as they headed west. "I fed him earlier, and he's now asleep."

"He's earned his rest." Paul turned and looked at the firm chin, the way her face shone in the afternoon sun. The bonnet cast shadows across her features.

Paul had come to help bathe his grandfather. He also took turns sitting beside him and had read to him. Nothing had worked. There were no signs that he understood anything going on around him.

"Perhaps if my grandparents have forgiven Emily she will come to stay with them now."

"I think they—that is—Grandmother Drake would like that very much."

The sun beaming into the small carriage made Pearl's heart sing with sudden joy. She had thoughts that burst inside her from time to time, and usually there was no one to share them with. Today she had Paul and without a second thought, she began singing in her clear, high voice.

> What a friend we have in Jesus,
> All our hopes and griefs to bear.
> What a privilege to carry
> Everything to God in prayer.

"You believe that, don't you?" Paul's hand let up on the rein. For right now he wanted to stop the carriage, wanted to stop time, wanted Pearl's voice to go on singing. It was as if she was meant to be here beside him. He'd never felt more sure of anything in his whole life.

"I believe God answers prayer, yes."

"And you've prayed for a change of heart in Grandmother."

"I have."

"And Emily and Ben have."

"Don't forget Luke and Kate. It's been a long time in coming, Paul."

Paul let the reins fall the rest of the way without fully realizing it. "And if I pray for something I want very much, do you think He will hear me?"

"He always hears us." Pearl turned and looked into his eyes. "It may not be the way you would hope, but He does hear, and He does answer prayer."

"But I must first believe."

If Pearl realized they had stopped, she did not let on. "Thee may believe more than thee realizes, my brother."

Brother. There was that term Pearl and the other Friends used. By her answering his question with the term, he knew she still felt he was part of the family. Nothing more.

"Does thee want to tell me what the prayer is about? It could be that others have this same prayer on their mind and hearts—"

"No," Paul interrupted. "I'm afraid not."

Pearl leaned over for one of the reins, without looking into Paul's eyes again. "Very well, then. I think we'd better pick up Ben, don't you?"

The rest of the trip was spent in silence. Pearl's smile had changed to a look of seriousness. She wished she knew what Paul was thinking, what he prayed for, but she would not, could not pry. She wondered if it had anything to do with Nancy Whitfield.

Ben sat on the front porch, whittling. The roses bloomed along the fence he'd put up a few weeks ago in anticipation of baby Clifford's learning to walk and wanting to go outside to play. He would be safe from the harm of the street, ever growing with daily traffic—he and the animals the Galloways owned.

"Yahoo!" he called, standing. "What's going on? I expected Emily and Clifford to be with you."

Pearl hopped down, not waiting for Paul to assist her, and ran to her brother. "The most wonderful thing has happened," she said, her eyes dancing. "An answer to many, many prayers!"

Ben cupped his chin. "And what might that be?"

Sarah came onto the porch, shielding her face from the warm sun. "Goodness, gracious, what has happened?" A spasm hit her, and she nearly doubled over from sudden coughing.

"Oh, Mama, Emily is with her grandmother, who wants Ben to come. Isn't it wonderful?"

After a glass of water, Sarah assured Pearl she would be fine and insisted Pearl return with Ben and Paul. In her hands were a loaf of freshly baked bread and a pie to help with the celebration.

The two men chatted from the front seat, but Pearl found herself staring at the back of Paul's head. He had a cowlick and she knew no matter how hard he tried to train it, the hair refused to lie down. She wanted to reach out and smooth the stubborn hair down, but refrained. He might not like it.

Her thoughts scampered through her mind as the old farmhouse, now even more weathered gray than when Emily lived there, came into view. Soon there would be even more reunion and perhaps with all the noise and celebration,

Grandfather Drake might recognize his world and loved ones once again.

The door opened, and Emily ran out.

"Oh, Ben. Paul. Pearl. I played the organ, Grandfather's favorite tune: 'Count Thy Blessings,' and tears rolled down his cheeks. I saw it with my very own eyes."

"And Clifford?" Ben jumped down, handing the reins to Paul.

"He's slept through it all. Of course he's used to my playing the piano at home."

"Oh, we have so much to be thankful for," Ben said, walking toward the house.

"Yes, we do," Pearl answered, falling in step beside Ben. "He does answer prayers, doesn't He?" She stole a quick glance at Paul, but he did not return her look.

Chapter 16

Within minutes, Ben and Paul had carried Grandfather into the parlor, where Pearl propped his head with pillows and covered his limp figure with a heavy quilt from his bed.

"Play, Emily. Play more hymns. He's responding. Thank God, he's responding."

Beulah Drake could barely walk, but she managed to make it to the parlor, where she sat in the Victorian chair. Her body was wracked with coughing, but she smiled, though clutching her chest.

"I never thought I'd see the day when our parlor would be full of people, Emily playing and others singing."

Pearl's voice, Paul's deep bass, and Ben's tenor soon filled the small room. A hand reached out as if Harrison Drake were trying to reach his granddaughter. Through tears, Emily played all the hymns she knew, the ones she had played over the years, the ones that meant so much to her, and those of her loved ones.

A sudden wail sounded from the bedroom floor where Clifford had been napping.

"I'll get him," Pearl said. "You keep on playing."

"He just wants to sing, too," Ben said.

"That child will never be left out when there's a party or singing going on."

" 'Rock of Ages cleft for me, Let me hide myself in thee.' "

Emily went from hymns to other old favorites: "Jeannie with the Light Brown Hair," "O Susanna," and "I've Been Working on the Railroad."

Grandfather had moved his right arm and appeared to be keeping time to the music.

"Look, Emily," Pearl cried. "He's trying to smile."

"Thee has brought such joy into this house again." Beulah shook her head. "So much hurt."

"This is turning into a regular prayer meeting," Ben said. "I think we should offer a prayer of thanks to our God for His wonderful mercy to us."

Pearl bowed her head and sensed Paul was watching her. She wanted to reach out, take his hand, tell him it was okay. Everything was going to be all right.

Later there was coffee, tea, Emily's cherry pie, and an apple pie that Pearl had made the day before. Pearl sliced the fresh bread Emily had made on Saturday and some of Sarah's raisin cake.

"God forgives, and so should I," Grandmother Drake said then.

It was late afternoon when Pearl cleaned up the dishes, Ben and Paul carried Grandfather back to bed and tucked him in, and Beulah was back in her bed.

"I will come often, Grandmother," Emily said. "I can come and let Pearl go home."

"If that is thy wish, then it is mine, also."

The two clung for a long moment, then Emily left on Ben's arm.

Clifford had fallen asleep in Paul's arms in the big chair by the wood stove. "I think this one needs to go home."

Pearl watched the little family make their way to the buggy and closed the door. It had been the most glorious day she could remember, and her heart leapt inside her. How good forgiveness feels. How beautiful Beulah looked. How peaceful Harrison was. This day would not soon be forgotten.

The following week was busy. Emily came by on Monday, Wednesday, and Friday. She played each day and Pearl left to go home to be with Mama. Clifford stayed with Emily, sleeping in his own little bed. Memories were made. Kind words were spoken, and Grandfather had even said a word: Emily. It was difficult to understand, but Emily knew it was her name and gave him a squeeze.

On the tenth day following the reunion, Harrison Drake slipped away in his sleep. He'd gone to be with his Lord one week after Beulah closed her eyes one night and did not wake up.

Luke came for both services. They were services of celebration.

Kate came and embraced Emily. "God calls those home He needs. And Beulah had made her peace."

Sarah had more times of coughing than not and Pearl and Ben knew she'd be called home soon, too. But Pearl couldn't bear to think about it.

A letter arrived on April 14. Anna was coming west, and she was coming to stay. At least Sarah would see one more child before she died.

Chapter 17

It was May, a few weeks after the first funeral, and Pearl had come home. Home to be with Sarah. In a weakened condition, she lay on her bed, accepting the meals brought to her, yet not wanting anyone to fuss over her.

"I'm going to be all right. You go fuss with the baby."

Pearl sat beside her mother and stroked her hair. "Mama, I cannot bear to see you like this."

"I know, Child." Her hand reached for her youngest child. "I would never cause thee any pain, if I could help it. I have but one request before I go to be with my Lord."

"What is it, Mama? I'll do anything I can."

"I want to know that thou are settled in life. Here you are doing for everyone, tending to the sick, teaching children, but what is it that you want?"

Pearl knew, had always known she wanted to marry, have children, to serve God—to be as happy as Emily and Ben, Kate and Luke. Yet God's plan still wasn't clear in her mind.

"Has thee asked for the desires of thy heart?"

Pearl looked away.

"As I thought."

"Mama, the person I have strong feelings for does not believe. He has said as much."

"Often people say they do not believe, when they do. It takes longer for some to recognize God's goodness, His faithfulness. I feel it to be so in this situation."

Pearl felt uncomfortable. She didn't like it when the attention was on her. She wanted to help others; she was a server as Luke had said the day he drove her to the Drakes' farmhouse.

"Mama, do you want a cup of tea?"

"Do not evade the issue," Sarah said.

"I'm not."

"You answered too quickly."

"I just want to make you feel better."

"Then sing for me. Thy voice is so clear. So beautiful. I can well imagine it is as the angels singing in heaven."

Pearl grasped her mother's hand and tried to hold back the tears. " 'Be Thou my vision, O Lord of my heart.' "

Pearl sang all the hymns she knew from memory, and when the words wouldn't come, she hummed. The creases on Sarah's forehead faded as a smile came to her lips. It was as if she were ready now. Ready to go home, and Pearl was leading the way.

The doctor came that day. He shook his head. "There is nothing more to do for her. Keep her warm. Comfortable. Give her clear broth. Her body cannot digest more."

Pearl read, sang, then talked about the farm in Iowa and what she remembered about her father.

"Mama, I remember that little chest Papa made. How thee loved it. And you were so happy you could bring it on the train to Oregon."

Sarah smiled, as if recalling earlier days, making a home for Jeb, the arrival of her babies. Each child was an added blessing. And God had blessed her even more by giving her grandchildren. She touched Pearl's arm. "Read the passage from Matthew."

Pearl knew the one Sarah meant. It was well marked in her Bible:

"Come unto me, all ye that labour and are heavy laden,
and I will give you rest.
Take my yoke upon you, and learn of me;
for I am meek and lowly in heart:
and ye shall find rest unto your souls.
For my yoke is easy, and my burden is light."

Sarah squeezed Pearl's hand. "That is the one. I will give you rest. I am not ready for the passage in John quite yet. I am waiting for my Anna to come." She closed her eyes, and Pearl slipped from the room. Though she tried to tell herself that Mama would live forever, she knew it could not happen. This consumption had taken over her body, and it would be a matter of days, possibly hours.

Pearl washed her hands thoroughly before starting the bread for tomorrow. Everyone could be susceptible to contracting tuberculosis, but if caution was taken, the household would survive. "God giveth and God taketh away" went through her mind. And Mama was ready to go. Her words of today indicated she knew her fate, and she was preparing herself.

The kitchen was quiet with Emily and Clifford napping. Pearl opened the window and felt the spring breeze on her face. This home, this place meant so much to her. Yet Mama was right. What was she to do about the desires of her heart?

Kneading the bread was balm for her soul. She punched and turned and punched it down more.

"My, but that will be the lightest bread we've had in quite a while." Emily stood in the doorway, smiling.

"Yes—I guess I got carried away."

"How is Mama?"

"Resting for now."

"I'll take the next shift, Pearl. You need to get away."

Get away. Was that what was needed? If she were to go, where would it be?

When dinnertime came and Paul hadn't arrived home, Ben said they should eat anyway. "He's probably finishing up the Powell house."

Pearl was cutting pie, and Sarah had finished a whole cup of clear broth and was resting again, when the phone call came.

"It's Judson Rome," Emily said, looking at Pearl.

Pearl's face turned white, the knife slipping from her hand. *Judson Rome? What could he want?* "I don't want to talk to him."

"Hear what the man has to say," Ben said.

Pearl reached for the receiver, a hundred thoughts whirling through her mind. Was it about teaching? What else? He already knew she would say no to another marriage proposal. She cleared her throat. "This is Pearl Galloway."

The voice sounded strange, almost hollow. "Miss Galloway, Judson Rome here."

"Yes?"

"I am in an awkward position and thought of you immediately. I know I can count on you."

"What is it, Mr. Rome?" No matter how many times he had told her to call him "Judson," she had never been comfortable doing so and wasn't about to do so now.

"I need a teacher for the fall term. I realize that's several months away, but the school board does like to prepare in advance."

"I am hardly a viable candidate," she said, feeling the shock from his request. "Have you forgotten your words?"

There was a long pause, but she knew he was there. She could hear his breathing. Her hand reached for the chair as she eased into it. All eyes were on her, watching, waiting.

"Oh, my, no. I was hard on you. I have done some rethinking and after speaking with my sons and Mary Alice, I realize how much they actually learned in the few months you taught at our little school."

It was good to hear that he finally recognized her worth. Still. . . .

"Mary Alice asks for you all the time."

"Is Mary Alice all right?"

"Of course. I remarried, and she has a mother at long last."

"Married? Oh, how wonderful, Mr. Rome."

"Yes, well, I married the new teacher and we're quite happy."

So that's why he was calling. His wife could no longer teach and with Judson Rome no longer heckling her, Pearl thought it might work. She glanced around the room, at the people she loved the most. Was this the window God was opening? Is this what He wanted her to do?

"What is it?" Ben finally asked, lurching to his feet. "Pearl?"

He took the phone.

"Hello. This is Ben Galloway, Pearl's brother."

Pearl remained motionless. Why couldn't she think straight? Judson Rome needed an answer. He was calling long distance. What was wrong with her?

Emily put a cup of coffee in her hand and the voice stopped. Ben put his arm around her shoulder. "We will return Mr. Rome's call later. After you've had time to consider the teaching position."

"And what you need now is a day off. I think you should get away from this house and have a fun day riding the streetcar, or shopping at the new farmer's market," Emily said.

Wasn't that what Emily had said earlier?

Pearl watched while Clifford banged on his highchair tray. Ben ate his pie, and Emily sipped her coffee. Was it time to leave this safe cocoon? Should she go back to teaching?

The back door opened, and Paul entered the kitchen. His bulk filled the doorway, and her heart nearly stopped. Paul. He was the reason she hesitated, even if only for a moment. She loved him, but it wasn't to be.

"Sorry I'm late." He hesitated, looking around. "Why is it so quiet? You all look—" His eyes widened. "Not Sarah?"

"No," Ben finally answered. "Pearl just got a phone call from Judson Rome. He wants her to return to teaching in the fall."

"Oh." Paul took the plate Emily offered and dished up his dinner. He glanced at Pearl, but she stared, transfixed into space, as if nobody were here.

"Did you finish the job?" Ben asked.

"Yes. It's done. They can move in on Saturday."

"Good. Take the day off tomorrow. I want you to take Pearl on a picnic down by Johnson Creek. It's not a request, but an order."

"It isn't as if I had to decide tonight," Pearl said then. She hadn't heard anything going on around her and spoke to no one in particular.

Emily nodded. "You're right, Pearl. You don't have to decide immediately. I'd think about it for a few days."

Pearl stared at the cup of lukewarm coffee. "I just wish I knew what to do."

"While you're thinking about it, why not go with Paul on a picnic tomorrow?" Ben said.

"Tomorrow?" Pearl looked dazed. "Tomorrow is Friday. It's a work day. I couldn't—I mean he couldn't possibly go—"

"It's all settled," Ben said. "Paul needs some time off, too. He's been working six ten-hour days and needs to relax, too."

"I'll go on a picnic only if Pearl brings along an apple pie." Paul buttered another slice of bread. "That's what it has to be."

They laughed, and soon Pearl was laughing. It felt good to laugh. She forgot the last time she had. Probably not since Christmas when every one had been here and they had all sung Christmas carols around the piano.

"Pie!" Clifford shouted, banging his fork on the tray.

They turned and laughed all the harder.

"Wouldn't you know pie would be his second word?" Emily said, poking an apple into his mouth. "Yes, our son does like sweets."

She lifted him and held him close. "Such a baby you are," she whispered against his soft, blond hair.

PEARL'S PRINCELY APPLE PIE

6 medium tart apples
¾ cup sugar
1 tsp. cinnamon

2 tablespoons flour
2 tablespoons heavy cream
(set aside)

Peel, quarter, and slice apples into a bowl. Cover with sugar, sprinkle on cinnamon, and dredge in the flour. Set aside while making the pie crust.
Pearl always used lard for a flakier crust.

2 cups white flour
1 tsp salt

¾ cup lard
5 tablespoons cold water

Place flour and salt into large bowl. Add lard and cut into flour until mixture resembles small peas. Add the cold water. Divide in half. Roll out bottom crust on a lightly floured board, using a floured rolling pin. Handle as little as possible. Don't try to make it perfectly round. Put in 9" pie pan. Dump in apples. Roll out top crust, making sure it's an inch larger in diameter than pie plate. Before putting on top of apples, pour the heavy cream over apples evenly. Put on top crust. Tuck under bottom crust and crimp edges.

Bake in 400⁰ oven about 45 minutes. Put cookie sheet under pie plate to catch drippings since apples expand as they cook and pie can run over.

Cut into six generous wedges. Top with ice cream, or pass a pitcher of heavy cream. Some prefer a slice of cheddar cheese. Enjoy!

Chapter 18

The Friday morning began with a clear blue sky without a trace of clouds.

"A perfect day for a picnic," Emily said, packing leftover fried chicken, a jar of dill pickles, bread and butter, and of course two wedges of apple pie left over from last night.

"I shouldn't leave Mama," Pearl protested, but Emily wouldn't hear of it.

"I am so much better now that the morning sickness has gone. I can handle Clifford and Mama just fine." She pointed toward the door. "I'll not hear another word from you except good-bye."

Pearl placed a blanket on top of the picnic basket and checked to see if Paul was finished patching the shed roof.

Paul came around the side of the shed, whistling. It was good to have a day off, and he couldn't think of a better way to spend it than with Pearl. He knew she worried about Sarah, hoped that her sister Anna would arrive soon and that Emily would have a healthy baby. And now the call from Judson Rome. She liked teaching. She loved the children. He sensed this was her calling, what God intended for her to do.

He'd thought a lot about God the past few weeks. He could see how one was guided by his belief that God would show him the way and care for him once that path was taken. A lot of the Scriptures made sense, though he often had to read a passage two and three times before he understood it. He had also started praying—a sort of out loud talking prayer when he was alone at night. He thought about moving on. If Pearl left, there was no reason to stay. He wanted to marry, and Pearl always came to mind when he thought of marriage, but if teaching was where God wanted her, far be it from him to stand in the way. Yes, he worried about things, also, but worry seemed to weigh heavier on women. He had never known why.

Paul changed to his Sunday pants, wore the blue shirt that Pearl had once said she liked, and slicked back his hair. After feeding Pandy and Mandy, he was ready. Now if Pearl didn't back out.

She came to the door, picnic basket in hand, and smiled. She was lovely in the yellow dress. Yellow like the sunshine; it was his favorite color.

"Are you ready?"

Pearl smiled. "Yes."

"Shall it be down by Johnson Creek?" he asked, assisting her up into the buggy.

"Yes, it's my favorite place."

"I feel I should be working." Paul took the reins.

"I feel the same way."

"You do need to think some things out," Paul said.

"Yes."

Pearl held her hands in her lap, wishing she could relax. Paul was her friend. A brother to her. Why was she finding it difficult to talk? Her feelings were strong, and she wished she could take them back and just be his friend again. It was easier that way.

"Pearl, what is it you want to do?"

His question caught her off guard. "I don't know." How could she say how she felt? That she wanted to have a home, children?

"I think you do know. You're afraid of something. Why don't you talk about it?"

"How is Nancy Whitfield?" Pearl hadn't gone to church the past two Sundays. She'd stayed home taking care of Mama.

"Nancy is moving to Seattle."

"Are you taking a job there?"

He stopped, letting the reins fall. Suddenly it all came together. Nancy. She thought he cared for Nancy Whitfield. Didn't she know, couldn't she tell that he thought of her day in and day out? Hadn't the picture at Christmas told her where his feelings lay—that it was her face that filled his thoughts?

"I'm staying right here, Gem."

"You haven't called me 'Gem' in a long while."

"Could be because I haven't seen much of you lately."

"Nor I you."

"Will you be happy in Stayton teaching?" He had to know. If so, he would live with it.

"I suppose so."

They crossed the road, and the horses slowed to a trot as they headed toward the creek.

They found a spot under a maple tree close enough to hear the creek rushing over smooth stones. Nothing more was said while Pearl spread the blanket and set the basket between them. Paul sat and moved the basket to the other side.

"Pearl, God's been showing me a lot of things lately—things I wanted to talk to you about."

She heard the words and wondered if her hearing was going bad. *Was this Paul talking? God had been showing him things?*

"I don't have the strong faith that Ben, Emily, or Luke have. I am seeking. Does that make sense?"

Pearl turned and their gazes met in a lingering look. The words wouldn't escape past the knot in her throat, so she nodded.

"I know what I want. I've known for a very long time."

"To build houses like Ben?"

Paul felt blinded by the sun overhead. Blinded by the bright yellow of Pearl's dress. Blinded by his love for her. "Yes, I am already doing that."

"What else then?" Her heart was hammering against her rib cage, and she tried to still it by clasping her hands tight in front of her.

"When you were away teaching, I was happy for you because I knew you were doing what you wanted to do. I liked writing to you. I enjoyed your letters."

"If you only knew how your letters got me through those days—"

"Pearl," he took her hand and held it tightly. "Let me finish, or I'll never get it out.

"I tried to like Nancy, but it wasn't right. That's when I first knew God was hearing my thoughts. It was as if He led me away from her. And then it was Christmas, and you came home, and everyone was happy and laughing and singing, and your presence made everything right again. I hadn't known until then—until I heard you laugh, watched you holding baby Clifford, heard your voice singing out, that I never wanted to lose sight of you again. Yet now I fear you are going off to teach again. And it should be that way if it's what you want. Just make sure that you really, truly want it."

Could she have heard right? Was this Paul sitting next to her, saying words she had always hoped to hear, but never thought she would?

His voice was speaking, but she could hardly hear it above the pounding of her heart.

"I have yet to hear what you want. It's your turn, Gem."

She'd lain awake half the night, listening to Clifford's even breathing, thinking she would never have a child of her own, but would mother other children, those she taught in the classroom.

She had accepted this to be God's will for her. She would call Judson Rome to give him her decision. That was the last thought she'd had before she could sleep.

"I know you're a good teacher," he said, as if thinking he had to break the silence.

"Yes, I am a good teacher, Paul."

"And you're a good nurse. Look how you took care of my grandparents when they were so ill. And now Sarah. Perhaps nursing is more of your choosing."

"Perhaps." She needed to say more, but the words were still forming in her mind. Her being was bursting with love for this man beside her. Love that she now knew he felt for her. God had answered her prayers. And in the best way possible. How could she have ever doubted Paul's faith? As Mama had said, "We cannot judge, Pearl Marie."

"My dream," Pearl began, "is not to go into nursing, though I would always be there for my family. It is not to teach, though the children are a special blessing. It is to marry a man whom I love and one who would love me back. One who would agree that God is important, and we would serve Him and our community. It is the way of the Friends, you know."

"Yes, I know." He had not let go of her hand.

"And I want a whole passel of kids!"

"Passel?"

"It's a southern term." She felt happiness bubble up inside her, and it was about to tumble out and encompass them both.

"I have questioned God about my lack of beauty, but I know that beauty does come from within, and to deny it is to say to God that He has not made a good creation."

"Oh, Gem. You're beautiful to all of us who love you."

She turned and touched Paul's face. "I have thought of thee for such a very long time. I have loved thee with all my heart, though I tried to deny that love for thee filled my heart and soul."

Paul leaned over, touching Pearl's hair, her cheeks, the strong, determined chin. "I prayed last night that God would direct my path today and show me the way, and I think He has. I truly think He has."

Pearl stood, throwing her arms into the air. "Oh! I cannot believe this is happening. I cannot keep from shouting. Laughing!"

Paul jumped up and took her hands. "My Gem, my beauty. Thank You, God, for giving Gem to me. For giving us such love."

The lunch was eaten, and then they watched as children came along and searched for crawdads in the shallow water of the creek.

"I think we need to talk to Luke about marrying us—" Paul began.

"After you ask Ben for my hand." Pearl looked up and laughed. "As if we don't know what he will say."

"Everyone's probably been wondering why this didn't happen sooner."

Pearl nodded. "I think I loved you from that first night you arrived from California."

"I think I loved you since the first time I ate your apple pie."

They stayed until the sun started its descent west, then they picked up the blanket and headed home.

"Love's tender path," Pearl said as the horses trotted down Foster Road.

"What does that mean?" Paul asked.

"It's something Mama said about her and Pa. I just remembered it. It was after he died, and she talked about how the path can be narrow and rocky in marriage, but if you truly love one and it's the one God intended for you, the path can be tender."

Paul smiled and took her hand again. He had not yet told her about his design, the house he would build. That would come later. Perhaps tomorrow.

Epilogue

The Galloway house once again bustled with activity. With the announcement of Pearl and Paul's plans, Sarah took on a better color. God had answered her fervent prayer: She now knew her youngest would be happy. One look at the couple, and she also knew God would bless this union. Paul was an earnest young man who had accepted the Lord into his life. Pearl, as far as Sarah was concerned, was the cream of the crop.

Kate, though close to the delivery time of her first baby, made the special wedding dress, a white organdy with full skirt and puffy sleeves. Luke would officiate, while Emily played the "Wedding March" and vows were repeated in front of the fireplace just as she and Ben had done three years ago.

Anna arrived two days after Paul announced their plans. A replica of Pearl, only smaller, she bustled through the house as if she'd always lived there. Clifford took to her immediately.

"He's going to be a feisty one," she said, tickling him under the chin. "One of these days I'll find someone and have a baby just like you!"

Anna, in a dress of sea-green taffeta, would be her sister's maid of honor. "It shouldn't be that an older sister does not marry first."

"Thee will marry," Sarah said. She sat in a chair close to the window where the June sun filled her weakened body with warmth.

But it was Albert who surprised them all. Arriving in Portland on the *T. J. Potter*, a passenger boat that carried people from the coast and Astoria down the Columbia River, he showed up on the porch two days before the wedding.

Albert was big and loud with a robust laugh. He hugged Sarah close and said he wouldn't have missed coming for anything. "And now you tell me I'm just in time for the wedding of my baby sister?" He laughed again. "Pretty good timing, if I don't say so myself."

There were more hugs, and Emily tossed more potatoes and carrots into the stew.

"Anna," Albert said, "you must come back to the beach with me. I'm on the North Beach Peninsula in Washington State. It's God's country there. We need nurses. Doctors. Teachers." He looked at Pearl. "Fishermen we have!" He laughed again.

Before Pearl could answer, he turned to Paul. "Come up there for your honeymoon. You'll love the place."

Paul grabbed Pearl's hand. "I think a boat ride to the coast is just what we should do!"

"I'm not losing my best plasterer, am I?" asked Ben in all seriousness.

"Oh, no," Paul replied. "We'll be back. This is home."

This is home, Pearl thought. "Yes, this is home. And now I am going to be building my own home. Praises be to God."

That summer, weeks after all the festivities, Sarah went to be with her Lord and Savior. Pearl had read the passage the night before she drifted off to sleep:

> *In My Father's house are many mansions.*
> *I go to prepare a place for you.*
> *And if I go and prepare a place for you,*
> *I will come again to receive you unto myself.*

"I will see you later," Sarah murmured, taking her youngest child's hand. "God be with you."

Anna's
Hope

To my friends on the peninsula, who love it as I do,
and especially to Jeanie Dunham,
who is an endless source of information and help.

Chapter 1

The *T. J. Potter*, loaded with passengers, cows, dogs, chickens, and assorted baggage, swooshed its way down the Columbia River. Most people were headed for Astoria and parts south. A few would ferry across the Columbia to Megler Landing on the Washington side.

It was to this place that Anna Galloway had promised to go. A nurse was needed to help the only doctor in the primitive area. Anna's older brother, Albert, had been most persuasive in talking her into leaving the comforts of Portland, her home with her younger brother, Ben, and all the other family and friends she'd just met in the two weeks since coming from Iowa.

After graduating from nursing school in Iowa City, Anna had worked at a hospital in Cedar Rapids. There she received word that her mother, Sarah, was dying. Could she come west to Oregon?

The time for a change could not have been more perfect. Joseph, the man she loved, had decided they could not marry. "You were meant to be a nurse, Anna, but I need a wife."

Joseph's words still stung, and now Mama's death added to the ache deep inside her. Perhaps she did like nursing too much, but it was a calling, and wasn't one supposed to listen to God's voice, the urging to be, to do?

The wind whipping off the river blew Anna's short curls—the few that stuck out from under the navy blue wool cloche she clutched tightly to her head with one hand. It was midsummer of 1912, and Anna wondered how it could be so chilly in July.

"I've never seen such a cold summer wind," she cried to Albert. "In Iowa, the corn would be growing overnight, along with the tomatoes in Mama's garden. I'm beginning to wonder about going to this place surrounded by water. I'm a farm girl at heart. I like land. A place to put my feet."

Albert, dark and ruggedly handsome, smiled at Anna. She was just a year younger than he was, but she had always acted older and had the upper hand.

"Yes, there is a heap of water." He fingered his short, well-clipped beard. "Soon we'll dock in Astoria. From there you'll take the ferry across the Columbia, then ride the railroad with its passengers and wide assortment of animals—whatever needs to be transported—west to the North Beach Peninsula."

"Once I get there, I'm staying put." Anna's chin jutted out with determination. She breathed deep gulps of air that nearly took her breath away. Whitecaps appeared, making her think of pictures she'd seen in books of the rolling waves of the Pacific Ocean. She never dreamed she'd someday see it, and now she was almost there.

Hills bordered both sides of the river, giving Anna some comfort. She pulled her long coat closer, her broad shoulders buffeting the wind. "At least there is *some* land."

"Of course, not much is inhabited by man."

"Oh!" Anna cried. Her voice seemed to be snatched by the wind and thrown to the depths of the river. She barely heard Albert's voice and had to shout into his ear or repeat her words. "Why did I ever let you talk me into this?" She tried to smile.

"Because you are needed. When Dr. Snow came to Astoria, asking for nurses, and nobody accepted the position, I thought of you. With five years' experience, you fit his request well."

"You haven't convinced me, Albert. All I wish is for this ride to be over."

Albert threw back his head and laughed the hearty, loud Galloway laugh. "Your journey is far from over, Anna." He chuckled again, then looked at his watch. "You'll probably arrive in Seaview by sundown."

Anna disliked it when Albert teased her. He had done so when they were children. That seemed so long ago now. Shortly after Anna had left for nurse's training at the University of Iowa, Albert had also left, looking for adventure in the Pacific Northwest. He'd never returned to Iowa and had no intention of ever doing so.

"How can it take so long?" Anna asked. She could have walked to the lower level where it was warmer, but it wouldn't have been nearly as interesting. Besides, she felt safer watching the waves, leaning in the direction the boat went. She marveled at how the river whipped up such monstrous waves, though she didn't want to admit it to her brother.

"It's farther west, that's why." He cleared his throat. "I'll be staying in Astoria, you know."

"What?" Anna turned and stared at Albert, but there was no laughter in the dark eyes now. "You mean you aren't going the rest of the way with me?"

He pointed across the river to where she saw the vague outlines of buildings suspended in the air. "That's the fish seining fields where I'll be working now. I don't live on the peninsula anymore."

"But. . . ," she sputtered. "Why didn't you tell me?"

Anna, fiercely independent, had been on her own the past several years now. She had a mind of her own—"a stubborn streak" Mama had called it.

She liked trying new things, but this was different. This place was at the end of the world.

Albert touched her shoulder, then hugged her for a brief moment. "I just didn't fill in all the details, but you'll do fine here. The most important reason is that you are needed. Besides, I thought you were ready for adventure."

Thoughts of Joseph flashed through her mind again, and she nodded. "Yes, I am wanting to do something new." How could she have forgotten?

"Excuse me," a voice said at her elbow. "I couldn't help overhearing." He offered a hand. "Peter Fielding. I'm on my way up past Seaview and can make sure you get off at the right place." His eyes met Anna's surprised gaze.

"You're going on the same train?"

Peter laughed. "There is only one way to get to the peninsula. We'll ferry across, then catch the Clamshell Railroad—"

"Clamshell railroad!" Anna declared. "Are the tracks made of clamshells?"

Both Albert and Peter laughed. Then, as if noting Anna's displeasure, Peter explained, "It's what the locals call it—the train that runs by the tide, and is never on time."

Anna raised her hand, wanting to add emphasis to her statement, and in that moment her hat flew off, sending her thick brown curls to dancing. She lunged for the hat, but Peter grabbed it. His dark, warm eyes seemed to mock her as he handed it over. Anna blushed deeply while putting it back on her head. "Thank you."

"You're certainly welcome." If he hadn't caught the hat when he had, it could have been over the railing and into the raging waters. It was the last gift from her mother, and she loved it dearly for that reason.

"We do need nurses," Peter said. "Doc Snow is overworked, and the only nurse we had left for California."

Anna found the young man disconcerting without knowing why. Words stayed inside her, a rarity in her case, since little ruffled her. She turned to Albert, hoping he'd carry on the conversation.

"Mr. Fielding, I'd like to take you up on your offer to see that Anna gets on the train and off at the Seaview Station. I understand there is a boarding-house nearby."

Peter smiled. "A short distance, and she'll love the proprietor, Miss Bessie."

The *T. J. Potter* turned and headed toward the bank. Astoria. The small fishing town on the Oregon side. Anna knew it was one of the earliest settlements on the West Coast and boasted the first post office. Fishing was the livelihood. Everywhere Anna looked there were boats and more boats. A few houses dotted the surrounding hills. Civilization. It looked inviting. Maybe she should stay here.

They pulled up to a dock with much bumping and clamoring about as people gathered their belongings. At last it stopped, and Anna knew she'd feel land under her feet. Firm, steady land. It would seem good, even if it was only for a few minutes.

Albert jumped into action. "I'll get your baggage, Anna."

She'd brought one medium-sized trunk. It contained two nurse's uniforms, a cape, her cap, and four dresses; two were good, two for everyday. Two pairs of shoes were in the bottom.

"I must get back to the seining fields," Albert explained to Peter. "I'd meant to see Anna settled in, but I stayed in Portland longer than intended and am a day late as is. I'm the assistant manager of the operation."

"But, Albert, when will I see you?" A sudden fear washed over Anna.

"I'll catch the ferry over a week from Sunday. See how you're faring." He bent down, brushing a quick kiss on Anna's cheek. Before she could protest further, he tipped his hat and was off, going up the gangplank. She turned to find Peter Fielding watching her, waiting.

"Here. I'll handle the trunk. We'd better get in line."

"And where is your luggage? How will you manage mine also?"

"I have none."

"None?"

"I went to Portland yesterday on business and am now returning home."

"I see."

The ferry was loading, and soon Anna was going from a large boat to a smaller one.

"Sometimes the *T. J. Potter* pulls up over at Megler Landing, but today there were people, like your brother, who needed to get off in Astoria, and passengers who needed to get on there."

Anna felt some bit of comfort in having Peter Fielding see to her needs, but she disliked being beholden to anyone. Yet there was something nice about him, especially the warmth in his eyes.

"It'll be a short trip across the river." Peter glanced at his pocket watch. "And I think the train will be ready and waiting."

"How far must I go on the train?" Trains Anna was used to. She'd taken the train on her ride out from Iowa. When Mama got sick, she could think of nothing but going to Oregon to see her one last time. Sarah had died a week later, and Anna was glad she'd come. Glad she'd left Iowa behind.

I'll forget Joseph if it's the last thing I ever do, she thought now. *Perhaps there is a life for me here.*

"Not too many miles. At least you're not going to the North End. We'll go past Chinook, Ilwaco, then Seaview. Just be glad you're not going to Nahcotta."

"Nahcotta?" *What strange names,* Anna thought. *Astoria, Nahcotta, Chinook, Ilwaco.*

"Indian names," Peter said then, as if reading her mind.

"Oh. Are there Indians, Mr. Fielding?"

"Of course. All civilized, to be sure."

"You're teasing me."

A smile played about his full mouth. "Maybe just a bit, but there are a few Indians living there. All friendly."

Before long the ferry arrived at Megler, and the train was waiting. Anna held onto her hat, lifting her heavy coat and dress just enough so she could mount the steps. Soon they were settled into adjoining seats.

"I will see you to the boardinghouse," Peter said, "perhaps borrow a horse from Bessie, as my family is waiting."

"Tell me about your family," Anna said.

"I have two children."

And a wife, Anna almost said. She had a habit of finishing people's answers, but she'd stopped in time. Not that she cared that he was married. She wasn't coming here to find a husband, though her mother had worried about her, begging her to find someone, settle down, but that was Mama. She supposed all mothers felt that way about unmarried daughters, and Anna knew Sarah had prayed often for all her children, wanting them to be settled and happy.

"What ages are they?" Anna glanced up to see a pained expression in the brown eyes. "Oh. Did I say something wrong?"

"No. You'll get a chance to meet them. Catherine is seven, Henry five."

"I will certainly look forward to that," Anna said, wanting to ask about his wife.

The train continued chugging toward its destination as Anna stared out the window. The exhaustion she'd felt earlier had abated some.

"Children are a blessing," Anna said then. She watched the different shades of green on the hillside as the train passed. She'd never seen such immense trees or so many. The various shades of green fascinated her. This was nothing like Iowa, where everything was brown with a few trees scattered across the land.

The feeling of desolation hit again. She thought of her family back in Portland. Brother Ben, his wife Emily with baby Clifford and another baby on the way. And Pearl, now married. How could her baby sister marry before she did? At least Anna had Albert. He was the one responsible for her coming here, leaving her to the whims of another person as if he didn't care a bit.

O God, Anna prayed. *Help this to work. Help me to be of use to someone. Guide my steps.*

She thought of the Bible buried deep in her trunk. A verse came to mind now—one Sarah had repeated to her many times as she was growing up on the Iowa farm. "Be still, and know that I am God" (Psalm 46:10).

"Anna," Mama used to say, "there is no way God can help you. You're never still long enough to hear Him."

Yes, God, I've not been still much of my life, but something tells me I am going to be still—very still—from now on. For once I'm going to rely on You all the way.

"You're smiling." Peter's voice broke through her thoughts.

Anna opened her eyes and found Peter Fielding's warm gaze on her. His look was expectant, and her heart gave a sudden lurch.

" 'Be still and know that I am God,' " Anna repeated then. "It's a verse my mother used to read to me, and somehow it seems most fitting now. I'm not sure why I came, or if I'll like it, but I guess I'll find out soon."

"You came because we need you, Miss Anna. As for the liking it, I think you will once you get used to the rain and wind."

Anna sighed. "I wish I could be more sure." She tried to relax, as she straightened her skirt of black bombazine. "Tell me," she said then, "what is the hospital like? How many rooms?"

"Hospital?" Peter looked perplexed. "We have no hospital on the peninsula."

"No hospital?" A strange feeling overcame Anna. Hadn't Albert said there was a hospital? Or had he? Perhaps she'd been so caught up in the adventure she hadn't even asked.

Anna finally found her voice. "I assumed there would be a hospital. How can I tend to patients if there is not?"

Peter shrugged. "Like Doc Snow does. You go to them."

"But how can I do that when I don't have a means of transportation or know where things are—"

"They'll give you a horse—"

"A horse!" Anna shrieked.

"Oh, no!" Peter hit his head with his palm. "Don't tell me you don't ride horses."

Anna just stared for a long moment. Of course she could ride a horse. She'd learned at an early age on the farm, but that had been eons ago.

"Do you want to go back to Portland?"

Anna considered that option, then shook her head. "I'm not a quitter, Mr. Fielding. I just wish I'd known ahead of time, that's all."

"Your brother may not have known."

Anna looked grim. "Oh, he knew all right. That's Albert for you."

She settled back against the seat, her mind whirling with thoughts. No hospital. No house where patients came. She'd be a traveling nurse. Riding on a horse, to places she knew nothing about. Well, Albert had been right about one thing: This area was far more primitive than anywhere Anna had ever lived. It would certainly be a challenge.

She closed her eyes and once more listened for God's voice, wanting to be reassured, but all she heard was the clickety-clack of the wheels as the train headed farther west. West to her new home. West to fulfill her career, to nurse those who needed help. Would she see Peter Fielding again? She doubted it, but time would tell. She adjusted her hat and leaned farther back in the cushioned seat.

Chapter 2

By the time the small train chugged into yet another depot, darkness had crept throughout the car.

"We're here, Anna." Peter Fielding stood, offering his hand. "I'll get your trunk, then walk you to the boardinghouse."

Anna straightened her dress and the hat and felt a tingle in her toes. She followed Peter down the aisle and down the steps, taking the hand he offered her. She shivered from the sudden chill of the night. No stars shone overhead. It was dark. Black and eerie. But there was a sound, a roaring noise she could not identify. Could this be the ocean? She sniffed the air. It smelled different, too, and she decided it must be the salt in the atmosphere. She wished she could see the ocean waves. Sudden fear of the unknown hit again.

"O God," she whispered, "if this is where I'm supposed to be, please help me to know."

"Did you say something?" Peter asked, turning as he placed Anna's trunk on a small rail cart.

"Only a plea to my Father above," Anna said. She shivered again. It was a damp sort of cold that chilled a body to the bone immediately.

"We've just one block to go, then you'll have a place to sleep and a spot of tea before you retire. You'll adore Bessie."

"A cup of tea would be delightful." Anna held her coat closer.

The house appeared. Shrouded in darkness, it looked immense.

Anna followed Peter up the steps onto a glassed-in sun porch.

He banged on the door. "I'm sure Bessie will have a room for you. She's come to expect travelers on the evening train."

The door sprang open and a large, buxom lady exclaimed, "Is that ye, Mr. Peter Fielding?"

Anna felt comfort from the voice, and her shoulders relaxed. She had an accent. She must be a Scot, just like Anna's nursing supervisor back in Iowa. She smiled and nodded.

"Brought you a guest, Miss Bessie—one who will be staying longer than a day or two."

"I wondered if the train might not bring some boarders to my home this night." She held out her arms, hugging the bedraggled Anna.

"I'm Bessie McGruder, head cook and owner of this place. Ye both come on in."

"This is Anna Galloway," Peter said. "She's the nurse Doc Snow's been expecting."

"Land a goshen, if he won't be happy to see ye."

"I was expected then?" Anna asked as she followed Peter and Bessie into the house. She hadn't been sure that he'd received her letter of acceptance.

"He did mention someone might come, but he's been disappointed before."

Anna tried to smile, but her face felt frozen, her body numb.

Bessie, as if reading Anna's mind, led her into the dining area. "Sit while I fix tea and a bowl of leftover soup. Don't always have soup left, but the good Lord knew I'd be a-needing some this night."

Anna nodded and sank against a thick bank of pillows in what looked to be a window seat in the combination dining-living room. Bessie turned to Peter. "And if ye'd be so good as to take that trunk up to the third floor—to the room at the far right, I'd be ever so grateful. I think this young lady would enjoy the view from there."

Anna heard the roaring sound, even inside the house, and wondered if she'd ever feel warm again. She wasn't sure how long she'd be staying at the boardinghouse, but a quiet peace came over her and she felt comforted by this woman who had thrown her arms around Anna when she didn't even know her. It was almost as if Mama had been there.

Though Anna hadn't been around Sarah in the past few years, she would always remember how her mother tended to her needs. Anna thought about the rainstorms that hit Iowa every spring with fair regularity. Everyone rushed out to pick as much corn as they could, filling the gunnysacks to over-flowing. Anna's arms had ached, but she couldn't stop. They couldn't sell it now, but would use it as feed for the horses and cow. Anna remembered her mother lifting her sodden dress from her shoulders, and then pressing a cup of hot tea into her hands. The warmth of the cup made her teeth finally stop chattering. . .

"I know how tiring that trip can be," Bessie was saying, bringing a tray in. "My son used to make it—" She turned away and a sudden stillness filled the room. "Not that God ain't a-takin' care of 'im, because I know the Almighty is. . ."

"Your son?" Anna asked, wanting to know more.

"He died. It was a fever that took 'im when he was twenty-five."

"Oh, I'm so sorry."

Bessie patted her hand. "Don't ye go a-feelin' sorry for me. I have family plenty enough right here, don't I, Mr. Fielding?"

Peter had come back down and nodded. "Yes, Miss Bessie has plenty of folks she thinks of as family, and we all think she's right special."

"Are you having tea?" Bessie asked.

"No. I must return home. Fetch the children from my neighbor, Doris Yates. I'll take ole Ned, if you don't mind."

Bessie hugged Peter briefly. "Sure thing. Ye can bring Ned back whenever. And give those two of yours a hug for me."

Anna wanted to say the same, but didn't feel it proper. She bade Peter good night, thanking him again for all his help.

"Such a loss," Bessie said, once the door was closed. "I don't suppose he told you about Callie."

"Callie?"

"His wife."

"No. I wondered why he had to pick up his children—"

"Died, she did. About a year ago. Right after Dr. Snow came. Doc tried everything he could, but the good Lord took her, and only He knows the reasons. As it says in the Book, the rain falls on the just as well as the unjust."

Anna set her cup down harder than she meant to. "Seems we all have losses." She thought of Sarah again, but it was different. Sarah'd had a full life; Peter's wife had been young and had left two children.

Bessie stood. "Now as soon as ye are ready, I'll show ye your room. I think ye will like it. Just last summer I put up pink rosebud wallpaper."

Anna loved the room the minute she saw it. Since it was on the top floor, the ceiling was slanted, yet it was spacious and airy. She liked the square brass headboard, the colorful quilt, the multicolored braided rug. A small vanity was in one corner, a massive wardrobe filled the wall opposite the bed. A faint smell of lavender made her smile, remembering that fragrance from years ago when Sarah had made lavender sachets for Christmas.

"I see ye is clasping your hands." Bessie set the lamp on a small end table topped with a crocheted scarf. "That's always a good sign."

"It's beautiful," Anna said softly. "I will be content here."

The older woman beamed. "I hope the train's whistle won't bother ye, but it can't be helped. That's why I put ye on this side of the house, hoping it wouldn't be quite as loud."

"I will be so tired, nothing will waken me," Anna said. Suddenly all she could think of was sinking into the bed, pulling the thick quilts up under her chin, and closing her eyes.

❄

It wasn't daylight that wakened Anna the next morning, nor was it the sound of the early morning train pulling into the Seaview station; it was the smell of bacon frying and biscuits baking that coaxed her from her sleep.

At first she didn't remember where she was, and then it all came back. This was her new home on the North Beach Peninsula, miles from brother Albert, and many, many miles from Portland, where the rest of her family lived. She'd made the decision to come here, so she would make the best of it. The Galloways had never been quitters. She'd do her best to help the sick in this isolated spot. Just knowing she was needed gave her some small comfort.

She bounded to the window with its white lace curtains and peeked out. Anna's breath caught in her throat at the beauty of the blue water with the frothy white waves. Mesmerized, she watched the waves rolling in, then rolling out, some more boisterous than others. The ocean stretched forever, as far as she could see, out beyond the blue horizon. She pulled herself away from the window. Enough lollygagging. There were things to do today. One of the first was to unpack, then iron her uniforms.

Anna chose a pale green muslin and tried to smooth the wrinkles out with her fingers. Wrinkles couldn't be helped, as she'd packed the trunk tight. Hurriedly, she ran a brush through her short hair, once again barely recognizing herself in the mirror. She'd chopped off most of her hair last week. It had been an impulsive moment and she wondered now if she might regret the decision.

Slowly, wondrously, Anna descended the stairs, taking note of the photographs, the artwork that lined the wall.

"Anna! And top of the mornin' to ye!" Bessie smiled at the boarders seated around the large, rectangular table. "This is Miss Anna Galloway, our new boarder and nurse!"

"Good morning," voices called out. Anna noticed all the boarders were older, with the exception of one young woman. Anna nodded and smiled.

"I trust ye slept well?" Bessie asked.

"Like I haven't slept in a year," Anna replied, looking again at the faces around the table.

After introductions, Anna took a small helping of scrambled eggs, two strips of bacon, and one baking-powder biscuit.

"Ye can certainly eat more than that," Bessie said, looking down the long table at Anna.

"Mama said one can always go back for more," Anna explained, dabbing berry jam on her biscuit.

"And in a boardinghouse if you don't get it while the gettin's good, you might miss out," said Miss Fern on her right.

"That's only when Doc comes," Mr. Webster added. He touched his short, straggly beard. "He's the one with the appetite."

After breakfast, Bessie took Anna's plate and shooed her on upstairs. "I have kitchen help. They'll take care of this. Take this day to rest. Unpack. Walk to the beach—though—" She looked out the window. "I don't think the walking will be good—not with that fog rolling in."

Anna looked out the bay window and sighed with disappointment. A walk to the beach had been on her agenda for the morning. However, there would be time for that later.

"When can I meet the doctor?" Anna asked then. She could be lazy one day—perhaps that would be permitted—but she longed to start work. She hadn't been nursing for three weeks now.

"Doc Snow comes for lunch, barreling through that door at 11:45 sharp. I can set my clock by him."

"There's plenty of time for unpacking—"

"And a tour of the house, if ye'd like."

Anna smiled. "I'd like that very much."

She followed Bessie up the winding staircase to the second floor, looking at the highly polished wood. She'd been too tired to notice last night and too hungry this morning.

"The captain bought this place before it was finished. The first owner died, and his wife moved back to Portland."

"The captain?"

"That's what I call my husband. He was a captain when I met him and a captain when he died." Bessie's eyes looked up. "The good Lord gave us twenty wonderful years."

Anna wondered how many years Peter and Callie'd had.

"Captain fell in love with this place—said it reminded him of his boyhood home back in Scotland."

"Was this before you were married?"

Bessie shook her head. "I met him on the *T. J. Potter* coming down the river just like ye came yesterday."

Anna thought of Peter again. Had God sent her here to care for two motherless children, or to be a nurse? She chastised herself for even thinking such thoughts. Besides, she still had feelings for Joseph.

"We have five bedrooms on this floor and a sitting room. Some call it a reading and writing study," Bessie went on.

The room, painted a sunny yellow, had two small sofas and a table with a checkerboard waiting, as if hoping someone would choose to play a game. The window beckoned and she looked out once more at the pounding surf, surrounded now by the incoming fog.

"The wood is the finest Douglas fir ye'll ever lay eyes on. Hauled up the river by the builder. He was a Portland businessman, ye know."

"It's all so beautiful," Anna said. Each room had vivid colors, drapes at the windows, and small throw rugs.

"Is this the captain?" Anna asked, noting she'd seen the picture of the same man in all the rooms thus far. He had a gruff look and wore a seaman's cap.

Bessie nodded. "That's my captain all right. He was lost at sea; storm came up that fast!" Her face looked drawn. "Never seen anythin' like it."

Anna gazed at the view from one of the windows and wondered how anyone in his or her right mind would want to go out in that water to fish. The Columbia River had been rough, but this ocean looked far more treacherous, and with the fog coming in, one could get off course easily.

The two women arrived at the top floor, and Bessie promised to show her the rest later. "Ye tend to the unpacking—whatever ye must do. Come down when ye like."

Anna hung her dresses and uniforms in the wardrobe and placed her shoes on the floor, her mirror and brush on the vanity. The window beckoned again, and this time she could not see the waves crashing against the shore, because of the fog, but the sound had a lulling, magical quality. She got a chill. Used to hot weather, sunshine beaming from sunup to sundown, as all Iowa summers were, Anna knew this cool climate would take getting used to.

She placed her Bible on the desk and pulled out the small chair. Withdrawing a small tablet, she wrote a note to Emily and Ben.

> *I have arrived in Seaview. It is so different from what I expected—so quaint. I'm staying at a huge boardinghouse. There is no hospital here. Imagine my dismay upon discovering that. The doctor needs a nurse, so perhaps I will be busy after all.*
>
> *I know God shall take care of me and has brought me here for a purpose. I hope to go to work soon.*
>
> *Emily, take care of yourself, and give Clifford a piggyback ride, Ben.*
>
> *Love to Pearl and Paul. I hope someone will come to visit me soon. I miss all of you tremendously.*
>
> *With warmest regards,*
Anna Galloway

Anna sealed the letter and took it with her as she descended the two flights of stairs. She saluted the photograph of the captain on the second floor landing, and noticed another man with a formal look. *President William McKinley*, the caption read. She remembered he had been assassinated in 1901, five years before her father died. She liked his strong chin, the bold, piercing eyes. He made her think of Papa.

A wonderful smell of beef stew and cornbread wafted in from the kitchen as Anna entered the main room. The table was set with blue willoware plates, cups, and thick, well-used pieces of flatware.

On cue, as the mantel clock gonged the quarter hour, the door opened and a tall, broad-shouldered figure came into the kitchen, filling it with his presence. "Is that beef stew I smell? Bessie, you're a darling."

His hand reached out to grab a chunk of cornbread, and Bessie playfully swatted him. "Oh, and be gone with ye! Can't ye even wait until we've sat and asked the Lord's blessing?"

"The Lord knows I'm thankful for my food, especially when I come here, my dear Bessie—" He stopped, and Anna turned to find herself looking straight into the eyes of *the* Dr. Snow, the man she had come to work with. She trembled unexpectedly as their gazes met and held.

"You didn't tell me we had company."

"That's because I didn't know she was a-coming until last night. Came up on the *T. J. Potter* and over on the train. Anna, this is Dr. Wesley Snow whom I've been speaking of. And Dr. Snow, this is Anna Galloway, all the way from Iowa State."

Anna stepped forward and held out her hand. His piercing gaze might have stopped one younger, but Anna had never been shy. "I trust you received my letter of recommendation?"

He towered over Anna, his square face showing surprise. Then he smiled as he took her hand. "Yes, I received it. My regret is there was not time to answer."

"I came on ahead, anyway," Anna said. "If you had no need for me, I planned on returning to Portland. I have family there." She wondered if she should mention she'd had second thoughts after the lengthy ride on the *T. J. Potter*. She decided not.

His eyes were intense, his face clean shaven. "You have a degree in nursing, I understand."

"Yes. I finished my schooling five years ago at the University of Iowa School of Nursing. Graduated with the class of 1907."

The eyes suddenly twinkled, and Anna felt herself relax. "My dear woman, you can be of use here. Do not think otherwise. It's just that I did not know when to expect you—"

"That's because my mother was gravely ill," Anna interrupted, "and I could not leave her side. She passed on a week ago."

"I'm dreadfully sorry to hear that." His face went somber. "I just said to Miss Lizzie Myles, my housekeeper, that what this peninsula needs is a nurse—and here you are!"

Anna felt her cheeks redden under his steady gaze. "I had thought there would be a hospital here, but Mr. Fielding, the young man who assisted me last evening, said there was none."

"Yes and there should be, but we use the boardinghouse here, and I've turned my home into a hospital of sorts. I can do operations and treat patients there nicely now. The rest of the time I visit the sick and do what I can."

"I am ready to start work straightaway," Anna said.

"Good. Good. I have a maternity patient who doesn't want to leave the peninsula. I'm a mite concerned about her."

The dinner gong sounded. Soon Mr. Webster and Miss Fern came down the stairs, while Cora, the younger woman, sauntered in from the porch. The table wasn't crowded, but Bessie said to wait until the weekend when the *T. J. Potter* brought more people to the peninsula.

Dr. Snow removed his coat and sat at the opposite end of the table from Anna. Soon everyone was chattering. She listened while he told about the beached whale he'd seen the day before. "Of course, there's never a thing you can do but let it lie there and rot."

Anna made a face. It was hardly the topic for meal conversation.

"I certainly hope you don't have a squeamish stomach—"

Anna looked him straight in the eye. "No. I assure you I do not, but what of the others?"

He roared then as if she'd said something amusing. "They're not even listening to me."

Anna turned back to her stew, noticing that the good doctor had finished both his stew and two chunks of cornbread. His face lit up when Bessie brought bowls of chocolate pudding with mounds of whipped cream on top for dessert.

"Bessie, each meal is better than the last."

Anna decided to say no more and hurried to finish the stew. It was good, but it was hard to swallow past the hard knot in her throat. She'd come prepared to like the doctor, but he seemed brusque, almost flippant. Finishing the pudding in three bites, Dr. Snow pushed his chair back. "You'll do, Miss Galloway. You look quite capable."

Before Anna could respond, he had stridden to the doorway. "I must go, but if you'd like, you can come first thing in the morning to my makeshift hospital. Bessie can give you directions. You brought uniforms, I trust."

"Of course."

He looked at her strangely, then asked, "Do all the nurses wear their hair short in Iowa?"

Anna felt remorse for her action when she'd whacked off the long, brown hair. She had been more than blessed with the thick Galloway hair that had a mind of its own. Many times she'd lamented trying to pin it up to her supervisor's satisfaction.

With it shorn, it would be so much easier to wash and brush.

"Do you have a problem with my hair?" Anna asked with sudden boldness.

He shrugged. "I suppose not, but—"

Anna's face flamed for the second time since meeting the doctor. "I cut it right after my mother died, as she wouldn't have approved."

"Hair is a woman's crowning glory; says so in the Good Book."

"Yes, so it does." Anna didn't know what else to say.

"But—" Wesley Snow smiled. "I think short hair might be a good idea. It's why I shave my face each day." He fingered his smooth chin. "Hair carries germs, you know." He stood and held out his hand again. "I look forward to having you work with me. I'll expect you in the morning, around seven. Now I must get on to my next patient."

Anna had a sudden impulse to ask if she could go with him. It would only take minutes to don her uniform, though it was wrinkled. She found she didn't want to wait until morning, but as he turned and walked back through the kitchen, Anna knew it would be better to go with a cleanly pressed uniform. And her cap might hide the fact that her hair was short.

Did Dr. Snow mean it, she wondered later, *that short hair was a good idea, or was he just being kind?* But as Anna was soon to discover, Dr. Snow was never kind for the simple sake of being kind. Anna wondered about his brusque, abrupt manner, yet she liked how he looked you square in the eye, his gaze never wavering.

"An honest man always looks you in the eye," Papa used to say. "If he cain't, don't trust him behind your back."

She stood at the parlor window listening to the surf and the sound of horses clip-clopping down the road.

Anna wondered again about Joseph, remembering that night when he'd broken her heart. "Anna, I will always remember you with fondness, but I love another. Besides, you have your nursing career ahead of you."

For a long while Anna had wondered what she would do without Joseph in her life, but looking back she realized she had done just fine, and would continue to do so. With fierce determination, she turned from the window and took her empty cup and saucer to the kitchen. Tomorrow was the beginning of a new and promising day.

Chapter 3

Anna rose with the dawn. She'd always risen early, but this was earlier than usual. Last night had been a restless one. She couldn't sleep for wondering how her day would go. Not that she worried. She knew she was a good nurse. She cared about people. She could talk to the patients easily, so she filled all the requirements Dr. Snow had mentioned yesterday. But it was a new challenge, and though Anna had always faced a challenge head-on, she was apprehensive now. She would do her best and surely he could expect nothing else.

Bessie's helper had the fire going in the cookstove. "You're up mighty early, Miss Anna."

Anna smiled. "I'm a bit anxious about my first day of work." She paused. "I'm sorry I don't know your name."

"Delia." The young girl bowed slightly.

"Well, Delia, I imagine we'll get to know each other rather well, don't you suppose?"

"Well, good morning to ye." Bessie looked surprised to see Anna standing by the sink. "The sun is barely up, and here ye are already." Bessie added water to the coffee-pot. "The sunrise was beautiful from my bedroom window. Means there'll be no rain, and that's a good sign for ye."

A few minutes later Anna huddled over the warmth from the stove in the dining room.

Coffee would warm her insides and her hands, too.

"Ye need some warmin' up, I see."

Anna nodded. "This is summer—"

"Aye. That it is, but mornings are always cold, even in summer. The ocean brings a wide variety of weather. The cold breeze comes off the ocean. Takes the sun to warm things up a bit. Ye'll get used to it."

In no time the coffee perked on the stove, and Bessie had potatoes sliced and frying. "It'll be oats this morning, scrambled eggs, bread, and potatoes."

Anna took her coffee out onto the sunporch. Her uniform, stiff from starch, was without wrinkles. The maid had insisted all it needed was a bit of pressing to make it presentable. As Anna looked at the sky waking up from its night of darkness, she prayed: "Lord, I come to Thee as Your child. Please be with me this day. Help me to do Thy will. Help me to be an asset to this community and to assist Dr. Snow in all ways."

"Trust in the Lord and he will direct thy paths" went through her head. She believed that with all her heart. God directed. God had pointed her in this direction, and He would be here to lean on.

Others came down the stairs, and Anna greeted Mr. Webster. He was hard of hearing so she had to raise her voice.

"It's a perfect day, Mr. Webster."

He wore the same shirt and pants he'd had on yesterday, but he'd clipped some of the straggly parts of his beard. "Yes, Missy, you're right there. But, then, it's always a perfect day at the beach."

Anna greeted every one, then went to refill her coffee cup. She offered to help bring the food to the table, but Bessie told her to sit down. "I'll handle it with Delia's help." Though Bessie didn't need to serve, she often did so. "I prefer to keep busy and just like to cook" was her comment.

Bessie asked the blessing, and everyone dug in. Though her plate was filled with food, Anna found it difficult to swallow. She'd never reacted like this before. Why was the job affecting her this way?

At last it was time to go. Anna put on the navy blue cape and pinned the cap to her hair. One of the helpers had brought the horse and buggy around and helped her up.

"We will see ye at 11:45 sharp," Bessie called from the doorway.

Anna nodded.

It had been a long time since living on the farm, and then she had ridden bareback, but taking the reins, she knew she'd have no problem with this gentle gray horse, as she called to him to giddiyup.

Since Anna had not been to Dr. Snow's home, she could hardly wait to see it. She'd heard it was right close to the center of Long Beach. The large home was the hospital, doctor's office, and waiting room. She was also eager to meet his housekeeper, Lizzie, who lived in, cooked most of his meals, and washed the necessary linens.

A sign revealed she'd arrived at the right house. Anna drove around to the back, and a form appeared to take charge of the buggy before she had a chance to light. "Doc Snow told me you were coming," the young boy said. He was not more than ten, Anna decided. She thanked him for his help and went to the front door.

Lizzie, the housekeeper, answered the knock. A short, full-figured woman, she had a warm smile and a firm handshake. "Dr. Snow is in the examining room—two doors down."

Dr. Snow appeared in the hallway. "Miss Galloway. You are earlier than I expected."

Anna tried to read his expression. Was he pleased or not? Perhaps he was not quite ready for her to arrive. "Everything was done that needed doing, so I came on ahead."

"Good. I appreciate both punctuality and efficiency in people. Come. I'll show you around what I call the infirmary."

It was primitive, but better than not having a hospital at all.

The waiting room, which would have been a front room, was rectangular and spacious. Two sofas, two low tables, and an occasional table filled the room. An oval throw rug covered the middle of the floor. The walls were a bright yellow.

"Very nice," Anna said. "My sister Pearl likes yellow. It does perk one up, don't you think?"

"Hmmm—" Dr. Snow seemed deep in thought. "I had nothing to do with the color. It was like this when I first came."

Anna followed him down the hall into a room with a long, leather-covered table. A desk fit nicely in one corner, and a small table with supplies in another. "My examining room."

"Adequate," was all Anna said. She wasn't about to make any extra comments. Clearly, he was a man of few words.

There was a water closet for patients and another room for minor operations. "We make do with what we have," he said, closing the door of the small operating room.

"I must check on a few patients. You may come with me, or stay here in case someone should need help. What would you prefer?"

Anna wondered if she would usually go with him, or stay in case of an emergency. Dr. Snow put his coat on, then stood, as if waiting for her reply. His eyes seemed to penetrate her and she looked away.

He paused. "Why not come with me—at least for today. I'll use the larger buggy and we'll be off."

Anna felt the stiffness of her uniform as he helped her into the buggy.

"We'll head up to Tioga Station first. I'm treating a man with chilblain. He's going to have to give up working at sea."

"Is that a common problem here?" Anna asked, remembering it was similar to frostbite, but not as severe.

"Yes, afraid so. Charlie works in the cold, damp air. He's getting too old for that—I told him so last month."

They rode on in silence, though Anna had a hundred questions rumbling through her mind.

He lifted the reins and paused for a moment. "Of course we'll head back to Bessie's close to noon. This is the day for her bean and ham soup. My favorite!"

Anna smiled as she stared at the doctor's profile. He was like her brothers Ben and Albert—and Jesse, too, she supposed, though she had not seen Jesse in such a long time—always thinking about food, *good food,* that is.

They reached the home, not much more than a shack, and Dr. Snow introduced Anna as the new nurse. Anna shook the man's hand and smiled, but couldn't help noticing the swelling of his hands and feet. His hands were clammy.

"Charlie, find a new job," Dr. Snow said, examining his patient. "You know what I told you—"

"Yes, doctor, but it's what I do. I can't stay indoors."

"He is a fisherman and works through cold and wet," he said, glancing at Anna. "Be careful not to warm up the hands too quickly." He turned back to his patient. "That's what causes the pain and tissue damage. I'll give you salve to help the itching and stop by next week, okay?"

There was one more stop before they headed back toward town and lunch at the boardinghouse.

"See how busy I am?" His face looked serious, but Anna caught the undertone of sarcasm, or was he in earnest? She did not know how to read him yet.

"The lady over on Shoalwater Bay—the one expecting a baby—I mentioned yesterday."

"Yes, I remember."

"Her husband wants her to go into Portland early, but she doesn't want to. I may get a call some night, but then again, they may deliver it themselves. Her neighbor has been known to assist in deliveries."

Anna enjoyed his sharing his practice with her, his thoughts on the local people and the various diseases and treatments he had given.

"You will undoubtedly see shipwreck victims while you're here. The ships get into rough water, or off course, and come in too close. When they go aground, we can save them, but often the whole crew is swept out to sea, and there's not a thing we can do."

Anna had never tended to a shipwreck victim, though she had seen a drowning. "I'm certain I can handle any situation," she said. "God brought me here for a reason, and I intend to fulfill my life's ambition."

"God." Snow said the name with disdain. "Not sure I believe in God. He took my mother, the only person who loved me and cared about what happened—"

"You have no father?"

"He was busy with his work and had no time for me."

"I'm sorry—"

"Don't be."

Anna moved away as if she'd been touched with a hot poker. Everything had been fine until she mentioned God. She couldn't help but speak of God, as He was very much a part of her life, and she couldn't exclude Him from her conversation as if He never existed.

"You don't pray for your patients then?" She had to ask it.

He turned and stared. "No, I never pray for patients. Why should I? It does no good. Weren't you listening to me?"

The words stung, but Anna ignored them. "I pray for patients. Is that going to be a problem, doctor?"

"You do what you want, just don't expect any miracles. We work with what we have, and that's about all we can do."

Of course Anna did not agree, but what was the point of arguing? It was a closed subject, and one she chose not to pursue. At least not now. He did not know her yet, nor she him; but there would come a time when Anna's prayers would be heard and answered.

"Do you usually say what's on your mind?"

Anna stiffened. Not one for thinking things out, Anna had been in trouble more than once for her outspokenness. It was because of that, that her mother had questioned her becoming a nurse. "Seems one would need to think, then act," she'd said, "when dealing with people's lives."

Of course Sarah had been right, and Anna had become better at thinking things out, then making a choice. Except for when she had cut her hair.

"You have a nice smile. I think the people will cotton to you just fine."

Anna's cheeks burned. A nice smile, indeed. Joseph had said it was her eyes that were her best feature. It certainly could never be her thick, unmanageable hair. Even short, it did what it wanted to.

"I speak without thinking," Wesley Snow said then, as if reading Anna's mind. "I apologize if I offended you before about your hair."

"It's quite all right." Anna held her head high and thrust her chin forward. If the truth were to be known—but far be it from her to divulge every bit of truth—his statement about God was far more offensive.

They passed the grocery store. Dr. Snow pulled on the reins suddenly. "Just remembered that Lizzie asked me to pick up some salt today. If I don't, my chicken will taste pretty flat."

"Do you want me to purchase it for you?"

He smiled, revealing even, white teeth. "That would be nice."

Anna held her skirts up, assuring Dr. Snow she did not need his assistance in getting down.

The store resembled the mercantile she'd shopped at in Portland. There was a bit of everything, and Anna could have looked all afternoon and not seen it all. One thing caught her eye: the candy counter—she should take back some lemon drops for Bessie, and crackers from the cracker barrel for her, but it was lunchtime and Dr. Snow was not a patient man.

"Can I help you with something?" the man behind the counter asked.

"Salt," Anna replied. "It's for Dr. Snow. He says to put it on the account."

The proprietor dug out a receipt box from under the counter, then glanced up. "Say, aren't you the nurse who came from Portland?"

Anna smiled. "That I am." She extended her hand. "Anna Galloway."

His grip was firm. "Name's Fenton. Glad to meet ya. Doc needed someone to help him out since we can't get another doctor to come here."

"It's a great place. I like it very much already."

He brought a huge container of salt. "Is that all?"

Anna nodded and started to leave just as two barefoot children came in. The older one came up, thrusting a penny on the counter. "Licorice, please."

Mr. Fenton handed him two strings of licorice and took the penny. His little brother pointed at the hard candy. "Me eat, me eat."

"And here's a piece of candy for you."

Anna laughed as he poked it into his mouth. Seconds later, drool cascaded down his face, mixing with rivulets of dirt.

Anna saw a copy of *The Oregonian* and was starting to pay for it when she heard a choking sound. Turning, she dropped the paper and rushed up the aisle as she saw the grubby-faced little boy turning red. His brother stood screaming. Fenton kept saying, "Oh my."

Anna turned the boy upside down and pounded on his back. The piece of hard candy shot across the room, landing on top of the pickle barrel.

The older boy stopped screaming, and Fenton clapped his hands.

"Oh my," he repeated. "I do declare. That happened so fast, I was standing there like a dumbbell. I guess you know what you're doing, being a nurse and all."

A lady who had just entered the store stood with gloved hand covering her mouth. "I wouldn't have known what to do. Thank goodness you were here."

Anna set the boy down, ruffling his hair. "You'll be just fine now. Don't try to talk when you're eating, or suck in when eating hard candy."

"He won't no more, Ma'am," the older child said, putting his arm around his brother who was still bawling like a newborn calf.

Anna picked up the paper, plunked down a nickel, and asked for five cents' worth of lemon drops. "For Bessie," she said.

Fenton pushed the money back to Anna. "You ain't paying for the newspaper or the lemon drops. Not this day!"

Anna left with her salt and other purchases and hurried to the side of the store where Dr. Snow waited.

"What was the screaming about? And what took you so long?"

"Which question should I answer first?" Anna asked, setting the purchases in the back.

He glared. "Tell me about the screaming."

After she relayed the story, he shook his head. "Well, I'll be. He sort of initiated you, didn't he?"

His full mouth turned into a half smile. She suspected he was amused, but she didn't care. She was needed here. She'd done her first act of nursing.

Soon they were on their way. "Tell me," Dr. Snow said, breaking the silence. "What do you think of young Peter Fielding?"

Anna swallowed. "He helped me get settled."

"He needs a wife."

"Bessie told me about Callie."

"You might be the one."

Anna's eyes snapped. "I am a nurse, Dr. Snow. I did not come here to find a husband, if that's what you're thinking."

"Good."

Anna was relieved to see the roof of the boardinghouse over the next road. She'd had enough of this conversation.

"I see a bit of temper in you, Miss Galloway."

"Only when provoked," Anna said, staring straight ahead.

"I believe we have arrived at Bessie's." He didn't look her way. "I'm sure you can put all of this behind you and indulge in the stimulating conversation around the table."

Anna was later to think about that moment, wondering if she could have been fired for her impolite manner before she even got a start at nursing here. Yet, she thought she caught the sound of a chuckle as the groom came up and took the horse to be watered. Could Dr. Snow have been amused by her outburst? Well, her affairs were none of his business or anyone else's. She would behave in a proper fashion, be chaperoned should she be courted, and certainly give it careful thought before ever agreeing to marry anyone. As long as she nursed to the best of her ability, no problems should arise. Of course to marry would mean the end of her career, and Anna enjoyed nursing far too much to give it all up. At least not yet. Not now. . .

Chapter 4

The discussion around the table was lively, especially after Dr. Snow reported on what Anna had done.

"Word'll get out," Mr. Webster said. "Our nurse here will be a celebrity."

Anna's cheeks flushed. "Don't be absurd. I did what anyone would do."

"Not so," Bessie said, passing around a plate of cranberry nut muffins. "I don't know if I'd a-done what ye did."

"A nurse is always prepared, right, Miss Galloway?"

Miss Galloway. She'd much prefer he call her Anna. Before she had a chance to answer, Bessie said that Peter had brought Ned back and wanted to stop by that evening so Anna could meet his children.

"I'm looking forward to it," Anna said, knowing Dr. Snow was watching her with an I-told-you-so expression. She took a big swallow of coffee, then began choking.

"Here. I'll tend to that." Dr. Snow got up and instead of pounding her on the back, acted as if he was going to lift her and turn her upside down.

"I'm—quite—all right—" Anna ran from the room, coughing into her apron.

When she came back to the dining room, Bessie had a twinkle in her eye, and Mr. Webster asked if she was okay.

"Dr. Snow said you could have the afternoon off. Not that much going on, it seems."

Anna was relieved. Having not slept well the night before, she knew a nap would help. If the fog lifted, she would walk to the beach and enjoy watching the tide coming in, or going out. She really wasn't sure how one could tell. It looked the same to her.

When Anna wakened from a short respite, she was happy to see the sun was shining. Its warmth filled her room, rejuvenating her. She remade the bed, then donned her cotton stockings.

She couldn't help but be disappointed that Dr. Snow had left without her after lunch. Bessie said he was being kind, thinking she needed her rest, but maybe he didn't want her around. How would she know? He was difficult to understand, and maybe she never would understand men.

Anna gazed at Joseph's photo atop her dresser. A lump came to her throat, as she picked it up and stared into the eyes. Somehow she wasn't quite ready to give him up. Maybe she should return to Iowa, try to see him once again.

The photo went back on the dresser as Anna slipped into her older brown high-tops and grabbed a hat. She'd borrow a cloak from the downstairs closet. "I often have guests who don't come prepared for a walk on the beach," Bessie had said yesterday. "Use any of these things. Anytime."

Anna chose a pair of warm brown woolen gloves. Even with the sun out, the wind could cut right through you.

Anna did not know about the ocean—the waves that sneaked up and drenched you in seconds—waves that carried people out to sea. She might have asked Cora to come, or anyone else, but the dining area was empty, and Bessie was nowhere to be seen. It must be rest time, she thought.

The water was close, just beyond a small copse of beach pines. Anna slipped down a well-worn path, her heavy shoes sinking into the sand. Once she hit the water's edge, she was glad she'd worn the heavy coat. The wind whipped around her, making the coat billow out. A thinner wrap would have been torn from her body.

Anna walked along, liking the way the water came in and out, sometimes closer, sometimes nipping at the soles of her shoes. Seagulls swooped down as if looking for a handout. She loved watching their graceful dives. Finally she knew she had to go into the water. It seemed to beckon to her.

Slipping out of the shoes and brown stockings, Anna left them in a pile close to the path and raced back to the water. She ran in, without thinking, then sucked her breath in. The water was icy cold! She hadn't expected it to be this cold. She grimaced and walked farther out. Perhaps one got used to it after a bit.

Another wave came, taking her breath away. Anna ran back from the teasing waves. Hearing a shout, she turned her head just as the biggest wave ever came and knocked her off her feet.

Gulping in huge mouthfuls of salt water, Anna tried to gather her bearings, but her dress was thick and now heavy and wet. She struggled just as another wave caught her in its clutches, carrying her farther out.

"Help!" she finally called, thrusting her head out of the water. "Help!" she called again, just as another wave came and pulled her under. Anna's life passed before her as she felt the water numbing her, taking her breath away. Papa. Mama. Sisters Lulu and Clara, whom she hadn't seen in so long. Albert, Ben, and Jesse. Jesse, her eldest brother, who had deserted his family.

Would she ever see him again? Ever be able to tell him she loved him in spite of his orneriness? Emily's face flashed through her mind. She'd grown to love her sister-in-law like a sister in a few short weeks. And Baby Clifford. Who couldn't love his chubby face, the happy smile. There was also Paul, Brother Luke, and Kate. She was pulled under again, her mind saying prayers to her Father above. . .

A voice shouted. "Here! Catch this!"

Anna felt something go over her head and she realized it was a rope. It anchored her and she felt the comfort of something solid.

"Hold on! We'll pull you ashore."

Having swallowed numerous gulps of salt water, Anna relaxed and let herself be pulled in. Finally she was out of the thrashing water and she sunk into a heap on the ground, breathing huge gulps of air. Another voice joined the first voice, but she was too exhausted to look up, to even thank her rescuer.

"We must get her inside, quick!" Anna felt the warmth of a thick, dry blanket. "It doesn't take long for exposure to set in. My wagon's close at hand."

"Anna! Can you hear me?"

From the depths of her whirling mind, she wanted to say yes, but all she could do was nod. The voices sounded familiar now.

"Bessie will get her warm in no time."

Anna felt herself being lifted into the wagon. She huddled closer under the blanket. Then the voice of an angel rang out.

"Anna, oh, Anna, why did you go wading when the tide is going out?" It was Bessie.

Soon she was assisted inside to the sofa in the parlor. Her clothing stuck to her, but Bessie pulled them off her while Cora's voice sounded in the background. "Here are the blankets."

"Good. Now fetch a cup of hot tea."

Anna's teeth began chattering, her hands gripping the edge of the blanket. Hair was pushed out of her face, while Bessie clucked over her.

"Child, I wish ye'd said something about wanting to go wading."

Anna glanced up as Cora placed a cup into her hands. The steam revived her as she breathed deeply of the pepperminty flavor.

"Drink it up," Bessie commanded. "It will bring warmth to the bones."

"Should I go for Dr. Snow?" Cora asked, hovering around the edges.

Bessie shook her head. "She's going to be okay. We got her barely in time. She'll be fine once she warms up. I'll get her in by the fire."

Anna opened her eyes again, but the room seemed to wave around her.

"Anna, don't go to sleep." The cup was taken from her trembling hands. "You must stay awake and talk to me."

"Bessie?" Why was her mind hazy? Why couldn't she focus on Bessie's face?

She was pushed to her feet and pulled into the room by the huge stone fireplace. "Talk to me," the voice commanded.

"I—" But Anna's teeth chattered so badly she couldn't say anything.

"Here. Sit. I'm bringing some warm beef broth. That may be better than tea."

Anna heard the words "fetch" and "doctor." But she wanted to huddle under the blankets more, wanted to sleep so she wouldn't need to think anymore.

"I lost my husband. I lost my child. I am not losing you, Miss Anna Galloway."

"But I am not a suitable nurse." Could that be her voice? Had she said that?

"Oh, dear God." Bessie lifted Anna's face, made Anna open her eyes. "Ye are speaking foolishly. I will not hear of it!"

Anna started to slip away, then heard the sound of her father. It was as if he was telling her to go back, to learn, to love. That she was needed here in this place.

She glanced up and finally focused on the older woman's face that bent down, staring at her.

"Anna! You're here. You're back among us! Praise the good Lord!"

Anna slept through dinner. Voices from the dining room table wafted in to her where she lay on the window bench. She strained to hear the words.

"Saved a child's life today, only to need to be saved herself!" Who was that? The voice sounded familiar. Anna lifted up on one elbow and heard another younger voice. Then she knew. Peter Fielding was here. Peter and his children. Her hand went to her hair, as she looked down at some sort of wrap Bessie had put on her. This would never do. She couldn't meet Peter and the children, or any of the boarders, looking like this. What a fright she was.

Anna rose from the couch, keeping the blanket around her shoulders as she tiptoed up the steps. If anyone saw her—those sitting at the end could see her—but she had to chance it. Quickly she hurried up the stairs. Once in her room, she stared at her face, still pale from the near-death adventure.

She slipped into clean undergarments and into the blue gingham. It had the fewest wrinkles. She ran a brush through the salt-laden hair and put on clean stockings and the shoes she'd worn on the trip here.

"Oh, Anna, you fool!" she said to her reflection in the mirror. "How can Dr. Snow trust you to care for patients when you can't even take care of yourself?"

Pulling in her breath, her fingers clutched the sides of her dress as she weakly made her way down the steps and to the dining room where people were still eating. Life must go on, and she wasn't going to let one almost drowning accident stop her.

Holding her head high, she entered the dining room and pointed to the large casserole in the center of the table. "I think I'll have a bit of whatever is in that dish."

Chapter 5

Peter Fielding stood and helped Anna to a vacant chair. "Quite a day you've had, Miss Galloway. I arrived just in time for dinner, and Bessie told me of your struggle with the tide. Of course I'd already heard about the boy's life you saved at the mercantile."

"You heard?"

Peter nodded. "This is a small town. Everyone knows everyone else's business. This latest part, including your rescue, will also be passed from pillar to post." His eyes were warm, not teasing her as Anna feared.

She looked at the two small faces, then nodded at Mr. Webster, Cora, and the others. "I am just thankful that someone rescued me, since I was beyond rescuing myself."

"I saw ye, Missy, from my bedroom window," Mr. Webster offered. "Went down and told Bessie right off. A neighbor done brought his wagon."

Anna sank deeper into the chair. "It was a dangerous thing to do. I'll not play heedlessly with *that* water again."

"Ye had no way of knowin', and not a-one of us thought to tell you about the dangers of the surf and those huge waves that sweep one right off her feet." Bessie's eyes looked moist.

Peter motioned for his children to stand. "Miss Anna Galloway, this is Catherine and Henry."

Catherine, with a pixie-shaped face, smiled, revealing a gap in her front teeth. "Hello, Miss Galloway." She curtsied. Henry hid his head behind his father's leg and wouldn't be coaxed into an introduction.

"He's been shy like this ever since Callie—" Peter's face went blank, "that is, his mama died."

Anna nodded, thinking of her own dear mother and how she might have felt if she'd lost her at such a tender age. "It's understandable. He needs time. And how old are you, young man?"

"He's four and I'm six," Catherine answered, flashing another big grin.

Anna had to laugh, remembering when she used to speak for Albert and how angry it made him. Suddenly she remembered the books she'd brought. Reading books, two tablets, and a small box of watercolors. Just the gift for these two. That would come later.

"Ye needs to eat," Bessie said then, "while the rest of us get chocolate cake."

"Chocit cake?" Henry finally found his tongue.

"Yes!" Catherine clapped her hands. "Chocolate is my absolute most favorite cake of all." Her eyes danced with excitement. Anna had a sudden impulse to reach over and pull the motherless girl close. It was apparent that it took very little to please her. It made Anna like her even more.

"Ah, I knew ye would open up to that," Bessie said with a nod to Henry.

They all sat and talked while Anna ate. Afterwards Anna took her cake and cup of coffee into the living room where she could sit and visit with Peter and his children. Bessie said she did not need to help clear the table, though she offered. Sarah had taught her children to always offer their help, no matter what the situation. Anna would never forget the words, the sage advice from her mother.

"I'd thought we might go clamming on Sunday. After church, that is." Peter sat across from Anna.

Anna thought of the water, the coldness of it, the gigantic wave taking her out to sea, and fear swept over her. "Clamming? Doesn't that mean we need to be in the water?"

Peter threw back his head and laughed. "Yes. Somewhat. We wait, though, until low tide, then dig in the high ground."

Panic seized Anna at the memory of only a few hours ago. "I don't think—I'm ready for the beach quite yet."

"Oh, yes, Miss Galloway," Catherine cried. "You must come. We can have a picnic and play ball, and it will be fun."

Peter cast a stern look, and she sat down and held her small hands in her lap, but her eyes hadn't lost their sparkle. Peter looked over the top of his daughter's golden head and smiled at Anna.

Anna felt the tentacles of fear closing in. Did she want to do this? Of course if they didn't go until Sunday, she had three days to prepare herself.

As if reading her mind, Bessie explained that low tide meant there'd be no danger of a wave coming anywhere close. "And I have just the thing to pack," she said. "Fried chicken, potato salad, and ginger cookies."

"Bessie, you're an absolute wonder."

"Oh, go on with ye. But what I think ye need to do is go out on the sun-porch and enjoy the sunset."

The four trooped outside to watch the glowing colors of a July summer night. The children insisted on sitting one on each side of Anna. They fit into the lawn swing nicely. Peter sat on a wicker chair across from the swing.

"Doesn't a red sunset mean perfect weather for tomorrow?" Anna asked.

"Oh, yes, to the sailor's delight."

"And I must go to work early," Anna said. "Enough time off for me." Anna glanced at Peter while he tied his son's shoe. She liked him. He was kind, and Bessie said he believed in God, that he hoped some day to find a Christian mother for his two motherless lambs. He was more open than the brooding Dr. Snow. She wondered if he had thoughts of Callie. How tragic to lose a wife at such a young age.

"I am glad you came to our little peninsula," Peter said, his voice husky sounding.

"I'm glad I came, too." Anna's cheeks flushed, but it was dark enough so no one would notice. "Does Dr. Snow ever go clamming?" she asked.

"I don't know, but I doubt that he does. He's far too busy."

"Maybe we should ask him to accompany us," though she knew he'd say no.

An awkward silence filled the porch. "I think teaching one person how to dig is enough for one outing," Peter finally said. "I'll take him another time—if he wants to go, that is."

"It was just a thought," Anna said.

"Someone's got to be there in case of emergencies," Peter added.

"Yes, you're right, I'm sure."

Long after Peter left, Anna thought about the evening, how comfortable she felt around him. It was as if she didn't need to prove herself, as if he liked her just as she was, impetuousness and all. With Dr. Snow it was different. She kept feeling he disapproved of her, no matter how hard she tried. No, it was definitely not a good idea to ask the doctor to go clamming, but Anna wondered if this was the real reason for Peter's comment.

Anna kept busy the remainder of the week. She removed a sliver from a baby's finger—the child would not sit still for the mother—helped set two broken arms—two different people—and assisted in a tonsillectomy.

"Those tonsils are the largest I've ever seen," Dr. Snow had said, holding them up with forceps.

Anna examined the inflamed tissue and nodded. "No wonder this child had sore throat on top of sore throat."

A lady came in to have a boil lanced under her arm. "The herbs I've been taking haven't helped," she explained, looking sheepish.

"Some of the people are superstitious and try old home remedies first," Dr. Snow said after she'd left. "I'm hoping my presence will prevent needless deaths.

"Speaking of deaths," Dr. Snow smiled at Anna. "I heard about a certain someone who let a wave knock her down."

Anna's face flushed.

"It's okay. You weren't forewarned. You saved that boy's life, earlier, so it was your turn to be saved."

"Yes, my guardian angel was watching out for me."

Dr. Snow scoffed, "It was George Webster who saved your life. Who knows what might have happened if he hadn't been looking out his window."

"Well, that may be true, but still—" Anna saw the tight-lipped look and decided to drop it. She believed that God often sends His messengers to intervene, but there was no convincing a person who didn't wish to believe. But Anna knew and would always believe that's what happened on that sunny afternoon in July.

"By the way, almost forgot. I have something for you."

"For me?"

"Yes. From the child's parents. His family was most appreciative and dropped by with a dozen eggs and a plate of homemade cinnamon rolls."

"What?" Anna exclaimed. "I expected no pay."

"That's how these people are. You cannot do them a good turn without their repaying you for your troubles."

Anna thought of the stack of unpaid bills in the file. People who could not pay. People who might never pay. Yet Dr. Snow would attend to their needs. She knew he'd never turn anyone away.

His manner was abrupt, but she could handle that. The main thing was the concern he showed for his patients. She noticed that right off that first day. Always curt with her, he turned on the charm for the next patient he saw.

That afternoon he nodded and smiled as he listened to a lady complain about her aches and pains.

"Comes with old age, Miss Connors."

She laughed. "I thought you'd say that, doctor."

He turned to Anna after the woman left. "The people are friendly, but set in their ways. Even if I offer advice, they go ahead and do what they've always done."

"Yes, I find it to be so," Anna said, "and I've only been here a short while."

She assisted Dr. Snow, often anticipating, even suggesting, a possible treatment. Once he had barked, "And who is the doctor here?"

Her cheeks had flamed as she hurried from the room. Her boldness had gotten her into trouble before; she couldn't let it happen now. She blew her nose in the empty waiting room, and tried to appear busy as she thumbed through the stack of charts on the various patients. Most names meant nothing to her. But they would, she vowed.

The remainder of the week, Dr. Snow seemed withdrawn, more brusque than usual. Perhaps it had to do with Lucinda, his betrothed.

Lizzie, the housekeeper, had brought up her name the day before. "That woman is the most spoiled I've seen, and I've certainly run into a few in my day."

"Lucinda?"

Lizzie stopped dusting. "They are to be married next June, when he moves back to Portland."

"Move? He's going to move? I thought he liked it here."

"I know, my dear girl, but Lucinda does not, and Lucinda is used to having her own way."

Anna wanted to question Dr. Snow about it, but thought better of it. Perhaps he did need to go back to Portland to practice, but what would the people do then? They depended on his knowledge, and most every one liked him. He put on a different face for patients as opposed to other people.

"I think he's in a snit because she's coming in November."

"She's coming here?"

"Why does that surprise you? She'll travel the same way you did, I expect. Probably come with a friend or a chaperone, though Lucinda certainly does not need a chaperone."

"She's come before?"

"Oh, my yes. Came last spring. Thought there might be a wedding in the new Methodist Episcopal Church not too far from the boardinghouse, but Lucinda soon let it be known she wanted to be married in a *huge* church with eight attendants."

"You know her well?"

Lizzie turned and stared at Anna. "I guess you didn't know."

"Know? Know what?"

"I used to be the cook for Lucinda Lawson's folks. I believe her mama sent me here to keep an eye on Dr. Snow."

"I had no idea."

"You don't need to go a-talking about it—though of course Bessie knows. Between us, we keep an eye on the good doctor, though more that he be fed right, rather than the fact that he might have a roving eye. Not that he'd have time for it, anyway!"

Anna knew that to be true. Dr. Snow rarely had a day off. There was always someone else to see, to "fix up better than new" as he always said.

"I'd never talk about Dr. Snow," Anna said then. "I do not believe in spreading rumors. You can trust me to keep my lip buttoned up."

Lizzie leaned over and impulsively hugged Anna. "I only been here a year, mind you, but I care for that man as if he were my own son. What he needs is to find is someone like you, Miss Anna."

Anna laughed. She wasn't quite right for the good doctor.

Besides, she wasn't looking for a man to marry. She gave Lizzie an impulsive hug. "I'm going to keep right on a-doing what I do the best: nursing."

Horses drew up to the side of the house. Dr. Snow had returned from his morning schedule. Anna busied herself by rearranging the bandages and medicines on the shelf. No wonder he had been agitated. Maybe he wanted to marry, but she also knew doctoring was his work, and he preferred a small town. Would Miss Lucinda ever come to realize that?

The door opened. He rushed in, and as Anna looked up, their eyes met. It was the first time she'd noticed an emotion other than a businesslike one. There was almost a kindness in his expression, before he turned and looked away.

"Stopped by to see if you're wanting to go to Bessie's—pick up lunch."

"I brought my lunch today. If you don't mind, I'll stay here, just in case—"

"Whatever you do is entirely up to you, Miss Galloway." He strode past her, muttering something as he refilled his medicine bag with supplies. "I'll be back presently."

Lizzie appeared in the doorway. "Thought I'd prepare a meat loaf, if you think you'd like that for the evening meal."

He paused, then stared at her strangely. "Lizzie, you know I eat whatever you fix and half the time don't taste it anyway. Not that it's your fault. It's just the way I am by the end of the day—being tired and all."

Anna busied herself with the charts, pretending she hadn't heard. She knew the feeling. She'd been so busy in nursing school that it didn't matter what she ate. Her friends often had to coax her to come to the table during meals. There were always other more important things to do.

"I'll be back." Again the door opened, and he was gone. Anna lifted her shoulders and told her heart to slow down. She had no idea why Dr. Wesley Snow had looked at her in such a way. His bold look had mesmerized her—at least for the moment.

It was time for lunch. She'd visit more with Lizzie Myles. It seemed she knew as much about the goings-on as Bessie McGruder. Suddenly Anna had an urge to find out more about Miss Lucinda Lawson, especially since she'd be coming soon. Perhaps her presence would make Dr. Snow smile more. He had such a nice, warm smile when he smiled. She wished she knew what made him so unhappy, so full of negative thoughts. Not knowing God as she did had some bearing, but it seemed to go further than that. Yes, perhaps Lucinda Lawson was just what the doctor needed.

Chapter 6

Sunday morning boasted a blue sky without a trace of the usual wispy white clouds that drifted across in lazy fashion. Anna bounded from bed, eager to attend the small church two blocks south of the boardinghouse. It was Methodist Episcopal, the one Bessie said Dr. Snow would be married in, should Lucinda change her mind and move to the peninsula. Anna had never been Methodist, but it didn't matter. To be attending the service meant so much. She loved to sing hymns and to pray amongst friends. The oft-quoted verse came to mind: "Whenever two or more are gathered in My name, there I am also."

She chose her best rose pink chambray with a delicate white lace collar and a touch of lace at the cuffs. The skirt was full, the waistline accented by eight pleats. It was clearly her best dress next to the sea green taffeta, the maid-of-honor dress Kate had made for Pearl's wedding in Portland. Anna was saving that for a special day.

Anna brushed her short locks until the hair shone. She found a tiny bit of ribbon that matched the dress and pinned it on one side. There. She had taken so long fussing with her hair and dressing, in between looking out her window, marveling in the beauty of the day, she was late to breakfast.

"Now this is the kind of summer day I am used to," Anna said, as she hurried to the table to dish up the last portion of scrambled eggs.

Mr. Webster glanced up from his plate of toast. "And isn't it today you're going a-clamming?"

Anna's heart sank. "Yes, we'll leave right after church." She was not looking forward to digging clams, but the children were so excited, she must be happy for their sake.

Bessie smiled. "Bless Peter's heart. He knows how I love clam fritters and chowder."

Anna took her second cup of coffee into the living room. She liked sitting on the window seat with its view of the ocean. Though it terrified her now, she would never tire of the frothy waves coming and going. It reminded her of God's might in creating something so huge, so powerful.

She set the cup aside and reached for her Bible. The leather of Sarah's worn Bible was soft.

She turned to Isaiah 30:15. "In quietness and in confidence shall be your strength." *In quietness.* Wasn't that why it was good to go off to a quiet spot to read, to pray?

It was now nearing nine. The service was at ten. Peter said to expect him at nine-thirty.

"You certainly look pretty." Cora slipped into the room and sat across from Anna.

"Why, thank you, Cora. Would you like to come to church with us?"

The small girl shook her head. "No, thank you. I am Catholic, you know, but I rarely attend Mass. Still, once a Catholic, always a Catholic."

"Oh." Not that it mattered to Anna. She thought it most important that all people believed in God. They could attend any church they wanted to. Sarah had instilled a deep and abiding love for God in all of her children. All believed, with the possible exception of Jesse, who had left his family and, as far as Anna knew, was still wandering hither and yon, falling in and out of love, making others completely miserable.

"Some children never grow up," Sarah had said about her firstborn.

But Anna, determined at a young age to always do what was right, to follow God in spite of the circumstances, now was living away from everyone, in this primitive spot that only a pioneer could love. Yet God wanted her here; she was very sure of that.

Anna'd been so busy working, busy thinking and worrying about others, she'd had little time for God. Now with a day off, she wondered what it would be like to be entirely free. Not that anyone was ever free. Still, she knew one must make time to read the Scriptures, for prayer, for contemplation. Since she'd come, she'd contemplated much, wondering what God wanted of her. Was nursing to be the way her life was spent, or did He have something else in store for her? Whichever, Anna felt blessed and open to God's way. She bowed her head.

"Lord, I pray for Peter and his children, for those who are sick, for Dr. Snow that he might believe again.

"And am I blessing You, God? Am I doing what You would have me do? I feel Your presence as I work each day. I am grateful for that—truly I am. . ."

The sound of horses hooves filled the still morning air. Anna closed her Bible and rose from the couch. The carriage pulled up out front, and from the sides, hands waved, voices shouted.

Peter came to the door, but Anna opened it before he could knock. His dark suit and red tie nearly took her breath away. She'd never realized how truly handsome he was. His eyes lingered on hers for a long moment.

"You look lovely in that pink dress, Anna." His eyes had an intense look, making Anna feel self-conscious.

"Thank you, Peter," she finally murmured. She flushed, but knew he couldn't see it as she went out the door ahead of him. Was pink her color? Not that she'd ever thought about such frivolous things before.

The children greeted her. Henry wore a suit he had outgrown and Catherine looked sweet in a yellow dotted Swiss. A battered straw hat sat atop the blond curls.

"I am so happy to see you," Anna said, squeezing first one pair of hands, then the other. It was then she realized she'd forgotten gloves. Tucked in the trunk still, she had meant to wear them, as proper ladies always wore gloves. Even Catherine wore gloves.

"Peter," she touched his shoulder. "I forgot my gloves. I'll be right back."

They were dark gloves, not ones for a summer day; still they were better than bare hands, Anna determined as she ran back down the stairs and out the door to the waiting carriage.

"I want to sit by you in church, Miss Galloway," Catherine said.

"Me, too," piped up Henry.

"Yes, you, too," Anna said.

"And what about me?" Peter raised an eyebrow.

"You can sit on the end, Daddy," Catherine said.

The church was small with wood plank floors, no stained-glass windows, but there was a warmth to it, and Anna was happy to note the piano in one corner. A slender blond woman went to the front and sat down to play.

Soon her fingers rippled up and down the keyboard, and Anna was enthralled as she hummed "What a Friend We Have in Jesus."

Anna remembered the church she'd attended in Iowa City. She'd wished that Mama could have heard the music, as she loved music so much. But then she'd found the Friends' Church in Portland.

The Reverend Keating, a tall, thin man with a warm, engaging smile, looked out over his congregation and led them in an opening prayer. Anna liked him immediately and knew she would come back to this church.

As Anna sat, listening to the sermon, she had to stifle her laugh as first Henry then Catherine squirmed. It was hard to sit still. They'd be more than ready for a trip to the beach.

After church, going back to Bessie's so Anna could change and pick up the lunch, the four headed up north toward Tioga Station, where Peter said the clams were more abundant.

"I brought shovels, buckets, extra coats, blankets, hats, gloves, a lantern, all the things one needs for a clam-digging expedition."

Anna felt overdressed in her old gray muslin, the heavy cloak Bessie insisted she would need, warm cotton stockings, and high-top shoes Bessie had also found.

"Don't want ye catching cold now."

As they started out, Anna chatted to the children, listening to Henry's story about the kitten he had found the day before.

"Did someone abandon it?" Anna asked.

"Ab-abdom?" he asked, screwing up his face.

"You know—leave him alone?"

"He was awfully hungry," Catherine offered. "We named him Fluffy."

"Because he has lots of fur?" Anna asked, her laugh filling the air.

"No, because he had none," Peter said, joining in.

Anna turned to stare at Peter. "You aren't serious, are you?" Her eyes were solemn. "I don't know if I could nurse a cat back to health. They aren't quite like people—"

It was Peter's turn to laugh. "No, he's a fine kitten; a bit skinny, but we can fix that up in no time."

"I don't know how to cook clams—," Anna said as she remembered what the outing was for.

"Don't worry. It's easy. First off, you have to clean them, then fix them."

"You'll show me?"

"Of course."

Now as they headed for what Peter termed the "best spot," Anna felt a sudden chill from a gust of wind that blew up from the ocean. She shivered, remembering her misadventure earlier that week. "The water is never warm in the ocean?" she asked. "Not even in August?"

Peter shook his head. "No. Never."

"But in Iowa the rivers and lakes are warm in the summer."

"They don't move like that, do they?" Peter asked, looking out over a wave smashing against an outcrop of rocks.

"No, guess not."

Anna had learned in the short time she'd been here that most people lived on what they gleaned from the ocean, the bay, and the rivers. Oysters fat and succulent, clams, crabs, salmon, sturgeon. Anna couldn't begin to remember all the things she'd heard. She'd never seen such huge fish as the mammoth salmon and sturgeon. In Iowa, fish were smaller, and bonier.

"Anna! Will you play tag with us?"

She turned and smiled. "Of course. What is all that sand for if we can't play tag? But it will have to be after I catch some clams."

"Dig for clams," Peter corrected her.

"Oh, yes. I keep forgetting."

Peter glanced at the profile of the woman he admired so much. Happy, energetic, she was always ready for the occasion, and the children adored her.

The beach was crowded. The tide was right, as Peter explained, and clams would be plentiful.

"We look for these bubbles in the sand," he explained, kicking at the sand with the tip of his boot. "When you see the bubbles, you start digging as fast as you can."

"As fast as I can?"

"How else will you get the clam?" Peter said.

"I—don't know."

"The clam tries to get away. It isn't stupid. It feels the movement—I guess that's what happens—and starts to burrow deep into the sand. We have to be faster and dig him out."

"How many can we get?"

"As many as we want. I usually stop at fifty."

"Fifty!" Had Anna heard right? "Surely you don't mean fifty."

"Why not?"

"But what do you do with fifty?"

"After cleaning, we can eat them fresh, chop them for chowder, eat more fresh, give some away. I promised Doris I'd bring her twenty or so." He leaned on the shovel, gazing at Anna for a long moment.

"But, how big are these clams?"

"You've never seen one?"

Anna shook her head. "I grew up in Iowa, remember?"

"But you've seen pictures."

"If I have, I've forgotten." She stared right back.

"Well, well, this will be challenging since you don't know what the thing looks like you're digging for."

Anna started to giggle. "I'll watch you dig for one first. Get an idea of how it goes."

"Okay."

They'd brought blankets for the children to lie on when they tired of playing in the sand. Catherine wanted to dig, but her father said she would not be strong or fast enough. "These critters are smart," he concluded.

The lunch, blankets, lantern, and extra coats and hats were far up on the ridge of grass where the children were told to stay. "You can play in the sand next time. Now you will just get in the way. Go!" He pointed.

Anna watched while they turned and trotted back fifty feet or so.

Peter was fast. In ten minutes he'd dug six clams.

"And I'm supposed to be that fast?" Anna cried.

"Sure. I know you can do it. You work with your hands all the time. You just scoop them out like so."

It was backbreaking work, but Anna finally got her first clam. She held it up and laughed. "See!"

"Put it in the bucket, Anna."

She dug fast and hard, but ended up with just five when it was time to quit.

"I can't believe you got that many," she said, looking into the bucket with the strange bivalves stacked like so many pancakes on a plate.

"Takes practice. You'll do better next time."

Anna wasn't sure there would be a next time. Her skirts were wet and sandy, and her hands cold because she'd discarded the gloves right off. It was too difficult digging with them on.

Anna was right about maybe never digging for clams again when she discovered later just how hard it was to clean them.

Sand and water were everywhere. The little buggers had a ton of sand in them and Peter said it had to come out. If not, the chowder or fried clams would have the gritty sand in them, and nobody could eat sand.

"This is more work than the digging," Anna said.

"I know, but you're doing a great job."

Peter said Bessie would show her how to fry them for dinner that night.

Shortly after she had cleaned the clams, doing as Peter showed her, Anna felt the muscles pulling in her back. It had been hard work. Very hard work. She guessed she'd have to go to back to nursing tomorrow to rest up.

Chapter 7

The clams were delicious. Anna decided they were well worth the work of digging, then cleaning them. Bessie was pleased, as were the rest of the boarders.

Anna couldn't wait to tell Dr. Snow about the excursion the day before and had brought enough for a meal for Lizzie to cook.

"I had an emergency yesterday," Dr. Snow said, ignoring Anna's comment.

"You did?"

"False labor. Mrs. Clayborne."

"Oh. Did you talk her into going across the river to the hospital?"

He glanced at Anna for a long moment. "She's a stubborn woman. Figures since she had Edward without a hospital, this one will be the same."

"And you think not?"

"I know not."

Anna let it drop. Sometimes she felt he was patronizing her. It was much better to keep quiet, to do what she knew how to do.

He left to go on calls, and Anna stayed behind. She wondered if Lizzie knew anything more about Lucinda, if she was still planning on coming.

"Yes, I am sure she is." She shook her head as she cut the clams into long strips. "It isn't good for a couple to be separated. The good doctor is brooding about this. As for Lucinda, doubt that she has ever not gotten her way, so time will tell."

Anna went with Dr. Snow to Bessie's for lunch. She later wished she hadn't. As they sat over dessert—a fresh plum crisp—the talk revolved around the appendix, how many had burst causing far too many deaths. "All because the symptoms are never recognized," Dr. Snow said. "The appendix is an unknown entity. One never knows why or when an attack will come on."

"Oh, but there are signs," Anna broke in. "Continual abdominal pain, sometimes a fever—"

"I know, Miss Galloway, but how many folks around here pay attention to some little pain or a fever?"

"That might be true, but isn't it our job to educate them?" she continued. "As far as I'm concerned, far too many die from a burst appendix, all because the symptoms are never recognized. Perhaps we should remove the appendix as a precaution—"

"And perhaps you, as a nurse, should leave diagnosing to doctors."

Anna flushed a deep red. "It distresses me is all."

"At least we know when we have smallpox or measles on our hands," Mr. Webster stated, as if wanting to take Anna's side. Anna wondered if Dr. Snow would make further comment on Mr. Webster's observation. She said nothing as she savored the last spoonful of crisp.

Dr. Snow pushed his chair back. "We must go back." He headed out the door with Anna following.

"I expect people don't realize how lucky they are to have a doctor who comes right to their door and administers to them," Anna said, wanting to appease him.

Dr. Snow's jaw was tight, his hands gripping the reins. "*Luck* is hardly the word for it."

"Well, you know what I mean."

"I'm not a saint," Wesley Snow snapped. "I'm just doing my job."

"As I will do mine," Anna added, staring straight ahead.

The remainder of the trip was spent in silence. The clip-clopping of the horse's hooves was like a song going through Anna's mind. *You will be tolerated. . .you will be tolerated. . .you will be tolerated. . .*

Later, when Anna talked with Bessie, she sighed. "I find it difficult working with Dr. Snow." They sat in the living room, in comfortable chairs looking out toward the ocean and darkening sky as a storm threatened.

"Why is that, child?"

"I'm far too outspoken. Such as this afternoon."

"Fiddlesticks! That's been forgotten for sure."

"I don't think so, Bessie." Anna straightened her shoulders. "He barely spoke to me all afternoon. Then there's the fact that he doesn't believe in God—"

Bessie looked Anna in the eye. "I've known Wesley since the day he arrived. He stayed right here for a month before the house was ready for him. We had lots of talks, and he believes in God, though he may not want to admit it. He's been hurt, that's all."

"Nor does he believe in miracles when it comes to people being healed."

"That may be, Anna, but ye have enough faith for the two of ye."

"He would barely speak to me this afternoon on the rounds." She had tried to get him to talk about himself, but there'd been nothing but silence.

"He just may not understand ye yet. You didn't ask about his life, now did ye?"

"If you mean about Lucinda—no. I know he's a bear where she's concerned."

"There's the answer. If he offers it, listen, but don't ever pry. He don't open up to no one, probably not even that wife-to-be of his, either."

"I'll never pry, Bessie." Anna knew she could find a job no matter where she went, but she already liked it here. It made her think of home—the small town where everybody was friendly and knew everyone else. In Portland, not one soul smiled when she went to the grocery store. This was beautiful land. She wanted to stay. She wanted to belong. And she hoped Wesley would find her satisfactory.

"Actually, I think he admires ye," Bessie said.

"Never." In spite of her denial, Anna's cheeks reddened. "I did not come here to be admired. I came to help."

"And so ye are." Bessie folded her arms. "Then there's Peter."

"Peter?"

"I can see how he feels about ye."

Anna bristled. "He needs a mother for his children."

"There are worse things than being needed."

After bidding Bessie good night, Anna went to the small room on the second floor, ran water from the reservoir into the small enamel basin, and washed her short locks with rainwater, as there was certainly no shortage of water here. Her thoughts turned to Peter. He had a troubled face and she knew he must be lonely since his wife's death. She wanted to be his friend, but doubted her feelings could go any deeper than that. Still, as Bessie said, one never knew for sure.

Later when Anna went to her room, she got to her knees.

"I pray for wisdom, God. For knowing when to talk and what to say, and for knowing when to listen. Help me be a good nurse. More important, help me to be useful to one and all. Amen."

Anna overslept the next morning. It was all because of the dream. She rarely remembered her dreams, but in this one she found Dr. Snow telling her to go and never come back. Her cheeks were wet with tears when she finally opened her eyes and realized where she was, in the little bed on the top floor with the slanted ceiling, and wallpaper with pink rosebuds. Home. This was home now, and she was thankful it had been only a dream.

When Anna entered the kitchen, she saw the dirty dishes and silverware in the sink. "You've already eaten?"

"Now don't you fret. Here." Bessie handed her a cup of steaming coffee, then a plate she'd kept in the warming oven. "I didn't waken ye, child, as I figured ye must need your rest."

Anna leaned over and with one arm hugged Bessie. "Oh, Bessie, you're so caring and loving. God has blessed you in a mighty way, and me for knowing you."

Bessie nodded. "Aye, I like to think I am doing what the captain would have wanted, but I sure miss his robust laugh, his hearty appetite, the way he could spin a yarn."

Anna thought of the captain and all the others who had drowned in the Pacific Ocean. There would be more shipwrecks. Hadn't the doctor said that yesterday? She hoped there would be survivors. She didn't want to think about sailors drowning and leaving loved ones behind.

Foregoing her second cup of coffee, Anna reached for her cape and cap. "I will see you at lunch." She wanted to ask Bessie what the soup would be, but knew that Dr. Snow knew and would be happy to tell her.

Lizzie met her at the doorway. "You're to meet the doctor at the Claybornes' cabin. There's to be a baby soon."

"The Claybornes' cabin? But where is that? I don't know my way around yet."

"It's down past all the houses." She pointed north. "About a quarter of a mile, or pert' near that far—there's a fence on the ocean side—you turn right there and go until you see his horse and buggy. Now go!"

A birth! Anna liked nothing better than to welcome a new baby into the world. It was one of God's best moments and a joyous occasion for the family. She hoped Dr. Snow's concerns were for naught and that all would be well.

She followed Lizzie's directions—surprisingly—and found the horse and buggy at the front of the house. A small child stood in the open door and clapped when he saw her.

Anna hopped down and hurried inside. The woman was moaning and writhing in the bed. "I can't stand any more pain, Doctor. Oh, please, please do something!"

Dr. Snow glanced up and shook his head. "I thought you'd be here before this."

Anna did not mention she had overslept. The woman cried out, and Anna leaned over and held her hand as another contraction hit.

The neighbor acting as midwife looked scared. "I been here all night long," she offered. "Nothin's happening."

"It must be a big baby," Anna said.

"Breech birth." Dr. Snow nodded.

"What're you going to do?" Anna remembered seeing a cesarean section performed at the hospital in Iowa City.

The woman cried out again. Anna took her hand and stroked her arm. "It's going to be okay. Try to relax."

The woman looked from Anna to her neighbor, then over at Dr. Snow until the next contraction seemed to rip her apart. The woman's fingernails dug into Anna's palm. Another contraction came immediately and another, but it was no use. The child could not come through the birth canal.

"Anna." Dr. Snow motioned toward a corner of the room. "We must operate."

"But we can't take the baby. Not here. There's not enough light, no supplies—"

The frown deepened. "To not do surgery means sure death, probably for both her and the child; to try the surgery could mean death, also."

"We need to transport her to your home."

"There isn't time, Anna."

"But—"

"We'll use the kitchen. It has more light. I'll help Mr. Clayborne move his wife to the table, then you can assist me while the midwife takes care of the chloroform."

Fear rose in Anna's throat. To operate here—under the poorest of conditions—seemed ludicrous, but Dr. Snow was right. They could not stand by and do nothing. It could mean death to both child and the mother.

Dr. Snow began issuing orders. "I'll need boiling water. Towels. Chloroform, antiseptic, my instruments."

Minutes later, Mrs. Clayborne lay on the sheet-covered table, sedated. Anna made a swath with the antiseptic on the woman's stomach. While handing the instruments over, Anna prayed that it wouldn't be too late for the child.

Anna wiped Wesley's forehead as he made an incision through the abdomen, then the uterus.

Mrs. Clayborne moaned.

"More chloroform!" he barked at the midwife. "She must stay sedated." Anna watched as he lifted the baby from the womb, then handed it to her, the umbilical cord following it. He cut it and nodded. "Here, take the baby."

Anna cleaned the mucus from the mouth and made the baby cry.

"Thank God, she's alive," the midwife said, bringing the small basket lined with yellow flannel in from the bedroom. "We'll set this close to the stove."

"A little girl," Anna said, holding the baby close. As her maternal instincts surfaced, Anna realized once again the miracle of birth. A longing filled her as she wondered if she'd ever experience this blessing.

"Anna," Dr. Snow's voice broke through her thoughts. "We have things to do. Let the midwife take care of her now."

Anna handed the tiny baby over, knowing the midwife would wash her off and wrap her in a blanket.

"Yes, Sir." Anna moved to the table and assisted Dr. Snow as he delivered the afterbirth and sutured the woman's abdomen.

Mrs. Clayborne lay still amongst the blood-soaked sheets as Anna cleaned up. Her husband's voice called out. "I heard a baby cry. Is it okay to come in now?"

"In a moment," Anna said, going to the doorway. "We'll make the bed up in there and you can help move her back. And, yes, you have a little girl. She's got a nice pink color, so it looks as if she'll be fine."

There was another cry, and the midwife held the child up. "I think she wants to nurse already."

Mrs. Clayborne moaned again, and Anna administered a bit more chloroform.

"That should do it," Dr. Snow said. "She'll come around soon."

"I couldn't stand it if anythin' happened to her, doctor," Mr. Clayborne said, taking his wife's limp hand.

"I understand, Mr. Clayborne." Dr. Snow looked at the worried husband and new father. "You must make certain she stays in bed. I hope you have someone who can stay with her."

"Maybe Nellie here can stay. Do you suppose?"

The midwife nodded. She'd put the baby back in her bed and watched her with a smile on her face.

An hour later as the baby slept, Mrs. Clayborne was transferred back to the bedroom, and Dr. Snow was leaving to visit a patient farther north. Anna took one more peek at the precious bundle in the yellow-lined basket, then stepped out into the late morning sun.

"What's yore name?" the little boy asked, following Anna outside.

"Anna." She leaned down and ruffled his hair.

"I think our new baby should be named Anna. I like that name, don't you, Pa?"

Mr. Clayborne came out and paused for a moment before going to the barn. "Yes, Edward, I think that's a right nice name."

Anna had never had a baby named for her, not as far as she knew.

"It's a good thing it wasn't a boy, then, because nobody wants to be called Wesley," Dr. Snow quipped, pausing before climbing into the buggy.

Anna left after making sure there was nothing else to be done. The birth had been a pure miracle, and the little one appeared healthy though she'd been through a lot. The first twenty-four hours were the most important.

As she drove back toward town, she felt thankful that Dr. Snow had decided to operate, even under the most primitive of conditions. If they'd waited much longer, little Anna probably would have been dead; the mother, too. She wished they could ride together and discuss the operation he'd performed, but there would be time for that later on. Lunch was out of the question, but Anna didn't feel hungry, anyway.

A bright sun burst out of the thin layer of clouds. Anna thanked the Lord for the day, for His creation, for the sweet-smelling air. What a story she'd have to tell Bessie. Not only the birth of the little girl, but she now had a namesake.

Chapter 8

D r. Wesley Snow left his last patient at dusk. He would arrive home long after darkness fell, but it was a fine night. No rain. Clear skies. He would enjoy the ride.

Once home, he handed his hat and coat to Lizzie and sat on the sagging couch in the waiting room. A child had vomited on it last week, and though Lizzie had cleaned it, the sour smell lingered.

Things looked dismal. Perhaps Lucinda had been right to leave him, to urge him to return to Portland. Busy with his practice, tending to the small population of the North Beach Peninsula, he would have very little time to attend to her needs. If it hadn't been for Lizzie Myles and the boy he had hired to care for the stable, he would not have a clean house or prepared meals. He looked forward to the noon lunch at Bessie's, but after a hard day of doctoring, he didn't care if he ate or not.

The house was cold, and he shivered. He'd had an eighteen-hour day. Nobody should have to work that long, "at least not anybody in their right mind," according to Lucinda.

Stretching out on the couch, he closed his eyes. He imagined he could smell Lucinda's fragrance. She liked rose perfume, and its smell lingered long after she left a room.

"Doctor, would you like the roast from yesterday's dinner, or shall I fix you something else?" Lizzie asked, after entering the room.

He waved her away. "Lizzie, I don't need you fussing over me. Go on and do what you want. I'll be fine."

She left the room, clicking her tongue as she did when she was perturbed with him.

Finally, he rose and went to his room to find his house shoes. The wardrobe held very little. There simply had not been time to shop before moving here a year ago.

He thought again of Lucinda with the sparkling eyes and the tinkling laugh—so different from Anna. Anna's laugh filled a room.

Anna. He had promised himself he would not think of her. His thoughts turned to her, he feared, because he was lonely. Because he wanted to share his life with someone—someday. Because, well, she could make him angry with her professional mannerisms. The big city was still in her, and the people they served were not big city with highfalutin ways. And yet there was an endearing quality about her. Honest and forthright completely. One knew where he stood with Anna.

Yet there was something else. Thoughts of Anna with that wild, unmanageable hair, the gaze that sometimes lingered when she thought he wasn't looking. The warm smile only tormented him, made his heart ache even more deeply. He wanted what he could not have, and he'd learned as a young boy how futile that was. His mother dying with the fever—his father standing over her, wringing his hands—praying to God to spare her life.

Wesley had a sister. He knew his father would have wanted more children, had his mother lived, but when she died the light went out in him, and he had little time or concern for his children.

It had been a lonely existence. The sister, Helen, was fifteen and soon left to marry a local farmer. After Helen and her new husband moved to Montana to homestead, Wesley was more alone than before.

"Help Father to talk to me," he had prayed in earnest. But even greater was his prayer to learn medicine, to know what to do for sick people, to help them get well, to continue learning about all the cures. Wesley read. What else was there to do? His father, a watch repairman, kept busy in the little shop in front of the house. Winters were cold in Michigan. Bitter. Wesley excelled in school, and nights, after doing his work for the next day, he would read for hours, often until dawn slipped up over the hill in back of the house. Once his father complained about the lamp oil, so Wesley started working at the local mercantile on Saturdays so he could pay for lamp oil and more books.

After graduating from high school and going on to college—at least his father hadn't minded that—reading gave him the opportunity to become even more reclusive. Wesley finished in three years and went on to medical school. Always, forever was the picture of his mother in his mind, with a long braid down her back. He had all but forgotten happy times when they had talked and laughed. His memory, now tattered, was of her lying in bed, moaning, tossing, and turning as the wicked disease claimed her life. Didn't God know that he needed her? That Helen needed her? It hadn't seemed fair, and a bit of him died the day his mother was buried in the cemetery west of town.

After graduate school, Wesley went to Oregon. A former classmate, and good friend, had moved to Portland, opened up a practice, and invited Wesley to come join in.

"There is an opportunity to practice what you've learned, Wes. Come on. I have space for you. There's a need here in Portland, a booming, growing town. You can leave the snow and cold winters behind. Here all it does in the winter is rain."

And so Wesley, with clothes packed in one suitcase, his beloved books in another, boarded a train and traveled to the Northwest.

He had stopped to tell his father good-bye but received the usual reception. Wesley knew his father wouldn't live forever. His shoulders bent from so many years of bending over watches, the straggly wisps of gray hair nearly broke his heart, but he had to leave. His father had always managed without anyone and would continue to do so.

"I'll write with my address," he said, hugging the old man briefly.

"I won't answer, you know." He looked back at his work and the conversation was over. Wesley had been dismissed as if he was one of the customers. No, the customers received more from his father than he ever had.

Wesley was so busy getting set up in the office he shared with Robert that he found little time for other pleasures.

One Friday after Robert had closed the small office on Woodstock, he eased into his chair and motioned for Wesley to sit, also. "You know, my friend, I never meant for you to come and do all the work. Not only do you see several patients a day, go to homes, and visit those who cannot come here, you do the books, light the fire each morning, and well, good gracious, when are you ever going to find time to relax?"

Relax? Wesley didn't know about relaxing. He had never known about relaxing. How did one go about doing that anyway when there were more sick people to see, calls in the night, the office to ready for the next day's customers?

"I want you to meet my sister's friend. She's a beautiful woman—loves parties and people. She'll do all the talking. Believe me, you need to do something besides be around sick people."

In the end Wesley had agreed to meet Lucinda Mae Lawson.

Lucinda had a way about her. She drew him out of his shell and ended up being the one whom everybody watched and listened to.

He knew he would never forget the emerald green dress she'd worn at their first meeting. He fell in love that night. Fell in love with her gaiety, her smile, the way she coaxed a few words from him.

"Come, Wesley, you must dance with me," she'd trilled, pulling on his arm. "It's really quite easy."

He loved the looks of her, the fragrance of roses, her bubbly personality. They were together from that night on. And then came the letter about the

North Beach Peninsula needing doctors. His first thoughts were that he already had a practice, a woman who would one day become his wife, a certain peace inside him, but a week later he changed his mind and wrote a letter. . .

Wesley shivered again. He should eat something, but it was too much trouble, and all he wanted was to go to bed and sleep.

The house still had touches of Lucinda. She'd insisted on hanging paintings and making it look like a home. She'd even brought a carpet on the first trip to visit him. Persian in design, it looked out of place with the plain walls of the front room, now serving as a waiting room. The rug belonged in an elegant parlor, the sort of home where Lucinda had been reared in Portland.

Wesley's thoughts shifted again to Anna. She was determined to be a good nurse. Dedicated in a way Lucinda had never known. Lucinda lived for the moment, whereas Anna lived for eternity. Lucinda had a definite stubbornness about her, but not quite as much as Anna. Her stubbornness reminded him more of determination. Dedication.

His hand touched the worn Bible on the end table, the one gift his mother had left behind—the only thing he had left of her. That and a faded picture.

God, I don't know You very well, if I ever did. Anna prays to You as if You were a good friend. Her faithfulness amazes me. I find myself dedicated to my profession. I know Anna is dedicated, also. She does not want marriage. Her desire is to be a great nurse. Please put thoughts of Anna from my mind, as I know it will bring nothing but heartache.

Focused. Wesley remembered Professor James telling him he must stay focused if he was to become a doctor. He would stay focused. He would not think of Anna again—at least not in that way. So far he had acted gruff to hide his feelings.

Wesley padded to the kitchen in search of something. He found bread, butter, and a slice of roast. He gobbled it down and sliced off another chunk of meat.

He sat in the dark, remembering his vow to make certain no more children would ever lose their mother as he had lost his. Callie Fielding flashed into his mind. He hadn't saved her. She'd left two children, just as his mother left two. She was younger, much younger than his mother had been. He had cried when Callie died. If only he could have known what to do. So much for keeping up his end of the bargain.

Then he had nearly lost a second one today. The Clayborne woman. Childbirth. Ordinarily, delivery was easy. But this one could not deliver in the natural way. If it hadn't been for Anna there, assisting him in the surgery, she might have died.

"It's a miracle," Anna had said. "An absolute miracle." This she was telling Peter when he stopped by the boardinghouse. Wesley couldn't help noticing how Peter watched Anna as she spoke. He knew, also, what he was thinking. If only his wife had been spared. But the look that was exchanged between Anna and Peter was more than that. He was certain of it.

Of course. Anna loved Peter. Peter needed her in a way Wesley did not. The children needed a mother. Anna would be a wonderful mother, just as she was a wonderful nurse.

He pushed the plate aside, noting it was nearly ten. After putting his dishes in the sink, he walked to the bedroom and fell across the bed.

Anna and Peter. Why hadn't he realized it before now? They would make a beautiful couple. And Peter's prayers would be answered.

Wesley turned off the light, but his mind would not go to sleep. Visions of Lucinda flashed before him. Then Anna's smile. Her laugh. Her eyes serious and ever so blue. Anna who cared for others and Lucinda who cared for no one but herself. There was no comparison between the two, yet he found both had entwined arround his heart and mind like ivy around a tree. What was he to do? How could he stay here? How could he *not* stay?

It was almost daylight before he slipped into sleep.

Chapter 9

July faded into August, and with August Anna found the weather more to her liking. There'd been three weeks in a row without a drop of rain. The trail going from the boardinghouse to the beach was dusty and powdery, making her think about Iowa and how she'd liked to trudge barefoot along the paths.

Each Sunday Anna went to the small community church near the boardinghouse. Sometimes she walked, but usually she accepted a ride from Peter Fielding. He came to dinner once a week, sometimes more often. Some Sundays they went swimming at the Crystal Baths. Other times they hiked in the woods, or picnicked in a meadow.

September came, and Albert had not yet come to visit, to Anna's keen disappointment. His notes always said he was too busy; the fishing was better than ever, but soon the season would be over, and he would need to find work. Then, he planned on a trip to visit Anna.

Pearl wrote on a regular basis. This particular morning, Anna withdrew the last letter from the pink envelope and read its contents again.

> *My Dearest Sister Anna,*
>
> *I wish you were here. There are many wonderful things to share with you, to tell you about.*
>
> *Paul is working long hours as a plasterer, and so I am alone, but not really. One is never alone when she has God.*
>
> *I fear our Emily is not doing well, but I dare not say anything to Ben as he has enough to worry about as is. Please include her in your prayers.*

Anna read the words again. As if she didn't already pray for Emily. She prayed for all of her family. She prayed for Peter, Catherine, and Henry. And, yes, even Dr. Snow, though she knew he would scoff if she ever told him this.

She rose, straightened the doily on the table, and carried her cup to the kitchen. Why did she have a problem with Dr. Snow? Why did she want to be with him when he clearly did not approve of her? Not that she wasn't a good nurse, but it was her manner he appeared not to like. Maybe it was her laugh. Sometimes it slipped out, and she had to put her hand over her mouth to bury it. She looked in the hall mirror, noticing how much longer her hair was. It stood out, making her want to use hair oil as men did. Anything to make it lie flat.

Horses' hooves sounded in the distance, and she grabbed the navy blue straw hat and jammed it down over the cantankerous hair. Bessie had found the hat in her closet and given it to Anna just yesterday.

Peter came to the door, as he always did. He nodded when he saw the hat. "New bonnet, right?"

"It's Bessie's."

The children hugged her, and soon they arrived at the church. Anna heard the music before she got down from the buggy. The words to the song came flowing over her as she sang the words aloud.

> "Constantly abiding—Jesus is mine;
> Constantly abiding—Rapture divine!
> He never leaves me lonely—
> Whispers O so kind,
> 'I will never leave thee!'
> Jesus is mine!"

"How do you know all the words?" Catherine asked, slipping her hand inside Anna's.

"I remember it from when I was in nursing school. The church I attended was huge with a pipe organ and a piano." Yet even as Anna remembered it, she knew she would rather be in this tiny church with her few friends, with the sound of the ocean in the background, than in the big church in the city. This was home. Her home. Peter was looking at her in a different sort of way, and Anna hurried on inside, Catherine on one side, Henry on the other.

They went to the front. This way the children seemed less restless. It was as if they knew Pastor Keating could see them, so they sat much more still. Peter slipped into the aisle seat, as always. He looked at Anna and winked.

The opening hymn was another favorite: "Rock of Ages."

"You know that one, too?" Catherine asked as they finished the fourth verse.

"Yes," Anna said. "I know most of them, I suspect."

The door opened, and heads turned. Anna gasped. It was the Claybornes. Mrs. Clayborne held her infant daughter as they made their way toward the front.

"A special blessing is in store for us today," Reverend Keating began. "We have the honor and privilege of welcoming one of our new arrivals: Anna Marie Clayborne."

Anna felt her insides tingle as she watched the couple walk up front.

"Anna, would you come and be a witness?" Reverend Keating asked.

Anna walked to the front and took the small baby in her arms. She was so very beautiful with her tiny rosebud-shaped mouth and a frizz of hair that peeked out from under a white bonnet. The flowing white gown engulfed the tiny body. Anna swallowed with pride. Big brother Edward had a too-large shirt and well-worn trousers. His hair was slicked back, and he looked proud and happy to be standing with his parents and baby sister.

The door opened, and Anna looked up to see the familiar tall, broad-shouldered man dressed in black suit and tie. The breath caught in her throat. What was Dr. Snow doing here? He'd never come to church before.

His footsteps approached, as Anna realized he was coming to the front. He stepped up to Mr. Clayborne and shook the man's hand.

Pastor Keating smiled and looked out at the congregation. "Dr. Snow—whom most all of us know—has consented to be this precious one's godparent."

Anna smiled and nodded toward Dr. Snow, but he was looking at the baby in wonderment.

The words were said, prayers offered, and then Reverend Keating said, "I dedicate thee to God, in the name of the Father, the Son, and the Holy Ghost."

Anna's heart swelled with pride. To have a baby named after her was one thing, but to be asked to stand up as a witness was even more wonderful and special. And the Claybornes, who had never come to the church, said they would come again.

The dedication ceremony over, Anna sat next to the children. They were extra quiet. Anna wondered if Dr. Snow would now leave, but the door did not open, and she knew he must be sitting with the Claybornes. Something about his presence had unnerved her more than ever, and she didn't know why.

Lord, Anna found herself praying, *I know this isn't the man You would have for me. Why can I not still these feelings then?*

With trembling fingers she opened the hymnal to the closing song.

"Be Thou my Vision, O Lord of my heart. . ."

Anna's voice sang out clear and true. Yes, she must keep her eye on the vision—her vision. Helping others, being there to assist Dr. Snow when needed.

The service was over, and Anna waited for those in front of her to move.

Peter got caught talking to Mrs. Farnsworth. Catherine and Henry had run outside to wait. She heard parishioners saying hello to Dr. Snow. Of course he would be greeted, as everybody knew him and respected him highly.

And then he was at her side. "Anna, good morning."

"Good morning, Dr. Snow. How nice to see you here."

"I was asked to come, and so I did."

She glanced up into his eyes, and it was as if the world did not exist. Voices hummed in the background, people milling all around her, but Anna saw nothing but Dr. Wesley Snow's face, his dark eyes that held her gaze.

"No emergencies during the night?" she finally asked, for want of something to still her pounding heart. This was ridiculous.

Before he could answer, a voice interrupted. "Dr. Snow! How wonderful to see you in church. We would love to have you come for dinner, if that's possible."

"Lily. It's good to see you're up and about on that leg."

Lily smiled and clasped his hand. Anna moved past and on up the aisle, the woman's voice penetrating her thoughts. "We do enjoy having company on Sundays."

"Well, I—"

Go, Anna was thinking. *Lily Hardin makes a good meal.*

Anna smiled and answered greetings as she headed out the door. The small slip of blue now filled half the sky, and she thanked God for the sun, for the warmth, for the wonderful day He had made. A sudden breeze came out of nowhere and lifted her hat.

Anna reached, but couldn't stop it from flying off. And then Peter was there, grabbing it and handing it over.

"To the rescue again," Anna said. "You're always catching my hats."

"I wish I could catch something else—"

Anna turned and asked him to repeat what he'd said, what she thought he'd said.

"Nothing," he said, grabbing Henry and tossing him into the air.

Before Anna could comment, Dr. Snow was at her side. "Had to turn down Miss Lily's dinner invitation since Bessie asked me yesterday to come for the midday meal."

"But this is Sunday."

"I know, but one does not refuse Bessie. Besides, she's making fresh peach pies. How could I possibly stay away from that?" His dark eyes twinkled with a teasing merriment that Anna found disarming.

That was true. Well, it would be a full house today as Peter and the children were staying.

The Claybornes came out then and Anna went over to give the baby one last kiss on the cheek.

"Thank you for asking me to stand up with you."

"It was Dr. Snow's suggestion," Mrs. Clayborne said. "We thought it a good idea, too."

The smell of beef roast filled the boardinghouse as the five entered. Anna knew the roast would be accompanied by slices of onion, whole carrots, and halved potatoes. Too bad Albert wasn't here, as he loved roast and especially peach pie.

Anna left Wesley downstairs talking to another guest who had come in last evening on the train. Slipping into her room, she put the damaged hat on the dresser and patted her hair into place. She would leave her best chambray on, but grabbed a pinafore to wear over it, since she felt led to help in the kitchen.

As Anna started down the stairs, she thought she heard a familiar voice, but it wasn't until she entered the dining room that her heart jumped to her throat. Sitting at the head of the table was her brother Albert!

"Albert! But I thought you couldn't come until November."

"What? And forget my sister's birthday?"

Anna stopped, her face turning red. "Birthday?" Then she remembered. She hadn't thought of it, not once. But Albert had. Twenty-eight. And unmarried.

"This is such a wonderful surprise!"

And then she knew that was why Dr. Snow had turned down Lily's invitation, why Peter had said he and the children would be there.

Bessie came from the kitchen carrying a birthday cake. "Surprise!" she called out. "I do love surprises."

"And I thought we were having peach pie," Dr. Snow said.

"And so we are," Bessie said.

It was too much. Anna grabbed for the back of the chair and tried hard to bite back the tears. Albert was there, throwing his arms around her. "I got someone to cover for me last night. Came in on the train, and you never suspected."

"Bessie said we had a guest, but I never thought—oh, Albert," and she hugged him again harder.

Anna knew her cheeks were still red when the dinner plates had been cleared and it was up to her to cut her cake. Such a day it had been. And Albert had to leave soon to catch the train back, so he'd be there for the morning work.

"This has been the most wonderful day ever," Anna said, accepting a small gift from Catherine. It was a picture she'd drawn with the new tablet and paints Anna had given her last week.

There were other gifts, but none as precious as the hand-made picture.

After another hug, Albert left to catch his train, Peter left with two very tired children, and Dr. Snow spoke of leaving, too.

"You can have tomorrow off, if you want."

Anna looked into his eyes for a lingering moment. "Thank you, but no, I'd rather come in to work, if that's all right with you."

"Of course."

Long after everyone had left and the house was quiet, Anna sat in her favorite spot and pondered over the day. It had been a wonderful day, a wonderful surprise, but she felt more confused than ever. Why had Dr. Snow looked at her in that intense way? Why had Peter said what he had in the churchyard? Why was her life suddenly seeming topsy-turvy? Was it possible, could she be falling in love? Yet, she couldn't let it happen. She'd come to be a nurse. Her career meant everything to her. Marriage was not even a consideration. She thought of Joseph. How long since he'd crossed through her thoughts, since she'd looked at his photograph. She knew now that part of her life was over. She was no longer an Iowa girl. She was a woman now, a woman who lived and loved the primitive beauty of the North Beach Peninsula.

As the stars beamed out of a dark sky, Anna thanked God for bringing her here.

Chapter 10

Peter glanced at the profile of the woman he admired, though he knew little about her except that she was happy, energetic, always ready for the occasion. He had done much soul searching last night when sleep wouldn't come.

He missed Callie, her sweet smile, the way she had taken his hand and pulled him close, nestling her head against his chest. Had it really only been a little over a year since her death? Somehow it seemed an eternity. He imagined his hands found her hair, burying them in the soft thickness. It had always been that way—ever since the Johnsons first came to North Beach. The young couple had known at first glance they would be together forever. There never had been anyone else for Peter. . . .

Peter got up and walked out of the bedroom. He didn't see how he could sleep in that empty, cold bed tonight. Thoughts of Callie wouldn't let him rest. He needed someone, yet wondered how he could even consider marrying again. Always, always Callie's face would get in the way. He thought of Anna—how it might be to turn and see her face on the opposite pillow. She would smile or laugh that loud, hearty laugh, and then he would remember a soft, tinkling one and—well—he didn't think he could ever love Anna in that special, tender way. Yet he needed her. The children desperately needed a mother, and he must think of them.

Doris Yates, his neighbor on the next farm, cared for them now—said it was no problem to add two more to her three. Her husband had died at sea three years ago, and it was a struggle eking out a living, but she managed okay. And of course Peter paid her some, but mostly helped out by doing things around the house that only a man could do.

When he'd returned from Portland that last time—after meeting and accompanying Anna—and picked up Catherine and Henry, she'd invited him to come for the next day's evening meal. It seemed he was falling into a pattern, and he didn't want Doris to make anything of it.

Peter added wood to the fire and paced across the front room. It was decision time, but he wasn't ready to make one. Would he ever be?

"Is Anna the one You've sent me?" Peter asked God. He'd never thought of her as beautiful, but there'd been a glow about her as she held little Anna up in front of the church. And later when they'd gone over for the birthday celebration, her eyes were still shining.

He liked being with her. She'd been such a good sport about nearly drowning, then gone clamming and worked right alongside him. It had felt good to have a helpmate again. Callie had loved clamming.

They'd come home late, and Anna had helped clean the clams. She loved everyone and everything. And she believed. That was important to Peter, whose grandfather had been a minister and had encouraged the young Peter in his faith.

The children loved her. He hadn't seen them smile as they did when Anna was around. Surely she loved them. Perhaps not him, but she cared for them. He was positive of that. She might have loved him if it hadn't been for Dr. Snow. He seemed to turn her head lately. Peter had noticed all right.

"I've prayed for someone, Lord. I need a mother for my kids. I need a wife, though I cannot love her as I loved Callie. Please do not ask that of me."

The fire had died down, and it was too late to put another log on. After their afternoon at Bessie's, the children had fallen asleep immediately.

Anna. So spirited. Talkative. Loud. Much louder than his gentle Callie. But she was good with the children, and they already adored her. Had she come to North Beach Peninsula to find a husband? Perhaps her job wasn't to nurse the sick and wounded, but to mother Catherine and Henry, to be a wife to him. He needed some sign to know she was the right one.

Peter picked up the oval frame holding Callie's picture. Her eyes seemed to look into his. Her smile was for him alone. They had always loved each other. Cared about each other. It was almost as if they'd signed a pact, promising to belong to no other. And they'd had eight glorious, beautiful years. Until the fever. Sometimes it seemed as if ten years had gone by since he'd felt her arms around him, her mouth raised to his. *Oh, Callie, I love you so. How can I pledge vows to another?*

Wesley Snow had not wanted to leave the boardinghouse. He had not wanted the evening to end. For some reason, he could not keep his eyes off of Anna. Once he had seen Peter watching him. And Bessie. She saw everything, but kept it to herself. Wesley knew he did not need Anna in his life now. After all, he was engaged to Lucinda.

He withdrew the letter he'd received just yesterday.

My Dear Wesley,

As the time draws near for my trip to the peninsula, I know I can convince you of what you must do. This nonsense has lasted a year now—I gave in to your whim of the heart—now it's your turn to give in to mine. I want us to be married at the huge Presbyterian Church in downtown Portland. It is the place to marry. We can have a most grand and elaborate wedding there.

Wesley let the letter flutter to the floor as he leaned back, hands on his chest. He didn't want a big wedding. It wasn't his way of doing things. He wanted to help people. Far better to donate money to the poor people who had nothing than to waste it on a lavish wedding with so much food, wine, and flowers.

As for his leaving the peninsula, he could not do it. He had just won the trust of some of the old-timers. How could he desert them now? Would someone come to care for them if he left? He leaned down and picked up the letter.

Darling, I do miss you, you know. We are going to have a wonderful life together, you'll see.

Papa has said we can honeymoon in the Caribbean, if you so choose. I think it's time you got away from the responsibilities of doctoring.

One more thing, darling, there is an Autumn Ball there close to your home. It's held in Long Beach each year. I am bringing a new gown and dancing slippers and expect you to make sure you can take off during that time. Let that nurse take over for you.

By the way, Lizzie sent me a picture of her. She's a homely thing, isn't she? I guess one must work if she can never hope to marry.

Wesley wadded the letter into a ball and threw it toward the fireplace. Imagine. Lucinda thought beauty was everything. She could not understand the inner beauty, nor would she probably ever understand.

The embers had died down and he looked at the letter, knowing it would be ashes by morning. He half expected Lizzie to come down, asking if he needed a cup of coffee or something. It was just as well. He'd much rather be left with his own thoughts.

Wesley closed his eyes and tried to visualize Lucinda, but for some reason, another face kept getting in the way. A wonderful, plain face to be sure, but one with a warm expression and eyes that danced. And most important was the laugh that started at the bottom of her toes and worked all the way up and out, filling the room with its raucous noise.

Anna. Oh, Anna, I love you more than I ever thought I could love anyone or anything. What am I going to do now? How can I marry Lucinda? How can I tell her no and make her understand my life is not in Portland, but here? Here with these people I've grown to love. People who need me. People I need back.

Chapter 11

September ended, and October came with the hint that winter wasn't far behind. Anna spent her evenings reading books Emily had sent. There were also books for Catherine, who was learning to read in school. Often, on Sunday afternoons, Anna would listen to her struggle with new words and encourage her to read and to always do her best in school. Bessie taught Catherine to cross-stitch, and she had made several samplers.

"You know what I'm going to do?" Anna said one afternoon. The inspiration had hit when the box of books first arrived.

"No, what?" Bessie asked.

"What we need is a library. Why can't we use one section of the living room here for books? Lots of people could use them."

Bessie smiled. "Yes. It's a wonderful idea ye have. I'll put out a plea for people to bring their books when they've finished them. We'll have the peninsula's first lending library."

Soon the shelves were full, and Bessie asked their neighbor to build more. Anna had made cards with holders for each book. The idea caught on and she felt good about it. One of the prized possessions was *The Lyric Music Series—the First Reader*. Bessie seemed to think it had been used in early schools.

As October drew to a close, Anna knew the beautiful Lucinda would arrive soon. She looked forward to meeting Dr. Snow's fiancée yet felt fear and trepidation without knowing why.

Thursdays were spent going over the ledger. So many unpaid statements. Never one to press, Dr. Snow accepted a dozen eggs, a slab of ham, vegetables, whatever a patient had an abundance of.

Anna ate the sandwich she'd brought that morning, wishing now for a cup of Bessie's steaming clam chowder, but not daring to leave, lest someone should come.

Perhaps she would travel to Portland on Thanksgiving to spend the holiday with Ben and Emily, Pearl and Paul. Pearl had written recently, excited with the news of a first baby due in June.

The fire bell sounded. Anna froze. The bell meant an emergency. Was it a

410

fire or some medical emergency? Anna prayed for whatever the tragedy might be. She hoped it wasn't a home fire where children might be trapped. Home fires were prevalent, and Anna held her breath, hoping it was only minor.

Minutes later, Anna heard the sound of horses pulling up out front, a voice crying out. "Burn victim! We need help!"

Anna threw open the door and ran out, staring at the small form in the man's arms. She gulped.

"Dr. Snow is on his way. Said you'd know what to do."

The small child couldn't have been more than two years of age. Anna swallowed as the tiny figure was hurried in. Her cries and moans filled the hallway. Anna pulled back the blanket and gasped. It was far worse than she could have imagined. The skin on over half the body was no longer pink, but blackened. The hair was gone and the only way one could tell it was a face was from the two tiny eyes peering out at her. Anna's fingernails dug into her palms.

"Lay her in the examining room at the far end of the hall," she finally commanded. Scrubbing up, she braced herself for this task, the worst she'd ever faced.

The nightgown must come off. And with it would come layers of skin. How could she do it?

"It's okay. You're going to be okay," she soothed, hoping the child could hear her. *O God, give me the strength I need. Keep me calm. Help me to do the right thing. And, please, bring Dr. Snow here quick!*

"How did this happen?" Anna asked one of the firemen standing by.

"House fire up out of Long Beach," the fireman said. "Couldn't reach the mother and another child. She's the only survivor. Father's off working. What a shock he's going to have when he returns."

"Oh, no."

How horrible, Anna thought, *to come home to find your home burned to the ground, no belongings left, and most of your loved ones gone.*

"Is someone trying to reach him?"

"Yes, the logging camp's been notified."

Anna started to touch the stockings on the tiny feet, but the child jerked and screamed louder. She fought back another wave of nausea. How could she handle it? If only Dr. Snow were here. . . .

"Found her in the crib—in a back room. Her backside may be okay and the wet diaper gave some protection."

Anna nodded. She'd seen burn patients before, but never one so young. She was just a baby who hadn't even started to live yet, and now it looked as if she might die. Of course, she wasn't the doctor; it could look worse than it was.

Dr. Snow rushed in, filling the room with his knowledge. "Here, Anna, let me see." He gasped, looking away for a long moment. "I'll scrub up, then we must remove the nightgown as slowly as possible. Be prepared. The skin is going to come, too."

They worked together, each looking away, hardly able to stand the sight. "We'll use this salve. It should take away some of the pain."

Anna opened the jar and put huge gobs on the tiny limbs. She felt her head swim and grabbed the edge of the table and held on tight.

Dr. Snow gave her a quick sideways glance. "Anna, go sit. Put your head between your legs, and stay for a minute. You look as if you're about to faint. I can't handle two patients just now."

Anna did as she was told. Dr. Snow recognized she was in shock. Though she prepared herself for some of the most gruesome of tasks, one could never be completely prepared. Ten minutes later she reappeared. The child needed constant care. She needed to be turned and given fluids to replace those she'd lost. She could not be left alone. They'd take turns staying with her around the clock.

It was hours later when Dr. Snow told her to leave. "If you can come back after a few hours' sleep, I'd appreciate it. You go now. Bessie is there to talk to. Cry if you must. You can't hold it in."

Anna nodded. "I'll be back."

"Anna?" He stepped out into the hall.

She turned and something about the expression on his worn face made her heart leap. "Yes?"

His face returned to the usual mask. "She may not make it. You must prepare yourself for that possibility."

"O God, please, no," Anna prayed. Covering her mouth with her hands, she sat in the nearest chair.

All was quiet when Anna arrived at the boardinghouse. A note was on the table: "Scones in the bread box; pie in the pie keeper."

Anna couldn't eat. All she wanted to do was forget the baby fighting for her life—the smell of burning flesh—the way it was not only in her uniform, but had saturated her hair, her cap, her nostrils. She knew as she threw the uniform in a heap in the corner of her bedroom that the smell would not leave her soon.

Four hours later, after a fitful sleep, Anna rose and fumbled with the buttons of her clean uniform. It was black and cold outside as she headed back to the hospital, not realizing she'd even arrived until Ned trotted up to the side. She hurried inside, and the smell of coffee revived her. Lizzie thrust a cup into her hands. "Here. Drink this before going in there."

So the child still lived. Her uneven breathing filled the room as Anna came, standing over the small form. Dr. Snow glanced up, as if just realizing she'd come and his eyes filled with relief. "Did you sleep?"

Anna nodded. "As well as could be expected under the circumstances."

He raised red-rimmed eyes to her. "She's still with us," he murmured.

"I see that. It's your turn to go get rest now."

He tried to straighten up. "Yes, you're right. I'll be upstairs if you need me." He ran a hand through his disheveled hair. "Let me know if her condition worsens."

"I will."

It was later that Lizzie reminded Anna of Lucinda's impending arrival.

"And the Autumn Ball is the next day, is that right?"

Lizzie nodded. "Heaven help us if Dr. Snow should decide not to go."

Anna couldn't think of fancy balls now as she forced fluids into the tiny mouth. The little girl moaned as she tossed and turned. Anna prayed that the pain would lessen. So tiny to endure such suffering. If only she could understand why these things happened. Would she live? And if she did, what would she have to live for? With a disfigured face and body, she would never be normal, never be like others. She'd be ridiculed and laughed at, yet Anna must pray for her recovery. The oath she'd taken said she would do everything in her power to help the sick, to administer to their needs, and she could do nothing less now.

Anna sat in the chair beside the bed. In a few minutes she'd apply more salve. She hummed a tune and the eyes fluttered open. "I love you, Rebecca," she whispered. She had to turn away, to keep the child from seeing her tears. The first twenty-four hours were crucial. Would Rebecca live to see tomorrow?

Chapter 12

Lucinda Mae Lawson boarded the *T. J. Potter* at the Portland docks that November morning. Dressed in her best purple damask with full skirt and gathered waist, she clutched her latest hat, a wide-brimmed affair with real ostrich feathers. Her gloves matched. Heads turned her way as she climbed aboard the sternwheeler that traveled from Portland to Astoria twice each day. This particular day she would go on the Washington side to Megler Landing, and then board the Clamshell Railroad to her destination in Seaview.

Soon she would be alone, having refused the accompaniment of her mother or best friend Mary Dugan.

"I must learn to do things for myself," had been her answer, and as always Lucinda had her way after much spirited arguing and pouting. The pouting—staying in her room one entire day—had unnerved her father so much he'd said, "I give in! What can possibly happen?" The one request was that she have a place to stay; hence a room rented in advance—the best room, of course—at Bessie McGruder's Boarding House in Seaview.

"Save your pretty frocks for when you arrive, and Wesley takes you dancing or partying," Mrs. Lawson had said yesterday, not agreeing with Lucinda's choice of traveling attire.

"Mama, I must look my best whether traveling or not," she proclaimed.

Now as Lucinda boarded, she waved good-bye. Her purpose was twofold. Not only would she be there to attend the Autumn Ball; she would convince Wesley Snow it was time to return to Portland; time to plan for their summer wedding. Surely he had gotten this place out of his system by now. She had waited a year while he played country doctor to the people on the North Beach Peninsula. She'd been more than patient.

Lucinda reminded herself that she did not fall for Dr. Wesley Snow because he was handsome, though he was in a rugged sort of way, but because of the prestige that would follow being married to a doctor. Such things were extremely important to her. Besides, it was time she married before tongues began to wag, saying she was an old maid. Twenty-two was not old, but she had waited long enough to receive the inheritance from Grandfather Lawson. His will stipulated she must be married before she received the legacy.

At last the boat was on its way. An hour later, Lucinda sighed, already more than a little weary from her trip, and they were only halfway down the Columbia River. It would be late before she arrived at her destination.

Two trunks had been carefully packed. The new gown—a rich blue satin with puffed sleeves—and new shoes, gloves, and stockings lay in one. Lucinda could hardly wait to show off at this annual dance. Surely Wesley would realize how fortunate he was to have her at his side.

She'd wanted to stay at his home; after all, their old cook Lizzie Myles was there to chaperone, but her mother put her foot down. "It is not proper, Lucinda, and I will not hear of your staying in the same home as your fiancé—not even if there were five chaperones. The boardinghouse it will be."

At last they arrived at Megler's Landing, and soon Lucinda was helped to board the evening train heading west.

"Goodness," she exclaimed to the passenger across the aisle. "I always forget how dusty and dirty these trains are."

"Yes, dusty it is," came the reply. The woman dressed in serviceable gray bombazine looked common. Plain. Something like that nurse who had come to work with Wesley a few months ago.

Lucinda turned and stared out the window. Undoubtedly she would meet her at the boardinghouse, as she lived there. And of course there would be that weird lady who ran the place. Bessie, with the strange way of saying *ye* for "you."

Lucinda held her left gloved hand to the window. The ring made a bump in the fabric. Her engagement ring. At first she'd hoped to marry by Christmas, but Wesley hadn't been willing to give up this inane idea to work in such a primitive spot. She could never live here. If she'd had any doubts, any reconsiderations, all had been dashed as she made this trip west, again. How Wesley could enjoy this remote area, why he hadn't wanted to stay in Portland and continue on with the practice, caused her much consternation. Should she marry such an insensitive man?

"My new dress shall need to be cleaned immediately after I arrive," Lucinda said, turning to look at the woman across the aisle.

"One shouldn't wear her best," the woman replied then. "Are you going far?"

Lucinda looked at her, noticing the smudge on her face. Her figure was full, her hair unkempt. "Yes. I have come to see my husband-to-be."

"Oh. And who might that be?"

"Dr. Wesley Snow. Perhaps you know him?"

"Dr. Snow?" The woman's eyes lit up. "Why, Dr. Snow saved my husband's life! It was just last month! Oh, my goodness, gracious, and to think you are to be his wife and all."

Lucinda straightened her shoulders and drew back. "I realize that is what my intended does best," and then the words slipped from her mouth before she could stop them. "If he tended to my desires, my dreams half as well, I wouldn't be coming here now with an ultimatum."

"Ultimatum?" The woman looked puzzled.

Lucinda, deciding she'd said more than enough, turned away and stared out the window again. All she could see was the lapping waters of the Columbia River and the fish seining camps, the horses pulling the heavy nets. The train chugged west and stopped suddenly. The lady descended at a place called Pt. Ellice. "Oh, please thank Dr. Snow for me again for saving my Ralph's life."

And then she was gone, and the train started up again, making its clanging, horrible noise. Lucinda withdrew a handkerchief from her purse and covered her mouth, hoping she didn't have soot in her hair, yet knowing she probably did.

Lucinda's mission would not be easy, but she was good at persuading people to do what she wanted. There were wedding preparations and parties to attend. Surely another doctor, one more suited to this place, could be found.

Lucinda covered her nose again as soot floated through the air in the travel car. There were several stops yet before she'd reach her destination.

She wasn't looking forward to having Bessie pry, or coming face to face with that short-haired, homely nurse. No wonder the poor woman had taken up nursing. Women chose careers when they knew they probably wouldn't marry. And she was old—at least as old as Wesley. But she was a good nurse. Wesley had mentioned it more than once.

The train stopped again, and a cow bawled. With the windows open, Lucinda heard the sound and caught the smell. Animals rode two cars back— whatever people brought with them. So quaint, this place. Lucinda would never become used to it. Already she was pining for Portland and its elegance, the party she would miss tomorrow evening. The dance here better be a fancy one. Surely it would be. Even country people must dress up at times.

With a sigh, Lucinda leaned back and closed her eyes.

The young boy who tended the horses met the train that evening. Bessie was expecting Lucinda and had reserved the fanciest room she had. It was on the top floor—across from Anna's.

The groom remembered Lucinda. She'd given him a nickel when he'd brought her trunk to Bessie's the last time.

She signaled him now. "I need help. You do live over yonder in that boardinghouse, is that not correct?"

"Yes, Ma'am." He bowed slightly.

"I have two large trunks. I'll need you to take them to the boardinghouse and on up to my room."

"Yes, Ma'am, I can do that."

Bessie had the room aired out and sent the lad up with the trunks. He had to make two trips, so Lucinda gave him two nickels. His eyes lit up as he pocketed the coins. "Thank you, Ma'am."

"Come," Bessie said. "Ye must be tired. Ye can have tea with me. Anna is not here yet, but I expect her soon."

"I want to see Wesley."

"Perhaps ye should wait until morning. There's a little girl fighting for her life."

Lucinda's eyes narrowed. "He knew I was coming."

"Yes, he did." Bessie poured tea into a delicate china cup.

Lucinda removed her gloves and hat. "I am a fright from that long, horrendous trip."

"A bath can be drawn for you."

Lucinda nodded. "That will be most necessary. After I have my tea."

After the bath and a change of clothes, Lucinda demanded to be driven to town to see her fiancé.

"Now?" Bessie asked. "It's terribly late."

Lucinda ignored her. "I assume the young man who helped me before can assist me."

Bessie assured her that was possible.

"I simply cannot go to the ball tomorrow night looking like this. Do you have a hairdresser on the premises?"

Bessie'd never had such a request. "There is one in Long Beach. I'm sure they can accommodate ye."

Lucinda sighed. "I suppose that will have to do."

"If ye are ready to go now, Miss Lawson, I'll call my groom. He'll be happy to take ye into town."

Lucinda wore a calico that had been beautiful once. It was wrinkled and she considered having it pressed, but decided time was wasting. She must go see Wesley now. The sooner the better.

Anna sat with Rebecca. It had been twenty-four hours and then some. The child clung to life.

Anna now waited for Dr. Snow to wake up from his rest. She must have dozed off because suddenly she heard a shrill voice. It filled the entire first floor of the infirmary.

"You didn't even come to meet me on the day I arrived!" the voice shrieked.

Anna trembled. Was it Lucinda? Dr. Snow's fiancée? But why would she come here? Wouldn't it have been better to wait at the boardinghouse?

Anna closed the door, but the voices grew louder.

"I cannot attend the ball tomorrow, Lucinda. I'm sorry, but I can't get away. I have a burn patient who needs—"

"The patients always come first."

"I took an oath—"

"And you also took an oath when we became betrothed. All I want is two hours of your time. Is that asking too much?"

Anna remembered Lizzie's words from the day before. It looked as if her prediction would come true, but she could stay, watch over the patient so Dr. Snow could attend the dance. She went down the hall.

"Dr. Snow, I can stay with Rebecca—"

"See?" Lucinda said. "I knew someone could relieve you."

He turned and held up his hand. "No. I cannot leave someone so critical—"

"She's a capable person," Lucinda broke in. "Let her take care of the little girl, and you come with me."

He looked at Anna again, then back at Lucinda. "No. I cannot, Lucinda. We can talk about this later."

"I won't be here later," Lucinda said. Even in the wrinkled calico, she looked exquisite. "I fully intend to be on the train that leaves Sunday."

"Very well. There's nothing I can do to stop you. We both know that."

"We're not talking about stopping," Lucinda said. "Nothing can make me stay in this place. Absolutely *nothing.*"

"That's too bad," he said, turning his back. "You do what you must, Lucinda, just as I do what I must. Now I have a patient I must check and a nurse to relieve. Anna's been here way too many hours." He started off down the hall.

Lucinda gasped and hurried after him. "Not before I have my say!"

He paused and faced the woman he thought he loved at one time. "Go ahead. I'm listening."

"This is an ultimatum, Dr. Wesley Snow. If you can't take me to the Autumn Ball, then we're through." Her mouth had drawn up into a pout. "I understand that you must care for your patients, Wesley. This is fine, but you can go back to your old office with Robert in East Portland. I cannot, I *will not* stay here. You have a month to decide. Surely they can find a doctor to take your place by then." She walked across the waiting room. "Either you come back to Portland then, or our marriage will be called off."

He stared at the woman before him. She was diminutive, a beauty dressed in calico and a large-brimmed hat with ribbons and lace. Her blond curls framed a heart-shaped face and he realized how beautiful she was. But her beauty was only skin deep.

Leave in one month, indeed!

Wesley never had liked threats, whether they came from his fiancée or someone else. Something recoiled inside him. He didn't do well with ultimatums. How dare Lucinda tell him what he could or couldn't do? Didn't she understand even a whit of what had brought him here—why he felt he must stay? Had his schooling meant nothing? Did she not understand a man must follow his heart, do what had to be done, what he felt led to do?

Lucinda would have her way. She cared for nobody but herself. He was born to serve, she to be served. It hadn't mattered in the beginning, but it did now. No. He would not be forced to return to Portland to practice. He liked it here. He was needed here. It would be a lonely life, perhaps, yet he knew it could never be so when there were people who needed treatment. People who brought him fresh fish, crabs, clams, and oysters. People who looked out for his needs as well as he did for theirs.

He pushed her words aside, the ones that stipulated what he must do. She stood waiting, eyes still blazing.

"I hope you will be very happy, Miss Lucinda Mae Lawson," he said aloud.

"Oh!" A sound of something hitting the floor, then the door banged once. It opened again as her voice rang out: "I don't want the ring anyway. It was just a cheap thing to begin with!"

Anna held her breath. She hadn't wanted to hear any of the conversation. Such things should be private, but with Lucinda she wondered if any matter was private. Lizzie Myles came out of the kitchen, wringing her hands. "That Miss Lucinda does have a temper!"

"Yes, well, I believe she may be leaving." Dr. Snow appeared in the doorway. He turned to Anna. "I'm sorry you had to hear this. You, too, Lizzie."

" 'Tisn't the first time I've been parley to Miss Lucinda's wiles, and I'm sure it won't be the last."

"Will she return to Portland?" Anna asked.

"Oh, I'm sure she will. After she creates another scene." He waved his hand. "You go on home now. You look exhausted."

Anna thought he did, too, but she didn't say it. Something made her want to reach up and press fingertips to the lines on his brow. The thought jolted her as she turned away suddenly, looked at Rebecca once more, then hurried out the door.

After Anna left, Wesley Snow thought, again, about Lucinda's display of temper. If he didn't attend the dance, she would leave the peninsula and never return. Somehow a sense of relief filled him at the prospect.

He sighed as he thought of Anna. Things had run smoother since her arrival. She was a stubborn thing, and maybe she was not beautiful like Lucinda, but she knew her work, and something drove her from inside. Sort of the same as he felt. He could tell by the concerned look in her eyes, the frown on her face. She worried about each and every one that walked through the door. She was here to take care of that cut, remove the sliver or fish hook.

She was dedicated. He could think of no better word to describe Anna Galloway. Yet, there was the situation with Peter Fielding.

Should she decide to marry—and he had a feeling that Peter would ask her soon—Wesley would lose her. Peter needed a mother for his children, a wife for his bed. He knew Anna loved them. She loved everyone. *Everyone?* A sudden warmth rippled through him. Strange, but he had never thought of it quite like that.

Anna probably cared for him, just as she did the many patients. Yes, hers was a caring heart.

He walked back to the patient's room and stared at the small child, actually no more than a baby. How could God make this tiny one suffer? How could he believe in a God Who allowed such things to happen?

Yet he found himself praying, uttering words he hadn't spoken since he'd sat at his mother's bedside. "God, please ease her suffering. Please, if there is any justice in this world. . ."

Chapter 13

As screams of anger, then sobs filled the house, Anna mulled it over, finally deciding to do something about Lucinda. Maybe she could explain why tending to sick people would always come before the desires of the heart. She knew Dr. Snow to be a wonderful, considerate person who would not hurt the woman he loved just to be cruel. He had looked forward to the dance; he had told Anna himself.

Anna found her lying across the bed, sobbing as if her heart would break. "Lucinda." She touched the young woman's shoulder. Lucinda flinched, then bolted up.

"What are you doing in my room? Can't a person have privacy around here?"

Anna swallowed hard. "The door was open. I thought perhaps I could help."

"You've helped enough already!" The cheeks were wet, the eyes now snapping. "I daresay you're the reason Wesley is staying here—"

Anna stepped back, her hand going to her throat. This could not be true. What was Lucinda talking about? No, it wasn't possible. Lucinda was distraught and was the type to strike at anyone who got in her way.

"I can bring you a cup of tea, if you like."

Lucinda shook her head, the curls bouncing. "I do not want any tea, and I do not want you to patronize me."

Anna stepped back. "I'm only trying to help."

"Oh, you nurses and doctors are all alike. You think you can solve the problems of the world by bringing someone a cup of tea, by holding her hand, mopping the perspiration off her brow."

At that word, she reached for a lace handkerchief and wiped her forehead. "I prefer not discussing it with you. The only thing for me to do—," she got up and opened the smaller trunk, "is to pack my things and go back to Portland where I belong."

"I wish you would change your mind," Anna said. "The North Beach Peninsula is a lovely place. It grows on you."

"I hate it here!" The voice rose shrilly. "And I especially hate people like you. So sanctimonious. Always so sweet and right. You have people eating out of your hand. I've never been that way, and I'm not about to start now!"

Anna stepped backwards as if expecting to get struck. She said nothing.

"You can stay here. Wesley can stay here, but I'm going back to Portland where my kind of people are."

"The doctor loves you very much—"

"And how would you know that?" She spun around and met Anna's steady gaze. "I suppose Wesley confides in you. Isn't that what doctors do with their nurses?"

"I—didn't mean to imply—"

"Well, if he prefers plain to beauty, then he's found the perfect mate in you."

Anna gasped as the words soaked in. "I suppose beauty does matter to most men. And perhaps that's why I never planned to marry, but chose a career instead."

"Don't make it sound any better," Lucinda said. "I said what I meant and meant what I said. Don't try to talk me out of it. If Wesley wants you, he can very well have you!"

Anna left the room without another word.

Lucinda threw clothes into the trunk. She had not wanted to talk to Anna with the smoldering eyes. She made her feel uncomfortable. How dare she think she could tell her how to feel? To act? As if it was any of her business.

She, Lucinda, was somebody. She wasn't a homely nurse from the state of Iowa. Lucinda's great-grandfather had come on a wagon train west; had settled in Salem, a community south of Portland. Later his son, Lucinda's father, moved to Portland, opening up one of the first ladies' shoe stores. Everyone knew the Lawson name.

Lucinda wouldn't be here now if it hadn't been for the stupid will. She didn't even want to marry, not just yet.

Voices came up the back stairs. Lucinda closed her door. She hated boardinghouses where everyone knew everyone else's business.

Anna slipped down the stairs, wondering if everyone had heard. Lucinda's words stung. Though she knew them to be true, they still hurt. Of course she wasn't beautiful. Anyone could see that. Freckles. Shoulders too broad. Mouth too small and just a thin line. What was it Mama had said once? "It's as if the bottom lip had disappeared."

Anna no longer had long tresses to make her look feminine. All men loved long hair—so she'd been told—but short hair was much more practical. She would ignore Lucinda's rantings. Lucinda was hurt. People said things when they hurt inside. She didn't want to go home, or face people saying she had lost the good doctor, the marriage had been called off.

Slipping into the kitchen, Anna moved the teakettle over to the heat of the stove. She needed a cup of tea while she sorted through her thoughts. If Mama was here to talk to, or Pearl—yes, Pearl understood about the plain part. She was even taller than Anna, with broader shoulders, but Paul loved her anyway. And Clara in Connecticut. Anna wondered if she'd ever see her sister again. She was the tallest of all, at least six foot in stocking feet.

Anna walked to the window and looked out at the whitecaps. She loved watching the ocean—all-powerful, yet soothing. She wished that Lucinda could find one thing she liked about the peninsula. It really wouldn't be that difficult, but Lucinda made things difficult. It was like Mama's saying: "You can lead a horse to water, but you can't make him drink." Or, "Pretty is as pretty does."

She clasped her hands and thought again about Rebecca. So young to be burned and not understanding why it hurt so much. Fires were such hazards. Why weren't people more careful?

Anna sipped her tea. A sound of thumping on the main stairwell startled her. It was Lucinda dragging the smaller of the trunks down the steps, thumping at each one. It never occurred to her that others were asleep. Anna thought about helping, but the less she saw of Miss Lucinda Mae Lawson, the better off she'd be.

The voice at her elbow commanded her to turn to face the red-streaked face. "I hope you and Wesley will be very happy together."

Anna shook her head. "If I marry, Lucinda, I can no longer be a nurse, and nursing is my career. It's what I want to do with my life." She hesitated for a moment. "Perhaps if you understood that, you'd know why Dr. Snow has to be a doctor. It's a definite calling."

"Calling!" Lucinda snorted. "He can feel led to treat patients in Portland as well as here!"

Anna put the cup back in the saucer. "Perhaps, but he wants to be needed, and this place would then have no doctor. Please, can't you understand?"

"No! Never!"

Bessie appeared around the corner. "I have some lovely scones if ye would like one with a cup of tea."

"When does the train come?" Lucinda asked, ignoring Bessie's offer. "I plan to be on the very next one heading east."

Bessie scowled. "At this hour? Go on to bed. Ye can catch the first one tomorrow. There's nothing tonight."

"See? That's what I mean. You can't depend on anything around here!" Her eyes blazed.

"I'll pack ye a lunch to take. That should help some."

"I don't want to spend one more night here, nor do I want to see Wesley again!"

"I could find an escort to the dance, if ye'd like. Especially since you brought your best taffeta dress and black patent leathers."

Lucinda whirled, her calico flouncing out around her. "I would not wish to go to a dance with someone I did not know and especially not someone from here. He would probably wear overalls!"

"I see this discussion is going nowhere," Anna said then.

She excused herself and slipped out the door, after grabbing a jacket from the hook on the glassed-in porch. It was late, but a full moon made it light. She needed to go walk on the beach, feel the sand under her sturdy shoes, hear the waves even better, taste the salt spray on her face. It was the best place where she could talk to God.

Tying a woolen scarf around her hair to hold off the wind, Anna tore off across the dirt road and ran toward the water.

There were things she must sort out in her mind. Were her feelings toward Wesley Snow more than just admiration? Surely not. She thought of that first day when he'd stopped at the boardinghouse for lunch. How much Bessie liked him and how well everyone thought of him. It became more apparent as she worked with him, went to homes to tend to broken bones, burns, raging fevers, women having babies, that all loved him. This was where he belonged. Why couldn't Lucinda understand that? Why couldn't she be happy that he was doing what God had called him to do?

Everything seemed to hinge on the dance. Anna closed her eyes and thought what it might be like to attend the dance. She had gone to a few dances in her life but none since she'd become a young woman. No, come to think of it, there was one in Iowa City, one Saturday night when she was in nurse's training. She hadn't danced with anyone, but enjoyed watching the others whirling out on the floor, the beautiful colors blending together as they danced from one end to the other. She wondered suddenly what it might be like to dance in Peter's arms. Or Dr. Snow. She trembled at the thought of Dr. Snow. It was laughable. She only thought of him now since Lucinda had put the thought into her head. She might dream about him all she wanted, but he would never think of her in any way except as a nurse. And a good nurse at that. Hadn't he said so more than once?

Deep in thought, Anna was unaware of a sneaker wave and soon her shoes were full of water.

"Oh! I will never remember to watch the waves," she said aloud. "One cannot take her eyes off the waves." Oh, well, what was a bit of water in one's shoes? She moved up on the sand farther, and it was as if someone was watching her. She knew, without looking, it was Lucinda. Lucinda already thought she was strange. She no doubt thought it weird anyone would walk on the beach at night and get caught by a wave.

Cold now, with her stockings full of water and sand, Anna walked back to the boardinghouse. She'd slip past Bessie and up to her room to change, but Bessie sat in the doorway, arms crossed. "I see ye been wading with your shoes on again!" The smile was impish.

"Yes, some of us never learn, do we?"

"Aye. I know how ye think things over. Ye get all caught up in the problems of the world and the problems of other people." She handed Anna a towel and took her coat and scarf. "Her Royal Highness has gone to bed, against her better judgment. She'll be up bright and early, or so she said."

"Lucinda is not the type to rise early," Anna said, not wanting to think about her anymore. "Think I'll go to bed, too."

Anna thought of Dr. Snow again as she tiptoed up the stairs, feeling the wet, hearing the squishy sound of each step. Why had Lucinda said such things? Now his face kept flashing through her mind.

She slipped into bed, too exhausted to read Scripture or say her prayers. She must go early tomorrow to take care of Rebecca.

Little Rebecca Sims died Saturday afternoon, at the precise time Lucinda boarded the train. Died with Dr. Snow at her side, before Anna came on duty again. He cried only a moment before pulling the sheet up over the burned face. Her father hadn't arrived in time to see her, but perhaps it was just as well. This child was not the one he'd left behind. Dr. Snow thanked God for His ultimate mercy. They'd done all they could, but it hadn't been enough. He hoped that someday there would be a way to help burn victims more. Or, better yet, perhaps fires could be prevented. There had to be some answers. There just had to be.

Chapter 14

Days slipped into weeks and with that came changes. Anna did not go to Portland for Thanksgiving and soon it looked as if she would not be going at Christmas. There was too much to do, with too little time to do it. A bad strain of flu had hit the peninsula, and even Anna came down with the debilitating symptoms. After the fever and achiness were gone, Anna was exhausted. Dr. Snow sent her home on two consecutive days.

"We don't want to give this to any of the patients."

She knew he was right, but had thoroughly expected to feel better. Working was what she needed to help her escape the lethargy. She was tired of the confining walls of her bedroom, the downstairs parlor. Bessie and the other boarders were sick, but nobody as sick as she.

"She just let herself get run down with too much work and not enough play," was Bessie's answer.

"That is true," Dr. Snow nodded in agreement.

It was lunchtime, and Anna was sitting in a far corner of the living room, gazing out at the gray sky. The day looked the way she felt. Still, she was perturbed that they were talking about her, almost as if she were a child who needed reprimanding.

Anna curled up and fell asleep, listening to the chatter of voices in the background. She wakened as a shadow crossed in front of her. Dr. Snow leaned down, pressing his mouth against her forehead. She jumped.

"Sorry." He backed off. "Just wanted to see if the fever was still there."

Their eyes met, and Anna tried to smile.

"I need you back at work, but I need you to get completely well so very much more."

He turned and walked away before she could answer.

Dr. Snow never did contract the flu, and Anna fully recovered two weeks before Christmas.

"Oh, Bessie!" she cried coming down the stairs one morning. "It's as if I turned over a page in one of my books. I'm starting a new chapter. I feel *good*." She stretched, then hugged the older lady close. "What would I have done without your chicken soup and endless pots of tea?"

"And prayers," Bessie added.

"Yes, and prayers."

"Did ye know the good doctor climbed the stairs every day, looking in on ye?"

Anna's face flushed. "No. I didn't."

"He was mighty worried about ye. Think he even said some prayers, himself."

Anna finished her second cup of coffee and rose to go. "I'm ready to go back now. How I've missed being out of the middle of things."

"There was a shipwreck a week ago, and ye didn't even know it—ye were still sleeping a lot. No victims this time. Just a crabber that came in too close and got stuck. Boat demolished when high winds came."

"Oh, no." Anna hated it that Dr. Snow'd had to tend to all the little details—bringing in food—changing linens—in her absence.

"He asked Lizzie to help."

Anna returned to work with renewed vigor. She'd never felt better, or more energetic. Peter and the children stopped by on Sunday, and they made the usual trek to church.

"And you never got the flu?" Anna asked.

Peter shrugged. "Strong constitution, I guess."

"We got sick!" Catherine said. "I yukked up in the kitchen!"

"Me, too," said Henry, not to be outdone by his sister.

It was good to be back, and Anna sang the hymns with gusto. Her voice rang out with "Blessed Assurance, Jesus Is Mine."

"I was worried about you," Peter offered on the drive back to the boardinghouse. They'd decided against going anywhere because Anna didn't want to overdo.

Bessie had fixed a meal to beat all. Glazed ham, corn fritters, her famous fruit salad, with dried-apple pie to top it off.

Later the children, Anna, and Peter went to the middle floor and played checkers and dominos.

"You look happy today," Peter commented after Henry had fallen asleep on the small settee.

"I am, Peter. I'm very happy and feel so blessed."

His hand touched hers. "I don't suppose you've been thinking about me—about us. Maybe missing us a little?"

Anna smiled. She was so very fond of Peter, Catherine, and Henry, but did her feelings for him go deeper? How did one know for sure?

"I'm glad you're part of my life," she finally answered.

He nodded. "I guess that's what I'm a-thinking, too."

Christmas was approaching fast, and Bessie said it would be the best one ever. "I'm going to make this old place shine!"

Anna helped Bessie decorate the downstairs. They set up a tree—a fine, bushy beach pine, which Catherine and Henry helped decorate with paper chains while she and Cora strung popcorn and cranberries. Anna was forever nibbling on the popcorn, but the cranberries were tart and not to her liking.

Emily sent more books—coloring books—crayons for the children, and decorations for the tree. They were shiny glass balls with silver centers. She'd packed them well, and not one was broken. Everyone thought they were beautiful.

Anna had tried to knit in the evenings, but she wasn't like her mother. Knitting was far from enjoyable. She'd get busy talking and have to rip out several rows. She finally gave up and bought gifts from the mercantile. Peppermint sticks for Ben, chocolates for Emily, who must miss the confections since she no longer worked at the candy factory. Chocolates, also, for family friends Kate and Pastor Luke. A bright red shirt for Clifford, a knitted sweater Cora had made for baby Hazel, who had arrived December 1. She gave both Peter and Dr. Snow pairs of socks she had knitted year before last. Maybe they wouldn't notice that one sock had an extra row. Bessie was the problem. What to give to her? At last she chose a new lace tablecloth for the small round table in the parlor.

On Sunday Bessie asked Peter to help her loop green garlands across the high ceiling in the parlor and a string of lights along the front windows. "I had these sent over from Astoria," she explained.

There was the baking of fruit cakes, sugar and ginger cookies, date bars, and a double batch of shortbread, a favorite from Bessie's native Scotland.

"The pies will be made the day before Christmas," Bessie proclaimed. "We're having a full house, as I've invited everyone I know!"

"Not everyone!" Cora exclaimed. "Surely not everyone."

Bessie nodded. "Yes. Guess ye don't know I had extra leaves for the table. I want no one to go without a good home-cooked meal. The menu includes turkey, ham, lots of sweet and white potatoes. Corn and peas. And Sally Lunn because that's what Dr. Snow requested."

Anna thought about what she liked. Mama had always made cut-out sugar cookies, so she asked if Catherine might not help her in the kitchen. After they were baked, Henry could help decorate them. It would be a festive holiday.

"What about Albert?" Anna asked then. "Maybe he can come."

"Already done." Bessie smiled as if she knew a deep, dark secret.

"What is it? Tell me, please tell me," Anna implored.

"He's bringing a lady friend, that's what."

Christmas Eve was spent around the fireplace while Anna read the story about Jesus' birth. Bessie offered prayers, then all had hot, spiced tea and lemon cake.

Christmas morning, which Anna had looked forward to for weeks, dawned cold, gray, and foggier than usual. As she bustled around, helping Bessie set the table, bells rang out.

"Oh, no, not today!" Bessie cried. "What's going on?"

"It's the bell at our church," Peter said.

"Aren't they pretty sounding, Papa?" Catherine asked, her eyes shining.

"Yes," agreed Anna. "Like bells of old, proclaiming our dear Savior's birth."

A sudden knock sounded, and Henry ran to open the door. When he saw the big man standing there, he stepped aside.

"Hello! Merry Christmas!"

"Albert! You made it!" Anna cried, running to embrace her brother. She looked perplexed. "Where's your lady friend?"

Albert laughed. "She couldn't make it. But, never mind. Look what I brought!" He set the box down. "Go ahead. Open it," he said to Henry.

Henry looked at his father, then back at Albert. "Go ahead," Peter said. "It's all right."

Henry bent down and tugged at the top. Albert leaned over. "Here. I'll help."

"Oranges!" Catherine said, after peering inside. "Oh, Papa, it's oranges!"

"Oranges?" Bessie exclaimed. "We haven't had oranges for so long. Nearly forgot what they tasted like. What a splendid gift."

Soon guests began arriving, and just before Dr. Snow came, Anna slipped upstairs to change into the sea-green taffeta. Her maid of honor gown. She loved it. Pressing down the folds, she turned sidewise to stare into the mirror. A comb in her hair, and she was ready for the banquet. Christmas Day. Such a joyous occasion, but it was what they were celebrating that meant more than anything.

Dr. Snow, dressed in dark suit and white shirt, looked handsome, and Anna smiled as their eyes met.

After all guests sat, Bessie, Anna, and Delia began bringing the food in. Bessie asked Peter to give thanks for this most blessed of all days, for the bounty of food, but especially for friends and family.

Chapter 15

I t was January 1913. Woodrow Wilson had been elected president, but would not be inaugurated until March. At the boardinghouse things had been quiet due to bad weather. Dr. Snow and Anna had kept busy tending to colds and broken bones.

On Saturday morning Anna was helping Bessie in the kitchen when the wire came.

"Imagine Miss Lucinda Lawson sending Dr. Snow a message here," Bessie said. "She has more chutzpa than anyone I've met." She looked up from the dough she had rolled out. "Hand me a knife, will ye?"

"Is he going to change his mind? About going back to Portland?" Anna asked.

"How should I know, Child? I don't know everything that happens around here."

"Not everything, but pretty close," a voice said from the doorway. It was Gloria, one of the boarders who had moved in last week.

Bessie began cutting the dough. "Aye, I know a lot that goes on, but I never, ever gossip about people."

Anna wished she'd never asked now. Bessie turned to put the two huge pans of rolls in the waiting oven and washed her hands. "Why don't ye two go out on the beach. It's the nicest day we've had in a month of Sundays."

"I think a walk would rid my head of cobwebs and stir some new blood in my brain," Anna said.

"You are so funny," Gloria said. "I like talking to you because you make me think about things."

Gloria wore a green and white gingham and a straw hat that in no way covered her blond curls. She was young, unmarried, and was shy around everyone else.

"You're fun to be with because you are a good listener," Anna answered.

Gloria and Anna walked across the road to the beach. They had taken along a small bag with apples and two of Bessie's oatmeal cookies. They found a nice spot and sat on the sand, knees tucked under them. The weather was almost hot, to Anna's delight.

"Do you really like nursing?" Gloria asked.

Anna nodded. "I hope to do it the rest of my life."

"And never marry?"

"And never marry." She wanted to tell Gloria about Joseph and how she had plans to give up her nursing when they married, but Gloria was onto another subject.

"I think it's a mistake to ignore that young man who comes around."

"Young man?" Anna sat up straighter. "Do you mean Peter?"

"He has two children. Bessie spoke with him on the sunporch yesterday." Gloria scooped sand into her hand, then let it sift through her fingers. "I wouldn't mind if he came calling on me. I think he's utterly handsome!" She smiled impishly.

Anna supposed Peter was handsome with that sandy hair and his dark eyes.

"I must go back," Gloria said then. "I burn real easy." She jumped up, brushing the sand from her skirt, and hurried across the road.

Anna put her knees up and hugged them to her chest. Such a gorgeous day. It didn't seem right to have the day off, but everyone seemed to be staying well, and Dr. Snow had insisted she rest up for the next emergency that came along. It had been a month since the flu, and she felt he was being too cautious.

Leaning back, she drew a deep breath and thought again about Peter Fielding and the children when a loud bell filled the air. Was it the fire bell? Was there a fire, or was it something else?

Seconds later Gloria hurried toward her. "Bessie says to come. It's probably a shipwreck, and you might be needed."

Anna jumped up and ran toward the house. A shipwreck. But where? And why so soon? And how could a ship wreck on such a nice day?

Bessie was on the phone. "The shipwreck's down at the bar. You're to go to Dr. Snow's—be ready for whatever."

"I must change—"

"No time for that. Just go, Child."

The horse and buggy were brought around, and Anna saw Gloria's round face all white and scared looking. She hoped there were no fatalities. Drowning victims were not pleasant to look at.

The fire bell still rang, and Anna feared the worst had happened. It was the first continuous one she'd heard since the fire that claimed Rebecca's life.

"A lot of people pray for shipwrecks," Mr. Webster had said one morning at breakfast. "Pray for one so they can get the good things that wash up on shore."

"But if lives are at stake—"

"People don't think about that part."

Bessie had assured her it was true. "Some are out to get all they can get, that's for certain."

"It's a steamer!" Anna heard as she neared town. People ran toward the water as if they could catch sight of the downed vessel, though it was several miles south.

Lizzie stood in the doorway when Anna pulled into the yard.

"I think I'll get used to this feeling of utter helplessness, but one never does. Doctor is on his way. He'll arrive around the same time as the victims."

Anna washed her hands and pinned her cap on. Before she left, Gloria had run down the stairs and out to Anna with it and the cape. At least she partly looked like a nurse.

Dr. Snow arrived minutes later, just as the fire wagon came with two forms in the back. "Put one in the operating room and the other in the examining room."

He told Anna to see to the one being taken to the examining room. She knew later it was because he was alive. The other man was dead. "Died of exposure," Dr. Snow explained. "The poor devil never had a chance." He covered his face with the blanket. "Not much we could do for him, but I think the other fellow has a good chance of making it. Thirty passengers are presumed drowned."

"Thirty!" Anna cried. "How do you know that?"

"It was the *Rosecrans*—a large ship. I don't know how these two got ashore, but ashore they came."

Anna brought the blankets and quilt stored in the closet. With Lizzie's help, they peeled the wet clothes from the sailor's body and bundled him up in thick layers of blankets. "We have to get his temperature up," Anna said. "If we fail, he will die of exposure."

"Not too many survive the ocean's waters," said Lizzie. "I lost a nephew at sea—my sister's boy. Rescued, but it was too late."

"I'm so sorry," Anna murmured, checking the patient's vital signs. It seemed everyone had lost someone at sea. All the old-timers, people who had lived here a long while.

Color began coming back to the cheeks, and Anna smiled. "Can you hear me, Sir? Do you know where you are?"

The eyes opened and a voice all raspy said, "I've died and gone to heaven, and you're an angel."

Anna smiled. "No, Sir. You're in Long Beach, Washington. I'm Anna Galloway, a nurse, and you're going to be fine."

Dr. Snow entered the room, examined the man on the bed, looked back at Anna, then at the sailor again. "His color is coming back. Good. Yes, he's going to live to tell about it. Too bad about the others."

It was hours later when the sheriff came to fill them in.

"Another body just floated up on shore."

Anna felt the tightness again. "Another one?"

"Yeah. Already the people are down there, looking for what else might be washed up on the beach."

Anna remembered Mr. Webster telling about a fellow who lived in Ocean Park finding a case of whiskey while another discovered German beer. Not that Anna thought these such finds, but it amused her.

"Once my grandfather found a beautiful trunk," Lizzie said in the doorway.

"But didn't it belong to someone?"

She shrugged. "In those days they said: 'Finders keepers, losers weepers.' "

Anna shook her head. "I wouldn't want to keep anything that didn't belong to me."

"If you don't take it, it just goes back out to sea and is lost forever."

Still, Anna thought it a strange practice. She wouldn't feel right taking something that belonged to someone else, something that had such a sad tale behind it.

"No more survivors, I fear," Dr. Snow said when the sheriff left. "It was out a far piece—in that bit of water where several have gone down before. Out past the bar, few can survive."

"I think we should pray."

Dr. Snow shook his head. "Pray all you want, Anna, but it will do no good. The Lord giveth, and the Lord taketh."

Anna's cheeks burned, as they did when her ire was up. He knew how she believed, yet persisted in saying it did little or no good. Anna went to check on the patient again. She would believe as she wanted. It was much better that way. She poked hairpins back under the heavily starched cap as she hurried down the hall.

Anna was happy to see the shipwrecked sailor up and dressed a few days later. Dr. Snow was still out checking on patients, but he had said the man could be released today.

"I suppose you can't wait to get home again," she said, nodding as the man, dressed in new clothes, stood in the doorway of the waiting area. Clothing had been provided by a fund set up for that purpose.

"Aye, Missy. The only one who lived to talk about it. Nobody will believe it. Guess I had the luck of the Irish."

Anna wondered what it would be like being the only survivor—seeing all your friends being swept away, buried at sea.

"I will never forget your kindness to me, your caring. It was your face I first saw and at first I thought I'd gone to meet my Maker."

"Oh, pshaw!" Anna's face flushed. Seeing a nurse under such circumstances gave some patients delusions, and she was used to it. She'd never be pretty, but that didn't matter anymore. Perhaps it had never mattered. She worked with what God had given her.

She watched the door close, and the man went to wait for the train that would take him to Megler's Landing. Soon he would be back in Astoria and on another ship heading to the mouth of the Columbia and back across the Pacific Ocean toward home.

The train went by, up through Long Beach. It stopped, and she looked out the window as the patient got on. He turned and waved, as if knowing she'd be watching. Others waited to board the train, while others "rubbernecked" as it went by. It was the highlight of the day for many.

Weekends were especially fun during the summer months when the train brought the papas from the city—papas who had not seen their families all week long. Once when Anna had been in Long Beach, she watched one father surrounded by his family. She choked back the tears and felt a wave of homesickness.

She watched until the train disappeared from sight, then went back inside.

Chapter 16

A pounding on the front door wakened Wesley Snow. He glanced at the clock beside his bed. Five-thirty in the morning? Small wonder he still felt tired. A frantic voice called out. "Please, Dr. Snow. Come quick!"

He stepped into his pants and grabbed the flannel shirt on the bedpost, throwing it on over his nightshirt.

Peter Fielding stood, holding a still form close. "Doc—it's my Catherine! She's got this red rash—hot as fire! I thought it would go away—but it hasn't."

"Bring her in."

While Peter took Catherine to the back examining room, Wesley scrubbed his hands. He remembered another night when Peter'd brought Callie. O God, was this a repeat?

The child said nothing as Peter laid her on the long table. "Honey, it's going to be okay." Yet even as Peter said the words, his heart almost squeezed shut. He'd told Callie the same thing when she lay so ill, but nothing had saved her. Not prayers, medicine, or his caring for her. He couldn't let Catherine die.

Dr. Snow came and felt the heat emanate from the affected area. He pressed her tummy gently. "Does this hurt, Catherine?"

She shook her head. "No, Dr. Snow."

"Does it hurt here?" He pressed against her inner thigh.

Again, she shook her head.

"She scratches it a lot—says it itches," Peter offered.

Dr. Snow nodded. "That might be how it spread."

Could it be contagious? he wondered. *If so, wouldn't Peter and the younger brother have come down with it? Of course it could have a two-week incubation period.* He decided they would treat it as if it were a contagious disease. In the meantime, he would read medical journals to try to find what it was. Oh, for a skin specialist, one who knew about such things. The main thing he must do was stop the raging infection inside that tiny body. If they didn't, she would die. Wesley wondered if Anna might know something about it. She'd been practicing in a large hospital in Cedar Rapids. It certainly wouldn't hurt to ask her when she got in.

Anna arrived an hour later, her cheeks flushed from the chilly morning ride. But she was as mystified as he was. "I have never seen anything like this, Dr. Snow." Her eyes looked from Catherine to Peter, then back at the doctor. "I think we should isolate her, though. At least until we find out what it is."

"That was the conclusion I'd come to."

Dr. Snow looked at Peter's sagging shoulders. "We'll do what we can, Peter. I'll call a colleague in Portland—see what he has to say."

"And I shall attempt to make our patient comfortable," Anna said. She tried to make Catherine laugh as she brought her water and juice—anything in an attempt to flush the disease from the tiny body. She also tried diverting her mind from the problem.

"Once you're through with this rash, we'll have to have another picnic. You'd like that, wouldn't you?"

Catherine nodded, her hand touching Anna's. "I want to get better because Daddy needs me."

Oh, yes, Anna thought. *We all need you. Dr. Snow can't let you go.*

When Peter had lost Callie, Wesley had felt responsible. He'd done everything possible, but she had died. His two children were all Peter had in the world. He must save Catherine.

Dr. Snow opened a second medical book. Old and falling apart, it had been a gift from one of his instructors. He looked under *Rash* and there it was. The words leaped out at him. St. Anthony's Fire, so named because of the redness—red as fire—and the heat as in fire—an infection which few recover from. The technical term: *erysipelas.*

He sighed. The new powder that had been discovered in Germany had wonderful powers, but would do no good here. It wasn't the fever they were fighting, it was the infection causing the rash. What could he give her? An open sore, a boil he could drain. Not so here.

Thoughts of Indian medicine men crossed his mind. Some of the herbs worked. The special medicines had not saved thousands from the measles epidemic, or those afflicted with smallpox, but this was different. He had little faith in herbs and special teas, yet sometimes a doctor was willing to try anything. Peter said he had given the child sassafras tea. Well, it wouldn't do any harm, but it surely hadn't done much good, either.

Wesley drummed a pencil against the medical journal. He needed something to take away the infection, but what? He doubted that anything would work, but somehow he couldn't get Anna's face out of his mind as she spoke earlier of God and miracles and how one must have hope.

Hope. How long since he had thought about hopes, dreams. Desires?

Had Lucinda taken the very life from him when she left? Yet he had felt relief that it was over.

He walked back to the room and inspected the rash again.

"I know what it is now, Anna," he said. "If I just knew how to treat it. What to do."

Anna's eyes lit up. "You *know*?"

He explained the medical term, the common term. "Never have I seen it, but this is what it is. Somehow Catherine got infected—perhaps while playing." He examined her closer. "I see scratches on the inner thigh. I wonder—" He motioned. "Get Peter in here."

"How did she get these scratches?" Dr. Snow asked, pointing to the red marks. "See? They are distinguishable, and it appears to be from rubbing against something. Do you have any idea?"

"She stayed at Doris's—my neighbor's—last week. They—she and Henry played in the barn with the animals. I think—" He paused, nodding. "Yes, I remember Doris saying Catherine had fallen through a hole in the loft. She landed on the hay and though scared, she really wasn't hurt. The hay cushioned her fall."

"That's it!" Wesley Snow stood and began writing frantically on the pad. "I remember the symptoms now. The hay irritated the skin—there are germs in hay—it somehow got into her body through these scratches. She has what we call erysipelas. It's also known as St. Anthony's Fire. Hence the heat, the color. I want you to know—" he met Peter's worried gaze. "I have nothing to treat this. I don't know if Portland would or not. I can call the hospitals there—see if they know how and what to treat it with. Just knowing is half the battle, Peter."

"Can you save her?"

"I don't—" Dr. Snow stopped, as if thinking twice before speaking. "We're going to try, Peter. We'll certainly try."

Peter dozed in the armchair while Anna sponged off the red area. It was just like fire when she lifted the blanket.

"Anna, about all we can do is keep her comfortable."

Anna stopped sponging the face. "Doctor, I remember a case now. We talked about it in class." Her eyes grew round. "That's why it's called St. Anthony's Fire—"

"Did someone named St. Anthony have it?"

"No, but he prayed for those who did. It was early—around the 1100s—and it was said that those who believed wholeheartedly were saved by his prayers, and those who didn't believe, died."

He sighed. "So there is no cure."

"I think a miracle is what we need here."

"Yes, I pray to God you're right."

Anna stopped and stared. *Pray to God?* Was he merely saying that, or did he really mean it? If only she knew.

Wesley went out, leaving Anna with the child.

Peter returned that morning, determined to stay until she was better.

And what if we cannot save her? Wesley had wanted to say, but the words that burst from Anna, the look on her face as she spoke of God, stopped him. For some unexplainable reason, he could not get her face out of his mind. A face that was not beautiful—one that was plain according to Lucinda—had taken on a radiance that jolted him to his toes. He dismissed the thought and hitched the horses and headed north.

They took turns sitting with Catherine. It reminded Anna of Rebecca and how she'd prayed for her recovery, all for naught. Anna knew Dr. Snow held out only a slim hope this time, but Anna was confident that Catherine would get well.

It was late when Anna climbed into the buggy and took the reins, praying for the little girl she had grown to love. Catherine was spunky—the apple of her father's eyes. Surely God would hear her fervent prayer. Catherine must be saved.

She stopped the horse and looked into the darkening sky. "God, I've prayed for many things in my life, but never one as needed as this. Please, oh, please save Catherine. Help us to know what to do for her. Amen."

A sudden peace filled Anna as she drove the rest of the way home. It was as if a heavy burden had lifted from her shoulders and she knew, yes, she knew that when she went back in the morning, Catherine would be better. She'd never been more sure of anything in her life.

The rash began to diminish at six o'clock the next morning.

Peter noticed first and jumped up, yelling and crying. "She opened her eyes. My Catherine opened her eyes."

They kept Catherine for two days, making sure she was stabilized. Peter left to go be with Henry when he knew she would be all right. In no time Catherine begged to be let out of bed, asking for her father, her brother.

"You must keep quiet," Anna cautioned her. She brought meals that Lizzie fixed, insisting she stay in bed. But the rash had all but disappeared, and the fire was gone. All that remained were a few scratches, as if reminding them of the illness.

Chapter 17

Spring came and with it Anna found golden daffodils, purple hyacinth, and a few weeks later red and yellow tulips bursting through the wet, sandy ground. She clasped her hands in anticipation, wondering what else might be planted in the flower beds around the boardinghouse.

She had grown to love the weathered old house with its gables, blue shutters at the windows, and widow's walk on the roof. Someday she might have her own house, but for now this was home. Her home.

One day in March Peter suggested a drive up the road to the north end. "We never did get past Ocean Park before." His eyes seemed to be teasing her today.

"I'd love to see Oysterville," Anna declared. More oysters were grown there than anywhere else and shipped to San Francisco on a regular basis. She'd read about how it once was the county seat, but bandits had come across the bay in the middle of the night, stolen the records, and taken them to South Bend. Yes, she wanted to see the end of the peninsula.

The day was warm with a gentle breeze. Anna laughed and waved heartily as they passed others on the plank road. "This is a perfect day for an outing!"

Catherine had rosy cheeks with little sign she had been at death's door a few months ago. Of course children were resilient and bounced back after an illness. Anna turned to smile, then laughed when Henry made a face.

"You laugh a lot," Catherine said, fingering the lace on the back of Anna's collar.

Anna turned to stare. "Oh, do I?"

"Yes, you do," Henry added. Now that he knew Anna he'd become quite talkative. Sometimes she referred to him as a chatterbox.

Anna squeezed the small hand. "If you think I laugh a lot, you should hear Albert. He is the jolliest one of the whole family. We call it the Galloway laugh, you know."

"I can attest to that," Peter said with a nod. "But 'tis true. The day *is* brighter when you're along."

The sun was out; birds sang from the trees as the horses trotted down the road. Peter drove the team of workhorses today since they were going so far. "This long trip is too much for ole Gopher," he had explained earlier.

Anna began singing songs she'd learned from Sarah, and soon they all joined in. "Yankee Doodle went to town, riding on a pony. Stuck a feather in his hat and called it Macaroni."

Anna leaned over and stuck a feather in the brim of Catherine's straw hat. She shrieked with delight, then stuck it in her father's hatband.

"I like 'O Susanna,'" Peter said. "Do you remember it, Anna?"

"Of course I do. It's the craziest song Stephen Foster ever wrote."

"Why, Anna?" Catherine asked.

Anna laughed. "Just listen to the lyrics and tell me what you think."

"O I's goin' to Alabamy for my true love for to see. It rained so hot the day I left, the weather it was dry. O Susanna, don't you cry for me, for I'm going' to Alabamy with my banjo on my knee."

"That's funny!" Catherine said. "How can it rain if the weather is dry?"

"That's exactly what I mean."

They sang on, including "Polly Wolly Doodle All the Day" and "Dixie."

"We may not be southern, but we need to learn the old songs," Anna claimed.

Once, the wind swept up, and Anna's hand instinctively reached up to hold her hat. It was a pink straw with a wide brim, another Bessie'd found in her closet, but it had ties under the chin and was perfect for a drive.

Peter chuckled, but looked straight ahead. "Thought I was going to have to rescue your hat, did you?"

Anna laughed again. She loved the view of the ocean with its magnificent waves, the trees, and brush alongside the road. Occasionally they would see a road and a house in the distance. She doubted she'd ever tire of its beauty.

"I'm thinking about taking on a new job," Peter said, breaking the silence.

"A new job? You won't be logging anymore?"

A frown creased his forehead. "I'll be working the cranberry bogs—a bit closer to home. The children need me, though my neighbor takes good care of them."

"Are you sure about this, Peter? I thought you liked logging."

"I'll still do that, just not as much."

"I see."

"You do like it here, don't you, Anna?" Peter said then.

"Yes," Anna replied. Somehow she could not imagine ever leaving here to go anywhere else.

Peter's gaze was intense. "It's just like I told you that first day when we were coming on the train."

"And you were right."

Peter let the reins go slack, then pulled over, though it wasn't necessary. Nobody was behind them on the nearly deserted stretch of road. "Would you ever consider giving up nursing?"

"Give up nursing?" Anna couldn't believe Peter could even ask the question. "No. I like my work. Why do you ask?"

He shrugged. "A nurse is dedicated to her job, right? This means you will never marry or become a mother."

Anna's heart nearly stopped. "But, Peter, nursing is what I know. There's such a need here."

His face was somber. Anna swallowed. She should have realized why Peter stopped by the boardinghouse so often these days. She felt little arms wrap around her neck, and though no words were spoken, she knew Catherine had heard.

Peter picked up the reins again. "We're almost there." The sun had gone behind a cloud, making the sky darken. Anna felt a sudden chill as the buildings of the town loomed into sight with the beautiful Shoalwater Bay to the east. It seemed she was replaying another scene from the past, as she thought of Joseph who had expected her to give up her career.

They stopped and sat along the bay, eating sandwiches and drinking lemonade. Catherine and Henry ran off to play on the sandy beach. Anna relaxed as she watched them. No worries had they. She leaned back, surveying the beauty before her. She could not imagine never marrying or having children, but perhaps that's what God would have her do.

Peter wasn't about to let the subject drop. "Suppose someone needed you terribly bad? Suppose there were children who needed a mother to care for them?"

Anna felt a smile tug at the corners of her mouth. "I don't suppose their names are Catherine and Henry?"

"And what if they are?" Peter leaned over and wrote her name in the sand. "Anna, surely you must know I get lonely. I'm not good with words—"

Anna wasn't good with words, either. At least not now. Peter needed her, but what of her needs? Did they matter at all?

"You look distressed."

"I do?"

"Perhaps this isn't the right time. Perhaps I should wait. I know how upset you are about the little girl who died—"

"Peter, I—" She turned away. She could not say the words that were in her mind and heart. She just couldn't. If he didn't understand now, how could she expect him to understand later? She wanted to be needed. Wasn't that why she had gone into nursing? But she also wanted to be loved. Love was important if one took that final step into marriage. Both had to love with their whole hearts. How could she expect anything less to work? Lucinda had not loved Wesley Snow. She didn't care about him at all. Anna loved Peter like a brother. She realized that now as she looked at him with the sun hitting his sandy hair. A marriage of convenience was not right, nor was it for her.

Catherine ran up and dumped a handful of small bits of driftwood at Anna's feet. "Just for you, Anna." Her small face beamed.

"And I found some, too." Henry added to the pile.

"Oh, you two are so wonderful to think of me that way." She hugged each of them, then looked back at Peter who seemed to be deep in thought. Of course he didn't understand, just as she didn't fully. One thing Anna knew was that Peter still loved his wife, or the memory of her. It was apparent when he said her name, the way he talked about her, the way he had not let himself open his heart to anyone. She supposed he had to her a bit, but not as he should. One must open his heart all the way. That was Anna's dream. Anna's hope. Some day there might be someone who would offer all of his heart, no strings attached.

The fog rolled in, and Anna gathered the wood, sticking it in the pockets of her coat, her dress, and the rest into the apron she often wore to the beach.

"We better head back." Peter grabbed the blanket and shook the sand out. They folded it together, neither saying anything. Peter helped her into the front of the wagon, while the children clamored into the back.

"It was just a thought, Anna. Just a thought," he said once they were on the way.

The children seemed oblivious to their conversation, oblivious to the fact that their father had just asked Anna to be their mother. If they had known, they would have urged her to say yes, assuring her they loved her, for she knew they did, just as she loved them. But one must have more than that. She couldn't help but believe that to be true.

"It's going to be very late when we get back," Peter said.

Soon Catherine and Henry fell asleep, and Anna was deep in her thoughts. A proposal. Mama would have said, "Yes, Anna, marry. Have children. You'll be a good mother. A good wife." She was certain Pearl and Emily would agree. And Bessie. Bessie who had loved her captain would probably say Anna needed someone. Yet Bessie might not agree. It was something to talk over with her. She'd know what Anna should do.

When they arrived at Seaview, Peter turned and took Anna's hand. "Thank you for going with us, for making our day special." He helped her down.

"It was a wonderful day—a wonderful trip," she answered softly.

Stars twinkled from above as she stood under the canopy of tree branches, praying to God she would say the proper thing, make the right decision.

"Peter, I'm fond of you and the children. It's just that—"

"Sh–h—say no more. Sleep on it." He bent down and brushed his lips across her cheek. "I'll see you in a few days."

Do you love me, Peter Fielding? Anna wanted to ask as she watched his retreating back and listened as the buggy drove out of sight.

It was late, and everyone had gone to bed, even Bessie. As Anna tiptoed up the steps, she thought of Peter from that first meeting on the *T. J. Potter*. He had been kind enough to help. He had taken her clamming, on picnics, on Sunday drives after church. Always courteous and polite. *But, does he love me?* she wondered again.

After her Bible reading and her evening prayer, Anna looked out at the dark sky. It was going to rain. She could always tell now. It didn't matter though, as the day had been flawlessly perfect for the drive.

The rain started up slowly, building to a roaring windstorm, and Anna snuggled under the heavy quilts, burying all but her eyes and the tip of her nose. The rat-a-tat on the roof calmed her somehow, made her glad she was inside where it was warm and cozy.

The storm matched the turmoil in her mind, her pounding heart. "Leave it to You, God, to send me a storm to quell my anxious thoughts."

Chapter 18

Monday morning came, and with it a renewal to continue with her nursing. Anna wanted to see Peter and the children again. She enjoyed them so much. Couldn't they go on as before?

Dressing quickly, she brushed her hair, which was growing out in all directions. It was especially contrary after a night of sleeping on it. She stuck in extra hairpins, as the cap wouldn't be able to make it stay down. Anna made her bed and headed down the stairs for breakfast. A smell of bread baking filled her with sudden hunger.

Anna nodded at Mr. Webster, Miss Fern, who had returned from an extended vacation, and Cora, who would be leaving soon. She'd decided to move back to New York where her parents owned a farm.

Bessie came with a platter of sliced ham, biscuits, and gravy. She asked the blessing, then hurried back to the kitchen for the coffee.

"And so, how was the trip up north?" she asked.

Anna glowed at the memory of the day. "It's more primitive at that end, though I enjoyed seeing Nahcotta. Peter pointed out where the train stops and turns around. And the bay! The water was as smooth as glass, nothing like the ocean side."

Bessie nodded. " 'Tis a different beauty up that way. Come. Let's sit in the parlor a minute before ye leave for work. I know something is troubling ye."

"You do?" Anna looked at the mantel clock. "I only have a few minutes."

"I know. I'll get to the point."

Anna felt uneasy without knowing why.

"Did Peter ask ye anything?"

She set her cup into the saucer hastily, sloshing coffee out.

"Peter talked to you?" She couldn't believe she'd be the last to know.

"Indeed not. Does ye think I'm everyone's mother?"

"But, how did you—"

"Know?" She finished Anna's question. "Child, I've lived long enough to know when people are happy, and when they are not. Peter has not been happy since Callie died. Only recently has there been a gleam in his eyes, a lighter step as he walks."

A knife seemed to twist inside Anna. "Oh, Bessie, I don't know if I can say yes to his proposal, though I am quite fond of him."

"It's the doctor, isn't it?"

Anna's heart quickened. "Why would you think Dr. Snow has anything to do with it?"

"I've been watching ye. Watching him. Noticing the way his voice changes when ye walk into the room."

"Oh, Bessie, no! Never. He loves Lucinda. I know he does. This has bothered him considerably—that they argued, and she left on an angry note."

"Then why didn't he go after her?"

"Because his work is here. This is his life. These people." *Just as it is mine,* she suddenly thought.

"Lucinda is beautiful. He could never love me in that way. Never." She knew her reasoning to be sound. "If there is any admiration from Wesley Snow, it has to do with my ability as a nurse."

Bessie just smiled. "His admiration goes much deeper than that, Anna. Trust me to know what I'm a-seeing."

Anna rose to leave, but Bessie's words rang through her mind as the horse clip-clopped down the street toward Long Beach.

Wesley Snow had already left when Anna arrived. Lizzie looked up from a pile of sand she was sweeping into a dustpan. "Doctor says he won't be back in time for lunch today—for you to go on and leave if nobody comes in."

"I can wait until he returns."

"Said he'd be gone all day. Oysterville's a fair piece, you know."

Anna removed her cap. "I now know how far it is, Lizzie. Peter drove me and the children up there yesterday. What they need is a physician for that end of the peninsula."

Lizzie shook her head. "Doubt one would come so far. It took a long time to find Dr. Snow. Most doctors prefer the cities."

Anna walked down the hall to the recovery room. As she straightened the room, she thought of Rebecca. It had been weeks since she had been here and subsequently died of her burns.

It was as if Anna could still see the small form, smell the stench of burning flesh, and was wishing and praying she could relieve the child's pain. She now prayed she'd never see another person suffer as Rebecca had. She often prayed for the father who had come home from logging to find not only his wife and older child dead from the fire, but to learn he had also lost his youngest the next day.

Anna checked the cabinet and noticed they were low on petroleum jelly and bandages.

"Do you know if Dr. Snow placed an order for supplies yet?"

"No, he didn't," Lizzie replied. "He mentioned it just this morning before leaving. Why don't you go ahead and send it?"

The supplies were sent from Portland, coming to the peninsula in the same way Anna had. Up the boat, across the Columbia, and then on the railroad. Anna could at least save him that task, as he'd be exhausted by the time he returned.

The day seemed endless. Not only did Anna not have patients to tend to, she had nothing else to do. The files were in order, supplies ordered, Lizzie had finished the cleaning and had gone to her room for an afternoon nap. Anna had straightened the furniture in the living room for the fifth time when she realized what was wrong. She hadn't seen Wesley Snow that morning, nor had she seen him yesterday. She missed him. She wanted to see him, wanted to make him smile, longed to reach up and touch the lock of hair that fell across his forehead. Wanted to tell him that she cared, though she knew she shouldn't.

It was Bessie's doings—she'd put the idea in Anna's head, filling her with notions about Dr. Snow. She shook her head. No, it couldn't be true. Bessie did not know everything, though she often professed to. How could she be in a quandary about this? It was Peter she should be thinking about. Peter who wanted her decision. Peter and the children who needed her.

She decided to write to Pearl. Maybe Pearl could shed light on the questions that tormented her heart so. She found paper and pen in the desk.

Dearest Sister, Pearl,
 How are you and the expected baby doing? Fine, I trust.

Anna chewed on the pen's nib. Now to go on with her question, but how was she to start?

 I am writing for advice. Yes, me, your eldest sister, asking the youngest member of the family.
 How did you know when you loved Paul? Did it come on gradual-like, or was it suddenly there? I thought I loved Joseph, and perhaps I did, in a way, but my feelings are much stronger for a certain person who will go unnamed. I do not want to make a fool of myself. I could not bear to do that.
 I implore you to write to me as quickly as possible and to please write personal on the outside of the envelope.

Anna paused for a moment. Her mail came to the boardinghouse, but she did not want the answer to go there. She would ask Pearl to send it General Delivery in care of Long Beach. Perhaps Tioga Station would be good. Or the Breakers Hotel.

She addressed the envelope and put it into the pocket of her uniform to mail later that afternoon.

Pacing back and forth, Anna wondered what she would tell Peter. He needed her answer, needed to get his life back in order.

When Lizzie rose from her nap, Anna excused herself, saddled the horse, and rode north to Tioga Station. The letter would go out today. She could conceivably receive an answer by next Monday.

She paused at the door of the post office, wondering if she should mail the letter. What might Pearl think about her older sister?

She bought a two-cent stamp and handed the letter over the counter.

"Aren't you Miss Galloway, our nurse?" the man asked.

Anna smiled. "Yes, I work for Dr. Snow."

"I'm happy you are here. Dr. Snow is much too busy for one man. It's nice that someone can relieve him." He smiled. "I heard about the little feller in the candy store. And it was my cousin who had the fishhook in his foot."

Anna laughed. "Every one seems to be related in some way here. I must be careful and not say anything for fear of offending a relative." It was the postmaster's turn to laugh now. "You are so right. I wasn't born here, but many were. Many will also die here."

Anna headed back. Her thoughts about Dr. Snow were ludicrous. He needed her far more as a nurse than as a possible wife. What could she possibly be thinking of? She had the sudden urge to run back in and ask for her letter back. What would Pearl think? And Emily? That she had gone daft? Nurses fell in love with doctors all the time, just as some students fall in love with their teachers. It was admiration, that was all.

How could she ever leave nursing? Her heart pounded when she saw the familiar wagon pulled up at the side. What was wrong? Had he changed his mind about going north? She stayed outside for a long moment and drew in deep breaths. She *did* love the doctor. Even so, it was something she'd keep buried deep inside her. Only she and God would know.

Chapter 19

Wesley Snow leaned over and turned off the lamp. It had been another long day. A momentous week. Spring had come and with it came more accidents. Fewer fires, thank goodness, but definitely more accidents. He'd felt such relief when little Catherine Fielding had pulled through. He'd seen her on Sunday, and she was as pretty and robust as ever. She and Anna were a pair. Anna must have been that kind of child, for she was certainly that sort of woman. Full of vigor, laughter, always seeing the best. That's what he needed; someone to remind him of the bright side of life. If one dwelled on the good things, the negative was much dimmer.

Anna. That smile. The eyes so intense, yet loving and caring. Her crazy, wild hair with a mind of its own. How fitting. Just yesterday, he had longed to reach out and touch her.

Why had he thought of that now, just before bedtime? Now when sleep should come, giving him the much-needed rest? And then Wesley Snow recognized there were times when he felt lonely. Bereft. He knew without wondering twice what Anna would say about that. And then it came to him. Swiftly and surely. He had not seen Anna Galloway today, and he knew how much he had missed seeing her. Missed the smile, the laugh that came from deep within.

He pulled back the quilt and slipped under the cold covers. He hadn't much time to think about it before, not even when he was betrothed to Lucinda, but it might be nice to snuggle up to someone, to share her warmth.

Wesley punched his pillow. What was wrong with him? At thirty he should be content in his position. Perhaps someone would come along one day, but for now he would concentrate on doctoring. He had things to do, people to help. He needed a wife, but not just yet.

It was an hour before Wesley found the needed rest, and then only after praying. Seeking forgiveness for straying, for those years of turning his back on God, for rejecting the faith his mother had instilled in him. He'd been bitter when his mother died, railing at everyone. This bitterness made him turn to study. And though he found solace in practicing medicine, there were times when his inner soul cried out for something more.

Wesley prayed, for the first time in a very long time, for God to help him, to guide his steps.

❄

Anna could not sleep that night. Exhausted from a twelve-hour schedule, sleep evaded her, as her mind whirled with a hundred scattering thoughts. She'd read the 139th Psalm twice. There was meaning for her there. She just had to find it.

> *O Lord, thou hast searched me and known me. . .*

She knew that to be true.

> *If I take the wings of the morning and dwell in the uttermost parts of the sea*
> *Even there shall thy hand lead me, and thy right hand shall hold me.*

Tears slipped from her eyes as Anna remembered that day in the ocean, the waves tossing her about as if she'd been a toothpick. God had been there. Her life had been spared.

She closed her Bible and asked for God's leading in the troubles of the moment. *God, I don't know when I first started loving Dr. Snow. Please take my thoughts away, and help me to love Peter who needs me. If it is Thy will.*

Anna wondered when she had first started loving Dr. Snow. It had crept up on her like a measles rash, only much, much slower.

Working with him, at his side, day in and day out, she noticed a gentleness, a fierce determination to be a good doctor. He lived to serve others. Anna had known dedicated doctors in Iowa, but Dr. Snow was different somehow.

Anna had realized long ago that knowing him at a deeper level would never materialize. She would admire and love him day in and day out, but it ended there. The thought that he might find her attractive never occurred to her. How could she possibly ever compete with the charming Lucinda Lawson? Then there was his manner. It was so often brusque and impatient, Anna had given up trying to please.

Did you ever stop to think that brusqueness is a cover-up?

Anna's heart pounded. Could that be? Why had it not occurred to her before?

But there was Lucinda, and she had not given up. She'd returned to the peninsula again in April, just as the rhododendrons were in full bloom. Anna had never seen such beauty, but beauty was wasted on Lucinda. She had a mission, and that was to win Dr. Snow back. She also had a vendetta against Anna, and Anna did her best to avoid her.

Lucinda was not one to discourage easily. "I want you, Wesley Snow, and I aim to get you one way or the other!" Her blond curls looked like fat sausages framing her pale face. The dark green taffeta dress swirled around her slender hips as she flounced from the building.

She left a week later, to everyone's relief. Still Anna wondered if Wesley was really over her.

The day after Anna's sleepless night, Wesley found her in the supply room, checking over the clean linens. "Are you hiding in here?" A smile lit up his broad face.

"Who, me?" She stifled a giggle.

"I want to stay here. Help these people. Portland has plenty of doctors. I'm needed here. Don't you agree, Anna?" He took the stack of towels and placed them back on the shelf. His blue eyes, with their warm gaze, reminded her of cornflowers that grew wild in the field close to home. They watched her now with an intenseness that baffled her.

She met his gaze and felt the color creep to her skin. Perhaps he was waiting for her to answer his question. "You are needed here, yes."

"I've done some thinking. Last night when I couldn't sleep. And you are needed also, Anna. You're good with the patients. They trust you. When I make my calls, someone always asks how my short-haired nurse is."

Anna laughed then. It had come from her depths, practically shaking the windows. She covered her mouth immediately.

Dr. Snow looked serious. "Don't hide your laugh, Anna Galloway. It's a wonderful, warm laugh. It cheers me up."

Anna looked down. He moved closer, his hands lifting her chin. She felt his warm breath on her neck. She fought back the impulse to touch his face, to bring it even closer. His gaze lingered.

"Anna, I need you," he said, breaking the silence.

"I don't think you know what you're saying," she finally said. She couldn't have heard right. This couldn't be. He loved Lucinda. She knew he did. It was a game of cat and mouse they'd been playing to see who was the most stubborn. She'd heard about the white satin wedding dress with its layers of tulle.

"Anna, must I say more?"

How could she respond? Her need was great, but others' needs superseded hers. Patients needed her. The peninsula needed her. Peter's motherless children needed her. Her family needed her.

But what of love? She wanted someone to love her. Need was necessary, but love was also important. How could she build a life on anything less?

Then there was his lack of faith, the most important reason of all.

"Anna?" Wesley Snow's voice was close, too close. "Say something. When you are quiet, I know you're mulling things over."

Anna pressed her hands to her side. Yes, Dr. Snow would know that about her. Hadn't they worked side by side for the past nine months? He observed his patients, just as he watched and understood his nurse. She would have been surprised if he had done any less.

She turned and raised her face to his. "I think your need is to continue being a doctor, whether it's here or in Portland. And Lucinda waits."

"That's over. She does not want to live here, and I do not want to live there. It's been settled."

Anna looked out at the empty waiting room. No one was there, but at any moment an emergency could arise. And if so, she would answer the call. "I have a calling, too, and it's just as great as yours. Women are not thought of as equal, and I hope that may change someday."

"Anna, Anna, I have never thought of you as any less just because you're a woman."

"If not, you are one of the few."

"I believe God has created all men to be equal, and I use that term *men* in a general sense."

Anna's heart pounded. *God created? Had he really said that?*

She met his gaze. "I think you are lonely, and I don't want to be someone who merely fills the void in your life, Dr. Snow—"

"Wesley."

"Wesley."

"Lucinda is incapable of loving anyone but herself. I learned after our engagement that she must marry before she could receive her grandfather's inheritance. I believe she has found someone who can fulfill that role."

"She was marrying you to inherit money?"

"Yes."

Anna walked to the other end of the room. She must keep busy. Perhaps get a cup of coffee. She straightened the doilies on the tables and stacked the few books. The waiting room always got so messy.

"I'm going to ask Lizzie to fix us something to eat." Dr. Snow turned and left the room. As darkness encroached, from a storm brewing, Anna's mind whirled with a hundred thoughts.

The sound of thundering hooves filled the air. The door flew open and a young man cried, "Oh, thank God, someone is here! I need help and quick!"

Dr. Snow and Anna ran out into the darkness. A hay wagon was pulled up to the door and inside a man lay writhing in pain. Anna bent down to investigate, then stopped. Peter Fielding lay in the wagon, blood coursing down his right leg. "Peter!" she gasped.

Wesley summed up the situation and ordered him brought into the examining room. Minutes later, the pants leg was cut off and a tourniquet was applied to the limb.

"Good grief, man, how did this happen?"

Peter's face was ashen, his eyes rolled in the back of his head.

"Clearing property. Wind turned and the tree came the wrong way. Tried to get out of the way—but it got his leg," the driver said.

Anna came with blankets. Peter was in shock, and the next few minutes were crucial. "It's going to be all right," she said, sponging his face gently. "You're going to be okay. Dr. Snow will see to that."

"My kids," he moaned, "I can't die and leave my kids."

Anna choked back sudden tears. "Peter, I'm praying for His mercy." She took his hand and prayed aloud, prayed for healing and that God would comfort him.

"Anna," Dr. Snow called, "I need your help here."

The blood had stopped gushing, but the cut was deep. Nasty. "Get the antiseptic. The large needle, then I'll need you to hold this while I stitch."

It seemed to take forever as Anna watched, and Dr. Snow sutured the gaping wound. He had administered morphine, and Peter was no longer in pain.

"He's going to make it. Another ten minutes and I wouldn't have been as positive."

Anna reached over, wiping the perspiration from his brow. "I knew it to be so."

"It's him you love, isn't it?"

Anna's heart thudded again. Peter? Did she love Peter? No. She had thought so once, but realized she loved him as a brother, would always love him as a brother. She trembled as her thoughts turned to Dr. Snow. They had much in common. Their love for and interest in medicine. In helping others. The love of this primitive area that time had all but forgotten. And he had mentioned God tonight in a loving manner.

More horses' hooves filled the night air, and Anna stared at Wesley. "Not another emergency!"

The door opened, bringing the coldness of the advancing wind, and a woman appeared in the doorway, screaming, "They told me he was hurt, and I feared, oh, how I feared the doctor wouldn't be in!" She gasped when she saw Peter's face. "Oh, no, Peter! Peter, please hear me!"

Dr. Snow put a hand on the woman's shoulder. "Mrs. Yates, he's going to make it. You must settle down; it won't do him any good to see you like this."

Of course, Anna thought, looking at the distraught face, wisps of hair pulled loose from the knot at the nape. Peter's neighbor, Doris. They had never met, but Anna'd heard a lot about her.

Doris stepped back, her eyes never leaving Peter's still form. "I take care of Catherine and Henry. They play with my own three kids—they're like family. And Peter—" her voice choked, "Peter is—oh—"

But her eyes said it all, Anna realized, as the woman bent over him again. She loved him. This was need, yes, but it was love, and perhaps Doris had not known it until now. The fear of losing him had brought it to the surface.

Anna washed her hands, the sobs she'd held back so long finally releasing. She felt a hand on her shoulder and took a deep breath.

"Anna, it's okay to cry. Why do you think God made tears?"

"I—I—," she turned and met Wesley's piercing gaze.

"There's no need to say anything." His hand brushed back a curl that had escaped from under the cap. "I guess I knew all along how you felt about Peter."

His words whirled inside her mind, as she realized what he thought. Of course he thought she loved Peter, that if she were to marry anyone it would be him.

Dr. Snow left the room to check on the patient. Peter's eyes were opening and Doris sat holding his hand, speaking to him in a low voice. "Doc says you're going to be fine as frog's hair—just need a few weeks to recuperate." She smiled through the tears. "And I'll be here a-waiting. You can count on that."

Dr. Snow wondered about love and need and how mixed up things could be. Clearly this woman loved Peter with her whole heart, while Anna loved Peter, and he loved Anna. The thought of losing Anna filled him with anguish. He could see that same fear mirrored on Doris's face. She'd lost one husband and did not want to lose the man she now loved. Why were there always complications?

Anna sterilized the instruments and washed the towels while she thought of Peter, his last words to her about getting married, giving Catherine and Henry a home. How she had not answered him and felt guilt for rebuffing him. She wondered now if he had been a mite careless and cut the tree wrong. She'd heard tell it could happen. Footsteps approached. Dr. Snow shook his head. "It was too close, Anna. Way too close."

"You are wrong about Peter," she said then.

"Wrong?"

Anna turned and looked into his eyes. She knew she would never tire of looking at the kindness, the concern, the way his eyes mesmerized her, the jutting chin, the clean-shaven face. She wanted to touch him—longed to touch him.

"I refused Peter's proposal last Sunday."

"You did?"

Anna nodded. "He—you see—we would never be able to agree on certain things, and I think of him as a good friend. I don't want to lose him as a friend—not ever—but I cannot marry a friend."

"Anna—" He came closer, his mouth against her hair. "If Peter isn't in line, let me be the first one there."

She didn't move—couldn't move. "There is no line."

"If there isn't, there should be."

She slipped into his embrace, asking God if it had been His plan all along—if that was why she had come to this place.

"I need you, Anna, it is true, but far more important I love you with my whole heart. If you think you could ever feel anything for me. . ."

Anna met his gaze again, and her eyes answered his question. "How about till death do us part?" she whispered, her head leaning against his thick chest.

The front door blew open as another gust of wind hit the small North Beach Peninsula, but neither the doctor nor the nurse noticed as they stood side by side as they had stood many times in the past. This time—as soon as arrangements could be made—it would be as man and wife.

A Letter to Our Readers

Dear Readers:

In order that we might better contribute to your reading enjoyment, we would appreciate you taking a few minutes to respond to the following questions. When completed, please return to the following: Fiction Editor, Barbour Publishing, Inc., P.O. Box 719, Uhrichsville, OH 44683.

1. Did you enjoy reading *Oregon?*
   ❑ Very much. I would like to see more books like this.
   ❑ Moderately—I would have enjoyed it more if _____
   _____
   _____

2. What influenced your decision to purchase this book?
   (Check those that apply.)
   ❑ Cover   ❑ Back cover copy   ❑ Title   ❑ Price
   ❑ Friends   ❑ Publicity   ❑ Other

3. Which story was your favorite?
   ❑ *The Heart Has Its Reason*   ❑ *Love's Tender Path*
   ❑ *Love Shall Come Again*   ❑ *Anna's Hope*

4. Please check your age range:
   ❑ Under 18   ❑ 18–24   ❑ 25–34
   ❑ 35–45   ❑ 46–55   ❑ Over 55

5. How many hours per week do you read? _____

Name _____

Occupation _____

Address _____

City _____ State _____ Zip _____

If you enjoyed

OREGON

then read:

Four Inspirational Love Stories
with a Dash of Intrigue by Tracie Peterson

A Wing and a Prayer
Wings Like Eagles
Wings of the Dawn
A Gift of Wings

If you enjoyed

OREGON

then read:

TUMBLEWEEDS

Four Inspirational Love Stories
with a Pioneer Spirit by Norene Morris

Cottonwood Dreams
Rainbow Harvest
Pioneer Legacy
A Heart for Home

Grace Livingston Hill Collections

Readers of quality Christian fiction will
love these new novel collections from
Grace Livingston Hill, the leading lady
of inspirational romance. Each collection features three titles from Grace
Livingston Hill and a bonus novel
from Isabella Alden, Grace Livingston
Hill's aunt and a widely respected
author herself.

Collection #8 includes the complete Grace
Livingston Hill books *The Chance of a Lifetime, Under the
Window* and *A Voice in the Wilderness,* plus *The Randolphs*
by Isabella Alden.

paperback, 464 pages, 5 ³⁄₁₆" x 8"

❤ ❤ ❤ ❤ ❤ ❤ ❤ ❤ ❤ ❤ ❤ ❤ ❤ ❤ ❤

❤ ❤ ❤ ❤ ❤ ❤ ❤ ❤ ❤ ❤ ❤ ❤ ❤ ❤ ❤

If you enjoyed

OREGON

then read:

Montana

*A Legacy of Faith and Love
in Four Complete Novels by Ann Bell*

*Autumn Love
Contagious Love
Inspired Love
Distant Love*

Grace Livingston Hill Collections

Readers of quality Christian fiction will love these new novel collections from Grace Livingston Hill, the leading lady of inspirational romance. Each collection features three titles from Grace Livingston Hill and a bonus novel from Isabella Alden, Grace Livingston Hill's aunt and a widely respected author herself.

Collection #7 includes the complete Grace Livingston Hill books *Lo, Michael*, *The Patch of Blue*, and *The Unknown God*, plus *Stephen Mitchell's Journey* by Isabella Alden.

paperback, 464 pages, 5 ⁹⁄₁₆" x 8"